Copyright © 2023 Tana Rose
All rights reserved.
ISBN: 9798390408094

For anyone who's ever wanted
To get it on with their boss

"Hating someone feels disturbingly similar to being in love with them."

-SALLY THORNE, *THE HATING GAME*

1
Lincoln

Sometimes, I hate my life.

I know what you're thinking. Believe me, I do. Poor little rich boy. Raised with a silver spoon in my mouth, attended ivy league college, met my business partner—the billionaire Cabot Harkness—there. After we graduated, we immediately started our company, and it was an instant success. I told you I know. I understand that in the eyes of many, I live a blessed life. That the life I lead is one to aspire to.

But Jesus, sometimes I just want to feel something.

That's the problem. For all the benefits I have in my life, I don't feel a goddamn thing.

I barely feel the pussy that's wrapped around my cock at this very minute. The girl bent over my desk has a fall of blond hair and a nice plump ass that jiggles with every one of my thrusts. One of my hands is pressed between her fabric covered shoulder blades, pinning her down, while the other grips her hip, just under where I've rucked up her skirt.

This is how sex is for me these days, always clothed, always fast and dirty. The girls don't mind. They know what they're getting into with me. I am Breaker's Point's most eligible bachelor since Cabot met his girl and became blissfully unavailable. The gossip rags delight in splashing me all over their pages, showing me with a different girl every time.

Because one thing I am not is monogamous.

So the girls know, and they don't mind, so long as they can say they got to fuck Lincoln George.

Soft cries bloom into loud moans, and my eyes flick up to my shut but not locked door. I know my personal assistant is out there, likely trying to ignore the sounds coming from in here, but she should be used to it by now. I only have sex here or if I'm feeling like I need a longer session, there's a sex club I frequent that provides everything I could think to use.

The girl—*Valerie, I think*—reaches back, trying to grip my hips to get me closer, to take me deeper, harder. *I don't fucking think so.* She gasps and whimpers when I slam her hand down on the desk and keep it there. "What did I tell you?" I growl.

She whimpers again. "Not to touch you."

"That's right," I snarl, squeezing her wrist. "You didn't follow the rules, and now you don't get to come."

Her gray eyes widen in surprise. "Wait. What?"

"Punishment," I groan as my balls tighten at the word. I fucking love it. Love the control and the submission that these girls give me, even if they don't realize it's happening.

"Linc, you can't be-"

She cuts off as my hips stall, my head throws back as pleasure races toward me. I come, filling the condom, while Valerie tries to buck her hips to reach that point with me, but she's not going to get it. She broke a rule. She doesn't get to come. Simple as that.

I grunt as I pull out of her, carefully holding the condom in place to make sure it doesn't slip. The last fucking thing I need is a pregnancy scare. Every woman I have sex with tells me they're on birth control, but I sure as fuck am not taking any chances. I always wear a condom that *I* provide, without fail.

She lays there, breathing heavy, pussy out and glistening like she thinks if she just waits I'll change my mind. It's never going to happen. *Ever.* My rules are the rules. I never bend them. I never break them.

She's still there by the time I've discarded the condom and straightened out my clothes. A glance at the clock tells me I have a meeting with Cabot in ten minutes, so I retreat to my private bathroom, and finish putting the finishing touches on my appearance.

I know what women think when they look at me. Sex on a stick. Lust personified. A tall drink of I'd-like-to-fuck-that. This isn't even me blowing smoke up my own ass. Those are actual comments made to me by women. I love it. I work hard on my body, on maintaining that persona.

It's imperative to remain as put together as I can.

I take a moment to smooth my dark hair and scrub a hand over my perpetual five o'clock shadow. I haven't been sleeping well, and it shows in the shadows under my bright blue eyes. Eyes I share with all three of my siblings.

I straighten my tie—green because it's Wednesday—and make sure my shirt is fully tucked into my charcoal gray suit pants before I leave again.

She's still in my office, sitting in my chair with her arms crossed over her generous breasts as she gives me an unimpressed look. "Are you serious?"

I stride to the door and hook my suit jacket off the coat rack there, slipping my arms through and smoothing out the lapels before I look back over at her. "You can find your own way out, I'm sure." When her full lips part, like she's going to argue with me, I hold up a hand to stall her words. "I am a very busy man, Valerie. I don't have time to coddle someone who cannot follow specific instructions. So, let me break it down for you. I gave you rules. You agreed to them. You broke them. You were punished. End of story."

Her mouth falls open and I swear I see a line of silver shimmer along the lower lashes. As if crying would ever sway me. "I thought it was part of the game," she whispers.

I lift a shoulder and reach for the door handle. "It was. And you lost."

Giovanna, my personal assistant, glances up as I step out, before lowering her eyes to her desk, waiting for any intrusion I might give her. I suppose it might be hard to look your boss in the face when you've just heard him fucking a woman, but really, she should be used to it by now. "Miss Peralta, will you see Valerie out please? If she raises a fuss, call security."

Giovanna's dark eyes flick up to the open door of my office, where I know Valerie is watching, likely with a disgruntled look on her face. I don't turn to look, though. I wait until Giovanna nods and murmurs, "Yes, Mr. George." And then I turn down the hall and head toward my business partner's office.

I haven't made it far when a honey sweet laugh reaches my ears, making my back tense and adrenaline rush through me. "Well, I'm glad you like them," says a voice that sets my teeth on edge, laced with the slightest southern accent.

"Seriously, Liv, you're wasted here. You should open a bakery. You'd make a killing on the donuts alone."

My teeth grit.

The laugh sounds again, as Liv—Olivia Hart—brushes off the compliment. "Oh, shoot!" she blurts. "Is that the time?"

Without another word, I hear the steady clop, clop, clop of cheap heels on the linoleum, and then the woman herself appears, darting out of the breakroom for this floor with a cup of black coffee in one hand, a plate of what looks like almond poppyseed muffins in the other, and a stack of files wedged into her armpit, precariously close to sliding out and spilling on the floor.

She pulls up short when she sees me hovering in the hallway with a scowl on my face. I can't help it. Anytime I'm around this woman, my mood sours. I think it has to do with how endlessly, relentlessly cheerful she is. She's so sweet it makes my teeth ache. Everyone knows teeth pain is the worst.

She arches one dark blond brow and shifts on her Target heels, drawing attention to her long slim legs and curvy as fuck hips. "Can I help you with something, Mr. George?" Her tone, while polite, is decidedly less sweet whenever she talks to me. That radiant smile she gives to everyone else, the one that reaches her amber eyes and plumps up her freckled cheeks, is nowhere to be seen.

It shouldn't bother me as much as it does. Olivia Hart doesn't like me. She's not the first and she certainly won't be the last. I roll my shoulders, like I'm shrugging off the weight of her dislike, and jerk my chin at the stack of paper under her arm. "Are those the charity initiative files?"

She gives a jerky nod, shifting again. "Yes."

"I'll take them." I reach toward her, intending to relieve her of the precarious pile, but she takes a step back and tips up her little pointed chin, to level me with a look that borders on a glare, but not quite.

"I can't give you them," she says, meeting my gaze.

I sigh and resist the urge to swipe a hand over my face. It would give too much away if I did. It's bad enough that I already sighed around her. "Give me the files, Miss Hart."

Her jaw tightens at my harsh tone. I watch her breasts rise, straining the buttons on her shirt, as she takes a deep breath, and lets it out. "I can't give them to you-" she starts.

I cut her off, reaching for the files again. "I am your boss, Miss Hart. You work for me. Give me the damn files."

Another step back as she thrusts the plate holding the muffins in my direction that's going to stop me. "Hold your britches, bossy pants. I work for Mr. Harkness, not you. He asked for these files, so I'm taking them to him. I can send you the digital versions when I get back to my desk, if you'd like?"

"Bossy pants?" Her cheeks flush pink as her teeth sink into her lower lip. Fuck. She has to know what the sight of that would do to any heterosexual man. An image of my teeth replacing hers, testing the plushness of her mouth, hits me, and I have to take a moment to force the thought away.

Olivia's gold eyes look away from me. "I'm sorry. I just... he needs the files. I'm already late taking them to him."

Another sigh puffs out of me. "Olivia." Her eyes widen at my use of her first name. It takes me a moment to realize I've never called her that before. "I'm heading to a meeting with Cabot to discuss the charities. They look like they're about to drop." I motion at her full hands. "I was trying to help you."

I keep my voice carefully disassociated, like it is anytime I interact with an employee. There have been too many times where a female has read too much into my actions, my words, and tried to seduce me, which results in me needing to fire them. I may be Breaker's Point's reigning man whore, but I don't fuck my employees. I don't need my work life to get messy.

I mean, messier than it already is, what with my tendency to bring women here to fuck.

Her cheeks go pink, and her plush mouth falls open in a surprised 'o' that invites a hard cock to slide through them. I push the thought away again, even as my dick stirs to life in my pants. "I'm sorry, Mr. George," she says, eyes dropping submissively to the floor. Her lowered lashes and contrite tone do nothing to combat the half chub I'm currently sporting. "You caught me on a bad morning."

I want to say something about how she seemed fine, chatting with Jake from marketing, but I don't want her to think that I care, because I don't. Of course, I don't. "We all have bad mornings, Miss Hart. It doesn't excuse inappropriate behavior."

She tips her chin down even farther as she nods. Fuck, I'd love to see her do that when she's on her knees in a waiting posture.

What the fuck is wrong with you, Lincoln? You don't shit where you eat.

"May I?" I motion at the files again and this time she doesn't move as I reach for them. My fingers curl around the paper, my knuckles brush against the side of her breast, and I hear her sharp inhale at the contact. A spark zings up my arm and I have to grit my teeth against the further swelling in my pants. From just barely touching her breast.

Fuck.

As soon as the files are secure in my hand, she jerks back and stumbles to the side, rushing around me to head to Cabot's office. I trail behind her, watching her heart-shaped ass in her ill-fitting skirt that looks like it was maybe fashionable thirty years ago, but now just looks dated.

I don't know much about Olivia. She's only been working here for a month, but I know that all of her clothes are second hand or bought at Target. Cheap versions of the nicer brands most of our employees splurge for. None of her clothes are tailored to her body, and thank God for that, because Olivia Hart dressed in clothes that actually fit her? Forget about it. I wouldn't be able to keep my hands off her.

She glances over her shoulder at me as she reaches Cabot's office, checking how close I am, if I'm following her. Spoiler alert: I am. Bobbing along in the wake of her scent that reminds me of a sun-drenched field full of wildflowers, soft and delicate and sweet.

I fucking hate that smell.

I can't get it out of my fucking head.

I've taken to mostly avoiding her in order to avoid the scent. But even though Cabot and my offices are on opposite sides of this floor, with the breakroom, a conference room and two other offices in between, I still catch whiffs of Olivia Hart and it makes me fucking hard every time.

Like now as I step into my business partner's office, I'm sporting a half chub that only gets worse when Olivia bends over to place the coffee and the muffins on Cabot's desk, skirt pulling tight over the curve of her ass.

"Mr. George has the files you asked for," she tells him as she straightens, sliding her delicate hands over her thighs to smooth out her skirt where it's ridden up.

Cabot looks up at her, a smile on his lips, but he doesn't dip his gaze lower than her face. Cabot has always been the consummate gentleman where women are concerned. He treats all the women in the office like humans, like they matter, whereas I hired my assistant based on the symmetry of her face and the size of her rack.

My point is that Cabot is the boss everyone wants. I am… not.

"Thank you, Liv."

She tips her head, sending blond hair sliding over her shoulders. "Is there anything else I can get you, Mr. Harkness?"

He reaches for the muffin and breaks off a piece before popping it in his mouth. My brows arch at the groan that leaves him. It's as inappropriate as I've ever seen him in any of his interactions with employees. "Jesus, Liv. Did you make these?" He shakes his head, breaking off another piece. "What am I saying? Of course you did. You might have missed your calling."

Liv laughs, nervous and shy, pink flooding her face as she looks away from him, down at the floor, hands clasping together in front. "Oh, heavens, no. I could never be a baker. I just like to stay busy."

Cabot grins at her. "I know. But you have a gift."

I clear my throat, hating the way they're interacting with each other, hating that he's making her blush in a good way with compliments. Unlike me. I always make her flush with frustration. Which, if I'm honest, is adorable as hell.

"Maybe you should bring some to *Verity*," I say her name like a reminder. To both of them. They shouldn't be fucking flirting when he's happily in love with another woman. Verity deserves better than that.

Cabot's eyes flash to mine, a brow arched at my harsh tone, but I ignore him. Moving to the window to look out. Olivia doesn't miss a beat. "I can wrap up some of what's left if you want to take it home to her."

I can hear the smile in Cabot's voice as he says, almost gently, "Thank you, Liv. That would be great. Verity will love these."

There's a click of her heels and then the soft closing of the door. My shoulders relax as I feel her absence, no longer bearing the weight of her presence. "Care to tell me what the hell that was?"

I shove my hands in my pockets and turn to face my business partner. "Nope." My chin jerks to the files on his desk. "Let's get to work, shall we?"

2
Olivia

"What was I thinking? What the hell was I thinking?" I mutter to myself as I tidy the break room. No one else on this floor does it, so it's almost always me that loads the little dishwasher, wipes down the counter and rinses the coffee pot at the end of the day. There's an espresso machine that I have yet to learn how to use that also needs a good wipe down, every so often. Once a week I go through the fridge and toss anything past its expiration.

I don't mind the act of cleaning, especially when I'm nervous. Or upset. Or frustrated. Basically, any time my brain is spiraling, I enjoy cleaning. I enjoy keeping my hands busy. Organizing the clutter helps me organize my mind.

Unfortunately, this happens so often here that there isn't much for me to clean up. I've already reorganized all the paper files, instituting a much easier to navigate system than what Mr. Harkness's previous assistant used, which seemed to be by account date and not by name. Don't ask me how she found anything.

My desktop is clean of unnecessary icons. My inbox is clear. I've already completed all the tasks assigned to me today and found a few extras that needed to be done. Now it's an hour from quitting time and I have nothing to do.

Crap on a cracker.

I need to learn to slow down and spread out my work. So I don't have to try to look busy, when really I'm just killing time.

"Oh, hey, Liv." I turn, dripping sponge in hand, and find Kirsten, the assistant for the Chief People Officer, lingering at the entrance.

I give her my best smile. "Oh, Kirsten! Look at you! You're glowing!"

She chuckles and smooths a hand over her round stomach. "That's what everyone says, but somehow when you say it, it sounds *true*. Maybe it's the accent."

I lift a shoulder and turn to rinse the sponge and then wash my hands. "Maybe."

Kirsten approaches, places a hand on my shoulder. "So listen, I know we ask you to come out every week and every week you say no, but tonight is trivia night at Chauncey's."

I'm shaking my head before she can finish. "I can't. You know, I can't." I wish I could. I wish I could just spend one night out with my co-workers, letting loose and forgetting about all of my responsibilities, but it's just not an option for me right now.

"Maybe next week," Kirsten says kindly, squeezing my shoulder as I reach for a towel to dry my hands.

I give her a smile I know isn't as genuine as the one I gave her before, nodding. "Yeah, I'll see if I can work something out." I won't. I know I won't. Because as much as it would be nice to go out and let my hair down, I'd rather go home even more.

"Well, I should go check if Mr. Harkness needs anything," I say with force cheerfulness. "Have fun tonight, Kirsten."

She gives me a sweet smile before heading to the drinks fridge and pulling out a can of sparkling water. "We will." Her warm, dark brown eyes flick over me. "Get some good rest tonight, Liv."

I dip my head in acknowledgement of what she didn't say. I look like shit. That makes sense based on how little sleep I've been getting, snatches of it here and there, usually while curled in the armchair in the living room. I wake almost every morning with a kink in my neck and sore muscles. But I still make myself get up with my alarm, slather concealer under my eyes to hide the dark circles there and then trudge to the office, in time to bring Mr. Harkness his first cup of coffee.

A yawn cracks my jaw as I plop into my chair. Yet another reason I need to have things to do. Staying busy helps to keep my energy up, helps to combat the exhaustion dragging at me, but when I have nothing to do but stare at my inbox waiting for a new email? Yeah, I start to feel that exhaustion.

"Miss Hart, can I see you in my office, please?"

Swallowing hard, I pick up my iPad and iPencil and head into Mr. Harkness's office. He smiles when he looks up at me and the tension that had been making my shoulders tight releases. I haven't worked for Mr. Harkness all that long, only a month, technically still in the probationary period, and he can let me go without notice.

I return his smile and lift my tablet, ready to note down anything he might need.

A tingle works its way over my spine, and I turn to see Lincoln George lingering by the windows, blue eyes focused on me, running from my perfectly smooth curls down my second-hand clothes and stopping on my three-inch black heels.

The tension is back, making my shoulders stiffen.

I have had little contact with Mr. George, Mr. Harkness's business partner. Anytime I need to set up a meeting between the two of them, I've talked with his PA, Giovanna, who is nice enough but definitely raised her nose at me. No number of compliments can soften that girl to me and believe me, I pulled out some of my best with her.

"You were late today," Mr. Harkness says, drawing my attention back to him. "Everything okay?"

I had been opening my mouth to apologize and explain, but at his question, I nod instead. "Yes, sir, everything is fine. There was an issue with my mother. I was only twenty minutes. I can stay late to make it up, if you'd like?" Though I don't know what the heck I'd do during that time.

He waves a hand and then leans back in his chair. "No need, Liv." He nods at one of two chairs facing his desk. "Have a seat."

Oh, no. Oh dammit. I'm being fired. That's what's happening right now.

Stupid Lincoln George told Cabot Harkness about what happened this morning, and now I'm being fired. I should never have called him bossy pants, but my southern sensibilities just had to rear their head when he'd gotten all snappish at me.

Nooooooo! My insides wail as I take a seat. My first two paychecks have barely made a dent in my mother's medical bills. I need this job.

I lay the iPad on my thighs and look up at him expectantly.

He steeples his hands in front of his face and eyes me. I can't tell if he's considering his words, or if he's trying to intimidate me by remaining silent. But either way, I wait him out. It's something I'm good at, sitting patiently. After about three minutes, during which I ignore the feeling of slate blue eyes on me and stare patiently back at my boss, he finally speaks. "As you know, Miss Hart, your position as my PA was intended to last at least three months as a trial." I nod because I had in fact known that. It was always a temporary position, but after three months of working together, I had hoped that he would decide to keep me on in some capacity. "Unfortunately-"

He starts and I can't stay quiet.

"I'll do better, I promise. I'll get up an hour earlier and make sure that I'm here early rather than take the risk of being late again. I'll stay late too. And I'll make a fresh pot of coffee every hour, on the hour. Please, I need this job."

Mr. Harkness's eyebrows rise in increments as I speak, and by the time I've finished, he's smiling at me again. "I'm not firing you, Olivia."

I sag back in my chair. "You aren't?"

"No. I'm pretty sure Verity would kill me if I let you go." My lips curl into a smile at the mention of his... wife? Girlfriend? His partner. Their relationship is complicated and not any of my business, but I know Verity is the center of a reverse harem and she's with singer songwriter Archer Daniels, MMA legend Holt Bracken, and a man named Nash Fahey, as well as Cabot Harkness. That sounds like too many penises for me. I hardly know what to do with one of them, let alone four. But all I can think is *get it, girl.* "She adores you," Mr. Harkness says, and I feel my cheeks go pink at the compliment.

"I like her too. She's always so sweet when she comes in."

Mr. Harkness's face goes all soft when he thinks about the love of his life and then he shakes himself to bring him back to the present and our conversation. "I'm not firing you, Miss Hart, but I do need to reassign you. Something has come up and I need to take a hiatus. I expect it to last at least two months, if not more."

I'm nodding along with him, grateful that I'm not being fired, but not sure what this means for me. Mr. Harkness looks up to my right. I follow his line of sight and flinch, because Lincoln George is a helluva lot closer to me than I thought he was. Like within a few feet of me. How had he managed to do that? Get so close without me realizing it. He's a big man. He shouldn't be able to move so silently.

"What we'd like to see," Mr. Harkness says, drawing my attention back to him. "Is you working with Lincoln."

Ice water douses me, making me shudder. This is the last thing I want. The absolute last freaking thing. He's a monster. A literal monster to the people that work under him. The marketing department calls him the Devil. They have mockups of him as Lucifer, with the horns and the tail and the cleft tongue. It suits him far too well with his black hair and big muscled build. The girls in customer service? Yeah, they scatter anytime he's near. He's even made the entire accounting team cry. All of them. Even Harold, who's been doing the job for forty years, and is the least emotional man I've ever met.

I've found Giovanna in the ladies' room sniffling more than once because of something he's said to her, some heartless comment, some demand he's made.

And then there are the women. The constant parade of women he brings into the office and has sex with, right there, where everyone knows what's happening, even if we can't see it.

We aren't deaf, buddy. We can hear it.

"You sure you don't want to fire me?" I mutter before I can think better of it.

Oh, shit.

I didn't actually just say that out loud. Did I?

My whole body flushes when Mr. Harkness burst out laughing, shaking his head like I made a joke. But let's be real here. That wasn't a joke. I'd rather be fired than work for Mr. George. The severance package would give me a little wiggle room for the next month while I found something else.

My gaze flicks up to Lincoln George, only to find him scowling at me. I guess he isn't any happier about this than I am. I'm sure that my request that Mr. Harkness fire me hasn't improved his mood at all. I try to give him a small smile, as if I had, in fact, been joking.

His face remains set in a glare.

Okay then.

I look back at Mr. Harkness. "What about Giovanna?"

"What about Giovanna?" The first words that Mr. George says scrape against my skin, his voice all sorts of rough and raspy.

I tip my chin up and meet his slate blue eyes again. "Is she still your personal assistant? Or am I replacing her?"

"Worried about her?"

"Yes, I am." Not to mention that any of the blowback would be on me, not on Lincoln George. The office gossip would probably be that I slept with him in order to keep working here, especially since I've only been here a month.

"No," Mr. Harkness says, for all intents and purposes ignoring his business partner. "You won't be replacing Giovanna. You'll still technically be working for me. It will be your job to keep me up to date on everything that is happening in the company. This will require you to attend meetings, take notes, and send me weekly reports."

I glance at Mr. George, curious about how he's taking this. If his face is any indication, he's not pleased with this. He probably feels like Mr. Harkness doesn't trust him to run the company in his absence.

But can he really be surprised? The man spends more time having sex in his office than working. Of course, Mr. Harkness is going to be concerned. Anyone in their right mind would be.

A knot forms between my brows as I wonder how in depth my updates will need to be. Do I need to report on every little action Mr. George takes? Or is it going to be more broad strokes? The episode of *The Office* where Jan asks Pam to keep track of everything Michael does for a day flashes through my head and I can just see the report now.

8:30 Arrive for work
9:00 Sex in office with blond
10:00 Make Marketing team cry
10:15 Make Giovanna cry
10:30 Sex with brunette in private bathroom
11:00-1:00 Long 'client' lunch

You get the idea.

I lick my lips and keep my eyes focused on Mr. Harkness. "Um… how in depth would the updates need to be?"

Cabot's lips twitch like he knows what I'm asking. "It would mostly be meeting minutes. You already take those for me, so it's not adding to the work you're already doing. Though," he winces in apology. "You will probably need to attend a few more meetings, a few client dinners and such."

My stomach drops. "Dinners?"

My boss's face softens as he nods. "Yes. I know it's not ideal, but if I can't be there, I need you to be."

Mr. George lets out some kind of growling snort, a cross between a laugh and a snarl. Mr. Harkness keeps talking, like his business partner isn't in the room. "We'll compensate you for any overtime, of course, Liv."

I wave my hand, still clutching the iPencil. I'm not worried about the pay. He made it clear when I started working for him that any additional hours I worked would be double time. And under normal circumstances, I would be thrilled with the prospect, but...

"We can hire someone to help you when needed," Mr. Harkness offers. My eyes flick to Mr. George, who has now crossed his arms over his chest and his glare has deepened.

I shake my head. "No, that's fine. You've already done so much for me. As long as the dinners aren't a surprise, I should be able to figure something out."

Cabot Harkness eyes me, his gaze shrewd. I wonder if he can tell I'm just barely holding on by a thread here. "If that changes, let me know."

I give a jerky nod, even though I will do no such thing. I'll just have to pay Harvey overtime or see if Claire can help. Regardless, I will not be asking my boss to hire an additional nurse to watch over my dying mother. It's just not something I'm comfortable with.

I'm already so lucky I found this job, so lucky that when I stepped into The Winslow Foundation—an organization focused on helping people find work after taking a leave of absence from school or work to care for sick parents or loved ones—I met Verity Winslow. She liked me enough to find me a position in her husband's company. Not only that, but with her husband himself.

Cabot and Verity have already done enough for me. I will not take advantage of their good hearts or good will any more than I already have.

Cabot watches me for a moment longer before clicking on his computer. "I'll send you a calendar with all the events and meetings I would like you to attend in the coming months, and you'll need to chat with Lincoln to see if there are any I missed or additional one's he'd like you to join him at."

I nod, feeling slightly numb. My eyes move to Lincoln against my better judgment, and I find him glaring at me with a knot between his brows, like this is somehow my fault. My gaze snaps back to Cabot to find him watching me. God, everything is wrong. This wasn't supposed to be the way it goes. My tongue darts out to wet my lips. "When... Um, when does this change take place?"

"Tomorrow," Mr. Harkness sends me a sympathetic look. "I know it's sudden, but I really need to have my focus elsewhere. Immediately."

Tomorrow? I have to work with this imposing, glowering man starting tomorrow. "And you don't know how long it'll be for?"

I know I need to stop talking. I just need to grin and bear it. Nod and say I'll handle everything. If it was anyone else in the company, I wouldn't have a problem with that. But Lincoln George *unsettles* me. It's not that he stomps around glowering at everyone, it's not that he brings women into his office to fuck them at all hours of the days, it's not that he's harsh and exacting in his expectations for his employees.

Sure, all of those things together are unsettling. They're unsettling, taken apart too. But the reason I find Lincoln George unsettling is that I struggle to be nice to him.

I pride myself on that ability. I've dealt with more condescending pricks than I care to count—men on the street, bartenders, doctors who think because of my blond hair and soft Southern accent, I'm an idiot. Women who haven't learned we need to lift each other up, not smack each other down. Strangers on the street.

I can find a nice thing to say about or to everyone. If someone insults me, I let it roll off my back and smile at them harder. Reminding myself that I have no idea what they're going through in their private lives, and I don't need to add to their pain the way they are adding to mine.

But Lincoln George? He strains that ability.

I can hardly look at him, let alone be polite.

It doesn't help that he seems to have taken an immediate dislike of me for no reason I can decipher. I smiled my best smile at him, held my hand out to shake, and he'd just glared at me.

That was the last time I tried to be nice to him. Now, I'm polite and professional. *Usually.* Calling him bossy pants this morning certainly wasn't ideal. But I'd been up most of the night, only snagging a few hours of sleep, so I didn't have my normal walls in place. In short, he'd caught me at a weak moment.

Cabot Harkness smiles at me, all charm and sympathy. "I don't, I'm sorry. Verity is… She's having a very slight problem with her pregnancy, and refuses to listen and take it easy, so that's my focus for the next few months."

Few months?!? Now it's months? At the start of this conversation, it seemed like it was just going to be for a short time. But now it's months.

My gaze slides to Mr. George again. "I'm so sorry to hear that, Mr. Harkness."

"Olivia, I've told you to call me Cabot. Many times."

My tongue darts out again as I tuck my crossed ankles farther under my chair. "It wouldn't be proper."

Mr. George snorts at my statement, and I feel my cheeks heat in embarrassment. He probably thinks it's silly. But Mr. Harkness is my boss and my mother always taught me to keep it professional when I'm at work. Calling my boss by his first name will not do that.

Mr. Harkness shoots him a dark look and then turns back to me. "Are you comfortable with everything I've outlined today?"

I nod before I let myself second guess it, before I can open my mouth and say I can't possibly work with someone who glares as much as he does. But I need the job. "Yes."

Cabot claps his hands together and beams at me. "Excellent. Why don't you spend the rest of the day moving your things to your new desk outside of Lincoln's office? And the two of you can meet before you go home to go over the schedule."

I force a smile at him and dig deep before standing. "Thank you so much for the opportunity, Mr. Harkness." I say as earnestly as I can, meaning the words. I really do. Like I said, he took a chance on me he certainly didn't need to. "I won't let you down."

"I know you won't, Olivia." The smile he gives me is fond, and it makes my shoulders relax slightly. His unwavering belief in my capabilities is bolstering. I get the feeling that he does genuinely like me and cares about my situation. It's not just lip service.

So I bob my head to him again with a genuine smile on my face that falls as soon as I slide my gaze to Lincoln. "Mr. George." I bob a weird half curtsy thing and then head to the door, feeling a set of slate blue eyes on me the entire way.

3
Lincoln

"This isn't going to work," I mutter, watching Olivia Hart's heart shaped ass as she exits Cabot's office.

"Why wouldn't it?"

"She's an assistant, Cab. Not an executive."

He leans back in his chair, lacing his fingers behind his head. "She's the best assistant I've ever had. I trust her to help you make decisions regarding the company." He sighs, tipping his head back to look at the ceiling. "Look, she'll do the work and she'll do it well. She can act as your sounding board just as well as I can. I'm telling you, Linc, she already knows more about this company than Giovanna could ever hope to, and she's only been here for a month."

"Well, Giovanna is an idiot, so that's not hard to do." Shit. I shouldn't have said that. I can tell by the way Cabot's brows have lowered over his eyes and his lips thin disapprovingly. Honestly, my assistant's lack of brains is entirely my fault. I'm the one who hired her based solely on the size of her tits and the sym-

-metry of her face. At the time, I hadn't cared if she couldn't string two sentences together. I'd just wanted something to look at.

And she's not an idiot. Not really. She does her job well. Keeps my calendar organized, makes appointments, picks up my dry cleaning when I need it. She does an excellent job of remembering my siblings' birthdays and sending them gifts on my behalf. She does the same with my mother and knows not to bother with my father. That asshole would likely send back anything that came from me, anyway.

I am, after all, the perpetual disappointment in his eyes. No matter how successful I become.

Cabot leans forward and slides a personnel file across his desk. This is not the first time he's asked me to look at Olivia Hart's file. When I make no move toward it, he sighs again. Like I am the most infuriating person he's ever come across.

"Olivia was accepted to Stanford on a full scholarship. She was double majoring in finance and marketing. Top of her class for three years."

My hand twitches, and I resist the urge to flip through her file. "What happened in the fourth year?"

He doesn't answer, just nudges the file closer to me, then pulls his cell phone out of his suit jacket, checks something on it, then ticks it away and stands, clearly done with this conversation. "She's smart. She's capable. She's trustworthy. She will not let you down. And I trust her to help you make good decisions while I'm away."

My jaw tightens, resentment flows through me. I love Cabot. He's as close to a best friend as I've ever had, but his implication here is clear. It all comes down to trust. He wants Olivia Hart to watch me and report back to him, because he doesn't trust me. He wants to make sure I don't fuck up our company while he's off forcing his wife into bedrest.

"I didn't mean that how it sounded, Linc," he sighs, like he can see the thoughts in my head. "I trust you to make good decisions, too. She's an excellent sounding board. Talk shit through with her before you make any big decisions. She will help, I promise. Especially if she sits in on all the meetings I suggested. She's quick, she does her homework. I've never had someone so prepared for anything working with me."

I take a deep breath in through my nose and let it out the same way. "Fine. But I swear the moment she stumbles…"

I let the threat linger in the air, and Cabot rolls his eyes at me. "She won't, but fine. If she has any major fuck ups—and I mean *major*, Linc—we can discuss moving her to a different department."

I grunt out my agreement. We sit in silence for a moment while Cabot wraps up his last-minute tasks. I'm not foolish enough to think he won't be just as hands on while he's working from home as he is now. I'm about ninety percent sure he'll have Olivia send him daily updates and every single message, contract and proposal that crosses her desk… and mine.

"You wanna meet for a game?" He asks suddenly, pausing to look up at me.

I arch my brows at his sudden question. "You can't be away from Verity for work, but you can for a game of basketball?"

He lifts a shoulder. "I gotta stay in shape for my girl somehow." He eyes me. "I'll have Holt and Archer come along. We can play two on two."

"That actually sounds great." I push to my feet. "Text me when and where." He nods, eyes already back on the computer screen. "I guess I'll go meet with my new assistant." I go to leave but pause when Cabot says my name just as I grab the handle.

"She won't let you down, Linc. I promise. Just give her a chance." I nod and wave at him over my shoulder.

I should take him at his word. I should just grit my teeth and bear it, being around her overly cheerful and sweet personality. But I wasn't lying when I said if she stumbles even once, I'll get rid of her.

Not because I don't like her, or I think she's incompetent. I know she's not. I can see how hard she works, how organized she is, how everyone in the building likes and respects her. She's a little ray of sunshine in a concrete jungle.

No, I'll get rid of her at the first sign of trouble because Olivia Hart is a distraction I don't need.

Olivia's bent over her new desk just outside my office. Giovanna is watching her with wide, worried eyes. I should take her into my office and explain the situation, but instead I just stop next to Olivia's desk and take a large inhale of her sunshine and wildflower scent.

"Whenever you're ready, Miss Hart."

She jumps slightly, like she was unaware of my proximity, spinning to face me with a hand over her chest as if she's trying to keep her heart inside the cage of her ribs. She recovers quickly though, chin tilting up as she uses a finger to adjust her glasses on her nose. Her tongue darts out to swipe her lower lip, a nervous habit I clocked almost as soon as I met her that never fails to send my blood rushing south.

"I'm ready," she says, squaring her shoulders. She picks up her ever present tablet, the one that most personal assistants with the company carry around, though I'm pretty sure I've never seen her without it.

I hold my hand toward my open office door like the gentleman I am most assuredly not. "Shall we?"

I don't miss that her gold gaze narrows slightly, warily as she circles around me and precedes me into the room. She takes a few steps until she's standing in front of my desk and then she pauses, waiting. I close the door with a click and note how her shoulders flinch at the noise.

Jumpy little thing. I know I make her nervous. I make most people nervous. Even the women I fuck. It normally doesn't bother me, but for some reason, seeing her twitchy like that makes my skin get a little itchy. I can't tell if I hate it or love it.

I keep my eyes on her as I stalk slowly through the room, noting the way she gets more tense with every second that ticks by where she can't see me. The anticipation must be killing her. I have a sudden flash of Olivia bound and blindfolded, completely naked, all that golden skin of hers on display for me, as she waits for my touch.

Fuck. See? This is why I can't have her around me. I'll be hard all the fucking time from just the *idea* of seeing her naked, feeling her skin, tasting her sweet pussy. But it's not like I could tell Cabot that.

Smoothing a hand down my suit jacket, I give up my slow stalking and round my desk, sitting heavily in my chair and purposefully keeping my eyes off her. Even in her ill-fitting clothes, she's a goddamn vision. A ray of gold sunshine in an otherwise dreary office environment.

"Send me the calendar that Cabot gave you." I don't soften my voice or make it anything more than a demand.

"I already did." My brows arch slightly at that, but I don't look at her as I pull up the calendar and compare it to mine.

"There's a lunch on the seventeenth with Rollins Industries. You should attend that. I have an appointment on Thursday, so I won't be able to make the dinner Cabot was supposed to go to, so you'll need to reach out and change the date."

I glance up and find her head bent toward the tablet, taking notes on the changes she'll need to make, honey hair slipping over her shoulder as she writes. She doesn't say anything, just nods with each change I make, each demand I voice. She takes a few deep breaths when I add three dinners to her schedule but doesn't argue.

While she makes notes about the schedule, I take notes about her. She clearly doesn't like working in the evenings. I haven't missed how she scowls at me every time I ask staff members to stay late, or work on a Saturday to finish up a project. She's been exempt from those demands, since, until now, she worked for Cabot, but that is about to change.

Twenty minutes later, I've rattled off every change she needs to make, and she's dutifully agreed to every one.

Just as I say, "I think that should get us through the first month," the tablet chimes and Olivia taps on it.

"Mr. Holton's assistant confirmed the need to change the dinner on the seventeenth. She says he can do it on the sixteenth for dinner or the following Monday in the afternoon."

I can't contain my surprise at that, brows climbing my forehead as she looks up at me to get my answer. She already reached out while also making notes of changes she needed to make to her schedule. Dammit. She really is as good as Cabot made her out to be.

That's going to make it difficult to get rid of her.

But I am nothing if not determined.

I nod and say, "dinner on the sixteenth. You'll need to be there too."

Her lips compress the slightest bit, and I can't say I even blame her. I've just added at least ten events and meetings she'll have to stay late or come in on the weekend for. And that is just for the next month. If Cabot stays away as long as he thinks he's going to, there will be even more.

She doesn't argue, though I can tell she wants to. Instead, she just makes a note on the tablet, and then looks at me with those honey gold eyes of hers. "Is there anything else?"

I halfway want to make something up just to make her stay, to make her linger in this room with me, but I also know I need her to go. Besides, I have an appointment coming in just a few minutes that Olivia doesn't need to be present for.

"No, thank you." Miss Hart dips her head at me in deference and it sends a shock to my cock, as her eyes lower submissively. Right on cue, Giovanna knocks on the door and pushes it open without waiting for a response.

"Mrs. Tate is here to see you."

My lips curl into a smirk as Olivia, already halfway to the door, glances over her shoulder at me, brow arched. "Should I stay?"

Giovanna lets out a squeak of a giggle, knowing exactly what Mrs. Tate is here for, before she smothers it and reaches out to snag Olivia's wrist, dragging her out into the hall without waiting for a response from me. "Trust me," I hear her murmur to Olivia as the doorway fills with a lush curvy body, long black hair, and legs for days. "You do not want to stay in that room for what comes next."

I should focus on my guest, should be already half hard as she saunters toward me, hips swaying suggestively, but my eyes latch onto Olivia as she looks at me again, a furrow between her brows, like she's trying to figure out what this meeting is about. *Don't worry,* I tell her with my eyes. *You'll find out soon enough.*

Mrs. Tate kicks the door closed behind her, cutting off my view of sweet honey and moves to stand just on the other side of my desk, exactly where Liv stood while going over my schedule. Mrs. Tate—Kathy—drops her gaze and folds her hands in front of her, then she waits. Just like I've instructed her to do.

Kathy Tate is older than me by quite a few years, nearing forty, but she's still hot as hell and doesn't get any sort of physical affection from her husband, thirty years her senior. And even if she did, it wouldn't be enough to satisfy her cravings, which just happen to align with mine.

Normally, her submissiveness would be enough to make my dick hard and I'd tell her to get on her hands and knees to crawl to me, take my dick out and make me come. But—my gaze flicks to the closed door, every inch of me attuned to the woman on the other side—it's not enough today.

I stand and circle my desk, while Kathy stays just as she is, like a good submissive. As I get closer to her, a wave of Olivia's wildflower scent hits me. It's not pure Olivia. There's a tint of Kathy's expensive powdery perfume laced through it, ruining it, but it's enough to get my dick to sit up and pay attention.

Hmm, I pull up an image of Olivia on her knees in front of me, pink mouth open, glasses sliding down her nose as she grips my cock and licks. *Oh, fuck.* Yeah. My cock likes that. A lot.

As I stand behind Kathy, I superimpose Olivia over her, turning her black hair to honey. They look nothing alike, and it won't be easy to hold the image in my head, but I should be able to manage it if I keep my eyes closed, especially with Olivia's perfume hanging in the air.

"Are you ready to play?" My voice comes out raspy with desire, and Kathy—*Olivia*—shivers.

"Yes, master," she whispers out, voice far too grating. Nothing like Olivia's soft tones and light southern accent. That won't do.

I stroke my hand down the back of her head, twisting my fingers between her long sky locks. "We're going to play a new game today." I tilt her head and lick from her shoulder up to her ear. "I want you to say nothing, be as quiet as you can."

I had kind of hoped that I could have Kathy screaming on my cock, that Olivia would hear it and know exactly what I'm doing during this meeting, but I won't be able to perform if every time she speaks, my dick goes soft.

So this will have to do. Besides, I'll make enough noise for the both of us.

"Do you understand?" Kathy, the good submissive that she is, nods her understanding. "Good," I say, releasing her hair and reaching for my belt. "Let's get started."

Olivia isn't at her new desk when Kathy leaves. All of her things are there, neatly arranged, but the woman herself is absent. I ignore the kick of disappointment. I wanted to see her reaction to the first of many trysts she'll be privy to. Will she blush and avoid eye contact? Will she stare at me with those honey gold eyes of hers, one eyebrow arched as she meets my gaze head on? Or will it be a combination of both? Flushed cheeks, teeth sinking into her lower lip, running her gaze over my hungrily?

I hate to admit how much I want it to be the last one. But the idea of turning on Olivia Hart is almost too much to bear, and my already sated cock goes half hard at the mere thought of it.

This is really not fucking good. I already had to think about her the whole time I was fucking a silent Kathy. This can't be the way my life is from now on. I can't just lust after a girl who is my employee and who seems to barely tolerate me.

It gets under my skin, how little she thinks of me, makes me feel itchy in a way I never have before. But I push it away. If I let every person who disliked me get under my skin, I would be in an insane asylum ranting about how there are ants all over my body, or some shit.

"Where's Miss Hart?" I ask Giovanna, who looks up at me like a frightened little mouse. Maybe I should feel bad for terrifying my assistant, but I can't help that I expect a lot of my employees, and never more than I know they're capable of. I might have hired Giovanna because she has a nice rack and a pretty face, but I also know she's capable. Otherwise, half of my shit wouldn't get done.

"She went to the breakroom to make a cup of tea."

I grunt a response and head back to my office before pausing. "Do you have her cell phone number?"

Giovanna's brows arch and she nods. "Yes. I'll send it to you."

I tip my head and retreat behind the door, grabbing my phone off my desk when it pings with Olivia's contact information, not just her phone number, but also her home address and her personal email.

I create a contact using the information, and then pull up a new text chain and add her to it.

Me:
Bring me a cup of coffee.

It only takes a second for the three dots to appear at the bottom.

Sunshine:
Cream and sugar?

Me:
Black

Sunshine:
Of course.

I blink at the display name I gave her, not really even sure why I did it, only that she's all gold, warm and soft. It's a ridiculous name, and one I immediately change to Olivia Hart in the contacts, like I should have done from the beginning. Though she'll probably put my contact information under something like Devil Incarnate.

I imagine that's how most of my employees refer to me.

She likely won't be any different.

Not more than two minutes later, there's a soft knock on my door and my heart rate picks up, knowing who is on the other side. "Come in," I call and keep my gaze on my computer as the door swings open and wildflowers and sunshine replace the powdery smell of Kathy's perfume.

I look up at her from under my lowered lashes, trying to get a read on how she's feeling after her first true introduction to what sitting outside my office is going to be like. But her face is carefully blank, devoid of emotion, as she bends and places my cup of coffee near my hand, but not close enough that I'll knock into it.

"Do you need anything else?" Her voice is just as impassive as her face, and it pisses me off.

It's the only explanation I have for what I do next. I reach out, take a sip of the coffee, and then spit it back into the mug before frowning up at her. "This is from a pot."

She nods, eyes wide. "You said 'coffee'. I assumed that meant drip."

I shove the cup back over the top of my desk. "Well, from now on, assume nothing. If you aren't sure what I want, then ask. I hate being disappointed. Go make me an Americano on the espresso machine."

I don't give a fuck about the difference between drip coffee and Americano. Caffeine is caffeine. But it's satisfying watching the knot form between her brows as her honey eyes narrow at me. Her lips part like she wants to tell me to stop acting like a spoiled brat, but she takes a deep breath, and everything melts off her face again.

She flashes a brilliant smile at me, one that I can tell is fake, because her left hand is clenched into a fist at her side. "Of course, whatever you need, Mr. George." And then she scoops up the mug and strides out the door.

An unpleasant feeling twists in my stomach. Something like guilt or shame, but it's overshadowed by the victory of getting under her skin, just like she's gotten under mine.

4
Olivia

I'm pretty sure my new boss is the Devil incarnate.

I know a lot of people say that about their bosses, but just hear me out. He's tall and dark and broad and so freaking handsome it's unnatural. Spooky almost. He's always dressed impeccably in a black or gray suit and white button ups. The only thing that changes is the color of his tie. Even then I know what day of the week it is by the color. Monday is solid maroon. Tuesday is navy with silver pinstripes. Wednesday is dark forest green. Thursday is the wildcard. He'll wear a random patterned tie, purple, gray, brown, silver. It's always different and I'm pretty sure I've never seen him wear the same tie on a Thursday twice. Granted, that's only been four Thursdays, but I feel like I'm onto something here.

And Friday he wears a black tie. Always.

I think it's because he likes to look as menacing as possible when he asks the entire office to stay late or informs us we'll need to come in on Saturday. When

I say 'asks' and 'informs', I mean *demands* and *demands*.

I only noticed the thing with the ties because I'd been concerned about my lack of clothing choices. I have exactly five outfits appropriate for working in an office environment at the moment. Some people might call it a capsule wardrobe. I call it being frugal. Or *poor*, if you want to be specific.

"Miss Hart?"

His voice cracks through the speaker on my phone, drawing my attention away from the screen of my computer. Giovanna glares at me from across our shared office space. I give her what I hope is a radiant smile as I push the button and lean closer to the speaker. "Yes, Mr. George?"

"My office now."

A shiver works its way down my spine, and I push away from my desk before standing. If my boss wasn't the devil, I would take a moment to check my makeup and fix my hair. But as it is, the best I can do is smooth my skirt over my hips, snatch up my iPad and iPencil and then stride on my black four-inch heels (one of two pairs that I own) into the devil's lair.

It really resembles a lair. Two walls of windows let in light and oh, boy, does this room need it. The other two walls are black. I think maybe black satin fabric? Who knows? They have a sheen, and they look expensive, not just normal paint. And the wood accents gleam like gold.

The devil is sitting behind his impressively large desk—compensating?—his gaze focused on the screen in front of him. My gaze drops to his tie. Black. Just like his soul.

I shift, but don't say anything to draw his attention to me. He knows I'm here. This is a power play. After just a day of working for him, I'm aware of his go-to move. So I wait patiently. And I wait. And wait. And wait until my feet start to ache in my cheap heels.

My gaze goes to the painting behind his desk, an abstract piece that I suppose is meant to evoke some kind of emotion, but to me it just looks like shapes. But shapes arranged into a pleasing format. I like the way the gold slashes meet the-

A throat clearing has my gaze dropping from the painting back to my new boss. His dark brows are arched over his blue gaze like maybe he'd tried to get my attention more than once before I noticed. I'm pretty sure that's not true, but I give him an apologetic smile, just in case. I straighten my head, realizing I'd tilted it when I was regarding the painting, and lift the tablet, ready to do whatever he would like.

"What can I do for you, Mr. George?" *Damn, I sound so professional right now. Good job, Liv!*

"Get better clothes." The demand is harsh and blunt. My mouth drops open, my brows lower. The tablet falls next to my thigh.

"Excuse me?"

He leans back, all arrogance and self-assuredness. "You need to buy some more expensive clothes, Miss Hart. For the next few months, you will represent Cabot Harkness at meetings, taking part in conversations with wealthy members of society, investors, and clients. You cannot attend these meetings looking like you got dressed in your mother's closet."

I look down at my outfit and my cheeks go pink because both the skirt and the shirt are, in fact, from my mom's closet. She hasn't been in the workforce for a few years, and she bought most of her clothes in the 90s and the outfit I'm wearing definitely shows that.

I can feel his gaze on me, scraping over me from head to toe, like he does anytime we cross paths. And I know he finds me hopelessly lacking, but I'm not exactly sure what I'm supposed to do about that.

"I'm not sure," I say to the tips of my shoes, "what you expect me to say to that?"

"Miss Hart, look at me." I lift my chin until my eyes are pointed in his direction, focused on his tie, but not looking at him. I'm too damn embarrassed. "*At. Me.*" He bites out with enough command that my gaze flies to his.

Victory flares in his slate blue depths and he shifts in his chair. "When I give you an order, like *get better clothes*, I expect you to nod your head and say, 'yes, sir'. And then I expect you to follow through. It's really not that complicated."

I blink at him, then slowly use my middle finger to push up my glasses. His gaze flits to the finger, then back to my eyes with a glower even more pronounced than it was before, but he doesn't call me on blatantly flipping him off. Though his hand curls into a fist where it rests on his desk.

"Where would you suggest I go to purchase these *better* clothes, Mr. George?" I ask lifting the tablet to pretend to take notes. This asshole may think he can make such ludicrous demands of me, but I'll be damned if I'll spend my hard-earned money on hundred dollar shirts, just to impress him and the men I'll be meeting with. How I look shouldn't matter in the slightest. I've never understood spending that amount of money on a piece of clothing when I can get something similar for ten bucks at Target.

Beyond not understanding it, I can't afford it. I've got a mountain of debt I'm trying to climb out from under—technically my mother's but it's not like she's going to pay it off—and spending anything more than ten bucks on a shirt is frankly not in the cards for me.

He waves a hand. "I don't know one of those boutiques that women go to downtown. Get things that are work appropriate, but also get some fancier dresses. We'll be going to a lot of dinners and events, and you'll need to look the part."

I haven't even bothered to write any of that down. "Are you serious?"

He leans back in his chair. "Yes."

I shake my head, dropping the tablet and pencil back by my sides. "I'm not sure if you know what I get paid, Mr. George, but it's not enough to allow me to go on some wild shopping spree just because you don't like the way I dress. Like most people not billionaires, I have bills and responsibilities that I need to take care of first and foremost. Expensive clothing is so far down the list of priorities, it's laughable for you to suggest this to me."

I'm not sure why I have to explain this to him. He should have at least some idea that not everyone has billions of dollars at their disposal, right? I know he was born into a wealthy family, but surely he understands that not everyone was that lucky.

I expect him to snap something at me, to scoff and tell me my priorities are skewed, that appearance is everything, but instead, he just nods. "Fine. The company will provide you with appropriate clothing."

I'm surprised I don't drop the tablet and pencil right onto his plush rug, I'm so shocked by what he just said to me. I just stand there staring at him, even when he looks back at his computer and, for all intents and purposes, ignores me.

I clear my throat to get his attention again. He ignores me.

I shift on my feet and wait. He ignores me.

I huff out a breath and fold my arms over my stomach. He ignores me.

Finally, I say, "Is there anything else I can do for you, Mr. George?"

He doesn't look up and I think he's going to ignore me again. But then he says, "no, that will be all. Thank you, Miss Hart."

Dismissed, I head for the door, only to stop with my hand on the knob when he calls out. "Oh, I forgot to mention there's a client dinner tonight."

I turn back to face him, tapping the tablet back to life as I pull up our joint calendar. The one we spent literal hours hashing out yesterday. "I don't have a dinner on the schedule."

I look up and meet his eyes. "It's a last-minute addition. Cabot would want you to be there, but if you can't make it, I'm sure he'd understand."

Asshole. He did this on purpose. I can just tell by the gleam in his eyes. Trying to make me fail right from the jump. "I'm sure you remember, Mr. George, that I need warning of any changes made to my schedule. I have responsi-"

"You got a kid?"

I blink at the blunt question but shake my head. "No."

"Jealous boyfriend?"

"No." That answer is a quick huff of laughter.

"You have another job?"

What the hell is he getting at? Does he not know about my mom? Has he not even bothered to read my file? Does he not know how I got this job?

I straighten my shoulders. "No, Mr. George. I don't have another job. I have-"

"Then I don't see what responsibility you have that would keep you from attending this dinner tonight. However, if you can't make it, then I completely understand. Cabot, likely, will not."

The threat is implicit in his voice. Realization hits me. "This isn't a sudden meeting, is it?" He blinks at me, a moment of surprise on his face. "You just conveniently forgot to tell me about it. I would guess you've known about this meeting for a while now, hmm? Cabot too. So if I don't go, it'll look like I'm shirking my duties to him."

Mr. George lifts one shoulder, a wolfish smile pulling at his lips. "It must have slipped my mind."

Goddamn it. Why does he hate me so much? Why is he trying to get me fired? I just don't understand.

The question is there at the tip of my tongue, but I know without even forming them, he won't give me an answer, not a satisfactory one anyway.

So I give him a tight smile and tip my head at him. "I'll be there."

He looks back at his computer screen, dismissing me. "I'll send a car to pick you up."

"No need. I'll make my own way."

I swear a muscle in his jaw flexes and tics, like the idea of that makes him angry, but he doesn't insist on the car. "You're dismissed, Miss Hart."

Such a freaking bossy pant. I roll my eyes at his tone, but leave the office, already making plans for what to wear. Maybe Claire has something I can borrow that will fool Mr. George into thinking I'm not some scrub. Even though I definitely am.

I trip almost as soon as I'm in the front door of my house. To be fair, my eyes had been on my phone, checking how much time I have to make myself presentable for the dinner Mr. George sprung on me. If I hadn't been, I might have seen the colorful array of bags littering the foyer. I blink at them.

Not one of them is a normal brown paper bag. No. They're all those sleek, satiny, glossy bags in teal, pink, yellow, white, black. Basically any color, and all of them bear a logo from one of the fancy boutiques that line the streets downtown. The ones that Lincoln George told me to go shop at like I can afford it.

"Claire?" I call down the hall, kicking a matte black bag with gold writing out of the way. "Did you win the lottery or something?"

"What?" Claire asks, curly red head popping into the hall from the living room, before the rest of her follows, lithe body carefully weaving through the shopping bags that extend even that far. "I was going to ask you the same thing." She motions with one long fingered, elegant hand at the bright array. "Harvey said these started just arriving this afternoon. At first he tried to tell them they had the wrong place, but your name is on all the sales receipts."

I clench my jaw as I unbutton my jacket, tossing it over the railing for the stairs. "How is she?" I jerk my chin toward where I can hear the faint sounds of the TV.

Claire glances back down the hall. "Fine. Sleeping at the moment."

I nod and look around at the bags. How are there so many? Why are there so many? "I didn't think he actually meant it," I mutter, toeing a bag out of the way.

"Who?" my best friend bends and pulls a plaid grey pencil skirt out of a bag, nose wrinkling in distaste. It's definitely not her style. Claire is much more edgy, leaning more toward ripped jeans and asymmetric tops than business wear. But it's exactly the type of skirt I would have picked out for myself.

"Mr. George." I sigh, running a hand down my face. "The asshole called me into his office this morning and told me to get better clothes." The fabric drops from my best friend's hand as she looks at me in shock. I nod. "I know! He had the gall to tell me it looks like I dressed out of my mother's closet."

Claire's lips twitch, her gray eyes twinkling. "Well, you did, didn't you?"

"Fashion is cyclical." I wave a hand in the air in front of me. "Give it a year and my current outfit will be the height of cool." Claire chuckles. "Anyway, he told me to buy a bunch of clothes at all those places we could never set foot inside, because we can't afford a single item of clothing in them."

I watch as Claire bends and snatches up a white lacy bra and a matching pair of panties. My cheeks heat as she holds them up. "How did all of this end up here?"

I roll my eyes and start gathering up the bags. "When I laughed at him and told him there's no way I could afford that, he told me the company would pay for new clothes."

Claire chokes on air. "I'm sorry. Are you saying your *boss* paid for these?" She waves the lingerie in the air. "Oh, my God. Did he pick out all of this for you?"

I frown. "No. Obviously not. He probably just had Giovanna call a few places and had them pick things out for me. I'd be surprised if any of it actually fits."

Clair's dark red brows arch over her pretty gray eyes. "There's only one way to find out."

I eye her while she looks at me expectantly. "No, don't say it-"

"Fashion show!" She squeals. "Fashion show! Fashion show, Livie!" Her hands clap to together as she bounces, pleading with her eyes.

I laugh, shaking my head at her antics. "I don't have time. Also, I'm not keeping any of it. Mr. Harkness has already done so much for me. I do not need thousands of dollars of clothing hanging over me."

Clair deflates, her long red hair sliding over her shoulders. "It's okay to let good things happen to you, you know."

That pulls me up short, from where I was bent over still gathering bags. "What?"

She lifts a shoulder and motions at the bags. "This is a good thing. A *kind* thing. I mean, sure, he could have been nicer about it, but Mr. George still bought all of this for you, Livie. He gave you these clothes. Maybe he's not rubbing your lack of funds in your face but hoping that this will help you succeed."

I frown down at the bags hanging from my fingers. What she's saying might be true and if it were anyone else but my bossy pants of a boss, I might be inclined to agree with her. But he hasn't made it a secret that he thinks I'm bad news. I can't even say I resent him for treating me like crap. It can't feel good to have his business partner tell me to watch him.

I sigh. "Fine. I'll keep *some* clothes, but not all."

In my bag, my phone vibrates, and I drop all the bags and turn to retrieve it. I frown at the message there. How the hell did he know I was planning on returning most of this?

Bossypants:
If I get even one refund notification, I'll be displeased.

Me:
What if they don't fit?

Bossypants:
They'll fit.
Dinner is at 7:30 sharp.
Do not be late.

I frown at that. The man has obviously never shopped for women's sizes, because a size eight in one manufacture might be a ten in another. It's less about the sizes and more about the fit.

"See?" Claire says, chin resting on my shoulder as she reads my conversation. "All this is yours, babe."

I tip my head back and sigh at the ceiling. "Why is he like this?"

Claire chuckles and stoops to pick up the bags I'd dropped. "Come on. I'll help you carry all this upstairs and help you pick out what to wear tonight."

I look longingly toward the living room, toward where my mother is no doubt sound asleep, or at the very least dozing. I want nothing more than to throw on a pair of sweats, reheat some leftovers, and curl up on the couch to watch *Jeopardy* with her.

But I need this job. Our savings ran out a few months ago, and the total owed on my credit card is through the roof, not to mention the enormous stack of medical bills that sit neatly on the little desk shoved in one corner of the dining room.

Claire nudges me with her shoulder as she passes by, heading toward the stairs. "Come on, Liv. Let's get you ready."

Hardening my resolve, I nod and gather up the remaining bags to follow her upstairs.

5
Lincoln

I spent too much time today picking out clothes for Olivia. Far too damn much time considering each item, wondering how they'd fit her body, if it would hide or hug her curves, pondering which I would prefer in the long run. Because as much as I enjoy looking at Olivia, I don't really want everyone else looking at her, too. The idea of it makes me itchy, a strange possessiveness I've never felt before creeping over me at the very idea of another man eyeing her appreciatively.

Still, when I see her standing outside the restaurant, in a pair of red-bottom Louboutin's and the long cream-colored coat I picked out for her, something stirs in my chest. She has a ratty old purse over her shoulder, and I frown at it, hating that I didn't think to replace that as well.

I bought her everything from shoes, to jewelry, to lingerie, but I forgot to get her a damn bag. Her arms are folded across her stomach, and she's turned away from me, her loosely curled honey colored hair falling to between her shoulder blades, just long enough for me to wrap around my fist as I take her from behind.

"Miss Hart."

She turns and that familiar squeezing hits my chest like I can't get enough air, as my body feels itchy, my skin too tight. My jaw clenches against the feeling, my gaze narrowing, and she takes a step back, away from me, one hand fluttering up to her chest.

"You startled me," she says in a small laugh, like she thinks herself ridiculous for her reaction.

I run my gaze over her face. She's changed her makeup, not much, but enough to make her golden brown eyes pop a little more against the darker color she's smoothed over her lids. She left her glasses at home, letting me see the liquid honey better. he's swapped her normal tinted lip gloss for a red lipstick, a color that I would love to see smeared on my cock after coming down her throat.

I shove away the image of Olivia Hart on her knees for me, but not before my dick swells in my pants, half hard from only that. Her brows arch as I give her a tight smile. "I apologize." Then I motion toward the door. "Shall we?"

She gives me a small smile in return, and then precedes me into the restaurant with my hand at the base of her spine. I can feel her heat even through the layers of her clothing. The gentle swell of her ass just below my palm calls for me to slide down just a bit to caress it, but I keep my hand where it is. Polite. Gentlemanly.

Cabot will kill me if I fuck Olivia.

If what he told me is true, Verity will kill me if I fuck Olivia.

I don't need the extra strain of dealing with her emotions when I inevitably grow bored with her and call it quits. If I can't get rid of her before then, she'll still be working for me, for the company, and I don't need those awkward interactions in my life.

Resolve renewed, I guide her up to the hostess stand and help her out of her jacket, intending to leave both our coats with the coat check, but my actions stall out, as soon as she's shrugged out of the fabric, offering me a shy smile over her shoulder.

The dress she's wearing doesn't show a lot of skin. It covers her from her neck to her forearms and hits just below her knees. There's a tie at her neck and a peplum waist that gives it a vintage feel. No, it doesn't show a lot of skin, but it *fits*.

And seeing Olivia Hart in clothes that fit, that hug those curves like a lover? Well, it's enough to make my mouth water. Literally. Not to mention the color, a deep cobalt blue, makes her skin glow and the gold of her eyes stand out even more.

On top of that, she's wearing something *I* picked out for her, something I imagined seeing her in, and it has my possessive nature roaring with pleasure. *This woman is mine.* I blink at the thought, wondering where the hell my resolve to not get involved with her went.

"What do you think?" Olivia asks, turning toward me as she smooths her hands down those shapely hips of hers, ruffling the peplum. "Do I meet your approval?" The words have a hint of brat in them, snarky, but they also sound slightly unsure.

I run my eyes over her again, since she invited me to look, and I don't miss the way her cheeks flush under my perusal, or the way she shifts on her heels.

"I think it fits."

She snorts out a laugh that has my ribs squeezing just a little and folds her arms over her chest. "It does. Everything does. I can't tell you how annoying that is. I've spent hours digging through racks of clothes to only find one item that actually fits. And you somehow managed to find me clothes that fit like a glove without even really trying."

Half my mouth quirks into a smirk. "It's a matter of quality, Miss Hart."

Another snort leaves her that has the other half of my mouth quirking up. *She's adorable.*

"Mr. George?" I turn toward the hostess, who's watching me with a look in her eyes that I recognize all too well. Hunger. She bites her lip suggestively as she runs her gaze over me, all but ignoring that my companion for the evening is a woman.

Olivia doesn't miss it either if the arch of her dark blond brow is any sign. "I'll show you to your table." I nod and place my hand on the small of Olivia's back again, taking a deep inhale of her wildflower scent as she moves slightly closer to me. "Seriously?" she hisses up at me. "I'm right here."

I chuckle, bending just slightly to murmur in her ear. "You're my employee, Miss Hart." It's a reminder for both of us.

"*She* doesn't know that," Olivia replies before pasting a smile on her face when she sees the table we're heading toward is already occupied. I swear softly to myself, and Liv glances up at me in concern.

We'd both gotten here early, but still we appear like we're late. I hate that. It sets me on the back foot for the meeting, even though if I know Jerome Kline at all, he won't treat this like a meeting until he absolutely has to.

That thought solidifies when he stands from the table, eyes running over Olivia in a way that has my hair standing on end, and my possessive side wanting to tuck her behind me to keep him from appreciating her curves the way I had not two minutes ago.

Olivia keeps her smile in place, extending one slim hand out to him as he stares at her tits hugged in cobalt blue. "Mr. Kline, it's so nice to put a face to the name. I'm Olivia Hart." Her voice is smooth and professional, even if she grimaces slightly when he uses his grip on her hand to pull her toward him, bending to brush a kiss on her cheek like they're old friends, like he has any right to put his lips anywhere on her.

"Olivia!" He booms boisterously. "What a delight to meet you in person. You're even prettier than I imagined." His eyes flick to me, and a wolfish grin curls his lips. "Though I shouldn't be surprised, Lincoln does like a bit of flash to keep him occupied." Olivia's mouth falls open and her cheeks flush an angry red at the insinuation that I only hired her to fuck her. It only gets worse when he says, "when he tires of you, come see me. We can work something out."

Jesus. What was Cabot thinking of having her come here, to this meeting that isn't even really a meeting? She gives him a tight smile and carefully extricates herself from his hands, even though he doesn't appear to want to let her go. "I work for Mr. Harkness. Lincoln and I are colleagues." She places a soft hand on my forearm as she says it. I don't know if it's a plea for me to not deny it or something else entirely.

I maneuver around her, offering my hand to Jerome Kline and effectively cutting him off from being able to touch her again. "Jerome," I say, squeezing his hand a little harder than I normally would. "Nice to see you."

The older man flinches just slightly at my grip and gives me a simpering little smile. "And you."

With one more squeeze, I turn to pull out Olivia's chair for her, across from the asshole who already propositioned her. Sure, this way he'll be able to stare at her all night, but at least he won't be able to touch her.

The very thought of that has my blood boiling. No woman should be forced to endure hands on her that she isn't dying for, isn't hungry for. Don't get me wrong, I've touched plenty of women, but they *always* like it. I've never put my hands on a female that wasn't panting for it. And at the first sign of her being uncomfortable, I stop.

I'm an asshole most of the time, but I respect a woman's right to choose what happens with her body.

As soon as she's settled, Olivia pulls her work tablet out of her bag and sets it next to her, ready to take notes. I'm sure she has all the files needed to meet with Jerome as well, and a small glow of pride at how organized and capable she is blooms in my chest.

I have no right to feel that pride, but it doesn't stop it from forming.

As much as I wish that Cabot wasn't right about Olivia, it's becoming increasingly obvious that he was. She is a credit to her position, to the company, and we're lucky to have her. Still wish like hell she wasn't my babysitter, though.

Jerome grins at her across the table, eyes crawling over what he can see of her body, and I have to curl my fist to channel some of the possessive energy flowing through me. How dare he leer at her like that? She's here with me.

You've never cared before, a small snide voice says at the back of my head. *You've brought countless women around this man and haven't once been upset when he makes a pass at them. Why would he think this is any different?*

Stupid fucking inner voice, being right. It's never bothered me before, because I know a lot of the women I sleep with are looking for the next best thing, someone to take care of them. I'm a foot in the door to wealthy men, but I will never be someone's meal ticket. As mentioned before, I don't do monogamy. So if the girl I bring to a business dinner wants to cuddle up with one of the other men attending, I don't give a fuck.

Maybe it's because Liv is here in strictly a professional capacity, but I hate the idea of him flirting with her, touching her. It doesn't help that I know she's fucking uncomfortable with the attention.

"How long have you worked for H & G?" Jerome asks, licking his lips suggestively.

Olivia looks up at him before she picks up the menu and looks at it. More for something to do than anything else, I suspect. "Not long. A few months." Her tone doesn't invite follow-up questions.

"And you're already tagging along to business meetings with the boss. You must be very… *industrious*. I look forward to seeing what you can do for me."

My jaw clenches at the implication. Fucking fuck. I shouldn't have brought her. Technically, Cabot didn't need her to be at this meeting. He suggested it might be nice for her to meet Jerome to put a face to the name, but it's really not necessary. She could have gone her entire career at H & G and never met this predator. It's more of an informal thing, meant to keep Jerome sweet on investing. Of course, he's going to assume that Liv is here for him.

I resist the urge to drape my arm over her shoulder and tug her into my side, claim her. It won't help the situation. Because although Jerome thinks Olivia Hart is here for him, he's the kind of asshole that wants what other men have even more. So if I claim her, he'll push harder.

Olivia slips on that mask I've seen her wear, that impassive, professional one she uses to avoid unpleasant interactions, and taps on the tablet screen. "I'm simply here to take notes, Mr. Kline." Her tone is cool as a breeze on a hot summer day. "I don't imagine I'll be doing anything for you."

I bite back a smile as Mr. Kline laughs his ass off, like she's flirting, playing hard to get.

The server comes up to the side of the table, and I take advantage of Jerome's distraction to reach under the table and give Olivia's stocking covered knee a squeeze of approval. I should have realized what a fucking mistake that would be. Electricity, hot and spiky, climbs up from where my hand rests, radiating up my arm and then down to my cock. She sucks in air on a quiet gasp, a faint flush stealing over her freckled cheeks, and her honey eyes find mine, wide and curious, like she's wondering if I felt the same thing she did.

Yeah, sunshine, I fucking did.

My thumb strokes over the silk of her stocking, wishing like hell I had direct skin to skin contact, but it doesn't seem to matter as Olivia's pupils dilate and her red painted lips part on a pant.

Fucking hell.

"Let me order for you," Jerome says, drawing our attention to him. I realize with a start that they're both looking at us expectantly, though in the next moment Jerome says, "she'll have the oyster Rockefeller to start and the lobster as the main." The server jots it down, but Olivia shakes her head.

"Sorry, I can't-"

"Of course you can! The company is paying, Olivia," he chides like she's an adorable idiot, who doesn't understand the way money works. "You deserve to have the most expensive thing on the menu."

"Exactly," I say, cutting him off so he can't be a condescending prick anymore. "I'm paying, Liv. So get what you want."

She gives Jerome a tight smile, and me one that's a little more loose and grateful. "I actually can't have shellfish. I'm allergic. Is there anything on the menu that you can be sure has no cross contamination?"

He nods. "Any of the meat dishes. They're prepared in separate areas of the kitchen."

Liv gives him a blinding smile and orders a salad to start and a steak with mashed potatoes for the main. I order the same as her, more because I haven't looked at the menu and it sounds good.

"I didn't know you were allergic to shellfish," I murmur to her.

She snorts out a laugh and glances at me. "You don't know *anything* about me."

My mouth quirks into a half smile. "True." *But I think I want to change that.* The server suggests wine pairings for our meals, Jerome and I accept. But Olivia sticks with water. I don't know if it's because she doesn't drink, or because she's a professional. I make a note to ask her about it later.

Liv is quiet for most of the dinner. She takes notes on her tablet, pipes up when necessary, and does a masterful job of ignoring or steering away from every single one of Jerome's suggestive comments to her.

Most of the women I've brought to dinners with him have twittered at his compliments, cooed over him when they hear how much money he makes—which he's dropped into this conversation at least three times already tonight—and inevitably about half of them end up pursuing him after they've come home with me for the night.

It's never bothered me before, but if Liv showed even the slightest hint that she was interested, I have the feeling I'd break Jerome's jaw.

An extreme reaction, to be sure.

Thank God the only thing she radiates toward him is annoyed professionalism and a fair bit of barely disguised disgust. I recognize it. She does the same thing with me. I don't know if that's a good thing, but I'll take it over her openly flirting with him.

At the end of the meal, Jerome throws his napkin on the table, and leans back, lacing his fingers over his stomach while he eyes Olivia like she's dessert. "Should we take this party somewhere else?"

Olivia arches a brow but doesn't look up from where she's already stowing her tablet in her ratty bag. "I have to get home." She glances at me with a small smile tugging at her lips. "But I'm sure Mr. George would love to have a drink at a bar with you."

I blink at her and resist the urge to growl into her ear about how I'm going to punish her for being a brat later. Jerome lets out a disappointed noise. "Surely you can come for one drink, Miss. Hart. You've hardly spoken all night and I find I would like to get to know you better."

I don't miss the delicate little shudder that rolls through her body. My hand curls over her knee again and squeezes while I turn my attention back to the man across from us. His hungry gaze is on her breasts. "Olivia is done for the night, Jerome. She's done her job."

He licks his lips. "Has she? Because as far as I can tell, neither of us has gotten what we want from her."

My teeth clench. Olivia's fingers slide over mine, still on her thigh, and she squeezes gently. Some of the rage flowing through me eases, and I flip my hand under hers, pressing our palms together as our fingers lace. It feels natural as hell, which is strange because I don't hold hands with women. It just doesn't happen. Girls have tried. I've never once been accommodating.

But here I am doing it with Olivia Hart. *My employee.* The one I vowed not three days ago to get rid of if I had the chance.

My hand slips from hers. "Olivia, go home."

She jerks slightly at the tone of my voice, the explicit command. But she doesn't hesitate to stand from her chair, looping her bag over her shoulder. "It was lovely to meet you, Mr. Kline," she says quickly, not offering her hand for a shake, even when he pushes to his feet and starts rounding the table to her. She looks at me as I stand, angling to put myself between the two of them. "I'll see you tomorrow, Mr. George."

I tip my head at her. "Tomorrow."

She spins and darts through the tables, disappearing before Jerome has a chance to put his hands on her again.

When I turn my attention back to him, he's scowling at me. "Not in the mood to share this one, eh?"

I blow out a breath through my nose, running a hand over the front of my suit jacket using the motion to push down the urge to hit him.. "Olivia isn't mine to share, Jerome. She's my employee. And she's a damn good one." I lean closer to him, lower my voice, and make sure he hears me. "She's off limits, Jerome. I don't give a fuck if you want to seduce the other women I bring around you, but Olivia Hart is not them."

His mouth falls open in shock, but in the next moment his eyes flare with determination and intrigue. I curse to myself.

So much for not claiming her.

Olivia's started dressing in outfits that match my ties.

I don't know if it's intentional or not, but every day at least one piece of her clothing matches the color tie I'm wearing. The only day she doesn't match is Thursday, since that is the one day of the week I allow myself to grab any random tie from the near hundred that I have.

Today is a Thursday, and I can tell it is because she's wearing a light brown tweed pencil skirt that hugs her curves like a lover, and a silky cream colored long-sleeved blouse. Her shapely legs are covered in sheer black stockings and her curly honey colored hair is in a high ponytail. A pair of large, round wire-framed glasses perch on the tip of her nose. I watch as she uses one finger to push them back up before her hand returns to her keyboard, typing away industriously. Without taking her amber eyes off the screen, she reaches for her cup of coffee, misses, and instead knocks her pen holder over.

"Crap." The hissed word reaches my ears. She picks up the pens on her desk and rearranges them into a neat bundle to slip back into the holder, before she scoots her chair back and bends to pick up a few that have fallen on the floor, her sumptuous ass pointed right in my direction.

I'm not proud of how quickly I get hard from just watching her bend over. If I'm being totally honest, it's damn inconvenient. Especially since I don't have a place to put all this sexual frustration.

No, that's not true. I have a phone full of women that would love a second shot at me. That would scramble to be here in a few minutes.

Olivia straightens, her face flushed, hair slightly messy from being held upside down. She shoves the remaining pens into the holder as she pushes her glasses back up her nose. She's the picture of a professional, and yet that flush on her cheeks and the slightly mussed hair? It has my dick hardening, imagining her in that state from me, that I've just fucked her so hard her glasses slid down her nose, her skin flushed, her hair messy from wrapping it around my hand as I railed her from behind.

Fuck.

I can't keep doing this. I can't keep staring at her, watching her, getting hard from just *looking*. I feel like a goddamn teenager all over again, popping boners at the most inconvenient times.

I need to get rid of her.

The dinner with Jerome only solidified it.

I'm not acting like myself. I held her hand under the table for chrissakes and that possessive edge I felt seeing her in clothing I picked out for her has only gotten work. Olivia Hart makes me feel like I'm losing control, and so she must go.

Still, I spend too long watching Olivia Hart. I know this. It was bad before, when she was Cabot's PA, but now she's there, right outside my office for nine hours of the day and I spend at least eight of those hours watching her, studying her, the way she chews on her lower lip when she's concentrating. The way she smiles at everyone who approaches her. The way she compliments anyone she interacts with.

It pisses me the hell off. She's never once complimented me.

Granted, I'd probably snarl back some sort of cutting remark about her trying to fuck her boss, but she doesn't know that, does she?

The sound of her phone ringing draws my attention back to her yet again. Normally when she gets a personal phone call, she declines it and goes back to work, but this time she glances at the screen and then flicks her gaze in my direction. I pretend to be looking at something on my computer and she takes a deep breath and picks up.

"Hey Harvey, what's up?"

Harvey? Who the hell is *Harvey?*

Olivia listens for a moment, before her expression falls. "Oh, no, if it's an emergency…" She nods. "No, I understand. I'll…" she flicks her gaze in my direction again. This time I meet her gaze, arching a brow. "I'll see what I can do," she says in a rush. "Thank you for letting me know."

She hangs up and sets her phone back down with a precise action. Then she stands from her desk, smooths her hands down her thighs and strides in my direction.

I lean back, waiting for her to come to me, watching the way her hips sway with each step. When she comes to a stop in front of me, I drag my gaze up her body, letting it linger on the swell of her breasts, the flush on her collarbone before I meet her gaze. "What can I do for you, Miss Hart?"

Jesus. My voice is absolutely dripping with lust. I clear my throat like that will help with the erection forming between my legs.

She, being the consummate professional, ignores my tone and lifts her chin just slightly. "I need to take the rest of the day off, and possibly tomorrow."

I run my eyes over her again, but this time I focus on her expression. She looks… worried. Really worried.

"You don't look sick," I say, looking back at my computer, but not seeing a damn thing on it.

"I'm not. It's a personal matter." A personal matter? She has to deal with a personal matter with the name of *Harvey*. Fuck that.

"No." I bite off the word.

"Excuse me?"

I look up at her again. "You asked if you could have the rest of today off and possibly tomorrow, and my answer is 'no', Miss Hart."

Her eyes widen and her mouth drops open. "You can't just-"

"Actually, I can." I stand from behind my desk, smooth a hand down the front of my suit jacket before I button it. "You are still within your three-month probationary period, which means you do not have access to the flexible paid time off. You haven't earned your right to play hooky." I come to a stop in front of her, too close for it to be considered professional. Her slightly sweet floral scent reaches my nostrils and I breathe in. Deeply.

She blinks up at me and oh shit, no. There are tears shimmering along her lower lashes. This girl has withstood everything that I've thrown at her, but this? Keeping her from Harvey is what is going to break her?

Something twists in my stomach, something awful close to jealousy and guilt, but I push that feeling away and glare at her. "Tears won't change my mind, Miss Hart. And they are highly unprofessional. I suggest you take a moment to get your emotions under control and then get back to work."

She doesn't say anything as I move back to my desk. She doesn't say anything as I lift my hands back to my keyboard and type absolute fucking nonsense into an email. She doesn't say anything when she turns on her heel and strides back to her desk, swiping up her cell phone, purse and jacket and then heading for the door.

I blink after her as she exits the office.

What the hell?

6
Olivia

"Oh, that prick of a man! That absolute asshole of a human being! That waffle stomper!" Claire snarls on the other end of the line. "I will tear his dick off and shove it down his throat. Just say the word, Livie, and I will do it!"

I let out a strangled laugh and shake my head, ignoring the curious glance I receive from the guy in line in front of me as I respond. "No need to deprive the man of his favorite body part, Claire. I honestly think he wouldn't know what to do with himself if he no longer had a dick." Claire makes a tsking noise and I get the impression that she's going to say more, but I cut her off by asking. "Are you sure you don't mind going to check on my mom?"

"Please, babe, I love your mother, and unlike you, my boss isn't a complete asshole."

I let out a breath at her reassurance. "Asshole he may be, but he's not wrong. I don't technically have access to any days off. Not for another month, at least.

You're sure you're okay with taking the rest of the day off?"

Claire makes some kind of noise. "Liv, seriously, stop asking. I won't even be taking the day off. Helena is letting me work from your house. I'll be able to keep an eye on your mom and still kick ass in the design world."

I nod, relief flowing through me. "Okay, good. Thank you. I owe you big time. I mean it." Honestly, I have no idea what I would do without my best friend. She is a constant source of support and love for me and my mother. And her flexible schedule and truly understanding boss means that she steps in for me more than I care to admit.

"Well, you can make me some of those brown butter bourbon pecan chocolate chip cookies, and we'll call it even."

I laugh. "It's a deal. Hey, I gotta go, babe. I'll see you later."

"Bye!"

I hang up and look up at the menu hanging behind the counter, trying to make my decision before I make it up to the harried looking barista. After Mr. Bossy Pants had denied my request to go home for the rest of the day, I'd needed a breath of air, and decided that grabbing a coffee would be a great way to 'get my emotions under control'.

"Insufferable jackass," I mutter under my breath, making the guy in front of me turn around to glare at me. My cheeks turn pink. "Oh, sorry, not you. Obviously. I don't know you well enough to know if you're a jackass or not. But all signs point to *no*." I give him what I hope looks like a genuine smile. "I like your tie. It really brings out the color of your eyes."

His brows lower and I get the impression he's trying to decide if I'm completely crazy, but then a smile breaks out over his face, and he smooths a hand down it. "Thank you. My niece picked it out for me."

My smile grows. "I guess that explains the hotdogs, then?"

He chuckles. "It sure does. She thought it was hilarious."

"Well, she has excellent taste." I'm not even joking. Sure, the tie has hotdogs and what look like little squiggles of mustard and ketchup on it, but the color really does complement the blue of his eyes. Eyes that are crinkled at the corners with amusement and, dare I say, interest?.

The barista clears her throat. "How can I help you, sir?"

"Oh, you're up," I motion to the front of the line, where there is now a vacant space. He grins sheepishly at me and then moves forward to place his order. Vanilla latte. Safe, basic, classic. He glances over his shoulder at me as he gives the barista his name. "Marcus." *Did he want me to hear it too?* I shake my head at the thought. He's probably just checking to make sure that I'm not foaming from the mouth or something.

When it's my turn, I step up and give the harried worker a smile. "Oh, gosh, I love your hair color! It's so pretty!" It really is. A light icy blue that I always dreamed about being able to pull off but know that I would never be able to.

She blushes and touches a strand of her shoulder length hair, almost self-consciously. "Oh, thank you. It's new. I'm not used to it yet."

I beam at her. "Well, you made the right choice. It looks so good on you."

She gives me a full genuine smile and something in my chest loosens a little, knowing that at least for a moment I made her day better, even if it's just a little.

I place my order- salted caramel latte with extra whipped cream. When she asks if she can get me anything else, I hesitate and then order an Americano black and a flat white. I leave a generous tip and then move down the counter to wait for my order. Marcus gives me a smile as I approach, but then his gaze flicks to just over my shoulder and I realize, for the first time, that I am not alone.

A huge stormy man is standing right behind me. And I mean *right* behind me, close enough that I feel the heat from his body, and then... oh then the jackass takes it one step further, sliding one of his big hands around my body until it's pressed against my stomach in a proprietary move that he has no right doing.

He's not my boyfriend, he's my boss, and the way he's pressed against me right now is entirely inappropriate.

Marcus's gaze flicks down to where the man behind me is holding me, then back up. His smile is strained. He turns around and ignores me, like we hadn't had some flirty banter not two minutes ago. Insufferable bossy pants jackass.

All thoughts of Marcus fade as Lincoln pulls me closer, bending his neck to say against the shell of my ear, "playing hooky, Miss Hart?"

I ignore him. There is no rule that says I have to acknowledge him when I am out of the office and on a break.

He growls when I don't respond, pressing into my back until I can feel his erection between my ass cheeks. My stomach flips and butterflies take flight, and I swear my heart stops beating and then picks up double time.

What the hell is he doing? He doesn't like me. Or at least I don't think he does. It's true that he treats me just like everyone else, but the hard length pressing into me tells a different story.

Maybe.

Maybe it has nothing at all to do with me and he just walks around hard all the time. I wouldn't be surprised given how often he has sex. Maybe its a medical condition. The opposite of erectile dysfunction. Which I guess would just be *erectile function*?

Still, it doesn't explain my body's reaction to him and his proximity. I want to melt against him. I want to turn into his solid form and raise on my tiptoes to press my lips to his. I want to go back to his office and let him bend me over his enormous desk and fuck me with his enormous cock. Or rather, my body wants to do that. My mind is still pissed off at him, and it's my mind that draws my arm forward and then back so I can jab my elbow into his side.

He grunts in pain, and then chuckles, low and dangerous. "Problem, Miss Hart?"

The barista behind the counter calls my name and I step away from him, forcing a smile to my lips as I take the cardboard drinks tray from her. "Thank you so much. Have a lovely day!"

Then I shoulder by the number one jackass and head out the door, pointing my feet toward the office at a fast clip. He doesn't even have to rush to keep up with me. Of course he doesn't. His legs are like twice the length of mine and I'm in *heels*. Granted, they're a pair that he bought me, so they're comfortable as heck, but they still force me to a relatively sedate pace.

"Won't Harvey be upset to find out you're flirting with other guys?" His question takes me so off guard that I stumble on a crack in the sidewalk and would have fallen if he hadn't caught my upper arm in a punishing grip to keep me upright.

I shrug off his grip and frown up at him, confused, as I start forward again. "Harvey? Why would he be-" Oh. *Ohhhhh*. He thinks Harvey is my boyfriend. And he thinks I was flirting with Marcus while I am in a relationship, because that is how low his opinion is of me. "How long were you standing behind me, listening like a creeper?"

"Long enough to hear you call Harvey 'babe', and then flirt with another man. Does he know you cheat on him?"

I laugh. Oh, how I laugh. So hard that I have to stop in the middle of the sidewalk and bend over slightly, just to get the hilariousness of it out. Mr. George just stares at me, the storm that is always on his forehead growing and growing the longer I laugh. "I don't see what's so funny, Miss Hart."

I chuckle one last time, shaking my head. "You mean besides *you*, the guy who parades a new woman around the office on a daily basis, accusing *me* of cheating?" I start toward the office again.

"Those women know exactly what they're getting from me. I don't promise them anything beyond what we are."

I nod and smile at Rupert, the doorman, as he opens the door for me. "And Harvey knows exactly what he's getting with me." I jab at the elevator button. I turn to him, opening my mouth to explain my relationship with Harvey, which is most assuredly not romantic, when he cuts me off.

"So he knows you're a little whore?"

My mouth snaps closed. Two things happened at that moment. One, hearing him call me a little whore in his raspy, rough, *angry* voice floods my panties in a way that I didn't think was possible. And two, hearing him call me a whore in that judgy tone makes me furious. Who the hell does he think he is?

His lips twist into a feral smile because he sees both reactions. I have no clue how he does, but I know he does. He moves closer to me, his thumb coming up to brush against my parted lips. "You like that, Olivia?" he murmurs. "You like being called a whore? A dirty little slut?"

I may whimper. I definitely whimper. His eyes darken to stormy blue, heavy with lust.

And then, because I have no self-control and apparently no shame, my tongue darts between my lips to flick the tip of his thumb.

"Fuck," he growls out, before leaning forward and saying. "If I were to put my hand in your panties right now, would I find out just how much you like being called a whore, Olivia? Are you wet for me, sunshine?"

My body sways toward him while my eyes flutter closed, unable to look at him while I give him my answer. "Yes," I whisper.

The elevator next to us dings as it arrives and the doors open. I jerk away from him so fast I nearly fall on my ass, but he grabs my elbow to keep me steady, and takes the drinks container from my other hand. Then he ushers me into the elevator and growls, "Get out," at the woman already in it who apparently came up from the parking garage. She scrambles past us just as the doors close.

Mr. George keeps one hand on my arm until the elevator moves, and then he slowly, leisurely uncoils his grip from me, and reaches out to hit the emergency stop button. The elevator shudders as it slows, and the lights dim.

"What are you doing?" I ask, already backing away from him, even though he hasn't moved in my direction. He bends and sets the drinks tray on the ground and when I'm pressed against the far wall with nowhere else to go, he moves in my direction. One of my hands goes behind me to grip the metal bar that lines the walls, and I hold out the other in front of me like that will be enough to keep him on his side of the elevator, but of course it does nothing, but give me the chance to feel all those hard, defined abs hidden under his dress shirt.

His big hands sweep up the outside of my thighs, dragging my skirt along with them, exposing the tops of my stockings and the garter belt holding them up. He chuckles low in his throat when he realizes that I've put on my lacy panties over the garter. "Do you wear this for me, Olivia? Hmm? Do you imagine me slipping off your panties and fucking you while you're wearing these?" His fingers pluck at the garter.

I don't answer. Even though, *yes*, that is exactly what I think about every morning when I put on my stockings. The ones he picked out for me. He definitely doesn't need to know that.

His hand trails upward to the apex of my thighs, brushing against the fabric that covers my aching core. He groans. "So wet, baby."

My only response is a whimper, full of need, while my hips buck farther into his hand.

"You want more? You want to show me what a good little slut you are?"

His slate blue eyes are focused on my face, reading my every emotion so I know, *I know* he sees the shame that drifts over me. I shouldn't like that. I shouldn't like being called slut and whore during sex. The one time I'd asked for it, my partner had been so uncomfortable with it, he'd lost his erection and no amount of my mouth on his cock could get it back. He'd informed me that there was something wrong with me for wanting that, that it was—*is*—demeaning.

Linc doesn't seem inclined to tell me I should be ashamed, and if the bulge pressing against the zipper of his black slacks is any indication, he's as turned on by it as I am. He tsks. "Never feel bad for something turning you on, Olivia. Never. Not with me. Not with anyone else."

Then his hand slips between my legs, tugging the fabric to the side. He plunges two fingers into my pussy with no warning, making my head tip back as I cry out, "Oh, fuck!"

"So wet," he praises, his head dropping so he can trail his lips along my jaw. "So tight. Such a good pussy."

He draws out and slams back into me, drawing out another moan. "Look at you, sunshine," he murmurs against my neck. "Look at how well your pussy takes my fingers, squeezes them just like a fucking whore. You gonna come on my fingers, baby? You gonna be my good girl and squeeze them with your tight pussy while you scream?"

Oh, God. His fingers are moving at a hurried pace, thrusting in and out of me so quickly that my breasts are bouncing with each one. But then suddenly he stops, his fingers still deep inside me, and his other hand comes up and smacks my cheek, light enough that it's nothing more than a brief sting, but hard enough to draw my attention. "Answer my fucking question, Olivia."

I whimper and shift my hips, my core pulsing around his digits still buried deep inside me. His free hand shifts from my face to wrap around my ponytail, tugging it almost painfully. "Answer my question and I'll let you come."

Dammit. What had his question been? I try to make my lust addled brain focus. What was his question? Fuck it. I can't remember.

It's a gamble, but I whimper out my answer. "Yes."

"Yes, what, baby?"

I look up at him with wide eyes, and he smirks down at me. "You have no fucking clue what I asked, do you?" He draws his fingers out and then thrust them in again, making me moan. "Too distracted by your greedy cunt to listen." He leans down until his lips press against my ear. "I asked you if you were going to come all over my hand." Thrust. "If you were going to squeeze my fingers with this tight pussy." Thrust. "While you scream. You gonna do that for me?" Thrust.

I'm mindless now. I know it. He knows it. But he still presses the issue. "When I ask you a question, you will answer it, Liv. Unless I instruct you otherwise. Understand?"

"Yes, I understand," I gasp out, curling my fingers in his shirt, trying to get him closer.

He smirks. "Good girl. And what about my other question?"

I shudder as his fingers curl inside me. *Focus, Liv. You need to focus so he'll finish this.* "Yes, I'm going to squeeze your fingers with my pussy when I come."

He growls out something I can't make out, but then he's really finger fucking me, his lips pressed against my neck. "That's it baby, show me what a good slut you are. Show me what you're going to do to my cock when I fuck you."

My hips are moving frantically, grinding my clit against his palm, while he opens his mouth and scrapes his teeth over my neck. I have a brief thought that the asshole better not leave a fucking mark, but then all thought disappears as the orgasm I've been chasing barrels into me, knocking the air from my lungs, making all of my muscles tense as I arch my back, head bumping into the wall almost painfully. "Oh, fuck," I moan up to the ceiling, as my inner muscles clamp down, suck his fingers, greedily wanting to keep them inside. *"Lincoln."*

"That's it, baby. So good. So fucking beautiful when you come." My eyes flutter open to find him still hunched over me, face just inches from mine, so close that when he exhales, I inhale his air and vice versa. His fingers pump in and out of me a few times, drawing out the orgasm, feeling out my tight muscles.

I blink at him. At my *boss*, who just made me come harder than I've ever come before, in an elevator in our place of business. "Holy shit," I breathe, reality slamming into me. *"Holy shit.* What the hell!" My hands push against him, but he doesn't go anywhere. Just keeps his hand wedged between my thighs, fingers stuffed inside me.

"I know. You fucking soaked my hand, Olivia."

I blink up at him again, confused by the way his words make my pussy clench and a fresh wave of arousal hits me. "You wanna come again, baby? Maybe this time on my cock?"

I shake my head in denial, even as my body betrays me, hips grinding forward just the slightest bit in anticipation. He chuckles and pulls his fingers from inside me, drawing a whimper out of my chest at how empty I feel without him there. "Not today, Olivia."

My brows narrow into a glare as I take a deep breath and try like hell to get myself under control. "Not *ever*," I correct, needing to re-establish some boundaries that have apparently just been smashed to smithereens by his dirty mouth and my needy vagina.

Another chuckle as he lifts his hand, dripping with my arousal, and offers his fingers to me. "You made a mess, Olivia. Time for you to clean it up."

"Excuse me?"

His slate blue eyes narrow and his jaw tenses as he stares me down. "What did we talk about? When I give you an order, you do it without questioning me."

I shake my head. "That was regarding *work*, Lincoln. Not to me sucking your fingers in a work elevator."

"It is regarding every fucking thing I say to you, Olivia." His other hand comes up and clamps over my cheeks. "Open."

I wish I could say that I refused, that my vagina didn't clench again as the pure command in his voice, that I didn't part my lips and let him slide his middle and ring finger between them. I wish I could say I didn't groan at the taste of myself on his skin and the way his eyes spark with lust as my tongue slid over his skin. I really fucking wish I could say that I didn't grind myself against his hard cock like a hussy, while I lapped up every ounce of my arousal from his hand.

But my mama didn't raise a liar, so I can't.

"Good girl," Lincoln says, when he deems me done. His hips press into me one more time before he steps back and smooths my skirt down over my hips, before reaching up to tweak my hair back into place.

I stand there, mouth slightly ajar, not fully grasping what the hell just happened, as Lincoln smooths out his own suit jacket, bends and picks up the tray of drinks that have probably gone cold by now, and hits the emergency stop button again.

The elevator lurches into motion as he glances over at me. "Close your mouth, Miss Hart. Or I might have to find something to fill it with."

I close my eyes as my head jerks, and I breathe out heavily. "Don't." The word slips past my lips, while panic tries to take over. I'm going to be fired now. If anyone finds out about this, I will lose my job, along with my health insurance and the income I so desperately need.

"Olivia." My eyes blink open just as the elevator slows to find Lincoln standing in front of me with a knot between his brows, his slate blue eyes focused on my face. "Everything's going to be fine." He dips his head and presses a soft kiss to the corner of my mouth just as the doors slide open. Then he turns and leaves me standing there, with the drinks tray in my hand. I stare after him for a beat.

"Come along, Miss Hart." He calls over his shoulder, making me lurch into action, stumbling along behind him on legs that are still trembly and weak.

I trail him all the way to his office, where I stop next to my desk. Thank God that Giovanna isn't currently at hers. I'm pretty sure she would take one look at my flushed as hell face and just know what happened. I take a deep breath to get myself under control, and then slide the drink tray onto my desk.

"Is one of those for me?" Mr. George asks, from far too close behind me, not quite touching, but he might as well be with how aware every single nerve ending is of him at the moment.

I swallow and nod. "Yeah. Yes. I bought you a coffee. It's probably cold now." I should reach for it, hand it to him, and then put the flat white I bought for Gi on her desk. But I just stand there, staring down at the three paper cups. *Shock.* I realize. This is some form of shock. It must be.

"How kind of you to think of me, even when you're pissed, sunshine." Lincoln's arm comes around me, grabbing the cup labeled as Americano, pressing closer, until his mouth is hovering just over my ear. "Good girl. To reward you, I'm going to fuck that pussy and fill it full of cum."

Jesus. I sway under the weight of lust and just barely catch myself on the edge of my desk. It shouldn't be possible for me to get so freaking turned on by just one sentence, but here I am.

Here I fucking am, bent over my desk, trembling with need while the man who put me in this state chuckles and walks away.

7
Lincoln

By the time Monday morning rolls around, I've run out of patience. Olivia Hart has avoided me since Thursday afternoon when she came on my fingers and gave me enough ammo for my spank bank to get me through… well, the weekend.

She'd called in sick to work on Friday.

And that pissed me off to no end. I *told* her she couldn't have the day off, that she hadn't earned it, and she ignored that. She should have been here. But then I'd thought about how fucking stunning she'd been in that elevator, crying out my name as she came, and I'd been willing to forgive her. Just this once.

How could I not when I fucked my hand more times than I care to count over the last three days to the memory of if it? To the feel of her clamping around my fingers like she never wanted me to fucking leave?

But as soon as I see her, she'll have to lean that she doesn't get to ignore my orders. Having her not show up to work on Friday has left me feeling out of control, and I need to get it back, need to know she'll follow my orders as my employee and as my... whatever the hell this is going to be.

Whatever it is, I know I'm not done with Olivia Hart.

Even if her staying home was her way of saying she's done with me.

I'd seen the guilt that had crawled over her face when she'd gotten that text shortly after she'd returned to her desk. No doubt it was that prick Harvey who apparently doesn't mind if she fucks other men.

Stupid fucking idiot.

Olivia Hart isn't someone you share with others. No, you keep her all for yourself. Your own personal whore to use as you see fit.

And that is exactly what I intend to do.

Sorry Harvey, I'm gonna steal your girl and make her mine.

Temporarily, I add as an afterthought.

Maybe I should feel bad about that. Maybe I should take a step back and not blow up her relationship with another man, but is it even a relationship if he hasn't told her in no uncertain terms that she belongs to him? If she feels okay flirting with other men she meets at coffee shops? If she lets me finger her to orgasm in an elevator?

I don't think so.

It's nine-thirty, and I'm about to call her into my office on the intercom so I can bury my face between her thighs, when the door slams open and there she is, my good girl in all her rage filled glory. I've never seen her angry before, but she is angry now. Oh, boy is she. And damn if it doesn't make her fucking stunning.

"You enormous prick!" she whisper-shouts at me. Apparently even furious, she's conscientious of where we are and the number of ears that might hear whatever she wants to yell at me about. Probably she's furious at herself for letting me finger fuck her in the elevator.

I don't respond to her words, instead leaning back and running my heated gaze over her. She's wearing a maroon pencil skirt with a black button-up shirt that has a neck high enough that it covers the bite I gave her on Thursday. I hate that she covered it up. I want it on display for the whole fucking world so that they know she belongs to me.

Temporarily.

I wonder what Harvey said when he saw that. I smirk, imagining it.

Olivia's brows raise. "You think this is fucking funny? You think threatening me, sending these pictures to Mr. Harkness is funny? It's my fucking *life*, Lincoln. You don't get to just-"

Wait. What the hell was that? "Whoa, whoa, sunshine, what are you talking about? What pictures?" I stand up from my chair and round my desk toward her. For the first time realizing that she has a manila envelope clutched in her hand.

She scoffs. "Don't pretend like you don't fucking know. I still open his mail. Or did you forget about that? 'I'm going to fuck that pussy and fill it full of cum.' Isn't that what you said?"

My brows arch in surprise while my dick stands up and starts paying attention again. Because the image that sentence evokes is something I definitely am interested in. And hearing Olivia say it while she looks so prim and proper is like a fucking wet dream. "I don't recall exactly, but I like that my words made an impression on you."

She snarls like that is the last thing in the world she wants. And my anger that had been at bay, replaced with the anticipation of seeing her again today, raises its head. "What the fuck is your problem?"

"*You*," she snaps back, not missing a beat. "You are my fucking problem. But you know what? I'm about to be *your* problem. I'm reporting you for sexual harassment. Thanks to you, I have proof!" She waves the envelope in front of me and then starts toward the door. "Hope you're ready to pay me a shitload of money, you perverted son of a -"

She cuts off when I swipe the envelope from her hand and retreat behind my desk, pulling the stack of paper from inside it. No, not paper. Photos. Of us. Together.

In the building's foyer with her tongue on my thumb, looking up at me like she wants me to fuck her right there.

In the elevator with my fingers buried in her pussy, her head tipped back against the wood of the wall, me watching as she comes undone.

In the office, just as I bent over and whispered in her ear that I'm going to fill her full of cum. The one piece of paper in the stack that isn't a picture has those words written on it in red ink like some kind of psycho killer letter. *I'm going to fuck that pussy and fill it full of cum.*

"Give those back!" She shouts, apparently done with moderating her voice to keep others from overhearing us.

I ignore her. The rage that had been simmering in my chest is now a full-blown boil. This fucking girl. She thinks she can fuck with me and not suffer the consequences? She thinks I'm just going to pay her to not take this public? If that's the case, she is fucking dead wrong.

"What the fuck, Olivia?" I grind out and she takes a step back at my tone. Her mouth snaps closed on whatever argument she was about to spew. "*What. The. Fuck.*" Repeat rounding my desk. "You think just because I gave you the best orgasm of your life you can blackmail me? You think I'm going to just roll over because of some pictures of two consenting adults fooling around in an elevator?" She stumbles back as I stalk toward her, but then tightens her hands into fists and lifts her chin to hold her ground.

"How did you get access to the security feeds?" I ask, stopping next to her, so close I catch her sunshine drenched field scent.

Her brows wrinkle, and she looks up at me uncertainly. Her honey eyes flick to the pictures strewn over my desk and then back up to me. "I didn't do this," she says carefully. "*You* did. You... You orchestrated that whole thing to get... to get Mr. Harkness to fire me. I know you don't like me, that you hate working with me. It... it has to be you."

It takes a moment for her words to filter through the rage running through me. Takes a moment for her expression to click in my head. For me to understand what is actually happening here. "You didn't bring those pictures here to blackmail me?"

"What? No!" She shakes her head emphatically. "They were in the stack of mail from Friday for Mr. Harkness. You did this to get rid of me."

A harsh laugh bursts out of me. "Oh, baby, that is the last thing I want. I want you right here, where I can fuck you anytime I want."

She swallows as a pretty blush covers her cheeks and she looks away from me, back to my desk. "You're hurting me," she mumbles. I realize with a start that I have both of my hands curled around her upper arms, tight enough that she'll likely have bruises tomorrow. I loosen my grip but don't let her go, instead sliding my hands over her shoulders until I'm cupping her face.

"You swear you didn't do this?" she whispers, looking back at me with wide, warm brown eyes.

I nod. "Yeah, sunshine, I swear."

She sighs and drops her head until her forehead presses into my chest. "It wasn't me either. I don't have a clue how to access the security feed. I don't even know who I would talk to about that."

I kind of doubt that seeing as she's all buddy-buddy with at least half the people who work in the building, one of the security guards could probably hook her up. But what I believe is that she wouldn't want anyone else to know about this. About us.

So the likelihood of her having someone print pictures of her in a compromising situation is nil.

I lace my fingers into her honey blond hair and tug her head up. "Tell me what happened, Olivia."

"Bossy pants," she chides gently. Her fingers stroke up and down my sides, making my cock stand up and pay attention, but I tell it to sit the fuck down because we have an actual fucking problem here. "There's not much to tell. I started opening the stack of mail for Mr. Harkness from Friday and over the weekend, and it was in the stack, addressed to him."

My brows lower, and I stride away from her to swipe up the envelope. "It's not postmarked. No stamp." Which means someone either used the interoffice mail system or dropped it on my girl's desk by hand.

She moves up next to me. "I didn't even think to check for that."

"No, you just jumped to the conclusion that I'm an asshole who wants to get you fired."

"In my defense, you are an asshole." She doesn't even sound contrite when she says it.

My lips twitch. "Touché, Miss Hart."

She fingers one of the photos, one where I have my teeth sunk into the flesh of her shoulder. "Someone knows."

"Someone knows," I agree. If I had been thinking clearly last week, I would have realized that even though there wasn't anyone in the elevator with us, the cameras would catch whatever we did. Frankly, I don't give a shit if the entire company knows that Olivia and I are fucking. Or *will be* fucking once I get rid of Harvey. Cabot will be disappointed, but he can fuck all the way off. What Liv and I do together has no bearing on him.

But I do have a problem with someone seeing her like this, in a moment where she was vulnerable and trusted me to take care of her. Some asshole in security watched while she came apart on my fingers and that is not something I cannot let stand.

"What are we gonna do?" she asks quietly, still staring down at the images on my desk.

I twist my head to look at her, look at the uncertainty on her face, the fear, the worry. Fuck. I don't want her to feel any of those things. I open my mouth to answer her, but a knock on the door has both of us leaping into action, sweeping the pictures into a neat stack. She slips them into the envelope. I take it from her and slip it into the top drawer of my desk.

"Enter." I call out as Liv moves to the far side of my desk and folds her hands in front of her.

The door opens, Giovanna pokes her head in. Her brown eyes sweep from me behind my desk to Olivia standing demurely eight feet away. "Your ten o'clock is here, Mr. George. Should I show them in?"

I nod, even though it's the last thing I fucking want. My only free half hour of the day has been wasted on this bullshit instead of with my head between Olivia's thighs, learning the way she tastes, seeing what makes her writhe in pleasure. "Thank you, Giovanna."

Her dark head retreats and Olivia moves to step out, shoulders tense, hands clenched at her sides. I have the inexplicable urge to reassure her, to ease her worry. "Miss

Hart?" She pauses and looks over her shoulder at me. "I'll take care of it."

Her lips curl into a small, strained smile. "Thank you, Mr. George."

I have zero fucking leads. *None*. And it's driving me crazy. How hard is it to track down the person who accessed the security feeds? Really fucking hard, apparently, when you're dealing with a company our size. There are thirty members of the security team alone, not to mention the entire board, upper management, HR personnel.

Those are just the people in the company who might have accessed them, who might have seen Olivia as she came on my fingers, who watched as I pleasured her and made her tremble. Who saw her in that vulnerable state. I hate the idea of that. Of anyone but me seeing her like that. Going forward, I'll have to be sure to only touch her where I'm sure there are no cameras. Like in my office.

"It might have been someone outside the company," Lance, the head of our security, says.

I arch a brow at him. "You want to tell me you think someone has hacked our security system?"

Lance's lips tighten, but he shakes his head. "I want to figure out who did this for you, sir."

I hated bringing someone else in on this, but I'm not equipped to hunt down a cyber-terrorist. Lance has an entire team dedicated to keeping our servers safe, so I had to bring him in. I showed him the pictures of me and Liv only after telling him if anyone else saw them, I would fire him without severance, and that I would make sure he never worked in security again.

He'd called me on being an overprotective asshole, but I apparently can't help it where Olivia is concerned. It's a new and disturbing feeling. One I choose to ignore even as it pulses through me.

"So figure it out, Lance," I practically snarl at him.

I'm beyond annoyed. I know without having a conversation with Olivia that this is going to affect her. She'll be less likely to be inclined to engage in all the activities I want to do with her. Now that I've had an *amuse-bouche*, I want the whole fucking meal.

I wonder if this was the intention of whoever sent those pictures, not to get her fired but to make her think twice about getting involved with me. It's possible.

But it's more likely that it was a threat to me, a warning, that someone is watching.

Cabot?

The thought has me pausing. My business partner has access to the cameras. He warned me to treat Olivia with respect, and he likes her. Would he send these as a warning to me? A way to get me to not pursue any sort of physical relationship with her?

I swear and reach for my phone, looking at Lance. "What the fuck are you still doing here? Go figure this out." His lips tighten and I can tell he wants to say something, but he keeps it locked behind his teeth. Smart man.

Lance is the second closest thing I have to a friend, behind Cabot. He's worked for me for years and I trust him with my life. But he knows I'll get rid of him without thinking twice.

The door closes with a snick, and I hit the button to call my business partner.

"Linc," he says when he answers, sounding jovial as fuck. "How's it going?"

I hesitate. I need to figure out if this was him, without telling him I got it on with an employee in the elevator, if he doesn't already know. "Cabot. How's Verity?"

"She's good. So fucking good. Being strong as fucking ever." His voice is soft, like it always is anytime he talks about his girl. He pauses, then asks, "How's Liv?"

I sigh and tip my head back against my chair. "She's..." *so fucking sexy when she comes on my fingers.* "Better at her job than I expected."

Cabot chuckles. "I told you she was. Did something come up? Do you need me to come in?"

I shake my head even though he can't see it. "No. No. I don't need you to come in. I just... I received some pictures."

"*Pictures?*" Cabot sounds normal, just confused. "What kind of pictures?"

It wasn't him.

I can tell just from his voice, it wasn't.

I run a weary hand down my face. "It's nothing. I'm handling it."

"What kind of pictures, Linc?" Cabot presses.

"Pictures of me in a compromising position."

He's quiet for so long I check to see if the call is still connected. It is. Finally he says, "is this going to blow back on the company? Do we need to prepare for that?"

I shake my head again. "I don't think so. Everyone knows I have sex. A lot of it. If it comes out, it won't be a surprise to anyone." It probably wouldn't, even if the woman in the pictures is my employee. I would walk away from the entire ordeal, relatively untouched. Olivia, on the other hand, would have to be let go, and the media circus, if it went public, would likely make it hard for her to get hired in another similar position.

Normally, that wouldn't bother me.

But then normally, I wouldn't be walking around in a near constant state of semi-hard for an employee. Sure, I have sex in my office, but I've never been tempted by someone who works for me. Even Giovanna, who is arguably stunning. I hired her because she's stunning, but I never once actually considered fucking her.

Cabot hums on the other side of the phone. "You're sure."

I nod. "Yeah. I'm sure. It's probably some kind of blackmail scheme. I imagine I'll have someone asking for twenty thousand dollars to keep the photos private."

Another hum from his side of the phone. "This is why you called? To give me a heads up?"

No. "Yeah. Just wanted to let you know in case it does go public. I know you're having Olivia report back to you on all my activities, but I don't think she'll tell you about this."

He chuckles. "No, I imagine that won't show up on her weekly reports." There's a murmur of a feminine voice on the other side of the line. "Verity wants me to invite you over for dinner sometime next week."

I both love and hate going to their house for dinner. Love it because the food is always amazing, and seeing my friend with the girl he loves makes me happy for him. I hate it because... I'll never have what they have. It just rubs in my face that I'm too fucked up to have a meaningful relationship.

Liv flashes into my head and inexplicable longing flickers in my chest. But I shove it away.

I can't have her like that. She wouldn't *want* me like that, even if I could.

"Yeah, man, that sounds great. I'll have Giovanna reach out about a day that will work."

Another murmur of voices on his side of the phone. "Great. Hey, did you give Al a heads up about the pictures?"

My stomach clenches uncomfortably, an unexpected wave of nausea sweeping over me. "I-I haven't gotten around to it yet."

"Linc-"

"I know." I cut him off. "Believe me, I know. I'll do it. Tomorrow's Thursday. I'll do it then."

I won't do it then, but Cabot doesn't need to know that.

He sighs, like maybe he doesn't fully believe me, but he's nice enough to not call me out on it. "Good. I have to go. Verity needs me. I'll see you next week."

He hangs up without giving me a chance to say goodbye and I set my phone face down on my desk just as a timid knock sounds on my door.

The nausea fades as anticipation rears up. I recognize that knock.

"Come in," I call and a moment later, the door pushes open. Olivia's head pokes around the edge and her honey-colored eyes find me behind my desk.

"Is now a good time?"

I nod, motioning her forward with my hand. "Yeah, come in."

She steps inside and closes the door with an audible click before striding toward me. My dick gets hard from just watching her hips sway in her tight skirt as she comes toward me. It takes everything I have to not bark at her to get on her hands and knees and crawl to me. She doesn't need that right now.

That thought only solidifies when she comes to a stop on the other side of my desk and laces her fingers together in front of her nervously. She doesn't meet my eyes. I don't like it. "I was wondering if you... If Lance found anything out? I saw he was in here with you."

I shake my head, leaning forward in my chair to brace my forearms on the top of my desk. "We haven't found out anything yet. You'll be the first person I tell when we do."

Wide, startled eyes meet mine. Finally. "Really?"

"Yes, really, sunshine." A knot forms between her brows at the endearment, but she doesn't tell me not to call her that, so I'll take it as a win. "This affects you as much as me. Of course, you'll know something as soon as I do."

Some of the tension in her shoulders fades and she blows out a breath. "Good. That's- Thank you. I appreciate that."

I hold out a hand to her, beckoning her around the desk. It's not a good idea, not in the slightest, not until we know more about what's happening and who managed to get their hands on those images.

Olivia eyes my hand like all the same thoughts are running through her head, too. She takes one step toward me, hand lifting like she's going to take it, but then she fists her fingers and retreats. "I don't think that's a good idea."

I arch a brow. "I think it's an excellent idea. Come here, Liv."

She shakes her head. "No. I-I don't want to."

"Well, that's a lie." My hand drops, landing on my thigh with a thud. "You want to. You're just trying to be responsible."

Half her mouth curls into a smile before she smothers it. "I don't want to lose my job."

"You won't," I say quickly, earning a huff of exasperation from her. If she rolled her eyes at me, we'd have a problem, but she manages not to.

"You can't promise me that, Mr. George. If those pictures come out..." she trails off, folding her arms around her stomach, and looking away from me.

She's right. Hadn't I just been thinking that if the pictures came out, she would be the one to suffer, not me?

She's right to protect herself from the eventual fallout of being with me. Doesn't mean I have to like it, though.

I nod, grudging as hell. "Fine. We'll see what we can find out and not pursue anything in the meantime. But this," I flick a finger between us. "It's not over."

Her jaw tenses as her chin tips up. "It's over if I say it's over."

I lift a shoulder in a shrug, a smirk pulling at my lips. "So don't say it."

A laugh bubbles out of her. A real life genuine laugh and it soothes something in my chest. I smirk at her as she shakes her head. "Just like that, huh?"

I nod. "Just like that." I lean forward and meet her gaze. "I promised you I was going to fill you with my cum, didn't I?" Her cheeks flush as her plush mouth parts on a gasp. Liv gives a jerky nod and my smirk grows. "Something you should know about me, Miss Hart. I always keep my promises."

8
Olivia

It's been a week since the photos crossed my desk. A week during which Lincoln George and I have worked closely with each other, attended three client dinners and one very long meeting on a Saturday with a group from Japan that was only in town for a single day.

A week during which he's kept his distance. During which he hasn't touched me more than what's polite. A hand at the base of my spine to guide me into a room, the brief brush of his fingers against my forearm to get my attention.

But nothing like what happened in the elevator. Not even close.

I should be relieved.

That moment of insanity between us has passed, and now we can just focus on work. Especially with those pictures hanging over us, but I every so often—more often than I care to admit—I relive that elevator tryst, the feel of him pressed against me, how he fulfilled fantasies I'd only ever acted out in my head, and how he hadn't seemed remotely turned off by using words like 'whore' and 'slut' while fingering me. It fact, I think it turned him on to do it. Whether it's one of his kinks as well, or he just enjoyed seeing it turn me on, Lincoln George definitely didn't seem bothered by it.

Which really is a problem for me. I get caught up in wondering what his mouth would taste like, because although his fingers have been inside me, he didn't kiss me, didn't thrust his tongue between my lips, or nibble on them, beyond that one soft press to the corner of my mouth while my brain was busy melting in my head.

I spend too much time wondering what his mouth would feel like, not just on mine, but everywhere on my body. I've never had my thoughts so consumed with another person like this. Sure, I think about my mother a lot. I have for the last few years, but I rarely spend this much time thinking about having sex with another person.

Or sex in general.

It's annoying as hell that my evil boss, Lincoln George, has reduced me to a hormone filled mess, after just *one* orgasm. One orgasm that should never have happened because he's my *boss* and we have to work together. One orgasm that just might have broken me for all other orgasms. Bossy asshole.

Believe me, I've tried in the last week to reach that same pinnacle, to get as high as he took me before I was flung over the edge. But even with the memory of his body pressed to mine, the feel of his hand on my throat, the thrust of his fingers inside me, the filthy things he rasped in my ear, I can't get anywhere close.

It was impossible to shut my brain off enough to do it.

While I was trying to recreate the feeling, I was also thinking about how I needed to be quiet to keep from waking my mother. I was thinking about the medication I needed to pick up the next day, the puff pastry chilling in the fridge, how I'm just barely going to be able to pay Harvey, even with the overtime that will be on my recent paycheck.

When I was with Lincoln, my brain shut off entirely, gave into his control and because of that, I could just enjoy the sensations he evoked in me. It's the first time in... *ever*, that I wasn't thinking about something else while also striving toward an orgasm.

I'm not really sure what I'm supposed to do with that.

Because it can't happen again.

Probably.

It won't happen again, I say to myself sternly. *There were pictures. Someone watched that happen. Saw you come undone under his hands and mouth.* Reminding myself of the photos of us together usually helps to quell the sudden and overwhelming need to have Lincoln George fill my vagina.

But it doesn't at this very moment. And I blame the man in front of me, standing behind his desk with his hands braced on the surface. He's undone his tie and rolled up his sleeves, revealing muscled forearms that make my mouth water and my thighs clench.

He's got a spread of marketing material on the desk in front of him, and there's a knot between his brows as he runs his slate blue eyes over the images, looking for any inconsistencies. I'm on the other side of his desk, tablet in hand, ready to make note of any changes he deems necessary.

Technically, Giovanna should be in here, doing this with him. But he sent her home an hour ago and ordered me to stay. So now it's nearly nine on a Friday, and I'm going to have to either beg him to let me go in twenty minutes or call Claire and beg her to go relieve Harvey.

My jaw tenses as frustration bubbles up. He must know I hate this. That I have other responsibilities and can't stay late on his whim. He must recognize that people have lives outside of this office, even if he doesn't.

That's something I've learned in the last few weeks.

Lincoln George is a workaholic.

For all that he's photographed all over the city with different girls at least three times a week, I'm just now putting together that those girls are his plus ones for work functions. Meetings with clients, charity events to show that H&G gives back. Every time he's been photographed, it's been while leaving an event. Don't get me wrong, I'm sure that he takes his dates home and fucks them when he's done, but the setup to the date isn't personal. It's always professional.

Something else I've noticed?

He hasn't had a plus one to any of the events he's dragged me to. Not since the elevator incident.

Just this afternoon, I saw an article in The Gossip, speculating about our relationship, wondering if Lincoln George, playboy billionaire, is off the market. At the very end of the article in which they dissected every bit of my appearance, they finally admitted they reached out to Mr. George, and Giovanna gave a statement saying we are work colleagues and nothing more.

I'm not sure why that stung.

I shake my head at myself now, at my ridiculousness, and open my lips to ask if he knows how much longer we'll be here. But he cuts me off, slate blue eyes shooting up to meet mine. "I can't figure it out. There's something off, but I've been staring at these too long to make it out." He straightens and jerks his chin at me. "Come have a look."

I sigh. I've already had a look. I saw the proofs before he did, and I thought they looked great. I'd told the marketing department that they were perfect and there was no way that Mr. George would have a problem with them. Color me wrong, because here we are literal *hours* after I delivered them to his office.

"Olivia," his voice is a warning. "This is your job. If Cabot were here, he'd be standing next to me. Get your ass over here."

The command has me pushing to my feet and rounding the desk to look down at the material with him. He's so damn picky that I am sure he's being an asshole just to be an asshole, so my lips part to tell him they look great, but he stops me with a finger against them. "No. Don't just tell me they're fine. *Look* at them. Take your time. And then tell me what you see."

I swallow and lick my lips. Only his finger is still pressed against my mouth, so I end up licking him, too. My cheeks heats, my entire face going red, but I pretend like it didn't happen, even as he slides his finger down, pulling my bottom lip with it. When it pops back into place, I can taste him.

I can feel his gaze on me as I look over the images in front of me. *Professional.* I will be a goddamn professional. I will not think about his mouth on my neck or his fingers inside of me, or how good it felt to just give control over to him.

Lincoln shifts closer, moving just slightly behind me. One of his hands braces on my hip as the hard length of his cock presses into my right butt cheek. I take a gasping inhale and am assaulted by his scent. Warm oak, oakmoss, vanilla citrus and a hint of bourbon from the glass he's been sipping from.

My vision goes slightly blurry. I'm not taking in a goddamn thing in front of me as the pictures all blend. My heart rate and breathing pick up as Lincoln's mouth brushes against the hollow behind my ear, not really in a kiss, but just hovering over that spot, his breath puffing against my skin, hot and moist.

"What do you see, Olivia?" he murmurs, low and deep and somehow so fucking erotic that a whimper pulls from my chest.

That involuntary sound is enough to have me blinking, pressing closer to the desk and away from him. He doesn't let me keep the space between us for long though, chasing after me, until the edge of the desk bites into my hip bones and his fully hard cock presses against my ass. One of his hands slides over the buttons of my shirt, between my breasts, until he's gently collaring my neck, tipping my head back against his shoulder. "I asked you a question, baby. What did we talk about before?"

I swallow and I'm sure he can feel my throat bob as I do. "When you ask a question, I need to answer."

"Good girl." He places a small kiss behind my ear. "So what do you see, sunshine?"

I shake my head as best as I can to try to clear some of the fog from my brain as I blink down at the copy in front of us. "I-I'm not sure."

He nips at that bit of skin, hard enough that I suck in a sharp breath, even as the bite of pain makes my nipples form stiff peaks behind my lace bra. "You better get sure."

"Lincoln." I husk. "We shouldn't. Someone might see."

His tongue darts out and tastes my skin, making him groan and his hips buck against me. "No cameras, Liv. Do you know what that means?"

Fuck. My thighs squeeze together as I shift on my heels, trying to relieve some of the ache between them. His fingers tighten on my neck, just slightly in warning. "Answer me."

My tongue darts out again, swiping over my suddenly sensitive lips. "It means no one can see us."

His nose nuzzles into the hollow he's been lavishing attention on. "That's right. No one will see if I push up this tight as fuck skirt, bend you over my desk and fuck you until I fill you up. No one will see if I do this." His hand slides down until he brushes against the hard peak of my nipple. He's not gentle when he pinches it. No, he's rough, pulling and twisting, making a sharp bite of pain and pleasure coil through my body. "Does my little whore like that?" He growls, pressing forward even more.

"Yes," I gasp out, writhing under his expert hands. "Oh, fuck, yes."

A pleased chuckle rumbles out of him, vibrating through my body deliciously. And then he's… gone. Cool air replaces his heat and my legs sag just the slightest bit until I have to catch myself on the edge of the desk to keep from falling. I hadn't realized how much he was holding me up until I didn't have that support anymore.

I blink in confusion, before glancing around the room to find him over by the bar, pouring two glasses of bourbon that I know costs an arm and a leg, because I've seen the receipts.

I just stand there watching him dumbly as he casually carries them over to where I am, like his cock isn't straining against the fly of his suit pants, creating an impressive tent. "You look disappointed," he says, handing a tumbler to me.

I don't reach to take it, just keep staring at him.

"What the hell was that?" I finally husk out.

He smirks, slides the glass onto the desk next to my hip, and then takes a sip of his drink. "Just reminding you."

"Reminding me," I parrot back to him, brows narrowing.

He gives a sharp nod and then uses the glass in his hand to motion at the marketing material. "Work first. Fucking later."

I shake my head, my sense coming back to me slowly. "There will be no fucking. I thought we were over this."

He moves in close, and my first instinct is to back away, to keep space between us. But I refuse to let him see me run from him, so I tip my chin up and meet his gaze with a glare of my own. "Over what, Liv? Me giving you the best orgasm of your life?"

It was. It really fucking was. But I scoff, and turn away from him, back to the marketing material. "That was hardly my best."

He hums in his throat like he doesn't believe me but says nothing else as I look over the pictures and fonts, the colors, trying to see what has him bent out of shape. The sooner I can come up with something, the sooner I can go home.

My brows arch as something catches my eye. I reach for the photo and pull it closer to me before grabbing another. With them side by side, the problem is obvious. "Here. This is what was bothering you." I motion at the two images. "The theme is *found family*, but everyone in the pictures looks like they could be related. It's like they didn't even try to find diverse models."

He blows out a breath and comes to stand next to me, looking down at the photos. "You're right." I don't miss that some of the tension in his shoulders eases, like it really had been bothering him. "That's what was bothering me." His head tips back to swallow the rest of his drink as I move away from him, intending to pick up my tablet and make notes of what needs to change on my way out of the office.

His empty hand snaps, catching my elbow before I can get more than a step away from him. "Where do you think you're going?"

I look down at his hand, pressing into the white fabric of my shirt and then up at him. "Home. I assume we're done for the night."

A slow wolfish smile curls his lips. "Oh, baby, we are so far from done. What did I say?" when I just stare up at him, he uses his grip to pull me into his body, bending his head until his lips brush my ear. "*Work first, fucking later.* It's later, sunshine."

I let out a shuddering breath and brace a hand against his abs, shaking my head. "We can't. Last time-"

"Last time we were in a public space. That's my fault. I should have kept control of myself long enough to remember the cameras. But there are no cameras in here, I've made sure of that. Everyone's gone home for the day." He drags his lips up and over my jaw to my mouth, speaking against my lips. "Come on, Olivia, let me make you feel good. Let me make you come. Be my good little whore."

My mouth goes dry, and I swallow convulsively to try to wet it. But all the moisture in my body has flooded my panties, and it doesn't work. He's just hovering there, bourbon on his breath as it puffs over my lips, my jaw, my tongue. I know he's waiting for my permission. It's a nice change considering he didn't seem to need it before, but the way he's looking at me, it's like he knows. He knows I'm going to say yes.

I probably am.

"Rules. We should have rules," I blurt out.

One of his dark eyebrows lifts in an arch as he pulls back just slightly to look at me. "What kind of rules were you thinking, Olivia?"

What rules indeed? I don't particularly want rules limiting the things he does to me. Just based on the one sexual encounter we've had, I know he'll do everything to make my experience more than satisfactory. But it feels like we should establish boundaries or something right?

"I guess I want some kind of assurance that you aren't going to fire me as soon as you fuck me. And is this a one-time thing or are you hoping to do it again? What exactly are you expecting from me in this situation?"

Lincoln's mouth curls into a smirk the more I talk. "I won't fire you after I fuck you, Olivia. I don't think I could even if I wanted to. But I can guarantee I won't wont to. I'd have to get Cabot's permission, and to do that, I'd have to explain why." He ducks his head to meet my eyes as I nod my understanding. "I'm not sure if it's a one-time thing or not. I suppose it depends on how this first time goes, hmm? If we both find it satisfactory, then we can go from there." Again I nod. "As to what I want from you? Nothing more than your complete and total surrender. I want you to give your body and your pleasure over to my control. To trust me enough to give you what you need physically. It won't always be pleasant," he warns, sliding one hand up to my jaw, tipping my chin up with his thumb so I can't look away from him. "I like to play games, to test my partner's submission, to see how far I can push before I reward you."

Oh, fuck. My thighs are slick now, arousal soaking through the lace of my panties. The more he talks, the slicker they get. I love the idea of everything he's telling me, everything he wants from me. I love the idea of giving up control to him, both mentally and physically.

"Do I need a safe word?" My cheeks flush when he chuckles, low and pleased and *dirty*.

"If you want one, we can have one. Though, if I'm honest, I don't think you'll need it."

He might be right, but since I want to be able to call an audible on this whole situation if it goes south. "Snickerdoodle," I say.

His brows arch at that. "You had that locked and loaded, didn't you?"

I lift a shoulder. "I was planning on baking some this weekend, so they're on my mind."

He nods. "Okay. The safe word is *snickerdoodle*. You say that and I'll stop whatever I'm doing, and we'll reassess both of our needs."

I let out a breath at that, at how accommodating he's being. "Good."

He presses closer, slides his hand from my hip to my ass, kneading the flesh there through my skirt. "Now that we have that settled, can I please fuck you? You've been driving me crazy all week."

I sway toward him, catch myself on his chest. "Yes." It's a breathy whisper that is only halfway out of my mouth before he slams his lips on mine. I can tell right away he's done waiting, done being patient and listening to my concerns.

He walks me backward, his lips devouring mine, hands running up and down my body, before plunging into my hair and tilting my head back, almost too far, but it gives him a better angle to thrust his tongue into my mouth, so I don't complain.

The backs of my knees hit something solid and the next moment I'm lying flat on my back on the couch, with Lincoln over top of me, my skirt hitching up as my thigh's part around him, until he's cradled between them, hard length pressed to my hot, soft center. We both groan. Lincoln braces himself on his forearms and holds some of his weight off me, and he thrusts forward, grinding against me again.

"Fuck," I hiss out, and his lips quirk into a smirk.

"Language, Miss Hart." I roll my eyes at him as my fingers scrabble with the buttons of his shirt. I want to see him without clothes, to see what I've only felt through layers of clothes. His hand curls around mine, stopping their movement, and I blink up at him, not sure why exactly he's stopping me.

But in the next instant he's up, standing next to the couch, slate blue eyes blazing down at me. "Sit up, Miss Hart." I do as he demands, shifting to slide my skirt down. "No," he snaps out. "Leave the skirt how it is. I enjoy seeing that plump pussy of yours straining the lace of your thong."

My entire body flushes at his words, and he chuckles. "You're going to have to get used to filthy talk, Olivia. A good little whore wouldn't blink twice at that." He doesn't miss the way my thighs clench at his words. He'd have to be blind to. Lincoln hooks a knuckle under my chin and lifts my gaze to him. I hadn't even realized I'd been staring at his fly. "You want my cock, Olivia?"

"Yes," I breathe, tangling my fingers together to keep from reaching for it. I'm learning how this is going to go. He wasn't joking when he said he wants my surrender. My only job here is to follow his orders.

"Good girl. Take it out."

His hand slides from my chin to the side of my head as I scoot forward on the couch, lifting trembling hands to first undo his belt buckle and then the closure of his pants. The zipper is unnaturally loud as I slide it down, before dipping my right hand inside his boxer briefs while tugging the fabric down with my left.

He hisses in a sharp breath as my fingers close around him, stroking slightly. "Fuck. That feels so fucking good."

I pull my eyes off his admittedly very pretty cock and look up at him. His head is tilted back, dark hair slightly askew, lips parted. His chest heaves under his white dress shirt. My fingers tighten, my pace picks up, catching the pre-cum slipping from his tip and using it to ease the way.

Lincoln's fingers tighten in my hair.

A sense of accomplishment flows through me. I'm doing that to him, making him feel good, like he made me feel good. I'm making his hips thrust with pleasure. His breaths come in sharp pants. And I'm doing it with just my hand.

I wonder if I can make him lose control.

I don't give myself time to think about it, to consider that he hadn't told me he wanted this. I lean forward and lick his tip, moaning when I get my first taste of him, salty and musky, with a hint of his soap. He groans when I take him into my mouth, his other hand coming up to clutch at my head.

Victory sings through me and I take him deeper and swallow around his shaft.

But in the next moment, he's pulled out. I'm on my feet, bent over the couch, with my hands braced on the back of it. Pain erupts on first my right butt cheek and then my left. Lincoln fists my hair and tugs me into a standing position until my back is pressed against his chest and his lips are on my ear. "Did I tell you to suck my cock, Olivia?"

He can't actually be mad about that, right?

I lick my lips, catching the flavor of him on my tongue. "No, you didn't."

Teeth scrape over my jaw. "No, I didn't. I guess my little whore just couldn't help herself, hmm? You saw my cock and just had to get a taste?"

I nod as best as I can with his hand in my hair. "Yes. I wanted… I wanted you to feel good. Like you made me feel in the elevator."

He goes still, lips pressing into my pulse point. "You're a little liar, Olivia. You wanted to see if you could make me lose control."

I must flinch or something because he lets out a low chuckle against my neck before biting down hard enough that I'll have a bruise when this is over. He licks the spot and then releases me, before stepping back enough to allow me to turn to face him.

His fingers cup my jaw. "I'll forgive you this once, sunshine. Because you're new to this. But you broke the rules of the game. If you were anyone else, I'd call it now and send you home without making you come. Do you understand?"

I give a jerky nod. "Yes."

"Tell me."

I lick my lips and fist my hands by my sides to keep from reaching for him. "I can only do what you tell me to do. No touching, or licking, or sucking that you haven't asked of me."

He nods, slate blue eyes following the path of his thumb as he traces my lower lip. "That's right." His thumb presses into my mouth. "Suck." I do immediately and he groans again, pumping the digit between my lips a few times, before sliding it down my chin, leaving a wet trail in its wake.

"You've had a taste, now I want one too," He murmurs. "Down on the couch." I drop like a stone, watching him as he kneels in front of me. One of his big hands circles my ankle, pulling it up onto the edge of the cushion before he does the same to the other, splaying my thighs wide. He leans forward and grabs my hands, his chest just barely brushing against my throbbing clit, making me moan. I blink my eyes open as he curls my fingers around the back of the couch cushion. "These stay here," he murmurs against my cheek. "No touching."

I swallow and nod. "Okay."

"I can tie them if that would be easier." He doesn't think I'll be able to follow his instructions.

I want to prove him wrong. I *will* prove him wrong. I shake my head. "N-No. I can do this."

A pleased smirk curls his lips before he kisses me. "We'll see."

Then his face is between my thighs. He uses one finger to hook the fabric of my thong out of the way, and unceremoniously licks from my ass all the way up to my clit. I have to bite my lip to keep from making too much goddamn noise, because it feels fucking stunning.

I see right away why he thinks I might fail, because after the first solid lick, Lincoln plays with me, teases me, flitting the tip of his tongue around my clit, while he circles my entrance with a finger. Always teasing, never giving me what I want, and it takes everything in me to not grip his hair and force him to give me more. Instead, my hips buck and wiggle, trying to get closer to him, trying to get him to give me what I need.

I'm a sweating, writhing mess by the time I gasp out. "Please, please, Lincoln."

He pauses in his torment and looks up the length of my body at me. "Please what, baby?"

"I need more. *Please*. I need *more*."

He licks me again, before resting his chin on my pelvic bone, looking up at me, looking sexy as fuck. "What do you need, Olivia? Hmm? You need my tongue, my fingers, or my cock?"

I shake my head. "All of them. I need all of them."

He chuckles. "Greedy little whore, aren't you?"

I don't argue with him, because at this moment I fucking am. "Yes."

His eyes blaze when I agree too easily. "Say it, Liv."

I meet his gaze and tighten my grip on the cushions. "I'm a greedy little whore. Please, Linc. Please."

Lincoln is looking right in my eyes when he shoves two fingers inside me. The sudden stretch borders on painful, but when he pulls out and thrusts back in, it explodes in pleasure. My back arches as best it can in the position I'm in, a low keening cry coming from my mouth.

"Is this what you need, sunshine?" Lincoln asks, adding a *third* fucking finger.

"More," I pant out. "Please. I need more."

"Fuck, you beg so pretty. I fucking love it." He keeps his eyes on my face as he dips his head and sucks my clit into his mouth, scraping his teeth over the sensitive bud. That's all it takes after all his teasing. I explode, calling out his name as my whole body tenses and my hands release from the couch to grasp at air, since I can't touch him.

Lincoln lunges up. My legs wrap around his hips as he thrusts into me, drawing out my orgasm as he fights through my squeezing muscles. "Put your hands back where I told you, Liv," He grunts as he bottoms out inside me. I do as he demands, squeezing so hard, I'm sure my knuckles are white. "Good girl. Good fucking girl. Fuck.

You're so tight like this, baby. I could come right now. Buried so deep inside you."

I come down from my release, and Lincoln begins to move as my muscles release their grip. His hands pinch at my waist, holding me where he needs me as he fucks into me. "Lincoln," I moan, feeling my pleasure build, coiling toward another orgasm.

He'd had his head thrown back, neck muscles flexing, but when I say his name he looks down at me, slate blue eyes clashing with mine. "I think that's my fucking favorite sound in the world."

I frown, not understanding. "What?"

His thumb finds my clit and circles, making my head toss back as ecstasy centers on that point of contact. "*Lincoln.*"

"Fuck, yeah. You moaning my name like that is my new fucking favorite sound."

I do it again and again, now that I know he likes it. And it seems like each time I do, he grows a little-less controlled, a little more frantic. His hips slam into mine, his face determined and full of pleasure all at once. Words fall from his lips, like he can't help himself. "Gonna make you come so fucking hard on my dick. You're gonna squeeze me so fucking tight. Gonna fill this pussy with so much fucking cum." Just like he promised after the elevator. "Fuck, yes. Olivia. Take it. Take my fucking cock, you little fucking whore." He pinches my clit on the last word, and it happens just like he said it was going to.

I come so hard, I scream. My vision goes spotty with lights, and my hands fly to grab onto him mindlessly, sinking into the muscles of his forearms as my pussy clenches around him, trying to hold him deep inside me. Not that he's going anywhere.

He pumps twice more, grunting with each thrust, before he grinds into me, the movement of his hips stalling out as he moans my name, followed by a long, "*fuuuuuuccckkk.*" I feel his cock pulse inside me, filling me with his cum. I have the very brief thought that I probably should have talked about safe sex with him, you know made sure we're both clean, but then he circles my clit with his thumb again, and an aftershock rolls through me, making my legs jerk as a much smaller orgasm hits.

He chuckles, entirely too pleased with himself as he leans over and kisses me. It's not a soft, sated kiss, more like he's trying to get us both ready to go again, moaning into my mouth as he grinds his pelvis against mine. I hiss against the friction against my too sensitive bundle of nerves and push back on his shoulder. "Too much, Linc."

He arches a brow at me and purposefully rolls his hips again. "You'll take as much as I say you will, Olivia. If I want to stay right fucking here, rubbing your little clit even though it fucking hurts, I'm going to do it."

There is no earthly reason that should make me clench around him, but it does. And I feel a dribble of our combined cum squeeze from my pussy. My nose wrinkles as he pulls back and out of me. The dribble turns to a gush, spilling over my ass cheeks.

"Mmm," Lincoln moans. "Look at that mess you made." I watch as he uses a finger to scoop it up, and I half expect him to thrust it back inside me. I've read about that happening in books and I'd be lying if I said it didn't turn me on. Instead, he offers his cum covered finger to me. "Clean it up."

Meeting his gaze, I use a grip on his wrist to pull him closer, before flicking my tongue out, catching the white sticky substance on the tip over my tongue, showing it to him, before I pull it into my mouth and swallow. Then I suck his entire finger in, all the way to his knuckle, before pulling back, cheeks hollowing until it emerges from my lips with a pop.

"Good girl," he pants. "You want more?"

I nod. "Yes, please."

He stands up, his half hard cock hanging out of his suit pants. "You covered me in your cream. Clean it off."

He doesn't have to tell me twice. I straighten up and lean forward, curling my hand around the base of his dick before sliding as much of it into my mouth and sucking as I pull back, like he's a popsicle. When his cock leaves my mouth, I sweep my tongue over his now fully hard cock, getting every bit of myself off him, while his fingers curl in my hair.

His hand replaces mine, and he taps his cock against my mouth. "Open up for me, Olivia." I do, and he slides in again. This time I have no control at all, his hands in my hair control the pace, as he slowly, slowly works his cock into my throat, groaning with each swirl of my tongue. "Swallow around me, baby," he urges me, and I do. Another groan pulls from him as his fingers tighten in my hair.

"Look at me, sunshine." I lift my eyes to meet his, and his thumb touches the corner of my mouth as he pulls back. "You still okay?"

I hum and nod, and the tendons in his neck tighten and stand out. I love it. I love that he feels that good because of my mouth, my tongue, my throat. "Good fucking girl," he murmurs. "Here's what's going to happen now. I'm going to fuck your mouth, you're going to gag on my cock, and then I'm going to fuck you again and come all over *my* pretty little pussy. Okay?"

Oh, Jesus. My eyes practically roll into the back of my head at his filthy words. My core clenches and I hum again. He takes it for the assent it is and after one more touch to my split lips, he says, "keep your eyes on me."

And then he precedes to do exactly as he said.

His hips power into me, balls slapping my chin with each thrust. My eyes water and I gag around his cock when he pauses as deep as he can get and growls out for me to swallow again and again. Saliva spills out of my mouth, drips onto my knees, but I don't fucking care. In fact, I use some of that when he demands, "touch your clit for me, baby. Get yourself close."

I'm already close, so fucking close, but I do as he says, getting the tips of my fingers wet with the spit on my skin, before circling my clit.

"Oh, fuck yeah. Look at you, my good little slut."

I moan, and my eyes flutter closed, only for his fingers to smack into my cheek gently. "Look at me," he all but snarls. When I do, I find his eyes latched on mine, even as his head tilts back in pleasure.

"Yes," he moans, and pulls out of my mouth. I've hardly gasped in a full breath when he yanks me to my feet, spins me, presses me onto my knees on the couch, one hand on the back of my neck bends me at my waist just in time for him to thrust into me from behind. His hand bites into the flesh of my hip, while the other curls into my hair, tugging back, making my back arch so he can hit all the pleasure points deep inside me.

"So good, sunshine. So fucking good. Gonna fuck this pussy all fucking night. Gonna make you scream my name over and over again." He tugs harder on my hair, making my scalp tingle with just the slightest bit of pain. And then he reaches between my legs and slaps my clit. I detonate.

I'm pretty sure I scream his name, but I think it comes out garbled, more air than voice, but he doesn't seem to mind, snarling out a "fuck yes" just as he pulls out enough to spray his cum over the curve of my ass, the swollen lips of my pussy.

When he's done, he slumps over me, breathing hard, His chest pressing into my back, his lips against my neck. My arms flop off the back of the couch, but my head stays where it is, with my forehead pressing into the couch cushions.

After we've both caught our breath, Lincoln kisses the nape of my neck and pulls off me. I turn my head just enough to see him out of the corner of my eye. He's leaning back on his heels, cock still out, staring at my naked ass.

"God, that is a pretty sight." I arch a brow, and he smirks before leaning forward, smacking a kiss on my hip, and standing. "Stay just like that, Olivia."

I nod and close my eyes. I have no clue how he can move to get off of me, let alone to move around his office. Exhaustion pulls at me after what he just put my body through. I hear the faint click of a phone taking a picture, and bolt upright, to glare over my shoulder at him. "Did you just take a picture of me like that?"

He doesn't even try to hide the phone in his hand. Just grins. "I think I might make that your profile pic."

My face flushes, and I jab a finger in his direction. "Don't you fucking dare."

He laughs and slides his phone onto his desk before he picks up two bottles of water and a damp cloth. "Don't worry, sunshine. That picture's just for me. I don't want anyone to see what belongs to me." A knot forms between my brows as he comes to a stop in front of me, holding out a bottle. "Drink this."

I take it from him. He drops the second bottle on the cushion next to me, before carefully, gently wiping between my legs. My first instinct is to knock his hand away, but when he sees me twitch in his direction, he tsks. "This is my job, baby. Aftercare. I wreck your body with a game and then I help put it back together." He taps the unopened bottle in my hand. "Drink."

I do, downing half the bottle in a few gulps. I hadn't realized how thirsty I was. When Lincoln's finished cleaning me up, he smooths my skirt over my hips and helps me turn around on the couch before settling beside me. His arm loops over my shoulder, tugging me into his side. Is this part of the aftercare, or does he just want to hold me?

"So my pussy belongs to you, does it?"

He looks down at me, his thumb rubbing back and forth on my shoulder. "For now, it does."

I hum and look away from him, taking another drink of water. "Does that mean your dick belongs to me?"

"Do you want it to?"

"I'd prefer if you didn't have sex with other women while we're doing this. Especially if you're going to be having sex with me without a condom."

He hums. "I'm clean. I assume you're on birth control?"

Why he would assume that I have no idea, but he's not wrong. "I am, and I'm clean as well. But you might not stay clean if you go around fucking random women."

He chuckles. "They're hardly random."

"Lincoln."

He twists his head to look down at me. "Fine. No one else while we play together. Deal?"

I nod. "Okay. Deal." I take another sip of water, feeling his eyes on me as I do so.

"What are you going to tell Harvey?"

I nearly choke on the water, but instead of spitting it out, it dribbles on my chin. "Why would I need to tell him anything?" I ask, swiping the moisture off my skin. "It's none of his business."

His gaze narrows, and his mouth opens like he's going to say something. But then he thinks the better of it, tugging me back into his chest. "Do you need to go home?"

I glance at the clock on the wall. "I'm already late. So…"

"So you might as well stay for round three?"

I laugh and shake my head, twisting my head to grin up at him. "Exactly."

9
Lincoln

Olivia Hart has consumed me. Every waking moment, I'm thinking of her, from sunup to sundown. I'm thinking of the next time I can get her alone, get my cock or my fingers or my tongue inside her. I'm thinking of the sounds she makes, how she submits to me so fucking beautifully. The way she clenches when I call her my good little whore or slut.

Fuck.

It's never really been my kink to degrade a woman like that. Sure, I like submission and I enjoy punishing and rewarding in turn, but I've never really gotten off on calling a woman a whore. Until Olivia. I know it has everything to do with how much she likes it. No, she fucking *loves* it.

It's obviously not something she's getting from Harvey or any other man she's fucking or has fucked. I didn't miss the small bit of shame the first few times, like she didn't think she should like it. But now, every time those words fall from my lips, every time I pant them against her ear or her pussy or her fucking tit, she does nothing but moan and beg for more.

Just like a good slut should.

I can't get enough of it. *Of her.*

It's a warning sign that I should put a stop to this, put her back in the realm of 'employee' and me, her boss. But I can't imagine a world where I'm not able to touch her the way I want. It's not like either of us are going to catch feelings. Olivia's dislike of me is clear, even if her body craves my touch. I'm not able to feel anything for anyone beyond general '*I don't completely hate you*' vibes. I wouldn't say even I love Cabot, and he's my oldest and closest friend.

I glance at my watch as I step out of the restaurant. One of the rare meetings that Olivia didn't need to attend with me, completed satisfactorily. Lance is already waiting at the curb next to the black town car.

As I slide into the back seat, I grab my phone and shoot off a text to Olivia.

Me:
Go to my office and call me in two minutes.

Sunshine:
Yes, sir.

The response is immediate and makes my cock throb. I hit the button to put up the privacy screen between me and Lance. The drive back to the office should take about twenty minutes, and that's more than enough time to play with Liv.

Anticipation thunders in my chest as the two-minute mark strikes. But she doesn't call.

My teeth clench.

I hate when my orders aren't followed. She knows this.

When another minute has passed with no call, I dial up Olivia and wait impatiently until her pretty face flashes on my screen. Her cheeks are flushed, like she already knows where this is going to go. "Mr. George," she says all business, letting me know she's not alone at the moment. Naughty girl, she'll pay for that. "How can I help you?"

"I need you to read some papers off to me. I left them in my office."

Her honey-colored eyes dart up and over the phone, as her teeth sink into her plump pink lower lip. She gives someone an apologetic smile before she's looking back at me. "Of course, Mr. George. One moment."

There's the rustle of air as the camera bobbles as she strides through the office, bringing me with her. As soon as I see the heavy wood of my door close behind her, I shake my head, a wicked smile pulling at my lips. "Oh, baby. You are in so much trouble."

She blows a piece of blond hair out of her face, rolling her eyes at me. "Listen, you try getting out of a conversation with Karen from finance in two minutes. It's impossible. The woman will not shut up."

I hum a laugh. That's as close as Olivia has ever come to insulting someone. Well, someone that isn't me. I watch as she rounds my desk. "Where are these papers you need?"

I ignore the question and slouch down in my chair, spreading my legs wide, cock already throbbing at the thought of what I'm going to have her do, what I'm going to watch her do. "Lincoln," she urges me. "Where are they?"

When I just cock my brow at her, she flushes even deeper. I love that I can do that to her with just a look. "There are no papers, are there?"

My mouth quirks up. "Take off your panties, Liv."

Her plush pink mouth falls open, eyes darting up to my office door. "No," I say before she can go to lock it. "Leave it. I'm on my way there, and I don't want to waste time with a key."

"But someone-"

I nod. "Yes, someone might come in. They might find you with your skirt around your waist and your fingers in your pussy while I watch." I wait as my words sink in, as she realizes what I want. "Are you going to be a good girl for me and make a wet spot on my chair? You gonna be my good little whore? Because a whore wouldn't care, Liv. They'd do what I say as soon as I say it."

A whimper pulls out of her throat as her eyes go glossy with lust. A second later, she props her phone against something on my desk and steps back, enough for me to watch as she shimmies her pink lace panties—panties I picked out for her—down her legs. "Good girl," I praise, gripping the base of my cock through my suit pants. "Now pull my chair up. Yes, just like that. Skirt up before you sit down. I want that bare pussy on my seat."

My breathing grows harsher as I watch her do exactly as I say, positioning herself with her knees wide, garters on display, pale thighs quivering and that swollen, glistening pussy front and center for me. "So fucking wet for me, aren't you, baby?"

She whimpers and nods. "Yes."

"Good. Now brace your feet on the desk."

She blinks. "What?"

"Feet up," I urge. "Knees nice and wide for me."

It takes some maneuvering. My chair has wheels, and it's one of those spinny ones. So it's a delicate balance, but Liv manages, splaying her legs on the edge of my desk and giving me the perfect view. I groan and fist my cock again.

"Okay, good girl, touch yourself for me. Show me how wet you are." Liv doesn't hesitate this time, trailing her fingers up her thigh, already glimmering with her arousal and right to her pussy. Her head tips back and she bites her lip at the first brush of her fingers against her clit.

"You're already so close, aren't you?" I growl out, resisting the urge to pull my cock out and stroke myself to the sight of her hips rolling on my chair, arousal dripping out of her clenched pussy. This is as much a lesson in control for me as it is for her.

"Yes," she moans out in a whisper, ever aware of her being in my office, of not making too much noise.

"Good. You're going to make yourself come as many times as you can in the next fifteen minutes while I watch."

She looks up at me through her phone, cheeks flushed red, chest heaving, straining against the buttons of her white blouse. "You understand?"

"Yes, sir," she gasps out, circling the tip of her middle finger around her clit.

"Good girl. Now finger fuck yourself until you come." A low sound emerges from my girl as she inserts her middle finger inside her, hips rocking up to help her take it all the way to the knuckle. A few pumps later, she adds her ring finger. Hips bouncing up and down as her left hand slides to play with her clit.

"So fucking pretty," I murmur, gripping my cock through my pants. "How does that feel, sunshine? Good?"

She nods and then shakes her head.

"Words, Olivia. I need words from you."

She licks her lips. "It feels good, but it's not enough."

"What would be enough?" My heart thunders in my chest, watching as she tips her head back, eyes half lidded as she looks at me.

"You," she whimpers. "You would be enough."

There's no stopping the pleased smirk on my lips as the caveman in me pounds on my chest. "Is that so? What part of me would be enough to satisfy you?"

She shakes her head, breathing coming more ragged as she gets closer and closer to her first orgasm. "All of you," she moans out. "Your tongue. Your fingers. Your cock. Any of them would feel better than this."

Fuck. My hand strokes up and down my throbbing dick, just once, to relieve some of the ache.

"Well, if you're a good girl and come three times before I get there. I'll give you what you need. Now, be a good little whore for me and come."

I'm not sure if it's the command in my tone or that I called her a whore, but her entire body tenses and her head tips back as her mouth opens on a silent cry. Her legs try to close, and I growl out. "Keep those fucking legs open, Liv. Let me see my pussy while you come."

I can tell it takes effort, that her instinct is to slam those legs closed while her hips buck along with her orgasm, but she manages to keep them mostly open, letting me watch as the movement of her fingers stalls out.

"Good girl. That's one. Now give me two more." Liv blinks at me, lips parting, and I think she's going to refuse me. I mean, she did just come once already. Does she really need me to fuck her when I get back to the office?

But then her fingers pull out and push back in, while her fingers circle her clit again, a determined little pout on her lips as her thighs tremble with aftershocks. I know it's probably too much, that her clit is sensitive and her muscles clench tight, but she does it. Because I fucking told her to.

It's not long until her head tips back again, fingers thrusting in and out, the sounds filthy and erotic. Small noises of pleasure pull from her chest, sounds that she tries to smother and keep quiet, but she can't. "Look at you," I murmur, granting myself another stroke of my cock. "Such a little slut for me, aren't you? Spreading your legs, soaking my chair. What a little fucking whore."

Again, the word acts like a detonator. This time she keeps her moan locked away behind a bit lip and I don't have to remind her to keep her thighs open. She just does it for me, giving me a front-row seat to her second orgasm.

"So fucking good," I breathe, and Liv lifts her eyes to me, a small smile playing over her lips. "This last one is going to be hard, baby," I murmur. "Your body might fight you on it, and you only have a few minutes, but I know you can do this for me, sunshine. I know you can make yourself come one more fucking time for me, so I can fuck you so hard when I get back to the office. You want that, don't you? My cock buried so deep in you, filling you up."

A mewling sound pulls out of her chest and she nods, fingers rubbing her clit frantically, thighs jerking uncontrollably when she hits a too sensitive spot, but she doesn't stop. Determination lines her entire body.

"Curl your fingers, baby," I encourage. I can tell when she does because her breathing hitches and her feet flex against my desk. "Rub that spot for me." She nods continuously as she does as I say. "Now jiggle your fingers. Yeah, fuck. Just like that. No. No, don't stop. It's doing what it's supposed to."

"Feels funny," she moans, but her fingers keep jiggling inside her, making her soft thighs wiggle too.

"I know, but it'll be worth it. Now alternate stroking and jiggling."

Liv does as I command, head lolling, hips bucking. "Oh, fuck, Linc," she moans, sounding distressed as hell, unsure about the sensations in her body. "Something's-"

"Don't fucking stop, Liv. I swear to fuck if you stop right now, I will never fuck you again." That lights a spark under her ass and she renews her efforts alternating between stroking and jiggling and I can tell when she's close, can tell when she's about to blow because her head snaps up and she locks eyes with me through the screen of the camera, eyes wide with surprise, before her mouth opens wide and she fucking squirts all over my chair, arousal gushing out from around her fingers as her whole body tenses.

I nearly come at the sight of it. I was able to talk Olivia through making herself squirt from the look on her face, for the first fucking time ever. But I push the need aside, even as pre-cum drips from my tip, soaking into my boxer briefs.

"Good girl, sunshine. That was three." Olivia blinks at me with heavy eyes, and I know I'm close to losing her to lethargy. "Keep fucking yourself until I get there." I lace the command with a fair bit of warning, letting her imagine what I do if I set foot in that office and she's not exactly as she is right now. It shouldn't take that long, though, since as soon as the words are out of my mouth, Lance pulls to a stop in front of our building.

I hang up the phone as I step out of the car, waving away Lance before striding into the building. Thank fuck for long coats that hide erections, because I'm sure without the fabric draped in front of me there's no fucking way I would be able to walk through the lobby without someone noticing my hard on.

I jab my finger against the button to call the elevator and wait impatiently for it to arrive. Fuck, my cock aches for release and I have to resist the urge to squeeze it again, to give myself just a little relief. I'll get all the relief I need when I get to my office.

The ride up is interminable, so fucking long, that I can't help but make an impatient noise in my throat, making the wide-eyed intern in front of me glance over his shoulder like he's worried I'm going to lunge at him and tear his throat out or something.

If I'm honest, I feel feral enough to do that to anyone that gets between me and the woman behind my closed office door.

As soon as the elevator stops on my floor, I push out, my long strides carrying me right to my office. Giovanna looks up as I approach, but her gaze drops immediately when she sees the look on my face.

Good.

Olivia looks up when I enter, fingers still buried in her pussy, a look of panic and arousal on her face. She relaxes when she sees it's me, head tipping back on a moan as her hand thrusts between her thighs. I pull up short, taking in the perfection of her in my chair, legs splayed open, pink pussy stretched around the three fingers buried inside her, arousal dripping down the curve of her ass to soak into my chair, just like I wanted.

"Such a good fucking girl," I growl, hand already moving to my belt. With anyone else, I'd take my time, order her to make herself come one more time while I watched, then I'd have her wrap those pretty pouting lips around my cock and suck me dry.

But with Olivia I feel unhinged, out of control, and I need to be inside her the next time she comes, need to feel her clenching around my throbbing cock. I circle the desk as I unzip my pants, my cock springing free, leaking pre-cum like fucking crazy.

Olivia's gaze snags on my erection, pink tongue darting out to lick her lips, like she wants a taste. I'm tempted, but I want her pussy, not her mouth. "Stand up. I want to see what a mess you've made of my chair."

Olivia does as I ask, pulling her fingers from inside her with a whimper and then dropping her shaky legs to the floor before pushing to her feet. Her skirt stays wedged up around her waist, which is probably a good thing, seeing as she really soaked my chair, along with her garter belt, her stockings, and a fair amount of the carpet.

I grin down at the puddle. "You made such a mess, baby." I can't even help that I sound proud of that fact. A deeper flush, that I know is embarrassment, floods her face.

"I've never done that before." She shakes her head. "I didn't even know I could do that."

"Most women can." I use a knuckle to tip her chin up so I can kiss her. She sags against me, letting me support her weight and maneuver her around the desk and to the couch. "You want your reward for being such a good girl for me today?"

Liv bites her lip, and again I have the fear that she's going to deny me, that she's going to tell me to fuck off, she's come enough for one day. But then she nods and whispers, "yes." My cock jumps where it's pressed between us at her agreement, and Olivia smirks. "I think you are too."

I huff a pained laugh and drop back onto the couch, dick pointing at the ceiling in invitation to her. My girl goes to straddle me so our chests will press together, but I catch her hips and spin her, before guiding her down so her back is to my chest, hovering over my stiff, throbbing cock.

Liv doesn't need me to tell her what to do, she doesn't even need to grip me to guide me to her entrance, she just sinks down, gracefully, the squeeze of her muscles exquisite torture as she drops. It's a tight fit, and it has to be at least slightly uncomfortable for her, but it doesn't stop her from bearing down and taking me in one swift motion, her slick arousal making the job easier. We both groan when her fine ass hits my pubic bone.

"So fucking good," she moans, flexing her hips to grind against me.

One of my hands curls around the front of her neck, pulling her head back over my shoulder, making her body arch deliciously, while my other hand urges her up, just slightly, making her take her weight on her already tired thighs. "Stay just like this for me, baby," I murmur against the side of her head.

I feel her swallow against my palm, before she whispers, "okay."

It's going to be tough. Her thighs are already trembling, weakened and soft from her earlier releases.

But she's so damn good at this, at following my orders, at being the perfect submissive for me, that I know she'll do it. The knowledge makes my cock twitch deep inside her and she moans. I brace her with my arm around her waist, holding her against my chest as I pull out of her, and then slam home again. A garbled noise leaves her, and I smile against her temple as I do it again.

"Feel that, baby? Feel how deep I am in you? Feel how good you grip me, like you never want me to leave your pretty pussy?" She nods, one hand scrambling to grip the backrest of the couch, the other looping around my forearm, scraping against the fabric.

Not for the first time since I started this thing with Liv, I wish we were naked. I want her skin on mine, to feel our sweat rub between our bodies as we fuck. But getting fully naked would make this seem like more than a quick fuck in my office, more than just satisfying our need for release.

At the reminder that this isn't anything more than fucking, I tighten my grip on her throat and let myself loose. My hips slam into her ass, making her entire body shake. The drag of my cock against all those sensitive places deep inside her as her moaning and writhing against me, but she doesn't drop, doesn't move a single inch from where I want her, so I can fuck her as deep as I want.

I wish I could keep fucking her forever, keep my cock thrusting in and out of her for all fucking time, because goddamn does it feel like nirvana, but my body is already wired too tight from watching Liv follow my every command, from making her squirt at my direction, from the tight squeeze of her muscles as I drop my hand to between her thighs and grab her pussy, fingers splayed on either side of where my cock is pounding in and out of her.

"This is mine," I growl against her temple, tightening my fingers around her throat as I tighten the other hand much lower down, feeling possessive and animalistic all at once. "You're my good girl. My fucking slut. This pussy is mine to use whenever I want. Isn't that right?"

Olivia nods, soft hair brushing against my cheek before she turns her head and takes my lips with hers, using her mouth to give me my answer while I've cut off her ability to speak. I inhale her, slide my tongue into her mouth like a madman, and then pull back and order. "Be a good whore and come for me." At the same moment, I release my grip on her neck and she gasps in a breath, just as her orgasm hits her.

Her inner walls squeeze tight as a loud scream pulls from her chest. "Yes, fuck yes, just like that," I grunt out. "Squeeze me so fucking-" I cut off as my balls draw tight and my cum releases into her in a torrent. "Olivia. *Fuck.*"

Olivia grinds down against me, drawing out her orgasm even longer and making me groan at how fucking good it feels.

We collapse. My head hits the back of the couch, and she slumps against my chest and shoulder, her face pressed into my neck. I take a moment to gather myself, to make my arms move, loop around her to hold her closer as she comes down. Her lips press into the underside of my jaw in a sweet kiss that has me tightening my grip on her, before I tilt my head down and nuzzle my nose along hers, kissing her sweet soft lips. I only do it once before I urge her up and off my lap until she's standing on shaky legs like a newborn giraffe in those red soled high heels.

I stand right behind Olivia's plush body, staying there as I tuck my cock back into my pants, still covered in both our releases. I should clean it up, I should guide her into the bathroom and take a wet washcloth to both of us, so we can go about finishing out the rest of the day not sticky or—in Olivia's case—dripping cum.

But I love the idea of having a part of her with me, of my cock smelling like her, and I love the idea of her staying just as she is for the rest of the day. "Stay here," I murmur into the back of her head as I caress the swell of her ass before sliding my hand down between her cheeks until I can fuck any of my cum that's dripped out of her back in with my fingers. Once I'm satisfied, I move to my desk and grab the slip of pink lace on the surface.

I help Olivia back into her panties, kneeling in front of her and placing a soft kiss against each of her thighs as I pull them up. "You're going to stay like this for the rest of the day. Dripping with my cum like my good little whore should always be."

I look up at her and find her honey-colored eyes focused on me, lips parted. When I arch a brow, she nods quickly. "Okay."

I lean forward and press a kiss to her clit through the fabric and then uncoil from my kneeling position before checking the time on my watch, while Olivia adjusts her clothing, smoothing her skirt over her hips and making sure her shirt is tucked in.

"We have about ten minutes before Jerome Kline will be here." Her movements still as I say the words, and that pretty flush that had been on her cheeks vanishes, just like that.

"He's coming here? Right now?"

I reach up and finger comb her hair, attempting to set it back to some semblance of order.

"He is," I say easily. "And you are going to sit through the entire meeting with him smelling like me, filled with me. He might want you, Olivia, but you are mine." There's a dark thread of possessiveness in my voice that I don't recognize. I've never felt like this with any of the women I fuck. Even the ones I go back to repeatedly.

Olivia looks like she wants to say something, but sinks her teeth into her lower lip instead, while she watches me. Finally, she shakes her head and takes a deep breath. "I guess I should go get the conference room ready." She smooths her hands over her hips again, before twisting to show me her back. "Do I look okay?"

I run my gaze over her, first to just make sure that she does indeed look professional, but my eyes snag on her swollen lips, her messy hair, the glow on her skin and the slightly wrinkled clothing. Anyone who looks at her will know she was just fucked hard and put away wet.

But God, I don't think she's ever looked more beautiful. It makes something tighten in my chest. Even more so when she quirks a brow at me, her lips pulling into a smile, the one that she almost never shares with me. "Lincoln?"

I hope she doesn't see the shudder that moves through my body as she says my name. Looking away from her, I clear my throat. "You look fine, Liv." My fingers curl around her shoulders and turn her gently back to the door. "Now go get to work."

I smack her ass to emphasize my point, and a surprised giggle bursts out of her.

Like an honest to God *giggle*.

I don't think I've ever made her laugh before. Not on purpose, and not when it's not at my expense.

It feels like I'm walking on air as she glances over her shoulder at me when she reaches the door, that smile still playing over her lips. "This doesn't mean I like you, you know," she breathes, but her eyes are telling a different story, so I smirk back at her.

"Sure, it doesn't, sunshine." I point at the door. "Work now. And I'll fuck you again later."

Her cheeks flush and she scowls at me before she yanks open the door. "Who says I even want that?" she comments just before the door closes.

A chuckle pulls out of me. So goddamn stubborn, that girl. Fighting this every step of the way. But she'll keep coming back because she knows only I can make her feel this good.

10
Olivia

It's been a hell of a week. Two weeks actually. Most of it is not so great. My mom took a turn for the worse midweek, and Harvey had to call her doctor in to adjust her meds, which stabilized her, but it's not as though it's going to save her in the long run.

When he called me, guilt, my constant companion these days gnawed at me. I should have been there. I should have held her hand and spoken with the doctor and learned about her new medications. I should have been there in case those were her last moments.

They weren't thank God, and now she's feeling better than she has in a long time, sleeping less, talking more, though she still tires easily. That's to be expected.

Harvey reassured me that if he thought my mother wasn't long for this world, he would have called me to let me know so I could be with her when it happens. We've talked about this, about the steps we'd both take to make sure my mother's last hours on earth are the best she can have.

I *hate* that I've had that

conversation. With both Harvey and my mother.

Work has been busy. Which is a blessing because keeping busy means that I don't have to think about my mom wasting away and leaving me all alone. Even as that niggling guilt eats away at me. *I should be with her.* But I can't afford to.

I have to work in order to keep paying Harvey, to make sure she has the professional care she needs.

I'm doing the right thing by being here. It just doesn't always feel like it.

Giovanna looks up at me from her desk across the room. "You're going to the charity event tonight?"

I bob my head in affirmation as I type my daily report to Cabot. It's the last thing I have to do before I head home to get ready.

"Are you coming?" I ask, almost as an afterthought. Giovanna is a tough nut to crack. I'd thought we'd have a pleasant working relationship once she got to know me, but she's still a little standoffish. It doesn't help that she never eats any of the baked goods I bring in.

Those normally go a long way to softening someone toward me. After asking around, I discovered that she's celiac—like truly allergic to gluten—and I've been researching recipes for gluten-free sweets. Hopefully, once I've perfected a recipe, she'll devour it, and like me a little more.

She snorts and shakes her head. "Not everyone is the favored pet of the boss."

Then again, maybe she'll always hate me.

I lift my eyes to her, peering at her from behind my wire-framed glasses. "You know it's my job to go with him to these things, right? It's not like we're dating." Even if we *are* having sex. "I'm mostly there to take notes for Mr. Harkness."

She rolls her eyes at me, like she doesn't believe that for a minute. Smart girl. I'm sure with her proximity to his office door she's caught some of the sounds we've made together.

It makes my stomach clench with anxiety. It's only a matter of time before someone realizes what we're doing. Only a matter of time before we're caught. When that happens, I guess we'll be done, and I'll be fired. No matter that he said he wouldn't do that to me.

The thought of that makes my chest ache in a way I hadn't expected. I don't particularly like Lincoln George, but I fucking love what he does to my body. How when I'm with him and we're in a scene or playing a game, he makes my brain shut off. The guilt that is my constant companion slips away. The worries about everything that plague my mind disappear.

I am one hundred percent using him as a coping mechanism. Self-medicating with orgasms to escape the reality that is my life. But the idea of not having that anymore? It makes me feel itchy and weirdly *sad*.

I don't want to give him up.

Sometimes, when I'm lying awake at night, listening to my mom's steady breathing as she sleeps, I think that maybe, just maybe, something is happening between us that is more than just fucking.

My desk phone rings, and I answer it while I continue typing. "Cabot Harkness's office." Silence greets me. "Hello?"

There's no response, so I shrug and hang up.

Only for it to ring again, a moment later. "Cabot Harkness's office." Silence again. "Hello? I'm so sorry, but I can't hear you."

I can feel Giovanna looking at me, head tilted in question. I meet her gaze and shake my head as I wait for a moment. When there's still no response, I say, "I'm going to hang up now, maybe try calling back on a different phone." Almost as soon as the handset meets the cradle, my phone rings again.

I eye it, knowing I need to answer the call, but not really wanting to. "Are you going to get that?" Giovanna asks.

I sigh and shake my head. "I think there's something wrong with the phone." Even as I say it, though, I pick up the phone. "Cabot Harkness's office."

"Don't hang up on me, you bitch!" The voice explodes through the phone, electronic and staticky. My breath catches in my throat and my heart thunders in my chest. "I'm gonna kill you. I'm gonna kill you," whoever is on the other end of the line singsongs, creepily. Goosebumps erupt on my skin and my scalp goes all prickly. I slam the phone into the cradle and then unplug it. I'll deal with the voicemails later.

I look up to find Giovanna at my side, brows pinched in concern. "What the hell was that?"

I shake my head. "Probably some asshole who thinks they're being funny." I make note of the time and jot it down before opening a new email. "I'm going to report it to security."

Giovanna reaches out to brush her fingers on my shoulder. "Smart. They should be able to trace the calls or something."

I'm honestly not sure if they can, but I need to do something, so I compose an email detailing the events and the time and send it before shaking off the unsettling situation and returning to my work.

"Miss Hart." I look up at Lincoln's brusque voice and find him striding toward me, fingers at the button of his suit, undoing it. There's an energy crackling off him that makes my knees clench together as my core goes warm and melty. "My office."

I don't glance at Giovanna as I push back my chair, pick up my tablet and follow in his wake. By the time I reach the door, he's already shucked his jacket and taken his seat behind his desk, leaned back, legs spread wide.

"Close the door, please." I do as he asks, still keeping my eyes off of Giovanna even though I can tell she's glaring at me. When I turn back around, he points to the spot between his legs, beckoning me over.

I should tell him no. I should put a stop to this, but I don't think I can. Because the truth is, I love it. So much. I love giving up control to him, letting him do whatever he wants, trusting that he'll make it good for me. I love letting my brain shut off, letting my worries go, even for a short time.

His slate blue eyes follow the sway of my hips as I round his desk, sliding my tablet onto its surface before I step between his knees. "Yes, Mr. George?"

I expect him to say something sexy and demanding, but he just runs his eyes over me in concern. "Lance just informed me you've been getting disturbing phone calls?"

I blink at him. "I-I-"

"Answer me, Liv."

"Yes. Just a few and just about five minutes ago? I reported it to security. How did Lance find out about it and tell you already?"

Lincoln curls his hands around my hips, tugging me farther between his splayed legs. "He's very good at his job. Which is why I know he'll figure out who it is. I don't want you to worry about it, okay?"

I melt, I can't help it. My tongue swipes over my lips while I nod. "Okay."

His thumbs stroke over my hip bones and a wolfish smile curls over his lips. "Did you do what I asked you this morning?" My breathing picks up. He means the text he sent at 6:30 this morning that simply read: No Panties. I hadn't asked for clarification. I didn't need it.

"Answer me, Miss. Hart. Or do you want me to check? Is that it? You don't want to be my good girl today?"

My tongue darts out again and his eyes darken as he follows the movement. "You'll have to check."

"Turn around." That surprises me, though I guess it really shouldn't. Haven't I thought about him bending me over his desk and slamming his cock in me a million times? Hasn't he already done that?

My heart rate picks up as I regard him, long enough that his hands grip my hips, and he roughly spins me. "You really want to play this game today, Miss. Hart?"

My palms press against the surface of his desk, catching myself. His hand presses between my shoulder blades, while his other keeps a firm grip on my hip, until I'm bent over in front of him. "Sure," I say as my cheek touches down. "Let's play this game today."

A low growl works its way out of him, and he stands from his chair, bending over me, pressing his chest into my back so he can whisper harshly in my ear. "Stay just like this, Liv. Don't fucking move, or you'll regret it."

There's a dark tone to his voice, one that sends a shiver of arousal down my spine in anticipation. His teeth nip at the corner of my jaw and then he straightens, removing his heat from me, removing his hands from me.

I feel him step away, move around the room. "I hadn't planned on using this tonight, Miss Hart. But since you seem inclined to play the brat today, I think it's time to show you what happens when you do." There's the sound of something thudding onto the desk next to me, on the side I can't see, and then he moves behind me, sits in his chair, scooting close to my ass. His thick thighs bracket mine, one on either side.

I'm halfway expecting a spanking. That's what doms do, right? Punish their subs with spankings and whips, bringing pleasure along with pain. So when his big hands dip under the hem of my skirt, I suck in a sharp breath, nerves firing all the way to my needy clit.

He chuckles low and dirty, as he slides his hands up, bringing the fabric with them slowly, revealing the tops of my stockings, the garter belt that holds them up and my lack of panties.

I bite my lip to stifle my moan when his teeth scrape over the curve of my ass. "Good girl, Liv. And look at you already so wet, dripping for me. I bet as soon as I said your name you got wet, hmm?"

I don't answer him, because he doesn't deserve to know that *yes,* just the sound of his voice gets me wet now. His ego is already big enough.

One of his hands leaves me, and a moment later, where I expected to feel his fingers or his cock, something foreign presses into me. It only takes me a second to realize its silicone and shaped like a dildo.

"Do you know what this is, sunshine?" Lincoln murmurs against my neck.

I wiggle my hips as he slowly works the toy inside me, pressing forward and retreating, slicking it with my arousal to make the going easier. "It feels like a vibrator."

He chuckles, breath puffing against my skin. "It is." Something in his tone tells me he's so fucking pleased with this, and I know in that instant that there's more to this than just him fucking me with a toy.

He presses the vibrator all the way in, and I feel it sort of lock into place. He didn't show it to me, but I can tell there's a clit stimulator, and that the dildo portion is relatively small, nothing like Lincoln's cock.

His heat leaves me as he stands back, eyes running over my bent form, the toy stuck inside me. "Fuck, you look so pretty like this, Olivia."

I smile against the desk, a pleased flush spreading over me. I can't help it. When he praises me like that, I just glow. His big hands cup my ass cheeks, massaging just slightly, and I stiffen up, preparing for a spank. It's not something we've done yet, but I've read enough smutty books to know that kneading the ass usually precedes a spanking. And he did call me a brat earlier.

Lincoln chuckles when he sees how I tense up. "Don't worry, sunshine. We aren't doing that today." He gives each cheek a gentle pat and then carefully smooths the fabric of my skirt back down. "Stand up for me."

I press my palms flat on the surface of the desk and press myself up, letting out a whimper when the toy rubs against me with each slight movement. Lincoln gathers my hair in one hand, holding it away from my neck, so he can nip the corner of my jaw. "How does that feel?"

I tip my head back and shift, testing it out. "Like it's going to drive me crazy."

He places another sucking kiss against my neck. "Good. You're going to keep that in all night."

"What?" I spin to face him and find a pleased smirk on his face. "I can't spend all night like this, Lincoln. I won't be able to form coherent sentences. That will be torture."

His grin only grows as he tucks a piece of hair behind my ear, his thumb scraping along my cheek. "You're right. It's not fair to ask you to stay like this."

I let out a relieved breath. "I can keep it in while I get ready, but once we're-"

Oh, holy hell. Whatever I'd been saying cuts off as the toy inside me vibrates, sending jolts of pleasure straight to my clit. My knees buckle and I have to grab onto Lincoln's jacket to not completely collapse to the floor.

Almost as soon as it started, it's gone. My breathing turns ragged, and my muscles feel weak. "Too much?" Lincoln asks innocently. "That was the highest setting. I think we'll avoid that until the end of the evening."

I blink my eyes open and straighten my legs before turning a glare on him. "What the hell, Linc!"

He laughs, then holds his phone for me to see the screen. I already know it's going to have an app for the vibrator inside me. He'll have the ability to turn it on at any time during the party, can bring me pleasure while I'm talking with a client or an investor, or hell, the bartender.

I shake my head at him. "You can't be serious, Lincoln. This is a *work* function. I can't be halfway coming through the entire thing."

He lifts a shoulder. "I don't see why not." When I just continue to glare at him, he just grins at me. "You can always use your safe word if this is something you really don't want. But fucking hell, Olivia. I love the idea of being able to make your pussy weep in the middle of a crowded room without even touching you." He grabs my hand and guides it to his cock, already thick and hard, pressing against the fly of his suit pants. Evidence of just how much he likes it. "I'll be so fucking hard the entire time, weeping pre-cum, needing to be inside you. It'll be torture for me, too." His lips press softly into my cheek before he drags his lips up to my ear to husk, "what do you say, sunshine? Are you gonna play with me?"

I blow out a harsh breath through my nostrils. I'm going to agree. We both already know that. Besides, I can always use my safe word if it gets to be too much, and retreat to a bathroom to relieve myself of the toy.

I love the idea of this being torture for him, too. Love the deliciously naughty feeling I know I'm going to get from being turned on beyond all reason in a room full of people dressed in their finest.

I lick my lips, and turn my face toward his, brushing my lips against his, before whispering. "Yes, I'll play."

Getting ready for a night out with a vibrator buried inside you is difficult, to say the least. Especially when Lincoln uses the app at random times to send pleasant gentle vibrations to me. Nothing as intense as he used in his office, but just enough to keep me constantly on edge, constantly horny and needing release.

I could have relieved the tension myself, could have finished the job, at any point while at home, could have sent him a text that said *snickerdoodle* and removed it. But damn if I don't want to show him I can do this, I can keep up with his games, take whatever he wants to throw at me.

So I "suffered" through curling my hair, applying more glamours make-up, putting in my contacts, and picking out a dress appropriate for the event. I chose an emerald green silky satin dress, with a plunging neckline, a tie at the waist and a slit that goes almost all the way up to my thigh. I consider wearing stockings and a garter, but decide I like the look better if it's only bare thigh that shows when I walk.

I think Lincoln will like it too.

Harvey whistles when I come down the stairs and my mother cat calls me when I step into the living room.

I'm cutting it close on time, so I don't linger with them, just press a careful kiss to my mother's cheek and wave at Harvey before I head out the door. Sometimes not having a car is a pain, but public transit in Breaker's Point is excellent, so it shouldn't take me that long to get to the hotel where the event is being held.

When I step onto the porch, I draw up short at the sight of a familiar black town car idling at the curb. As soon as I snap the door closed behind me, Lance, the head of Lincoln's security, steps out and rounds the car to open the back door for me.

"Miss Hart," he murmurs, offering me a hand to help me into the car.

"Lance," I say back, taking it and sliding in. I expect Lincoln to be waiting for me, but the back seat is empty. I push away the disappointment that I won't have any time with Lincoln before we're surrounded by people and lock my seatbelt into place.

At that exact moment, the toy inside me buzzes faintly, and my breath catches in my throat and my knuckles go white. Pleasure assaults me. It's everything I can do to not come right there in the back seat.

Just when I'm on the verge. It shuts off.

Stupid asshole.

I'm not going to survive this night.

By the time we pull up in front of the event, I've nearly gotten myself under control. Sure, I'm still clenching and horny, but I'm not quite so needy as I was before. There's a red carpet in front of the hotel, with photographers and journalists taking pictures of the Breaker's Point's most illustrious people and celebrities as they enter the event.

Lance doesn't drop me off there. He circles around the building instead, and I ignore the way my stomach drops. Of course I don't get to walk a red carpet, I'm no one. Technically, I'm here working, not to enjoy myself.

Lance glances into the rearview mirror and he must see the disappointment on my face because he explains, "it's for security, Miss Hart. With the phone calls you received earlier, we didn't want to make you more of a target."

I almost smack myself on the forehead. "Oh, of course. That makes total sense."

Half his mouth quirks up into a smile before he maneuvers the car to a stop in front of a pair of double doors at the back of the building. I hear him send a text and assume I'm supposed to get out, so I reach for the handle. Before I can push the door open, one word whips through the car. "Wait."

I freeze with my fingers three inches from the latch. We wait for another minute until Lance receives a message, and then he climbs out, scanning the area before rounding the car to help me out and hustle me into the building.

Lincoln is just on the other side of the doors. His slate blue eyes run over me from the top of my softly curled hair to my deep red lips, down the plunging neckline of my dress. His eyes linger on the sliver of thigh peeking through the skirt. I swear something close to a growl leaves him.

I can't blame him. I'm feeling just as possessive. Lincoln is always handsome, always effortlessly sexy in his suits, but in a classic black and white tux? He is debonair as fuck.

He nods to Lance and holds out a hand to me, tucking my fingers into the crook of his elbow.

"You look beautiful, Miss Hart." Lincoln's husky voice scrapes over my skin, makes me clench on the toy buried inside me. He's not usually so giving with his compliments. But then I guess maybe knowing I have a vibrator inside me has him feeling kind of amorous.

I lick my lips and ignore the way my chest is heaving from just his proximity. "Thank you, Mr. George." I smooth my hands down the front of my dress. "You have excellent taste."

His lips brush against the shell of my ear. "That's right I do. And I'm going to taste you later."

Oh, God. This man is going to kill me tonight. I can already tell. "Promises. Promises," I murmur back as he guides me toward the rumble of many voices laced with classical music.

Another of those almost growls sounds from his chest. "We need to go over the rules for tonight's game."

I blink up at him, allowing him to draw me to a stop just outside a set of doors. I can hear the party on the other side. "Rules? Besides me needing to keep the…" I glance around and lean closer to him to whisper. "Vibrator in all night, and you having the ability to turn it on at any time?"

He flashes a pleased smile at me, one thumb stroking along my cheek. "That was the game before I saw you in this dress and realized what a problem it's going to be."

My chest glows with the possessive tint to his voice. "My new rules are: no one touches you but me."

I frown. "I'm not sure how I'm going to manage-"

"I don't care how you manage it. You're doing it. If anyone but me touches you tonight, you'll be punished."

I lick my lips and nod slowly. "Okay. What's the second rule?"

Lincoln leans forward until his lips brush against the shell of my ear. "You can't come until I say so."

11
Lincoln

Olivia looks up at me with her gorgeous wide honey eyes, and I can tell she wants to say 'no.' If I'm honest with myself, even I think this might be too much for her. She doesn't have much experience with these sorts of games and if she makes it to the end of the night without coming, I'll be so fucking impressed I'll have no choice but to reward her.

But fuck, I can't wait to hear her beg me, plead with me to let her come.

It's going to be the sweetest sound.

I wait with an arched brow for her to agree to my new rules. When she'd been bent over my desk this afternoon, I truly hadn't intended to add any more. I was just going to play with her all night, was just going to turn the toy on if she decides to chat with any of the male attendees, or if I grow bored, which in this crowd is sure to happen. I have the feeling that watching Olivia struggle to hide her building orgasm in a room full of bedecked and bejeweled people is going to be the highlight of my week. Hell, maybe my year.

"I can use my safe word at any time, right?" Disappointment flickers through me at her hesitant question. This is too much. I'm pushing too hard.

But I'm quick to nod. To reassure her. "Yes. Of course, use your safe word and the game stops."

She's still thinking about it, likely weighing her ability to keep herself from coming while not giving the game away against the punishment I'll dole out to her if she refuses.

We haven't gotten into that aspect of gameplay that much. She's been such a good submissive for me I haven't felt the need, but now the idea of it has my already stiff cock throbbing. I halfway hope she fails, so I can introduce her to the pleasure of a careful flogging.

Finally, Liv sighs and nods. "Okay. I agree with your new rules."

I want to kiss her, want to take her sweet mouth with mine and draw out all those delicious noises I'm pretty sure she doesn't even realize she makes every time I taste her. But the last thing I need before I step into this room is to have bright red lipstick smeared on my lips. The same shade of red that my personal assistant is wearing.

It's going to be torture keeping my distance from her all fucking night.

But at least I'll have control of her pleasure.

"Good girl," I murmur in place of kissing her and smirk as she preens under the praise. My fingers press her hand into the fabric of my jacket briefly before I turn to the doors and pull one open.

Liv and I slip into the room relatively unnoticed. Most of the focus is on the doors that lead to the lobby of the hotel, watching as new local celebrities and some international ones arrive.

Olivia draws up short as she takes in the room. The sheer number of people. There's a stage on the far left side of the room with a dance floor right in front of it that isn't being used for dancing at the moment, just people milling around. On the edges of the empty space are circular tables draped in white linens and already set for dinner.

The decor is simple, tasteful, even with the twinkle lights strung along the ceiling in starburst patterns. Olivia eyes the number of people. "So how firm are you on the no touching rule? If I accidentally brush against someone, does that count? Or is it a hands only thing?"

She sounds really concerned about it, so I throw her a bone. "Arms brushing is fine. I'd prefer if your fine ass didn't accidentally touch someone's crotch, but absolutely no hands or intentional touching."

She nods, determination settling over her face, like she's going to enjoy the challenge. "Fair enough."

I chuckle and guide her to a table near the front of the cluster. I'd scoped out the set up earlier, so I know where our seats are. They'd put Olivia next to Jerome Kline, and damn if I was going to let him get that close to her tonight, so I swapped our place cards, messing with the old school male-female set up, but if anyone has a problem with it, they can suck a bag of dicks. The only people who will be close to Olivia tonight are myself and an elderly lady with soft white hair and a beaded silver gown named Fiona Marks.

"I've never been to an event like this," Olivia says, her southern accent a little stronger as her nerves take over. I watch as she shifts on her heels and her eyes flutter closed as her mouth parts on a pant. Good. I'd been worried that she'd grow used to the feeling of the toy inside her, that it wouldn't be quite as much torture as I hoped, but it's still affecting her.

"Nervous?" I ask, my hand settling against the fabric of her lower back.

She quirks an eyebrow at me. "For more than one reason, Mr. George."

Across the room, I see a flicker of dark hair and a bright red dress, and my heart stops for just a moment. It can't be her. She'd told me she wasn't coming tonight, swore up and down that she wouldn't be here. And I believed her. Why would she lie?

"Lincoln?" I look back at Olivia to find her head tipped back, honey gold eyes on me. "You okay?"

I smile at her and nod. "Of course. Let's get you a drink, shall we? It should help with those nerves." I guide her over to one of the bars bordering the room, watching as Olivia carefully maneuvers herself to avoid touching anyone even though I'd told her that brushing against someone wouldn't count against her.

When we reach the bar, I have to resist the urge to put her in front of me, cage her against it with my body, and keep anyone else from getting anywhere near her.

Instead, I fish my phone out of my pocket, open the app, and flick it onto the lowest setting as I bend and murmur in her ear, "good fucking girl." She gasps and flushes, hands flying to grip the wooden bar top in front of her to keep her knees from buckling. I shut it off almost as soon as I started it, tucking my phone away again, while Olivia glares up at me.

"Asshole," she mutters as the bartender comes to a stop in front of us. "Crap," she winces. "Not you. You seem lovely."

I stifle the growl that tries to sound, eyeing the young guy behind the bar like he's a bug I'm going to squash if he so much as smiles at my girl. He must feel my intention because he just gives her that polite customer service smile and says, "no problem. What can I get you?"

Olivia orders a prosecco. I order a scotch.

She's shaking her head as we retreat from the bar. "I'm going to lose this game. And how the hell am I supposed to work if I can't concentrate on anything but that at any moment you can-" she cuts herself off and downs half the glass of wine in a couple gulps.

"You'll do fine, sunshine," I reassure her, but she just rolls her eyes at me, a small smirk playing around her lips. I growl. "Such a little brat today."

Olivia huffs and moves away from me. I watch her retreat, allowing her space. It'll make the game that much more enjoyable for both of us. I'll be able to watch as she tries not to fall apart from a distance, my finger on the button bringing her to ruin.

Anticipation sings through me, makes my heart rate ratchet up. I smirk as I watch Olivia dodge someone's hand when they try to get her attention.

Who would have thought that Olivia Hart would be so much fun to play with?

.... ♥ ....

By the time that dinner is served, Olivia is a sweaty fucking beautiful mess. I've kept my eyes on her almost the entire night, watched as I turned on the toys buried inside her and her mouth pauses in whatever she'd been saying, eyes going glassy.

Every fucking time my cock throbs, knowing that she's getting closer and closer to falling apart. Every time I flick on the toy, her fingers tighten on the glass in her hand until her knuckles go white and I watch as she takes deep breaths, like she's willing away her orgasm with each inhale and exhale. As soon as I turn it off, she seeks me out with her pretty honey eyes and glares at me, even as her cheeks flush.

When the host for the evening urges everyone to their seats so that dinner can be served, Olivia practically falls into her chair. Her knees are likely weak after the hell I've just put her through. I settle next to her, leaning slightly to the side to murmur, "how are you?"

It's a genuine question but also slightly taunting.

Her jaw tics, pulse thumping crazily in her neck before she turns to look at me, meeting my challenging gaze with one of her own. "I'm fine. I can do this all night." She leans closer until I can smell her sunshine and wildflower scent and her breath puffs over my cheek, and then my ear as she murmurs. "But can you? I'm so wet right now, Lincoln. Don't you want to feel?"

My cock throbs, leaking pre-cum, and it takes every ounce of my control to not shove my hand under her skirt and into her pussy to feel exactly what this is doing to her, what I am doing to her. "Don't be a brat," I murmur back, before holding my phone up. Her honey eyes widen as I hit the button to turn it on, the faint buzzing reaching my ears.

Olivia's mouth opens on a gasp when I turn it up, the buzzing getting louder as her hips shift restlessly against her chair, despite her best efforts. "Linc," she groans. "Please."

"Please, what, sunshine?"

Her gaze flicks around, making sure no one is paying any attention to us. "Please, can I come?"

My eyes slip closed at the question, so sweetly asked. It's on the tip of my tongue to tell her yes, because of that alone, but in the next moment, she whimpers. And it's not a whimper of pleasure, but one of distress. "

"Lincoln!" *Jerome Kline.*

My eyes fly open, and I jab the button to turn off the toy. Olivia sags into her chair, eyes focused on her napkin, avoiding Jerome entirely as he says her name. "Not yet," I say to her quietly. And she nods, looking relieved as hell. I can't even blame her. The last thing I want is for her to fall apart in front of Jerome fucking Kline, even if he has no clue it's happening.

I stow my phone back into my pocket and shift in my chair until I'm facing the man who will undoubtedly put a dampener on my game with Oliva while we're at the table with him. And maybe even longer now that he knows she's here.

The man is annoyingly persistent in his pursuit of her. No amount of me telling him it won't happen seems to work.

"Jerome!" I say, holding my hand out to him. He takes it and gives it a hearty shake, but his beady little eyes are on Olivia. "Great to see you."

"And you." His tongue swipes over his lips. "What a *pleasure* to see you again, Olivia."

I twist slightly to see her give him a weak smile. "Mr. Kline," she murmurs before reaching for her water glass and taking a sip, so she doesn't have to say anything else.

He waits, expectantly, but my girl turns away from him entirely as Fiona Marks takes her seat, engaging the old woman in conversation, that I have no doubt will occupy her for the entirety of dinner.

It takes me a while to realize that Olivia isn't eating. She does a good job of pushing the salad around her plate, so it looks like she is, but I don't see her lift the fork to her mouth once. When the main course arrives, I shift more fully toward her, watching as she grips her fork. But once again, none of the food makes it to her mouth.

I have no idea why, but it pisses me off that she's not eating, like she's not taking care of herself. I lean over into her side until my shoulder brushes against hers and my mouth is right next to her ear. "Is there something wrong with the food?"

She twists her head slightly, almost enough that our mouths would brush, but she keeps a distance between us. I hate that she does. "I'm worried about cross contamination," she murmurs. "There's a seafood risotto on the menu. I brought an EpiPen, but an allergic reaction and a trip to the hospital would kind of ruin our game, wouldn't it?"

I frown. How did I not think of this? "Did you ask?"

She shakes her head, but I'm already looking for a server, waving them over. "Yes, sir, how can I help you?"

"My companion is allergic to shellfish. Is there something she can eat that we can be sure hasn't come into contact with any seafood?"

Olivia shakes her head. "It's really not-"

"Olivia."

That's all I have to say to have her mouth snap shut. I look back at the server expectantly. She flicks her gaze between the two of us before bobbing into a bow. "I'll check with the chef and verify that the food on her plate is safe."

I nod at her, and Olivia gives her a shaky smile. "Thank you."

"Are you enjoying yourself, Olivia?" The woman next to me tenses as Jerome uses my interruption of her conversation to insert himself.

She gives him that polite, slightly detached smile. "I am. Though I am here in my capacity as Mr. Harkness's assistant."

Jerome guffaws like she told a joke and nudges me with his elbow. "Yeah, I bet. I bet you're here as Cabot's assistant and nothing else."

I fist my hand in my lap and just barely manage to not punch him in the mouth.

The server comes back and bends slightly between Olivia and me to report. "The chef has assured me that what is in front of you at this moment has had no cross contamination."

Olivia gives her another smile and carefully lifts a forkful of mashed potatoes to her mouth. She tastes it, swallows, and waits. Just in case the server and the chef are wrong. I watch her too, looking for any signs of distress from anaphylaxis, though I don't know what that would look like, anyway.

I watch as she tastes the rest of the food on the plate like this, carefully testing to see if she'll stop breathing. I've never been so tense watching someone eat before, on the edge of my seat, ready to leap toward her purse and the lifesaving medicine there.

When she tastes everything and nothing happens, we both relax. Olivia goes back to her conversation with Mrs. Marks, and I zone out while Jerome talks at me, though he has a hard time keeping his gaze off of my woman.

I seriously consider cutting all ties with him, plan what I would say to Cabot to explain it away and imagine never having to sit by while he runs his hungry gaze all over Olivia. It's a beautiful thought, but a dangerous one. Jerome Kline is one of our top investors. We can't afford to alienate him. The fact that I'm even thinking it is a bad fucking sign.

I've grown too attached to Olivia. More than I intended. More than I can.

I should work to distance myself from her.

So that's what I do.

As soon as the last course is served, I leave her at the table. Leave her with Jerome Kline one seat away from her. My stomach twists uncomfortably as I walk away, heading for the closest bar.

I keep my gaze away from her as I order a drink and watch as the bartender pours it. "George!" A boisterous voice says from nearby, making me turn toward the crowd. I catch sight of Olivia standing abruptly from her chair, smoothing her hands over the skirt of her dress before my view is interrupted by Owen Thatcher. He gives me a grin. "I was hoping I'd run into you at this thing."

"Well, here I am." I give him a strained smile and then turn my attention to Olivia, weaving through the crowd, carefully avoiding touching anyone. She stops next to an older gentleman and smiles widely at something he says to her. By her reaction alone, I can tell it's nothing I need to be concerned about.

Fuck. I shouldn't be concerned about anything that has to do with Olivia. We fuck. That's it. I shouldn't be considering cutting ties with Jerome, or gouging out the eyes of anyone that looks at her. I shouldn't have the urge to wrap her up in my arms and press her close to me in this crowded room.

I sure as fuck shouldn't be so worried about her allergy that I hardly ate anything until I knew it was safe for her.

Goddamn. Olivia Hart is fucking with me. With my control.

And I'm not sure that I like it.

My body tenses as I see Jerome weave toward her, unsteady on his feet. I have to grit my teeth to stay put, to not head him off. I can't run to her rescue anytime this man decides he's going to make a pass at her.

Jerome's hand brushes against her forearm to draw her attention back to him. That possessive edge in me razors to life, wanting to beat the shit out of the pervert for touching her. I watch as Olivia pulls away from him, giving him a strained smile as she surreptitiously wipes the back of her hand on her skirt, even though he touched her arm through fabric.

My jaw ticks.

"Everything okay, Lincoln?" I draw my attention away from Olivia, even though it's the last thing I want to do and give Owen Thatcher a winning smile.

"Everything's fine." But in the next moment, I've thrown back the rest of my drink and slid the glass onto a nearby table. "Excuse me for a moment. I see someone I need to say hello to."

I don't wait for a response from Owen. Everything in me is demanding I go to my girl, that I mark her, claim her. But really, I'm just going to take her into a hall and fuck the shit out of her, fill her with my cum, before sending her back into this party.

Yeah. *Fuck yeah.* I like the idea of that. Of her being around all these assholes while dripping my cum down her pretty, pale thighs.

"Meet me in the back hall," I murmur in her ear as I pass by, grinding my cock against her ass like it was an accident, when it's anything but. Olivia, for her part, keeps talking, though I catch a small stutter in her speech when I squeeze her hip and then continue on. I don't linger in the party, don't wait to push through the door that Liv and I entered through earlier. I can feel her gaze on me, tracking my movements as I go. Smart girl, she'll know exactly where to find me.

12
Olivia

"Meet me in the back hall." The demand is growled in my ear and accompanied by a firm hand on my hip, squeezing in warning like if I don't show up, he'll punish me.

I mean, he probably would, but I have no intention of not meeting him out there, because if the erection he'd pressed into my ass as he whispered in my ear was any indication, Lincoln is on the verge of giving us both what we need. And God do I need it. Even after sitting through dinner with Jerome Kline.

I've nearly come so many times in the last few hours I've lost count. It's not even from him using the vibration of the toy. It's from the feeling of his possessive gaze on me all fucking night. Well, that and the delicious filthy naughty feeling of being so fucking close to coming in this room full of people.

It's not quite exhibitionist behavior, but it's damn close and I never would have thought it would be a turn on for me, but apparently it is.

I wait for three minutes. It's probably too long in Lincoln's mind—it's too long in my mind too—but I get the impression he doesn't exactly want me to flaunt that we're about to get it on while everyone else dances the night away.

When I've estimated that enough time has passed, I smile at the elderly man in front of me. "I'm so sorry I see someone I need to say hello to. I'll find you later so we can continue our conversation."

He blinks and nods at me, reaching out like he's going to pat my hand, but I dance back and away from him, keeping him from making contact, because Lincoln told me not to let anyone touch me. I hope like hell Lincoln didn't see Jerome touch me, or if he did, maybe he'll think the touch itself was punishment enough. I certainly do.

I casually make my way through the room, back to the door that we entered through before, and slip out into the hall. As soon as the door clicks shut, the noise from inside becomes muted. I glance left, then right, but don't see Lincoln anywhere.

Blowing out a breath through my nose, I pick a direction, heading farther away from the party. When I round a corner, I find him. But he's talking with a gorgeous dark-haired woman in a deep red dress. I duck back around the corner, and then peek my head back, just in time to see her press a kiss to his cheek, leaving behind a smear of red lipstick.

She steps away from him, flicks her eyes in my direction and smirks at me, then saunters off, hips swaying in her form fitting dress. Lincoln watches her go, his jaw tight, before he turns and looks back at me, with one brow arched.

Apparently, I'm not as stealthy as I would like to think I am.

"Sneaking around?" He growls at me.

I step out from around the corner and move toward him, acutely aware of the toy between my thighs, even more so when he pulls his phone out of his pocket. "No. You told me to meet you out here. I just didn't want to interrupt you if you got a better offer." I don't do a great job of hiding the hurt, the jealousy in my voice. Half his mouth quirks up as he hits the control.

I stumble to a stop, one hand shooting out to brace against the wall as my hips buck in response. I whimper as I sink my teeth into my lower lip to keep from shouting. Apparently, now that I know I'm alone, except for Lincoln, my body knows it doesn't have to hide what it's going through.

The need to come is so strong that my lips part on a small sob. As soon as that happens, Lincoln shuts off the app, tucks his phone away and curls his finger at me, beckoning me closer. I take a deep breath, straighten my spine, and move until I'm standing in front of him.

Slate blue eyes burn into me as he tucks a strand of hair behind my ear. "There is no better offer than you, right now, sunshine. Besides, I wouldn't abandon our game when you've been playing so beautifully."

"Good," I breathe, and he chuckles, bending his head to skate his lips along my jaw, down my neck. My hand grip the lapels of his jacket and I tug him closer, backing up until I'm pressed against the wall, and he's pressed against me. After the torture of being turned on all fucking evening, of him bringing me to the edge only to keep me from going over, my body is essentially a live wire, sparking at the barest of touches. And now here he is, pressed against me, cock hard and throbbing against my hip.

Goddamn, I need to come.

I don't see him do it, but the toy starts to vibrate again, making me whine.

"Please, Linc," I gasp out as he bites at my neck. "Please. I need it."

"You want to come, baby?" He growls against my neck. "You need it?"

I nod frantically, clamping down on my orgasm. Because as much as I want to come, I want to follow his orders more. "Please, Linc. *Please*. I can't think about anything else."

He hums before he sucks my flesh into his mouth, scraping over my neck. "I'm not sure you deserve it." A sob breaks from my lips at his words. I'm going to lose this game. I'm going to fail. "You let him touch you."

I blink, trying to focus on who he means when I can only think about my release, and it takes me a moment to realize he's referring to Jerome Kline patting my forearm to get my attention.

I shake my head. "You can't be mad about that, I didn't-"

"Did another man's hand touch your body? The body that belongs to me, Olivia?"

The vibration against my clit is nearly unbearable. "You can't expect me to go through life without ever touching another man. It was an innocent touch!" I pant out.

"No touch is innocent when it comes to a little whore like you," He growls, pulling back to look at my face. "But now you understand you must follow my rules, so if you beg pretty enough, I'll let you come. Would you like that? Hmm?"

I nod again, hips thrusting shamelessly against his thigh. "Yes. Yes please, Linc. Please, I'll be good. I promise."

His slate blue eyes crinkle slightly at the corners as he smirks at me. "I know you will be Olivia. Now get on your knees and ask again."

I only hesitate for a moment, glancing down the hall. Anyone could come this way, literally anyone. It's not exactly private, and the floor is not exactly clean, but I need this orgasm. My body has been in a state of arousal for hours and I'm wound tighter than a spring. So I drop to my knees, keeping them slightly spread, hands resting on my thighs like I know he prefers. I keep my chin dipped down in submission. "Please, can I come, sir?"

"Not yet." Another sob rips out of me, even as my hips shift. Lincoln hooks a finger under my chin and tips my face up to him, swiping away the tear that escaped my eye along with my sob. "No crying, either. We don't want to ruin your makeup. We don't want them to know what we're doing out here, do we?"

I shake my head. "No, sir."

His knuckles stroke over my cheek. "Good girl. Now take my cock out."

My hands are moving before he's even finished the command, fumbling for his belt and zipper while he chuckles. "So greedy aren't you, baby? Such a little slut for my cock." I nod again, as I slide my hand into his boxers and fist his long throbbing length, pulling it out. He groans at the slide of my hand along his length, but it cuts off on a hiss as my tongue darts out to taste him. In a flash, his hand curls in my hair, making my scalp tingle, and tugs me back. "Did I tell you to put your mouth on me?"

I stare up at him. "If you don't want a blow job, why am I down here?"

"Oh baby, I always want a blow job from your pretty mouth, but I don't want to smear your lipstick." His hand delves into the inner pocket of his suit coat and he pulls out his phone. "You are on your knees because that is where I wanted you. You took out my cock because I want you to stroke it with your hand while you're down there. Understand."

"Yes, sir." I know better than to hesitate. I curl my hand around his cock and stroke, just like he told me to, maintaining my grip when he opens the app that has been tormenting me all night and changes up the pattern of vibration. A scream pushes against my closed lips as I try to stifle it. It comes out like a keening wail, instead.

"You ready, my good little whore? You ready to come while on your knees for me?"

"*Yes. Yes. Yes,*" I chant, body going tight with anticipation.

"Beg me for it."

"Please, Lincoln. Please let me come. I need it."

I'm already halfway there when he says, "come for me, baby."

I thought it would feel like a release. I thought after hours of fighting off this orgasm it would be a relief to have it, but instead it hurts, a sharp spike of pain on my over sensitive clit that radiates up and through my body before culminating in pleasure so intense I must black out. Because the next thing I know I'm against the wall, my legs are wrapped around Lincoln's hips and he's shoving inside me in sharp quick thrusts, jaw clenched as he battles through the tight squeeze of my muscles.

"Fuck, Liv," he grunts out. "Fuck, you feel so good. So tight. Squeezing me like you never want me to leave."

My arms curl over his shoulders and I hang on for dear life as he ruts me into the wall. His breathing is harsh, puffing against my neck as he powers into me with jerky movements of his hips. "I think from now on I'm only going to fuck you after you've come, when you're so fucking tight like this. *Fuck, yes.*"

His hips stall and I feel him come deep inside me, lashing me with hot ropes of cum. His hands flex on my hips as he grinds deeper into me, before pulling back, dragging his lips over my cheek to my mouth. I want him to kiss me, so fucking bad, but I know he won't. That deep red of my lips needs to remain unsmeared for now. His breath puffs against my mouth, and he laughs softly. "God, you're perfect."

With that seemingly benign statement, he lets one of my legs drop, keeping the other wrapped around his hip. He slides the vibrator I hadn't realized he was holding down the crease where my hip meets my thigh and then he carefully works it back inside me.

I want to protest. Want to beg him to please not put me through that again, but I know he'll just tell me to use my safe word if I want the game to stop. He'll be disappointed in me if I do.

"I fucking love the idea of keeping my cum inside you with this little toy," he husks, eyes focused on the teal silicone peeking out from between my legs, before he lifts them to my face. "Still good?" There's obvious concern in the question, like he's actually worried this might be too much for me. It makes my chest feel strangely tight with emotion.

I nod. "Yes, still good." He rewards me with a grin so bright I have blink against it.

"That's my good girl." He drops my other leg, helps me rearrange the skirt of my dress and then tucks his half hard cock away. When we're both fully covered he cups my shoulders and squeezes just slightly, kneading muscles I hadn't realized were tense. "Go take a moment in the restroom. And then come back to the party." I nod my ascent. "My earlier rule still applies, Liv. No one touches you." When I don't answer right away, he ducks down until he can meet my eyes. "I mean it, sunshine."

I nod my understanding and he releases me, turning from me and striding away with quick steps, like he has to hurry to get away from me, to put distance between us, or he'll turn around and fuck me against the wall again.

The thought makes my lip twitch up in a smirk, but then I shift on my heels and the toy inside me rubs all those little pleasure nerves and I groan. I'm honestly not sure I can take much more of this torture.

By the time I return to the party, I'm a messy ball of need all over again.

Lincoln smirks at me like he knows exactly what's happening to me, but I ignore him. Sliding gingerly into my chair and giving the other occupants at the table a smile that I hope doesn't say, 'my boss just fucked me to within an inch of my life.' But I'm not sure I manage.

Lincoln slides his hand onto my thigh, caressing first and then squeezing gently. I half expect him to finger me right here, but he just keeps it there, possessively gripping my thigh for the rest of the evening.

As soon as we're in the back seat of the car, speeding toward my house, Lincoln shoves up my skirt and pulls the toy out of me. I flick my eyes toward the front seat, but find the partition already raised, so I turn my attention back to the man beside me.

His fingers plunge into my pussy, replacing the vibrator he just removed. He groans, feeling how wet I am with a combination of his cum and my arousal. "God, you feel so fucking good, sunshine. I need to be inside you."

"God, please yes, Linc." There is no playing, no game as I reach to undo his belt, as I pull his cock out and he helps me straddle his hips, positioning the tip of his dick at my entrance before gripping my hips under my dress and helping me sink down slowly.

"Look at me, Liv," he groans, head tilted back against the seat, tendons in his neck straining. "Look at me while you take my cock."

My eyes fly up to meet his. Our noses bump, our breaths mingle. And for some reason, this feels so damn… *intimate*. The enclosed space in the back seat doesn't allow for a lot of distance between our bodies, not that we'd let there be, anyway. I slide my arms around his neck to brace myself, but also to get him closer. His hands splay on my back, pressing me into his chest as I roll my hips slowly, languidly.

"Yeah, baby," he moans. "Just like fucking that. So fucking good. Your pussy was made for me."

He says, all of that while staring right into my fucking eyes. The intense contact makes my arousal spark and bloom. Something shifts inside me, and I see an answering shift in Lincoln. "Tell me you want me, Olivia," he whispers against my cheek.

"I want you," I whisper back. "Fuck, I always want you. Probably always will." It feels like more than just saying I want his body, his dick, but we both know what this is, how far this will go.

"Me too." The words are almost ripped from him. "Me fucking too. I can't get enough of you. I never want to leave-" He cuts off on a groan, and I don't know if it's because he didn't want to finish whatever he was saying, or if something just feels particularly good. Either way, he laces his fingers into my hair in the next moment, tugging my mouth to his, where he kisses me in the same languid way we're fucking. Slow and steady, like he knows my entire body is tense, on the verge, and he doesn't want to push me over too quickly.

Then he pulls back. "Come for me, sunshine." I would have thought that this orgasm would be painful, powerful, after the torture I've been under tonight, but at his words it blooms smooth and sweet at the base of my spine, growing until I'm a shuddering, shaking mess on top of him. I moan his name. A moment later he moans mine, his hips pressing tight to me.

I collapse against him, my forehead resting on his shoulder. I might doze off like that, with my hands curled between our chests. Lincoln rubs his hands up and down my back, kneading my sore muscles as best he can. When he's worked out as many knots as he can find, he laces his fingers with mine, lifting my hand to kiss the back of it before he lets out a kind of breathless laugh.

"Goddamn, sunshine. I could spend a week fucking you and not get enough."

I smile against his neck and then press a kiss to the corner of his jaw. "Me too."

What neither of us say is that what we just did felt a lot less like fucking and a lot more like something else.

And he didn't call me his good girl or little whore once.

13
Lincoln

I probably shouldn't be here. If she's sick, it's not any of my business, but I can't help but feel that she isn't actually sick. I think I pushed her too hard with the last scene, the vibrator, the dinner, the fucking in the car after.

I took care of her, made sure she was clean and hydrated. Hell, I'd even given her a mini massage to help ease her muscles, sore after being tense for the entire evening, from clamping down on her need to come. God, she'd been so good. Doing exactly as I'd said, and holding it off until she was shaking, nearly crying.

No one else noticed a thing, but I sure as fuck did.

I thought everything was fine. With the way she kissed me, so gently in the car before she climbed out and made her way on unsteady feet to her front door, I thought she handled the entire game like a fucking pro.

Apparently, I was wrong, seeing as she wasn't at work today.

So now here I am, standing on a

porch in East Breaker's Point, well out of the downtown area, away from the waterfront. The house that Olivia lives in is small, two stories, with a tiny well maintained front yard, cheerful robin's egg blue paint and crisp white trim. It looks freshly painted, within the last year or so.

I'm sure Liv did it herself, keeping her house as tidy as she keeps the rest of her life... Well, except for me.

I press my finger on the doorbell, but don't hear the chime, so I lift my hand and knock, too. Twenty seconds later—*I counted*—the door yanks open and Olivia blinks up at me. My breath leaves me in a whoosh as I take her in, starting at her bare toes, painted a pale pink with white daisies on the big nails. Up her charcoal gray leggings that hug her like a fucking lover, to her oversized wide neck white t-shirt, draped off one shoulder, baring her collarbone and the strap of a white lace bralette. My eyes rest on a spot of ink on her forearm, a bundle of dahlias, done in pinks and purples.

I frown at the tattoo, unaccountably angry at the sight of it. How did I not know she had a tattoo? And on her arm, of all places? I've been inside this woman, and yet, this is the first time I'm seeing her *forearm*? How the hell is that the case?

Because you always fuck her in your office with your clothes on, asshole. You've never bothered to take your time with her, to strip her bare and learn every fucking inch of her.

Liv clears her throat, one hand gripping the door, the other holding the frame like she needs their support to interact with me. My eyes leave the tattoo and travel to her blond hair, piled into a messy bun on top of her head, strands falling all around her exhausted face.

"So you *are* sick." The words just fall out, propelled by relief that I didn't actually scare her away, that our game wasn't too much for her.

Her dark blond brows draw together as she scowls at me. "You came here to make sure I wasn't lying?" Her voice is rough, husky, like she'd been asleep when I knocked.

I tip my head at her. "I came to make sure you were okay."

A surprised laugh rolls out of her as she releases the door frame to run a hand down her face. The movement is exhausted, wrist limp and floppy. "Well, I'm fine, as you can see." She shifts like she's getting ready to close the door. "I should be back at work tomorrow."

"Liv," I say, pressing my hand into the door before she has a chance to slam it in my face. I have the inexplicable urge to take care of her, to figure out whatever has her looking this exhausted and fix it. "You don't look fine. What's going on?"

She just stares at me, honey brown eyes wide. Her pale pink lips part and I think she's going to actually answer, but then she shakes her head. "I really can't handle whatever this right now, Lincoln. I don't have the brain power."

I frown, stepping closer, almost to the lip of the door frame, close enough to feel the warmth from inside, and catch a whiff of something baking, along with a heavy dose of Liv's wildflower scent. Her head tips back, keeping her gaze on my face.

"Tell me. Is it Harvey? Did that asshole do something?" My eyes run over her again, making sure there aren't any fresh bruises on her skin. Bruises not left by me.

"Are my ears burning, or did someone say my name?" A masculine voice says from inside the house, getting closer with each word. Liv's head tips even farther back as she shifts, turning sideways in the door to look at the intruder to our conversation.

My body tenses, ready for a fucking fight, ready to beat the shit out of the asshole who touches Liv, who hurt her. But I blink when he comes into focus. This is not who I expected. Not at all.

Harvey is big, broad shoulders, solidly built. His teeth flash white in his weathered face. His hair is all gray, and there's a twinkle in his pale blue eyes, framed in laugh lines and crow's feet. Harvey is at least twice Olivia's age. He's also wearing scrubs and a wedding ring. I might not have seen Olivia's tattoo before today, but I sure as fuck know she doesn't wear a wedding ring.

Olivia sighs and tips her head toward me. "Harvey, this is my boss, Mr. George. He came to make sure I'm actually sick and not gallivanting around the city playing hooky."

Harvey grins at me while he gives Olivia's arm a fond squeeze. My jaw ticks. "Ah, well, as you can see, our girl is here, and feeling a little under the weather." His blue eyes move from her to me and back again. "But you made the trek out here. Do you want to come in for a cup of coffee? Olivia made some absolutely delicious turnovers this morning. Cherry. My favorite."

Olivia's shaking her head, already pushing Harvey back into the house. "No. Nope. He doesn't have time-"

"Actually, I do." A wolfish grin pulls at my lips. "I would love a cup of coffee." I don't really understand what's going on here, but I'm going to find out.

Her teeth clench as her nostrils flare. I can tell she wants to say no again, push me back out the door and wash her hands of this entire situation, but her southern hospitality wins out. "Fine."

Harvey chuckles and squeezes both her shoulders, massaging just the tiniest bit, and I have to fight the urge to yank his hands off her and punch him in the nose. But a moment later, he slides his hands off and starts back down the narrow hall. "Come on, Mr. George. I'll show you to the living room while Liv gets the coffee."

I move farther into the house, brushing by Olivia, who closes the door, and stays there, her head pressed against the wood, muttering something under her breath that sounds something like, "fetching coffee in my own freaking home."

But when she turns around, she's got a fake as shit smile plastered on her face. "Go ahead." She waves a hand down the hall. The kitchen is to the right of the door, the dining room to the left, so the living room must be at the back of the house.

"Do you want help?"

Wordlessly, she shakes her head and moves into the tidy kitchen. There's a tray full of turnovers on the counter, but otherwise the space is spotless. The entire house is spotless and the scent of lemon cleanser hovers under all the other smells in the house.

Olivia may be feeling sick, but that hasn't stopped her from scrubbing every inch of this house this morning. Yeah, there is definitely something wrong.

I head in the direction Harvey went, but Olivia's voice stops me. "You're not sick, are you? You're feeling okay?" I turn to face her and find her in the kitchen's doorway, shifting uncertainly on her bare feet, worry clear on her face.

Is she worried she got me sick? Is she *concerned* about me?

My chest feels tight at the idea of Olivia caring about me. I shake my head at the thought. I've never needed one of my fuck buddies to care. It's always just about mutual satisfaction. Sure, there has to be some amount of trust between partners when we play the games I play, but I've never needed them to care about me.

I've never cared about them either.

This is a new feeling, and I'm not entirely sure I fucking like it.

"No, Liv. I'm not sick." Her teeth sink into her lower lip, and she nods before turning back to the kitchen. I watch her for a moment as she pulls out a tray and carefully places three mismatched cups on it.

I could stand there and watch her move around her kitchen, but at that moment, Harvey calls, "Come on through, Mr. George."

I note the way Liv's cheeks flush when she realizes I'm still watching her. It pulls a smirk to my lips that is still firmly in place when I swagger down the hall and into the living room. Where it promptly falls. Because this room, though called a living room, looks more like a hospital room. There's a couch shoved against the far wall, blocking a fireplace that looks like it hasn't been used in ages. I make note of the blanket and pillow, neatly folded and stacked on one side of the cushions. There's an armchair in one corner, a TV hung over the mantle. But the majority of the space is taken up by the mechanical hospital bed in the center of the room.

Harvey is standing next to it, hand curled around the frail wrist of the tiny occupant, as he counts seconds on his watch, checking her heartbeat.

"Who might you be?" Warm honey-colored eyes, so like Olivia's, scrape over me from head to foot.

This woman has to be Olivia's mother. The resemblance is uncanny, even with the hollow cheeks and pale skin. Even with the scarf wrapped around her head, and how painfully thin she is.

They have the same chin, the same nose, the same eyes. I'm sure if I could see her hair, it would be honey blond like her daughter's.

Yes, this is undoubtedly Olivia's mother. And she is undoubtedly dying.

Suddenly, things make so much more sense. Verity's attachment to Olivia. Cabot's insistence that I read her file. The lingering scent of cleanser in the air. The way Olivia was worried about me being sick, not because she cares about me, but because she didn't want me getting her mother sicker than she already is. How Olivia always looks tired, even after the weekend, like it wasn't restful for her at all. All the times she clearly wanted to argue with me about staying late or coming on a Saturday.

God, I'm a fucking asshole.

Harvey carefully sets Mrs. Hart's hand down and looks up at me. "Don't be shy. Take a seat."

His prompting makes me move, has me stumbling forward, hand out, as nerves—*I can't believe I'm fucking nervous right now*—flutter in my stomach. "Lincoln George," I say as Mrs. Hart lifts her tiny hand and places it in mine. I don't squeeze. God, I'm terrified if I do, I'll break something. Instead, I bend at the waist and lift her cold hand to my lips, brushing a kiss over her knuckles.

She lets out a surprisingly girlish giggle at the contact, so I do it again. And when I straighten, she's beaming at me, a pretty flush, so like her daughter's, on her previously pale cheeks. "Well, aren't you just the gentleman," she says, voice thick with the southern accent that only dusts Olivia's. "I'm Caroline Hart." She motions to Harvey, still standing on the opposite side of the bed. "And this is Harvey, my jailor."

My brows arch as I look at the older man, who just chuckles, shaking his head before he meets my eyes. "I'm her nurse. I take care of Caroline when Liv is working."

I almost ask why he's here now, if Olivia is at home, but then I remember how tired she looked when she answered the door and all I can feel is grateful that she has someone here to help.

"Please," Mrs. Hart says, motioning with one limp hand. "Have a seat. I apologize for the state of the living room, but it's unfortunately unavoidable." I wave off her apology as I unbutton my suit jacket and sit on the couch, being sure to not disturb the carefully stacked blankets.

"Please, don't trouble yourself, Mrs. Hart."

"Ms," she corrects. "Never did get around to marrying Olivia's father."

Surprise filters through me, but I keep it off my face. "Ms. Hart."

Her hand flutters over her chest, and then up to touch the scarf wrapped around her head self-consciously. "If I'd known we were going to have company, I would have freshened up a bit. I don't know why Olivia didn't warn me we'd be having a visitor."

"I didn't know he was coming, mama," Olivia says as she enters the room, tray in her hands. I stand to help her, but Harvey is already there, taking it from her and sliding it onto the foot of Ms. Hart's bed. "If I had, I wouldn't have answered the door."

"Olivia!" Ms. Hart scolds, flapping a hand at her daughter, like she would have affectionately smacked her with her knuckles if only she was close enough. "Apologize!"

Olivia sighs, taking a mug of coffee from the tray and offering it to me. "I'm sorry, Mr. George," she says sweetly, as I curl my hands around the warm cup, brushing my fingers over hers as I do. "That you're so distrusting you had to come all the way out here just to make sure I'm actually sick."

"*Olivia.*" Her mother sounds exasperated. "That is no way to talk to your boss!"

My lips twitch. "Yes, Olivia. That is no way to speak to me. I might need to punish you for insubordination."

A flush moves over her cheeks as she scowls at me, and I can tell she wants to tell me to shut the fuck up. To not say things like that in front of her mother, but she keeps the words trapped behind her lips. *Good girl.* I mouth the words at her from behind my coffee cup, and she spins, stumbling away from me to the other side of the bed, where she perches next to her mother, who leans her head on her daughter's shoulder.

Seeing them side by side makes their familial ties even more apparent.

"What really brings you to our side of town, Mr. George?" Harvey asks, drawing my attention away from the mother/daughter pair. I can feel Olivia's glare on the side of my face, daring me to tell these two people who so obviously love her that I'm here because I'm fucking her.

I give the older man my best smile. "Liv here has made herself indispensable, and when she didn't come in today, I got worried. I know I could have called-"

"I wouldn't have picked up," she says, and then squeals when her mother pinches her thigh. I chuckle. Such a brat. I'm glad to see I'm not the only person who gets to experience it.

"But since we were at that charity event last night, I just wanted to verify that everything was okay in person." I finish, glancing at Olivia, hoping she gets my meaning.

The scowl that has been present on her face since I stepped inside her house melts, and she nods. "Yeah, everything is fine. It was just a late night, and I woke up with a migraine."

"Poor girl couldn't stand any light when I got here this morning," Harvey says. "Had all the curtains down, the lights off, the TV, too."

"I was bored out of my mind," Caroline says, in a way that lets me know she doesn't mean it in the slightest. "I put her to bed with some maximum strength painkillers."

"And now here I am, better than ever." Liv lifts her coffee cup in a toast before she takes a sip. "And you can go back to work."

"Olivia June Hart, don't you dare be rude to our guest. I taught you better than that." Caroline turns her smile back to me. "I'm so sorry, Mr. George. I do not know what has gotten into my daughter today."

Olivia grumbles something that none of us can make out. Ms. Hart ignores her. "You can stay as long as you like. I'd enjoy the company."

I grin at her, then at Olivia, shifting back onto the couch to get comfortable. "Thank you, Ms. Hart. I do believe I will take you up on your kind offer."

Harvey leaves soon after I arrive at Olivia's urging. She tells him it doesn't make sense for both of them to be here. The older man runs his eyes over her, no doubt taking in the dark circles and the way exhaustion hangs on her and reiterates that he could stay if she needs more rest.

She waves off his concern and ushers him out the door after promising that she will call him if anything changes. I don't know Olivia all that well, but even I can tell that is a lie. She could be exhausted down to her core, and she would still make her body give more, make her mind focus, emptying her cup over and over.

I chat with Ms. Hart all afternoon. I keep expecting her to doze off, to fall asleep, but she stays awake until nearly dinner time. We mostly talk about the documentaries she's watched. Her body might be breaking down on her, but her brain is still as sharp as ever.

At some point, she has Liv fire up an old DVD player and she puts on *Sixteen Candles* while Ms. Hart explains that it's one of Olivia's favorite movies. Both of our phones vibrate through the entire movie. I know without looking that it's work and by the pursing of Olivia's lips it is for her too. Though at some point all the blood drains from her face and she flicks her gaze up to mine.

The fear in her eyes makes me want to bundle her onto my lap and hold her until she feels safe again. But then she looks at her mom, who has her gaze on her daughter, and she forces it away, smiling before asking if Ms. Hart needs anything.

Just after that, I get a text confirming dinner for Thursday.

Though innocuous and expected, the message is enough to sober me up, wiping away the warm glow I'd had from spending time with a family unit that so obviously loves each other. It makes my chest ache in an unfamiliar way to see the emotion and care between the two of them.

Ms. Hart asks me to stay for dinner.

I agree.

Liv gets up to go to the kitchen and I stay where I am, though my gaze follows her hungrily. "My daughter is too good, Mr. George." I turn my attention away from the hall that Olivia retreated down and back to the tiny figure on the bed. "I worry about her, about what's going to happen to her when I'm gone."

I suspected Caroline Hart is dying, but hearing her state it so blandly makes my heart clench all over again. She looks at me with those eyes so like her daughter's. "Olivia is a giver. She will pour and pour and pour, and when her cup is empty, she'll drill to find more to give. Look at her now, working for you, caring for me. She thinks I don't see how she doesn't sleep at night, but I do. I wake up at all hours and hear her moving around the house, baking, cleaning."

A knot of concern tangles between my brows. "She needs to do a better job of taking care of herself."

Ms. Hart reaches over and pats my hand, her skin dry and cool against mine. "I agree, and she needs someone who can take care of her. Especially when I'm gone." She sighs and shakes her head, leaning back. "Harvey will try. He cares about the both of us, but at the end of the day, Liv *pays* him to care. Claire is a good girl, fierce and protective, and I know she'll do what she can. But Liv will need more. She needs more *now*."

I'm not really sure what to say. Maybe she's waiting for me to promise I'll take care of her daughter, that I'll make sure she gets through the pain of losing her mother, but I can't make that promise. I refuse to lie to a dying woman. I'm a bastard, but I'm not that much of a bastard.

Ms. Hart waits, like she thinks I'll crack, but when I don't, she sighs again, shaking her head. I can hear Liv in the kitchen, crooning to herself to the background noise of something sizzling in a hot pan. "She's been better recently."

My gaze shoots back to the woman in the bed next to me. "What?"

"She's been sleeping better recently. Don't get me wrong, it's still not enough. I worried when she had to go back to work, that it would be too much, and for a while, it seemed like that was the case. She was more tired, a little irritable. But since she started working closely with you, she's been... happier."

Here the older woman pauses, eyes lingering on me, assessing my reaction to her words. I try to keep my face carefully neutral as I ask, "She does?"

A small smirk curls Ms. Hart's lips, and I know I did a shit job. She tips her head at me. "She is. And she would never tell you, because she complains about you as much as she praises you, but you make her happy."

The way she says it tells me that this woman knows that there is something more than just a boss/employee relationship here. *Of course she does, you idiot. CEOs don't show up at their employees' house when they call in sick.* I definitely showed my hand here.

My stomach lurches at the realization that maybe to Liv this means more. Maybe she feels more than just pleasure at my hands. I mean, sure, a good orgasm can do wonders for a person's mood, but how Ms. Hart says I make her happy? That tells me there's more to it than that.

God, please don't let it be more than that.

God, please let it be more than that.

I'm torn.

Ms. Hart's eyes flutter closed before she opens them again, pinning me with a hard look. "Olivia has a good heart. The *best* heart. Don't hurt her, Mr. George. If you do, I'll come back and haunt your ass. You see if I don't."

A surprised laugh pulls from my chest, even as the ache there grows. "I'll do what I can to make sure that doesn't happen, Ms. Hart."

She eyes me, her lips pursing into a thin line, like she knows the bullshit I just spewed, but she doesn't call me on it. "See that you do, Mr. George. Now, leave an old woman alone so I can get some rest. Go bother my daughter."

I do as she says, uncoiling from the couch and leaving her alone. When I glance over my shoulder at her, I find her eyes already closed, chest rising and falling gently. I pause at the door of the kitchen, watching as Olivia stir something in a pot, the steam from it lifting the tendrils of her hair just slightly. She's so goddamn pretty like this, dressed down in comfy clothes, bare toes pressing into the hardwood floor, shirt falling off her shoulder.

I have the sudden painful need to see her in my kitchen, wearing my shirt and nothing else. She'd be making eggs at the stove for breakfast, and I'd come up behind her and wrap her in my arms, inch the hem of the shirt up until I could grind against her bare ass.

She glances over at me and flushes, almost like she can sense my thoughts. When she flicks her gaze down to the fly of my suit pants, and back up, the flush deepens. But she shakes her head. "Not here," is all she says, turning back to the soup.

Disappointment swoops in my stomach. Not because she told me we can't have sex here in her house, but because she thinks that's why I'm here. I step farther into the kitchen. "That's really not why I'm here."

Olivia's jaw tightens, and she adjusts the heat on the stovetop, and then slides a lid over the pot.

When she doesn't say anything, I shift on my feet. "I think I'm going to head out."

She turns to face me, propping her hip against the front of the oven. "You told my mother you'd stay for dinner."

Something like guilt coils in my gut. "She's asleep. She won't know I didn't stay."

Liv's arms drop, and I swear I see a flicker of disappointment cross her face before she wipes it away. "I'll walk you out."

I nod and let her precede me to the front door, where I expect her to just open it and usher me out. But she steps onto the porch, and I follow her. *I think I'll always follow her.*

That thought comes unbidden and unwelcome. I push it away and look at the painfully beautiful girl in the evening light.

Olivia folds her arms over her chest, leaning against the post of the front porch. "Why did you really come here?" She keeps her voice low, like she's trying to keep her mother from overhearing, but Ms. Hart is asleep, pulled into exhaustion by the weight of her illness.

I move closer to her. Her honey eyes watch me warily as I come. I don't answer her question in favor of brushing my finger over the tattoo on her arm. "Does it mean anything?"

She looks down, watching as I stroke a pink bloom, then a purple one. "I like Dahlias." Her chin jerks toward the small flower beds at the front of the house. I follow the movement and find a neat row of the flowers in a variety of colors.

Her house is the only one on the block with a splash of color. All the other yards are green and browns.

It's so like her, that bright pop, that extra little flourish.

"Linc," she says, her tone of voice making me look at her, to see what her expression can tell me about how she's feeling. "What are you doing here? We don't have the kind of relationship where you just drop by."

A shot of pain hits me. One that I smother before she can see it, but by the way her face softens, I think I might not have been fast enough. Fuck, what the hell is wrong with me? I can't be this guy. The one that gets all tangled up and attached to his fuck buddy, his good little whore.

No. I can't tell her I came all this way to check on her because I was worried I'd pushed her too far. That I came here to make sure she's still in this with me. That she'll still let me touch her.

If that spike of pain, that ache in my chest proves anything, it's that she already has too much power. Fuck. That I'm here at all is proof enough of that.

"Why didn't you tell me? About your mother?" My voice is hoarse.

She sighs again, looking out at the front yard before she licks her lip, and then nibbles on it, trying to figure out how much to tell me. "You never asked. Also, it's in my employee file. Mr. Harkness knows. Verity knows. I assumed you did too." Half her mouth quirks up, but it doesn't hide the hurt she's feeling. "Guess I overestimated how much you care about me, huh?"

Christ. My heart clenches all over again. "Liv. We can't-"

She nods and waves away my concern, the words I was going to say to let her down easy. "I know. Believe me, I know." She doesn't say anything else, just stares out at the night, the sounds of the city filtering through softly.

I don't know how I never realized how tired she looks. How exhausted. She does a good job of hiding it, I suppose. She's always so freaking kind to everyone around her. Patient. Gentle. Uplifting. Even to me once we broke through that initial barrier.

I can't imagine she's getting more than a few hours of sleep at night. Sleep that is likely interrupted by getting up to check on her mother, to make sure she's still breathing. And fuck, I can't even imagine living like she does at this moment.

The fear and uncertainty. The long nights and long days. And I know I've done nothing to help her. To ease her.

"You're so fucking strong," I say, unexpectedly. They're definitely not the words I'd intended to come out of my mouth.

She casts me a wary look, one that says she doesn't trust what I blurted is true. "I don't feel strong. Mostly I just feel... brittle. Like I'm one knock away from shattering entirely."

The thought of that leaves me feeling cold. I'm going to be that knock. I'm going to do that to her. If we keep going like we are. If I let this bloom into more, I'm going to break her.

That realization doesn't stop me from reaching for her, pulling her into my chest as tears fill her eyes. Her arms wrap around my waist while I cuddle her into my body. We stay like that while Olivia cries quietly into my shirt, and my hand smooths up and down her back, comforting her how I wish someone had comforted me in my darkest moments.

After a while, she pulls back just enough to peer up at my face. "If you hadn't come here today, you never would have known about my mother, huh?"

Guilt pricks at me, but I don't see the point in lying to her. "I might have found out, eventually. But, Liv, I never would have guessed you were living with something like this."

She nods, presses her forehead into my chest. "People are extraordinarily good at hiding their damage when they want to, Lincoln. It's why I try to be nice to everyone, be kind. Be gentle. Even the ones that are assholes to me, or to those around them. You can't tell by looking what another person is going through. You can't look at someone on the train and know their mother is dying, or they were up all night with a sick baby, or they just had their heart ripped out by a person meant to love them."

My arms tighten around her, lips finding the crown of her head in a tender move that is so unfamiliar to me. "I try to give everyone a little grace, to not take it personally when they snip at me. And I hope like hell they feel a little better by the time our interaction has ended."

Jesus, she's so good. So nice. And her way of looking at the world is beautiful. So much about her makes sense now, how she's always complimenting those around her, bolstering them, lifting them up when it would be easier to snap back or ignore them.

She knows what it's like to be living through a hard time, to be struggling. I wonder if she's wished for someone to lift her up the same way she does to others.

"Linc?"

"Hmm?"

"I know the answer is going to be no." She tips her head back to look at me. "But do you want to stay?"

I blink at her, my lungs seizing as my heart beats erratically in my chest. "Stay?" I wheeze out.

I see the disappointment flicker in her eyes, but her little chin lifts in determination. "You know, stay the night? Sleep in a bed together. Wake up and have coffee together?"

My lungs constrict further at the thought, and I can't tell if I want it more than anything—to hold her all night, make sure she sleeps, wake up next to her—or if it terrifies me. The way I can't get in a full breath makes me think it's probably the latter. And when Olivia lets out a little laugh, bitter and humorless, I know she can tell it too.

She pulls away, moving to her front door. "Nevermind. Forget I asked."

I tuck my hands into my pockets to keep from reaching for her again, because as much as the thought of staying scares me, I still miss the heat of her body, still want her close.

She glances over her shoulder at me. "Goodnight, Lincoln." She whispers just before she pushes open the door and retreats inside, shutting me out on the other side.

I stare at that slab of wood for far too long, hating that I didn't jump at the chance to hold her all night, but also knowing I can't. We've already gotten too close, too attached. When I started this thing with Olivia, I thought I would tire of her, bored like I do with every other woman. But it's the opposite. The more I have her, the more I want her.

Not just for sex. I want to be the person she cries to when things get too hard. I want to be the person who makes it better for her. Who holds her all night. Who gets up to check on her mom, so she doesn't have to. I want lazy Sundays and late nights. Coffee in the mornings and curling up on the couch at night with a glass of wine and our favorite show on the TV.

I want a relationship with Olivia Hart.

I want a relationship with her, and I can never have it.

I'll never be able to give her what she needs, what she deserves.

If I were a better man, I would end it now, break it off before we get anymore attached. But I'm not a better man.

I can't have everything I want with Olivia, but I can keep what we do have. I can keep her body, her pleasure, her submission. I just have to shut myself off from those softer emotions, keep myself from getting too attached. Keep her from getting too attached too.

I take one last look at Olivia's closed door before I move off her porch, rebuilding my walls, shoring them up so that when I see her tomorrow, I won't feel this ache in my chest.

14
Olivia

If I thought it was hard working for Lincoln George before, it's nothing compared to now.

Things have been… strained for the last week.

I guess Lincoln George coming to my house and realizing I'm more than just a hole for him to put his dick in, has really freaked him out. He didn't touch me for three days after that. Three days of working closely together. Three days of sexual tension wound up tighter than a spring. Three days of biting back frustration with him, because although I pride myself on being patient and kind, he always pushes my limits.

And not in a good way.

He's been surly and closed off. I thought when he finally called me into his office, when he finally touched me, that things would get better. But they didn't. It was a quick fuck, with me bent over his desk, palms flat on the surface, not able to touch him. He made me come, he came, and then he shoved a bottle of water at me, cleaned me up in the most efficient way possible and went on his merry way.

Ever since then, it has been like that. I don't know if it's a new game that I don't know the rules of. If it is, I don't want to do it anymore.

Maybe he doesn't want to do this anymore, either. Maybe he's decided that now he knows I'm a human with people to care about—with a dying mother—he finds me disgusting.

But by the way his eyes still track me, I know that's not the case. He watches me like I'm prey, like he's just waiting to pounce. Which is strange, seeing as we've been having more sex than ever. It's just… always rushed and proficient. Almost like the number has increased because he isn't getting what he needs from our time together. Quantity over quality seems to be the name of the game.

I think I'm ready for this game to be done, though.

Something has shifted for me. Something that I didn't expect. It started the night of the torturous gala. With the way he held me after, made me look into his eyes as he moved so deep inside me. It was long and languorous sex, even in the back of the car. I'm not sure if we could call it fucking because with was… strangely gentle. Like he didn't want to break me after the torture of the night, like he wanted to show me with his body how much he appreciates me, how much he actually cares.

It freaked me out, to be honest.

I went home exhausted from the tension of the night, feeling weighed down, but I couldn't sleep. I kept thinking of the way he said, "look at me while I'm inside you, sunshine." His voice was all pleading and soft. By the time morning rolled around, I'd slept maybe two hours and had a migraine the size of a Mack truck.

So I'd called in sick, and he showed up at my house.

And ever since then, Lincoln has been *weird*.

There's no other word for it.

It doesn't help that there have been more strange phone calls to my office and my personal cell. If I don't pick up, they leave a message. I've been getting emails as well, all threatening. All creepy as fuck.

Everything I receive I send to Lance, since he told me to do that. I'm not sure if Lincoln knows it's still happening, but he hasn't talked to me about it, not since the first one.

Maybe he knows, and he just doesn't care.

I shake my head against the thought and focus on my weekly report for Cabot. I had to beg for some information from Giovanna since I missed Wednesday, and I also sent an email to Lincoln asking him for some details that I know I missed at the gala.

His response was clipped, a list of bullet points. No greeting or sign off.

It hurt, but I shoved that feeling aside and focused on work.

Giovanna stands from her desk, hooking her coat off the back of her chair as she flicks off her computer screen. My weary eyes find the time at the corner of my screen and find it's after five already. I still have work to do, so I know I'll be here for at least another hour.

Thankfully, I cleared it with Harvey already, but I shoot him a text to just make sure that he's still good with it and promise to pick up dinner for him and his husband on my way home.

"Goodnight," my office mate mutters as she passes my desk. She's been moderately more pleasant to me, since Lincoln seems to have erected a wall between us. He's called on her more in the last two days than he has the entire time I've worked for him, and she's no doubt noticed the change.

"Night," I reply, turning my attention back to my screen as my fingers fly over the keyboard.

An hour later, I'm just finishing up one of the financial reports to attach to the email for Cabot, when Lincoln's door opens. My gaze flies up to clash with his, where he's drawn up just outside his door. He looks surprised to see me, but the expression melts, hides behind a mask of indifference that hurts more than when he's glaring at me.

I lick my lips before offering him a strained smile and turning back to my work. I halfway expect him to just walk on by, continue about his business like he has for the last two days, but he tucks his hands into his pockets and leans against his doorjamb.

A flush spread over my cheeks as I feel his gaze on me, hungrily running over my shape, my curves. He clears his throat and my head whips in his direction. "Giovanna went home?"

I don't try to hide the disappointment his question makes me feel before I turn back to my screen. "Yep. It's after six. I think most people have gone home."

I see him shift out of the corner of my eye. "You don't need to be home tonight?"

"Harvey's with my mom. He offered to stay until 7:30 so I could catch up." I see him nod, like he suspected as much. Frustration bubbles out of me in the form of a question. "Is that really what you want to talk about?"

"Pardon?"

I twist my chair so I'm facing him, pinning him with a look that I hope like hell says, 'don't play dumb.' But just in case it doesn't, I mutter, "don't play dumb, Lincoln."

His brows arch. "I'm not sure I follow."

A laugh bursts from my chest, humorless and... *hurt.* Yes, I feel hurt.

This wasn't supposed to happen. I wasn't supposed to catch feelings, but I did and now this man, this infuriating, emotionally closed off man, has the ability to hurt me.

"Nevermind. I don't suppose it really warrants a conversation, does it?"

He pushes away from the door and saunters over to me, hands still in his pockets. "What are you talking about, sunshine?"

I don't look at him, keep my gaze focused on the computer. "Don't call me that. It feels a little too personal for what we've been doing lately."

He doesn't say anything. Of course he doesn't. Instead, he grabs my wrist and tows me out of my chair, into his office where he kicks the door closed, before pressing me against it, his hands grabbing my face roughly and holding me still as he devours my mouth.

The moan that hums in my chest is involuntary, but he snarls at the sound, alternating between nipping at my lips and fucking my mouth with his tongue. He doesn't say anything. But I know this is his way of trying to reassure me that he still wants me.

I should push him off, should demand that we talk about this. But my body is arching into his, between my legs is slick with arousal, my nipples pebbling where they press into his chest. His hands loop around my ass and lift me off my feet while I wrap my arms over his shoulders.

We kiss the entire way to his desk. I expect him to sit in the chair, to have me straddle him, but as soon as I'm on my feet he spins me, presses me almost painfully into the surface, the sharp edge biting into my hips and he grinds against my ass. His big palm at the base of my neck forces me down, until I'm bent against the surface, just like I was when he filled me with the vibrator.

But this time there is none of the gentle care. He's rough as he yanks up my skirt, exposing my sopping pussy to the cool air. One finger slides up and down the string of my thong before he gives a painful yank and there's the ripping of fabric.

He grunts when he feels how wet I am. I'm sure he can see it too, dripping down my thighs. I've never had a problem with a little roughness. If this is the game he wants to play today, I'll take it, so long as it doesn't extend beyond this moment, so long as it's followed with some kind of gentleness.

His hand smacks into my left cheek, followed by my right, one after the other, repeatedly, making me jerk against the desk to get away from the sting. I'm sure my skin is red, heat blooming over them as he continues to spank me.

I let out a sob when the blows ease, but gasp when he thrusts inside me, mouth hanging open in a silent scream at the pleasure of being filled so roughly. The only connection point of our bodies is where he penetrates me, his movements hard and powerful, like he can't really control himself.

"Touch yourself, Liv."

I blink at the order. "What?"

"I'm so fucking close to coming, so if you want to come too, touch your fucking clit." The way he says it feels off, the words feel off, everything feels wrong, but after weeks of giving in to Lincoln, of following his instructions, my hand moves of its own accord, finding and rubbing my clit, sparking my orgasm in mere seconds. I clamp around him as I howl.

"That's it, my good little fucking whore. That's it. Just. Fucking. Like. That." His hips pump into me with each word, until he stalls out, buried deep in me, hands flexing, one on the back of my neck, the other on my hip, while my own release fades.

Linc sags over the top of me, his forehead pressing into my shoulder, and I think maybe now he'll break out of character, that he'll be softer with me, like he was before. The aftercare he usually gives me is almost my favorite part. It's the part that makes me feel like he cares. But it's been lacking recently.

Don't get me wrong, he still shoves a bottle of water at me, watches while I drink it, helps me smooth out my clothes and my hair so I'm presentable for going back to work. But his motions are almost stilted, forced. Like he resents needing to do them at all.

For a while I thought it was part of a new game, but if it is, I don't like it. I'm going to have to tell him that this isn't a game I'm comfortable with. I need to feel like he at least partially cares about me, about more than just getting me off.

Because as much as Lincoln George infuriates me, I've started to care about him. I mean, how could I not when I watched him charm my mother and Harvey? When he bent and kissed her knuckles and flirted with her on what had been a very bad day for her, for me.

He doesn't know it, but my mother hasn't stopped talking about him since. She asks me about him every night when I go home, and wonders if he's going to come for a visit. She's put on lipstick every day this week, just in case.

Lincoln George's visit has made all the difference in the world to how my mother feels, and it shows.

Linc's mouth hovers over my skin. I can feel the rapid puffs of his breath. Normally, he would place a kiss there, a nip, a lick, *something*, before pulling back, but he doesn't now. He just heaves himself off and out of me. Cold air rushes in to fill the space, making me shiver as his cum drips down my thighs.

A paper napkin flops down in front of my face. "Clean yourself up," he orders.

I blink at the white object, still trying to come down from everything he did to me. My ass stings and my eyes do, too. Fuck. *No.* I can't cry here. I can't do that in front of him.

But then I hear the door to his private bathroom close and I realize it won't be in front of him. Because he's already left, retreated without even giving me a bottle of water, without soothing the skin that he ravaged with his palms.

Anxiety and pain make my chest tight, make my breaths all shuddery as my lower lip trembles. I bite it as I straighten, reaching for the napkin he unceremoniously dropped on the desk, and I use it to clean up his cum from between my legs.

Rather than drop the soiled paper into the trash, I drop it onto his desk. If he wants to be an ass about this, then I'll be a brat. I smooth out my skirt, make sure my shirt is buttoned and tucked in. I use the screen of my phone to make sure my hair and makeup are okay, swiping my fingers under my eyes to remove the mascara smeared there.

And then I sit in his chair and wait.

And wait.

And wait.

Finally, after fifteen minutes, he comes storming out, all brooding and angry. "You're still here?" He all but snarls at me, pausing just outside the bathroom door.

I link my fingers together over my stomach and arch a brow at him. "Aren't you done playing this game yet? Isn't the scene over?" My voice comes out a little husky and a lot shaky, my body still wired from what he did to me, with no chance to come down.

"Game?" He asks, tilting his head at me like a predator. "What game do you think we're playing, Olivia?"

I wave a hand. "The one where you're a dominating asshole all the time. It didn't use to be like this. You actually..." I swallow hard and look away from him. Not sure I want to tell him that before he made me think he cared about me at least a little. But recently I've felt like just one of many women, like the girls he fucks and kicks out without any sort of aftercare.

"I actually what, Olivia?" He snaps out.

I shake my head, teeth sinking into my lower lip as I stand, tipping my chin up in defiance. "If this is how it's going to be now, then I'm done."

The words hang between us. Silence fills the room while Lincoln glares at me. "You're done with what exactly, Liv?"

"You," I say, fisting my hands at my sides. "I'm done with you. Jesus, do you think I need this? That I need you to be an ass to me all the time? I looked up dom/sub relationships. You're supposed to do aftercare when a scene is over, but lately it never... It seems like it's *never* over, and I'm tired enough, Linc. I don't need to be in this constant state of anxiety over whether or not you're going to bite my head off, if you're going to call me a whore and actually treat me like one. I don't fucking need that. I have enough shit going on in my life to deal with. So if you can't take the time to help me come down, to take care of the bruises and welts that you leave on my body, then I am done."

He takes one big, menacing step toward me before he pulls up short. "We're done when I say we're done, Liv. And I say we're not fucking done yet. You're going to keep coming in here crawling for me, sucking my cock, and taking my cum like a good little whore. We aren't fucking done yet."

A humorless laugh bursts out of me as I shake my head. "I'm done, Lincoln. I'm not doing this anymore."

He growls and takes another step toward me. I back up, circling his desk to put space between us. "Olivia-"

"Snickerdoodle," I say, and his mouth snaps shut around whatever he was going to say, whatever angry, demanding thing he was going to spout. "*Snickerdoodle*, Lincoln. Do you hear me? I am not playing your game anymore. It's over. I don't want to keep letting you treat me like this." My voice catches. *"I can't."*

He looks like he wants to say something else, like he has words bubbling up his throat and only the tight clench of his jaw is keeping them back. But he respects the use of my safe word. Keeps whatever argument he wants to say locked away.

After Lincoln started this with me, after we came up with the safe word and I realized what he needs during sex, what I need during sex, I did a lot of research. I know that for most partners, use of a safe word would be a full stop to a scene, and they would sit down and talk about what went wrong, how they can do better in the future to create a safe and pleasurable experience for everyone.

I wait to see if he's going to do this with me. If he'll drop his walls enough to at least try to work this out. Talk to me like an adult would. But he just nods, dark hair falling over his brow. "Fine. We're done."

My chest seizes as a lump crawls up my throat. I hadn't thought he would give up so easily. But then, I don't know what else I expected. He goes through women like most people go through underwear. That he's done this with me for so long is a miracle.

I am replaceable. Of course I am. Convenient, sure, but still replaceable.

I tip my chin even higher when what I want to do is have it drop to my chest, to let the tears threatening to overwhelm me have their way. I want to hit him, scream at him.

I can't do any of that. I entered into this with my eyes open. I knew what I was getting into, so the least I can do is keep my chin up and my shoulders straight as I round his desk and head for the door. "I'll see you Monday, Mr. George," I murmur as I snap the door closed behind me.

15
Olivia

It's been a week since I broke things off with Lincoln. I hesitate to call it a 'break-up' because we were never really together. We didn't have a relationship beyond the physical, beyond fucking.

What I realize now, a week later, is that I wanted one.

With him.

It's so freaking strange. I don't even like the guy. And yet I can't stop thinking about the soft way he'd tuck my hair behind my ear, fingers brushing against my cheek, when he was done ruining me. I think about how he sat and chatted with my mother for hours until she dozed off, and then I think about the absolute panic on his face when I cried on his shoulder in a moment of weakness and asked if he wanted to stay over.

That was the moment, I realized. The moment things changed for him. The moment he slammed up his walls and tried to put me back in to the fuck buddy category. Things were getting sticky with

with emotions, and he couldn't handle it.

I keep telling myself that's fine. That to him, the idea of actually being with me is so abhorrent he'd rather just end things doesn't hurt.

I can't blame him for not wanting to get emotionally, as well as physically, involved with an employee. I can't blame him for being hesitant to feel proper feelings for me. Hell, I would be lying if I said I didn't have reservations of my own.

But I know without a doubt that I can't let him treat me like I'm easily disposable. My self-confidence is fragile enough as it is, and I can't let him shatter it.

Doesn't stop my body from craving him, the pleasure and escape he provided. It's like now that I know he can give me moments where I'm not weighed down by my responsibilities and worries, I feel even more bogged down.

"Excuse me?" I look up at the woman standing next to my desk. She's wearing a white bodycon dress that hugs her curves and sets off the deep tan tone of her skin. Her black hair hangs in a sleek sheet to her lower back, glossy and full. She has a perfect cat's eye liner on her dark green eyes and a smug little smirk on her too puffy lips. "I'm here to see Lincoln."

I just stared up at her, struck dumb at the sight. It's been a long time since he's brought a woman here. But then I suppose it's been a week since I broke things off, so he probably feels like it's been long enough. I'm sure he's fucked other women in the last week, but I thought he would respect me enough to not rub it in my face, to not do it twenty feet from where I sit.

Giovanna clears her throat, knocking me out of my reverie.

I take a deep breath and force the stinging at the back of my eyes and at the tip of my nose away. "Yes, of course. Let me just see if he's available." He is. I know he is. There's nothing on his calendar for the next forty-five minutes, except for this woman, apparently.

I could call him. I could pick up my desk phone and buzz through. But I don't. Maybe I'm feeling petty. Maybe I want to look into his face and realize that yes, we are truly over, and this is his way of proving it to me. I stand and smooth my hands down my thighs. "What's your name?"

The woman looks at me with a slightly surprised expression, like she hadn't expected me to ask. "Amelie."

I give her what I hope looks like a genuine smile but feels brittle as hell. "Oh, what a pretty name! It's so fitting. You're gorgeous."

A pleased flush blooms on her cheeks as she looks down almost demurely. "Thank you."

I round my desk and head toward the closed office door. Giving her one more encouraging smile over my shoulder, I rap twice on his door and don't wait for him to tell me to enter, just push it open. Stormy slate blue eyes meet mine.

I ignore how they soften slightly, widen just a bit when they see me. "Olivia-"

I don't let him say more. "Amelie is here to see you, Mr. George." I feel her press close to me. Her shoulder nudges mine as she slips past me and into his office.

He stands abruptly. "Olivia-"

I force a cheerful smile. "I was just about to run out to grab lunch. Can I get you anything? A burger from Sapphire?"

He shakes his head. "No, thank you. I have a lunch meeting. We *both* have a lunch meeting in an hour."

Well, shoot. I was planning on running out of the building as soon as this door is closed. Because the last thing I want is to sit outside this room while he fucks that woman. I swallow and grab the handle of the door. "Right. Yes. I meant that I have a few errands to run before lunch, and I'll meet you there."

Before he can protest—and what is he going to do, really? Call me a liar and *make me* stay at my desk?—I close the office door. I've collected my jacket, that cream-colored one he picked out for me, and purse. I don't want to wait for the elevator, so I head for the stairwell, pushing open the door before I hear him call my name after me.

He doesn't actually follow me.

I tell myself that's a good thing as I clomp down a few floors before taking the elevator the rest of the way down the building.

I wander for an hour and consider taking the rest of the day off. It shouldn't hurt this much, but it does. *We weren't even really together*, I have to keep telling myself. Three weeks of good sex shouldn't make this separation so hard.

I was the fool who got involved with my boss, with a well-known womanizer. What was I thinking? I should have known better than to do it. I should have put a stop to it before it even started, but something about Lincoln George felt... *inevitable*. As though no matter what I said or did, we would have always ended up entangled with each other.

I arrive at the restaurant at one o'clock on the dot. Lincoln and the client—fuck, what is their name?—are already seated. I resist the urge to look at him, to see if he has that lazy smile he gets after he's been sated, that afterglow from good sex.

It's only after I settle into my chair that I realize I have no fucking clue what the hell I'm supposed to be doing here. I don't have my tablet with my notes for each meeting. I don't have any of the files we'll need. In my rush, I let Lincoln and Amelie chase me out of the office and now I am woefully under prepared.

On top of that, I'm pretty sure I won't be able to form a coherent sentence with Lincoln burning a hole into the side of my head, like he's willing me to look at him. He finally clears his throat. "Miss Hart."

I have to look at him, or else I'll look like an asshole, so I twist my head in his direction and keep my gaze focused on the knot of his tie. "Yes, Mr. George?"

He holds something up in his hand. "You left this on your desk." My tablet. He's holding my tablet. "I thought you might need it."

I reach to take it from him, hoping like hell no one notices how my fingers shake. He doesn't release it right away, holding on until my eyes flick up to meet his. It's the briefest of contact, but it hits me like a goddamn Mack truck, stealing my breath before I yank the tablet away and give him a tight smile.

"Thank you, Mr. George." I look at the client, whose name I didn't even hear, and the tight smile turns into something more genuine. "This thing might as well be my brain. We wouldn't be able to discuss your needs without it."

They chuckle and I pick up the menu to stare sightlessly at the words. I'm quiet for the entire meeting, and Lincoln seems to understand where my brain is at, at least to some extent, because he carries the weight of the conversation, while I make notes on my tablet, chiming in when he asks for a certain statistic or fact.

We shake hands at the end of the lunch, and Lincoln escorts me from the restaurant, hand hovering over my back like he wants to touch me but doesn't.

It's torture.

If I didn't need this job, I would quit.

As it is, I make a mental note to look for something else, *anything else*. Though I'm sure nothing will pay as well as this.

"Olivia," Lincoln says, finally making contact with my body when his hand curls around my elbow, dragging me to a stop next to his black town car. "I didn't fuck her. I wouldn't do that to you."

I swallow and keep staring ahead. I want to believe him. But it doesn't matter. Even if he didn't have sex with Amelie, at some point, he will revert to his old habits. I can't let him think I care, that it hurts me. "It doesn't matter if you did, Mr. George." His fingers tighten on my arm, and I can feel him wanting to say more. "I wasn't able to complete my errands," I say before he can say anything else. "I'll meet you back at the office."

"Olivia. Sunshine, please." I shake my head and yank away from him, frustration boiling. I want to shout at him to never call me that again, that he doesn't get to call me that. But instead I move away from him, keeping my chin high, just like when I walked out of his office.

"I'll see you later, Mr. George." Before he can say anything else, I whirl away from him and get lost in the crowd.

"Miss. Hart, come with me, please."

My knee jerk reaction to the command in his tone is to tell him to fuck off. Well, that's not true. My knee jerk reaction is a flood of arousal between my legs and then to tell him to fuck off. I'm still recovering from our... break up. Is it a breakup if we weren't actually dating? Just having the best sex of our lives?

Or I guess *my* life. I can't say if that's the case for him. I honestly have no idea how he feels about it, about us. If he feels anything at all, or if I was just a convenient hole to put his dick.

"Liv," Giovanna's voice breaks me out of my reverie, and my face flames. She arches a brow and tips her head meaningfully down the hall. I follow the line of her chin to find Mr. George already standing at the elevator, literally checking his watch, and tapping his foot. My gaze moves back to Gi. "*Go,*" she mouths at me, eyes widening.

Right, because although I made the colossal mistake of sleeping with my boss, he is still my boss and I need this job. I give her a small, grateful smile and hook my coat off the back of my chair before grabbing my cell phone and my purse and following him.

He's holding the elevator open for me, waiting until I slip inside to release the door. We don't say anything, haven't said anything to each other beyond the bare minimum to get through working together ever since Amelie came to the office. I've also managed to not be alone with him in close quarters.

Sure I've been in his office with him, but I haven't ridden in the car with him to any of the events we've attended in the last week, usually making the excuse that I need to run home before I can go to whatever fancy occasion we've been roped into. I sure as shit haven't been in an elevator with him. It brings back too many memories of the first time he touched me.

His nearness is a tangible thing, not like a caress. No, nothing about Lincoln George is soft, not to me. Not when I haven't felt him in weeks. No. His presence is more like a hammer or a hard cock, pounding into me, trying to weaken my resolve to not fall back into his arms, back into the state of constant uncertainty that I was in before.

Sure, during the games I could shut off my brain, let him take away the worries and responsibilities that plague me, and I could actually truly just sink into the feelings, the sensations, the pleasure that he awoke in my body. The first time I hadn't needed to be in control in a long ass time.

But it never ended. I told him I couldn't be in that in-between state, between lover and employee, girlfriend and fuck buddy, lust and genuine feeling. I need more than what he was able, or willing, to give me.

He shifts just slightly closer, and I move away. A magnet repelled by the wrong side. I can feel his gaze on the side of my head, but don't turn to look at him, keeping my eyes focused on the shiny elevator doors. On our silhouettes together. Dammit. We look almost too good together.

I might hate it.

No, I *do* hate it.

"Olivia," he says, his voice hoarse. I shake my head against the need dripping from my name. It's not genuine need. Its lust, desire. He doesn't actually need me. He needs a convenient fuck. And I won't do it anymore.

"Where are we going?" I ask, keeping my voice perfectly level.

He sighs, but thankfully takes the change of subject. "I need your help picking out a present."

"A present?" He grunts an affirmative. "For who?"

His slate eyes glance at me, and then he looks away. "My sister. Francie."

I puff out a breath as the doors slide open to the lobby of the building. His hand presses into the small of my back for the shortest and somehow longest moment of my life as he ushers me out and toward the front door. I want him to keep touching me. I want him to never touch me again.

I am a bundle of contradictions.

There's a black car waiting at the curb with a familiar face waiting by the back door. "Lance!" I'm surprised that the head of security for Lincoln is driving us around, but then I guess that is his job, to some extent.

A wide smile pulls at his lips as he tips his head to me. "Miss Hart."

I wave a hand between us. "I told you to call me Liv." He nods in acknowledgement, but the way his gaze flickers to Lincoln tells me he's not going to cross that line. The smile on my face turns forced. "How are your girls?"

Another of those genuine smiles as his eyes go soft. "Good. So good. Nina gets bigger every day. I'm pretty sure she's the smartest baby to ever grace the earth." He reaches for the door handle and pulls it open for me, offering me a hand to help me climb in. His touch doesn't linger and as soon as I'm in the car, I scoot to the far side to give Lincoln space to climb in after me.

As he does, I keep my focus out the window, watching the cars pass by us. I'm vaguely aware of him giving Lance the name of the store he wants to visit, and then silence falls over the interior as the car pulls forward.

I keep my gaze focused out the window, even as my body heats and readies itself from just his proximity. I resist the urge to squeeze my thighs together. If I do, he'll know. He'll see that infinitesimal movement, and know I'm wet right now from just sitting next to him, from the brush of his hand against the small of my back.

I need to stay strong, to not fall back into the pleasure. I need to remember how it felt to have him pull away from me as soon as he finished fucking me. If we were just a one-night stand, then I wouldn't care. But we weren't. We aren't.

Whether he wants to admit it or not, we were *more*.

Not enough. But more.

"Can I ask you a question?" His rough voice comes out of nowhere, startling me from my quiet reverie.

"Sure, why not?"

"What's with the baked goods?" I can feel his gaze on me like a caress, running over my exposed skin, before it lingers on my face. "Every morning you bring in scones, or Danish, or donuts, or breakfast cakes. Why?"

I slide my gaze in his direction to gauge the intent behind the question, but I only find genuine curiosity, so I answer him. "You know my mom is… not doing well. I don't sleep much because of it. I want to be awake if anything happens, if she needs me. Baking gives me something to do. It keeps me busy enough that I can keep from falling asleep."

My cheeks flush as I say this, realizing that some people might find that sad, I guess. So I force my lips into a smile. "Plus, people tend to like you if you give them baked goods. It smooths the way for easy interactions. Well, for most people, it does."

His lips twitch like he knows I'm talking about him, since I'm pretty sure he hasn't eaten a single baked good I've brought in. "Have you thought about hiring a night nurse?"

I roll my eyes at the question. "I can barely pay Harvey. There is no way I could afford to pay two full-time nurses."

"What if the company-"

"No," I say, the word erupting from me, cutting him off. Frustration bubbles in my stomach. "No. You don't get to do this." I hiss in a whisper. "You don't get to pretend like you care now, Lincoln. You didn't care when you were fucking me, you don't get to act like it now. I am fine. My mother is… fine, all things considered."

I lean away from him when I see his hand shift toward me on the seat. "Besides, I add. She's not covered by the H and G health insurance. We pay for it out of pocket."

He frowns at me. "What do you mean, she's not covered by your insurance? She should be."

I lift a shoulder. "Technically, she's not my dependent."

Lincoln's eyes burn into the side of my head as I keep my gaze outside the car. I can't look at him.

If I do, I might say fuck it, and let him go back to fucking me and treating me like I don't matter when he's done.

I deserve better than that.

"There must be something you can do," he says, stubbornly.

I let out a weary sigh. "Believe me, we've done everything we can. I petitioned that she is, in fact, my dependent since she can't work, and I provide for her, but the insurance company denied the claim."

He hums in his throat and when I look at him, he's staring out the window, his hand on the seat between us, like he'd reached for me, but stalled out halfway there.

Good. I don't need him touching me.

Lance pulls up in front of a jewelry store that I know just from looking is so far out of my price range, I could never afford even the least expensive piece in the place. Lincoln strides to the door without waiting for me, but he holds it open, like he's a gentleman. I feel the heat from his palm as he hovers it over the small of my back, but doesn't touch, and then we're inside.

I feel immediately uncomfortable.

A woman wearing a dark blue suit with a cream-colored blouse greets us. "Mr. George. Lovely to see you again." She slides her gaze to me, runs it from the top of my head, down to my shoes, and seems to deem me acceptable. Most likely thanks to the clothes Lincoln bought for me. If I dared to set foot in here in my real clothes, I'm sure I would be ushered right back out again with a 'we don't allow your kind in here.'

You know, *poor*.

Because stores like this learned nothing from *Pretty Woman*. They didn't need to.

"What can I help you with today?" She has her eyes on him, and I don't miss the hungry glint to them, the knowing smirk. Has she had sex with him? Did they do it here, in this very store? Or did he take her out first? Is this why I'm here? For him to show me he's desirable, to make me regret breaking things off with him?

I shake the thought away. It doesn't matter. We aren't together anymore.

We were never together.

"Rings," Lincoln says, and the woman's smirk falls as she looks at me again, this time with curiosity.

"Rings? Like an engagement ring?"

I'm not sure if this question is for me, or for Lincoln, but I don't actually know the answer, so I look at him. He doesn't look at me. "It doesn't matter what type of ring. My sister is particular. I'd like to see all of them, please."

"Oh," The woman grins again. "Your sister." She leans toward me. "You're very lucky to have such a doting brother."

Lincoln opens his mouth, likely to refute our sibling status, but I beat him to it. "I am, aren't I? My big bro takes such good care of me."

Linc grumbles something I can't make out. I ignore him and motion to the woman, who is now eyeing me less like I'm a bug and more like she's going to finagle a lot of money out of me. Or rather, out of my *brother*.

"If you'll follow me." She strides across the open space, hips swaying provocatively in her blue suit pants, and the way she glances over her shoulder at Lincoln with her teeth sunk into her lower lip tells me they have had sex. Maybe even in the small private room she brings us to. There's a table in the center, covered in black velvet, with three chairs surrounding it. She motions us to two of them, and then folds her hands in front of her. "I'll pull what we have in stock that I think you'll like."

I round the table trailing a finger over the velvet tabletop, before taking a seat. Lincoln waits until I'm settled before sitting next to me, a glower on his face. "Oh, come on bossy pants," I whisper. "It's a little funny."

"My sister?" he snarls. "My fucking *sister*, really?"

I frown. "It's not like it matters, Lincoln. We aren't..." I hesitate to say *together* because we weren't *really* together even while we were having sex. Maybe if I think it enough, I'll actually believe it. "We aren't anything anymore. This way, if you want to fuck her again, you can. Something tells me she'd be more than happy to oblige you."

His slate blue eyes fly to my face, and I pretend like I don't notice, keeping my eyes on the bright display cases lining the walls, with jewelry sets that I'm sure are somewhere in the hundreds of thousands of dollars. "Jealous, sunshine?"

I snort just as the door opens again. "Hardly."

The woman—I should probably learn her name—has two trays of rings in her hands and she slides them onto the table. She gives us a smile as she settles into the seat across from us. "Now then, what did you have in mind?"

I glance at Lincoln to find him still scowling, and I sigh, turning back to her. "I can try all of them on, right?"

She nods. "Yes, of course." She nudges a tray toward me. "If you don't see anything you like here, I can pull some more. Or we can bring in one of our designers and they can work with you to get something perfect."

Lincoln shakes his head, finally leaning forward. "That won't be necessary. I love my sister, but she doesn't need a custom piece. What we have here will be fine."

I frown, looking down at the rings. I suppose he could be right, but what if none of these are something Francie would wear? When I don't immediately reach for either tray, the woman does it for me, plucking one out of the velvet holder and reaching over to pick up my right hand. She slides the ring on my pointer finger. "What do you think?"

I frown again, looking over at Lincoln, trying to get some kind of reading on him, on what he wants to get for his sister, but there's just... *nothing*. "Linc?"

His slate blue eyes meet mine, his lips thin out and he gives a shake of his head. "No."

The woman has a strained look in her eyes. I smile as brightly as I can. "I guess, not this one. But I'm sure we'll find something that meets my brother's approval."

She gives me a tight smile and picks up another ring.

16
Lincoln

I thought bringing Olivia here, running this errand with her, would be a good way to completely end our relationship. To put the final nail in the coffin of our very brief but passionate affair.

I was an idiot. A big fucking idiot.

We aren't anything anymore. Those words had nearly gutted me. I'd had to work to not physically double up as the pain hit me. But she's right. Of course she's right. We aren't anything anymore. That's what this was supposed to be. The end of our... whatever we were together. This was supposed to help me get over her.

It did the opposite.

Watching her try on rings for me, sliding them onto her finger, the way she held out her hand and tilted her head to see the glitter of the stone better as she considered what would best suit my sister? God, it did something to my insides. And now I can only imagine sliding a ring onto her finger for real, making her mine in a way that announces it to the whole fucking world.

I know the ring I'd get for her, too.

A round moss agate center stone, with asymmetrical diamond accents around it, five on one side, tow on the other, with even smaller diamonds spiking out from it, making it almost look like a snowflake or an ice crystal.

She'd practically glowed when she'd seen it on her finger, and I'd felt a returning glow, right in my gut.

The ring I'd settled on was much less ornate. It had to be because, rather than telling her the truth, I'd told her it was for my little sister, Francie. I can't exactly buy an engagement ring to give to Francie.

So now here I am strolling along the boardwalk, a breeze pulling at the loose strands of blond hair around Olivia's face, and I'm imagining getting down on one knee to ask her to marry me. It's a fantasy. And while I've lived out some of my best fantasies with Olivia Hart, this is not one of them.

It'll never happen.

But what if it could?

I push the thought away, making the ache in my chest worse. I rub at it idly, as if that will help with the emotional pain I have no right feeling.

I know I can never marry her. I wouldn't want to do that to her in the first place, but my other responsibilities… I push that thought away and instead focus on what I can accomplish, what I can do.

I never would have thought I would miss her so damn much, especially while she's right there in front of me, but I do. She's like a phantom limb that I can still feel, but I can't fucking touch.

As much as I thought today would end everything I've been feeling for her, it hasn't. It's only made it worse. Olivia Hart may be done with me, but I sure as shit am not done with her. I can't be.

I drop my hand from the never-ending ache until it's between us, brushing against hers in the barest of touches. Dammit. I feel that slide of skin all the way to my toes. I need more. My pinky hooks around hers and she jerks at the contact like I surprised her. I suppose I did. We've spent all day together and I haven't touched her. It's been torture.

I use that small point of contact to tug her to a stop, to bring her closer, until we're nearly pressed against each other just a sliver of space between us. Olivia doesn't look at me, just keeps her eyes focused on the knot of my tie, purple, because it's Thursday.

"Come back to me, sunshine," I murmur before I can stop the words. "I know I fucked up. I'll do better this time."

I watch as the tip of her pink tongue darts out of her mouth, wetting her lips. Her free hand comes up to press against my chest, over my shirt, under my jacket. What I wouldn't give to have her skin on mine, "I can't." Her whisper sounds broken, full of resolve but also pain, an ache that echoes in my heart.

"Please."

She shakes her head again, sending her glasses sliding down her nose. My fingers itch to push them back up for her, but I keep them where they are. And she fixes them herself, disengaging from me to turn and look out over the water, scanning the horizon with her gorgeous gold eyes. "You aren't able to give me everything I want, what I need."

Probably not. I know better than anyone all the ways I'm lacking. I've been told it enough times by someone who was supposed to love me unconditionally. It doesn't stop me from asking, "What do you need, Olivia?"

She glances at me, before quickly looking back at the view, a faint blush on her cheeks. "You've been holding yourself back. I know we started as just sex. I know it's mostly physical, but I wasn't lying when I said you'd changed how you behaved when it was over. You went from caring for me to just discarding me." She sighs and swipes a strand of hair away from the lip gloss on her mouth. "I'm smart enough to know, to have figured out now, that you were likely catching feelings. That you were withholding the aftercare part because you didn't *want* to care. So you were portioning yourself out for me. Little tiny pieces. I can have the sex, but not the aftercare. I can have the lust, but not the feelings. I can have your body, but not your heart. Crumbs, Linc. You were giving me crumbs. I don't want crumbs." Her voice is soft as she says this. "I want the whole cake."

I blink at her, something close to fear blooming in my chest.

"You don't know what you're talking about, Liv." She really fucking doesn't. No one wants all of me. I'm too fucked up, too damaged. She's just barely scratched the surface of my damage. It extends far beyond my needs in the bedroom and has everything to do with the way I pushed her away when she got too close, when I started to care about her.

It's better if she views me as an uncaring asshole, then to give her the power to hurt me.

Not to mention if she ever found out about- I cut off the thought, not wanting to give it a voice in my head while I'm with her.

Olivia turns to face me, one of her hands coming up to cup my cheek, her thumb stroking over the stubble growing in even though I shaved last night. "I *do* know what I'm talking about. You aren't as bad as you seem to think you are." Half her mouth quirks up into a smile, and fuck, I want to kiss it. "You aren't as bad as you want everyone to believe. Why do you push everyone away?"

I have to swallow around the feeling of being seen. It's uncomfortable the way her gold eyes look past the bullshit and *see*. No one has ever done that, except maybe Cabot. But even him I keep at a distance, separate. I love my siblings, but since I'm the oldest and our parents are nightmares, they've always looked at me as a protector, someone separate. I didn't mind—*don't* mind—but it means that I've never really let myself go around them, never showed them the broken pieces of me.

Yet here is this woman who I've known for all of a month, calling me out on my deeply seated bullshit.

"I'm not worth getting to know, Liv," I say softly, harshly, even as I lean my cheek into her palm. "I'm really fucking not."

She tsks and shakes her head sadly. "I know that's not true, Lincoln. And my heart aches that there's any part of you that thinks that it is." Her other hand comes up, holding my face steady so I'm forced to look at her. That's not true. Her touch is gentle enough that I could pull away if I wanted, could look out to the sea. But I can't look away from her. No matter how hard I try, I'm always brought right back to her with her warm honey tones, her soft eyes, the spray of freckles over her nose.

She stares me right in the eyes, her gaze unwavering. "You are worth it, Lincoln George. Let your walls down and let someone in. It doesn't have to be me. But *someone*, please. It'll be worth it. I promise."

My throat tightens, feeling like I have a bone lodge sideways in it, and my nose tingles. I swallow down the feeling and reach up to press her hands more firmly against me. "I want it to be you, Olivia. Please, I'll try for you. You're worth it."

The smile that spreads over her pink, glossy lips is so bright, I nearly stumble back at the force of it. She fucking glows, radiates happiness, and I can't believe I'm the one that put it there. How the hell did I manage that with only my rusty confession?

Liv doesn't let me go. Instead she presses closer, so close her breasts smoosh against my chest and her hands slide from my cheeks to around the back of my neck as she pushes up onto her toes and drags my face down to hers.

Her kiss feels like stepping into the sunshine after a long period underground in the dark. There's nothing tentative about it, nothing hesitant or nervous. She's just so fucking warm and soft and loving. I don't deserve to be kissed like this. Don't deserve to slide my hands around to the swell of her ass, pulling her firmly against her as my tongue plunders her mouth. I don't deserve her sweet honey taste on my tongue or the moan that she breathes into my mouth. I don't deserve a damn thing about Olivia.

And I know it's only a matter of time before she finds that out, before she realizes what a colossal mistake it was—is—to be with me.

17
Olivia

Lincoln is trying. I can tell he's trying because he's officially meeting Claire for the first time tonight. My bestie has been pestering me for days to meet him, vet him. I've put her off for as long as I can by telling her it's still new. We're still feeling each other out. I don't want to scare him off.

"As your best friend in the whole entire world, it is my duty to meet him before you catch too many feels for him, Livie. If my bullshit detector finds out he's an asshole, it needs to be now, and not six months down the road. I don't want to see you get hurt."

I sigh and cast a look at Lincoln, who's in my living room chatting with my mother, like he's been doing for the last two weeks. Ever since, we agreed to really give a relationship a shot. He's come home with me every evening, so I can check on my mother and relieve Harvey. He usually eats dinner with us before giving me a chaste kiss and leaving for the night.

He never stays.

Any sex we have is done

at the office or in the car on the way to my house if we're feeling particularly amorous.

Lincoln must feel my eyes on him because he looks up with a brow arched in question. I tip the phone away from my mouth. "Claire is being a pest." I hear her protest on the other end of the line. "And she wants to meet you."

A quick grin flashes my way. "Makes sense. I'm sure she wants to make sure I'm good enough for you."

My mom smacks her hand on his forearm, quick to reassure him. "You are! Claire," she raises her voice as much as she can. "He is! He has the Mama Hart stamp of approval."

I swear I see a blush tint Linc's cheeks at my mother's words and he *ducks his head*, like he's suddenly shy. I roll my eyes at him, and then lift my phone back to my mouth. "Do you want to come over? He's here now."

Lincoln shakes his head before she can answer. "No, let's go out. My treat."

Claire must have heard him, because she says, "Yes. Let him take us out. We can do that thing where we get one of everything on the menu."

I laugh and shake my head at her. "We'd never be able to eat it all."

"That's what doggy bags are for, babes! We'll have lunches and dinners for a week!"

"I don't know," I hedge, looking at my mother, who frowns at me. It's one thing to leave her for work, it's another to leave her so I can go out on the town with my bo- with the guy I'm seeing and my best friend. I don't think I can do that to her.

"Olivia Jane, if you are thinking of declining Lincoln's invitation because of me, I will whoop your butt." She runs her fingers over the blanket covering her legs. "I will be just fine for a single night."

I can tell by looking that she will not take no for an answer, so I roll my eyes and say, "fine, we'll go out." Claire squeals on the other end of the phone while my mother gives me a satisfied nod.

Lincoln is already pulling out his phone. "I'll find a nurse who can come spend time with you, Caroline. Someone who might be open to more night shifts for us." He looks up at me, gaze burning. "I foresee a few more date nights in our future."

I shake my head. "No, I can't afford-"

"Did I say you would be paying, sunshine?" My mouth snaps closed and my eyes narrow. He sighs and softens his tone. "Just let me do this for you. *For us.* Please."

"Gah," Claire says from the other side of the phone. "I think I'm already ready to give my stamp of approval. Marry the man, Livie. Marry him, or I will."

Lincoln takes us to a tiny restaurant off the beaten path. I'd expected him to impress Claire by getting us into Tourmaline, where you have to have a reservation six months in advance, or *Niche* where the crème de la crème of Breaker's Point dine when they want to be seen.

But this place is small and cozy. There isn't a sign out front, so I have no idea what it's called. The atmosphere is homey and sweet. Claire looks around, a little disappointed when we step into the restaurant, taking in the simple decor. There are only about ten tables, making it an intimate space. And there isn't a single celebrity in sight.

Her brows arch. "We're sure this is where he wants to eat?"

I look at the other diners and try to ignore the uncertainty in my stomach. "It's where Lance dropped us off, so I'm fairly certain-" I cut off when a smiling older woman bustles across the restaurant toward us. She's wearing a long, flowy black skirt, and a cream-colored blouse. Her gray streaked hair is loose and in gentle waves around a face lined with many laugh lines.

"Olivia?" she asks, coming to a stop in front of us.

I nod, surprised that she seems to know my name. "Yes."

She beams. "You're just as pretty as he said you'd be." She reaches to take both my hands in hers. "My name is Candice. My husband and I run this place." Her brown eyes slide to my best friend. "And you must be Claire. Lincoln phoned and said he's running just a little behind, but he wanted me to get you settled. If you'll follow me?"

She releases my hands and spins to weave through the tables, bypassing the only empty one and pushing into a private room just off the kitchen. There's a window that will let us watch as they work, but it's separate enough that we'll have privacy for our conversation.

Candice motions at the table already set for three, complete with glasses of wine. I drop into a seat and Claire takes the one on my left, while Candice braces her hands on the back of the chair that Lincoln will sit in.

"We have a *prix fixe* menu planned for you with wine pairings included. Lincoln informed us of your shellfish allergy, Olivia, so we've made sure it's not anywhere on the menu for anyone tonight. There is no cross contamination."

Again, disappointment flashes over Claire's face. "So we don't get to choose what we eat?"

The smile on Candice's face dims somewhat before its back. "Not tonight. But I promise you it will be worth it. Let me know if there's anything else I can get you." She bobs, almost like she's curtseying to us, and then leaves the room.

Claire wrinkles her nose as she picks up her wineglass. "Bit presumptuous, isn't it?"

I laugh and pick up my own glass to take a sip. God, that's good. "What happened to 'marry him or I will'?"

She shrugs and looks around again before leaning forward. "That was before he took us to an unnamed restaurant in the middle of nowhere, Breaker's Point, Livie. He's a billionaire. He could have gotten us into Tourmaline! But he brought us here, where we're immediately shuffled into the back, out of sight?"

I sink my teeth into my lower lip and glance around. "Isn't this a chef's table? It's like an honor or something to be seated this close to the kitchen, where we can watch them make our food."

She rolls her eyes. "I would rather have sat next to Jonah Graves at *La Niche*, to make him fall in love with me."

I chuckle. "You and your obsession with Jonah Graves."

Claire arches a brow at me. "What? He's hot! And he's got that hockey butt you could bounce a quarter off of. Plus, he's a total player, so it wouldn't be that hard to get him to take a bite." She straightens in her chair and adjusts her breasts, so they sit higher on her chest. "Look at these, Liv! They're perfect and they're wasted tucked away back here!"

I laugh. "Well, Lincoln hired someone to be with my mom for the entire night, so maybe after this Linc can use his clout to get us into Gothic."

Claire's eyes widen, and she nods emphatically. "Yes. Please. Let's do that. I need to get my groove on." She settles back into her chair, content now that I've dangled the carrot of dancing in front of her.

But her first concerns stick with me. It is a little weird that he brought us here, rather than to one of the well-known restaurants. He didn't pick us up, didn't even meet us out front. And we *were* hustled into the back like a secret.

"Hey, babes," Claire says, drawing my attention to her from where I've been glaring at my glass of wine. "I was just being pissy. I'm sure there's a reason for being here. He'll explain it. And the smells coming from that kitchen are amazing, so I'm sure the food is good."

I push my hair back over my shoulders and nod. "You're right. Let's just enjoy this." I pick up my glass and take another sip. "How's work?"

"Great. Really, really good. We just closed a deal with the marketing department of the Guardians. I'm going to be designing all the new merch."

I nearly spit out the wine I just pulled into my mouth, but just barely manage to swallow before I screech. "What?!?" Claire blushes and shakes her head, embarrassed for some unknown reason. "Holy fucking shit, Claire! That's huge!"

She nods and grins. "I know. I know! I'm also terrified. So fucking worried I'm going to be awful at it."

"Impossible," I say, shaking my head. "You are a stunning designer. And you'll make sports gear for women that is actually cute."

"I know, right? It's getting better, but there's still room for improvement."

We talk about what it means for her, the ideas she already has. By the time Lincoln enters the room, we're both on our second glasses of wine and have had nothing but bread to eat. "I'm sorry," he says as he rounds the table to press a kiss to my forehead. *My forehead.* Not my lips. "Something came up I needed to deal with."

He takes the empty chair next to me, while I offer him a stained smile. "It's fine."

"What was it?" Claire asks, tone bordering on combative, no doubt the alcohol coursing through her veins making her bold. Who am I kidding? She's always bold. "What was it that came up?"

His gaze flicks to me and then over to her. "Something was delivered to the office that needed to be handled immediately."

That gets my attention, and I sit up straight, a jolt of panic moving through me. "What was it?"

Lincoln turns to face me, reaching out to cover my hand with his. "It doesn't matter. It was picked up by security, and one of Lance's guys is handling it."

Claire's narrowed gaze moves between the two of us. "Would either of you care to share what's happening?"

"It's an ongoing investigation," he says, thumb stroking over my wrist. "We aren't really supposed to talk about it."

I frown. Is that true? Are we not supposed to talk about the pictures and the phone calls? If it is true, then I guess it's a good thing I haven't.

"Hey!" Claire growls. "I'm the best friend here. If there's an investigation regarding my girl, I need to know about it."

I flick my gaze up to Lincoln, and he gives me a small nod. I turn in my chair to my best friend and take her hand in mine. "It's not that big a deal," I say, trying to reassure her, but Linc's growl makes it clear that I'm lying. "I've been receiving some... *disturbing* phone calls and apparently deliveries now, too. It's been reported to the police, and they are working on figuring out who it is."

Claire gnaws on her lower lip and flicks her eyes between the two of us. "When did it start?"

I feel my face flush a deep pink. I can't tell her the first time we heard anything from them was after Linc destroyed me in the elevator with just dirty words and his fingers. Nope. My best friend does not need those details. "Not long after I started working closely with Lincoln."

She frowns, and I squeeze her hand in reassurance. "They're going to figure it out, Claire, I swear."

Lincoln's hand comes up to touch between my shoulder blades. "I have my security team working overtime on it. And once we know who it is, we'll crucify them."

Claire's brown eyes flair at the promise In Lincoln's tone, but she still looks back at me, uncertainly. "And they haven't attacked you physically? It's just the phone calls and the deliveries?"

I nod, decisively. "Yes."

She lets out a breath and leans back, releasing my hand to reach for her wine. "Okay. Okay. But the second it escalates to anything more than that, we're wrapping you in cotton wool and locking you away to keep you safe."

"Agreed," Lincoln rumbles from behind me.

I roll my eyes at their overprotective natures but can't deny that I get a warm spot in my chest. Also, this is a good sign. That they agree on this. I'd been worried that she would assume Lincoln is trying to hide me, especially with this restaurant and this private room.

Almost as if she can read my thoughts, my best friend slides her gaze over to the man next to me. "What made you pick this restaurant?"

Lincoln's hand slides up my back until he can play with strands of my hair. "This is my favorite restaurant.

Candice and Marco are masters at what they do. The food here is truly spectacular." He smirks. "Let me guess, you thought I'd take you to Tourmaline? Or some equally hard to get into restaurant to flex about how much power I have?"

Claire arches a brow and then nods, a grudging smile on her lips. "Yep."

Lincoln shrugs. "Next time I'll do that. But since this dinner is for you to get to know me, I thought bringing you to a place I actually like to eat would be better. Tourmaline is a great place to see and be seen, but the food is subpar at best. Especially compared to what Marco creates here."

"Oh, aren't you just the sweetest," Candice beams as she pushes through the door carrying three plates and I nearly choke on my tongue because I'm not sure anyone has ever called Lincoln George sweet. "He's been coming here once a week for the last five years."

He smiles at her as she places down the first plate in front of Claire, and then me and finally Lincoln. That done, she steps back and clasps her fingers in front of her. "The first course tonight is an appetizer of smoked beets on a crispy walnut crust topped with a horseradish cream." With one hand motioning at the table, she grins. "Enjoy."

The first bite has me moaning and next to me Claire is nodding. "Oh, okay, yeah. Yes, I get it. This is phenomenal," she mutters out between quick bites. "Do you think I could get a second one?"

Lincoln laughs. "I'm sure they'd do that for you, but there are four more courses, so you might want to hold off on that request."

The entire meal is exquisite, and I can't for the life of me figure out why more people don't know about this place. I've certainly never heard of it. But then I suppose it's hard to hear of a restaurant with no name.

We talk through the whole thing. There are no lulls in conversation besides when Claire asks Lincoln about his family, and he pauses like he's considering how much to tell her. But it only lasts for a few minutes before he's talking about his siblings—all three of them. The pride he feels in them is apparent in his tone.

Not one of them went into business like he did. Kyan is a tattoo artist with his own shop. Francie is in PR and Zayne is a musician. When he mentions a band name that is fairly familiar to me, Claire squeals her delight. "Oh, my fucking God. I can't believe your brother is the front man for Brigades of Menace."

Lincoln's lips turn up into a smile. "He is. I can get you tickets the next time they're in town. Backstage passes too."

Claire is nodding emphatically. "Yes. Yes, please. Let's do that." She points a finger at me. "Dating him is the best thing you've ever done. I knew putting up with your ass for so long would eventually pay off." Her face goes serious. "Don't fuck it up."

I know she's not saying that to me, but Lincoln, so I turn toward him and catch the flicker of guilt in his eyes before he meets my gaze and says, "I'm going to try my hardest not to."

18
Lincoln

I'm not sure I've ever been as happy as I am right now. It sets me on edge, just waiting for the other shoe to drop, or the shit to hit the fan or one of the other countless sayings that implies something bad is going to happen.

I try like hell to not let it affect my time with Liv. She doesn't need to experience the swirling cocktail of fucked up emotions in my stomach.

It doesn't help that whoever is tormenting my girl seems to have picked up their game. Hardly a day goes by that she doesn't receive a phone call or a delivery. Thankfully, Lance has started having all packages for me or Cabot go to security first, so Liv hasn't seen them.

But I have.

Countless pictures of her, usually with her eyes x'd out. Some of them have just her head cut out. All of them have some form of a threat attached to them.

It drives me fucking insane that we can't seem to find out who it is. There are no leads we can follow, no threads to pull to make the scheme unravel. I can't protect her from the phone calls on my office line. I wish like fuck I could, but it's a business. *My business.* I have paid to have her personal number changed multiple times, though. It works for a while, but eventually they always find her.

Liv doesn't know about those deliveries, and if I have my way, she never will.

My arms tighten around her and she nuzzles further into my chest, with a contented little sigh that makes my ribs feel tight. I bend my head to brush a kiss over the top of her head. And she tips her head back to look at me with a soft smile on her face, before turning back to the movie on the TV on the far wall.

I brought over a new smart TV with all the streaming services downloaded and put it in Liv's bedroom upstairs, so she could watch things without waking her mother.

She sighs, watching as a boy and girl sit and talk together on top of a dining room table with a cake between them. "The first time I saw this movie, I thought this was the pinnacle of romance," Olivia laughs. "Like he showed up out of the blue after finding out whatever he could about her and then gave her a cake on her birthday."

I cuddle her closer, brush my lips over her temple. "It is pretty romantic," I murmur. "He was curious, wanted to know more, tried to find out what he could about her. A day later, he breaks up with his girlfriend for some girl he's never even talked to and goes and gets the girl."

Liv hums. "Actually, when you say it like that, it's kind of creepy. He stalked her for a whole day and then made major life-changing decisions based on what he found out. The only reason it worked is that she liked him back. And—let's be real—what girl in their right mind wouldn't want Jake Ryan?" She flaps a hand in front of her face like she's trying to cool off. "That boy is hot."

I pinch her side and she squeals and jerks like she's trying to get away from me. "I'm sorry, sunshine. Who did you say was hot?" I tickle her sides hard as she laughs and scrambles to get away from me, but I've got a good hold on her, so she doesn't go anywhere.

"You!" she finally shouts out and my fingers still their torment. "You, Linc." She shifts around until she's straddling my hips, arms draped over my shoulder as she presses a kiss to my lips. "You're the hottest boy I've ever been with."

I grumble at her use of the word 'boy,' but choose to ignore it when she sweeps her tongue into my mouth so sweetly to slide along mine. I'm still getting used to this. To the easy affection between the two of us when we aren't at work. At the way she cuddles into my chest at every opportunity, rains kisses on me.

It's getting harder and harder to avoid it when we're at work. Anytime I'm around her, I want to be touching her, to brush back the hair from her face, or lace my fingers with hers. It's not a drive to be sexual with her, it's the need to shower her with affection, claim her for the world to see, remind her how much I cherish her.

I have to work doubly hard to shove that second instinct aside. It's not something either of us are ready for, and it's not something I'll ever be able to do. No matter how much I might want to.

The credits have stopped rolling by the time Liv pulls back and sighs. "You should go."

My fingers tighten on her hips, and I pull her closer. "No, I should stay."

She chuckles and kisses me before pushing off my lap. I want to grab her, to hold her in place, but I let her stand with my hands still on her hips, until she gets too far away and I have to release her.

Her lips tighten, and I can see that she's considering. But then she shakes her head. "No, you should go. I'll need to check in on her frequently, and I don't want to disturb your sleep. You need it."

God, she's so fucking thoughtful.

"Liv, please," I groan, typing my head back. "Your mother will be fine."

Her honey gaze sharpens on my face, and I know I've said the wrong thing. "No, actually, she's not going to be fine, Lincoln. I have limited time with her."

She pulls her hair into an angry little bun, like she's readying for a fight, and I stand, reaching for her, needing to smooth this over. The last thing I want is for her to be upset with me. "I know. I'm sorry. That came out wrong. Of course, you should spend as much time with your mother as you can. I just… I miss you when we're apart." I cup her elbows, try to bring her closer to me. But she resists, even as she softens, just slightly, dropping her hands down to smack against her thighs.

"I miss you too. But... You're going to be here long after she's not, and I have to... I have to prioritize her now, Lincoln."

I nod. "Yeah, of course. Of course."

I pull her into me, and she comes willingly, nuzzling into my chest again. I wish there was something I could do for her, for them. Something to make this easier or to fix it. If there was a way to heal Liv's mom, I would do it. But I've already reached out to the top minds in the field, already had them look at Caroline's medical records and their opinion is the same. Months at most.

The last doctor I talked to said it's a wonder she's lived as long as she has with how aggressive her cancer has been. It's not a wonder, it's Liv. Liv and how much she loves Caroline, how much Caroline loves her.

Liv tips her head back until her chin is propped on my chest. There's uncertainty in her eyes when she suggests, "Maybe I can stay over at your place one night? Maybe after the... after that dinner with the board of Houser?"

I smooth the loose hair she didn't catch in her angry bun back from her face. "Stay? Like all night?"

Half her mouth curls into a smile. "That's generally what staying over means." When I don't say anything right away, the smile drops from her lips, replaced with embarrassment. "Sorry," she mumbles as she tries to move away from me, but I hold her in place. "I can see you're not into the idea."

I chuckle. "No, sunshine. You misunderstand me. I'm very into the idea. So fucking into the idea. I was just thinking of all the things I'm going to do to this tight little body of yours when I have all night and all of my toys at my disposal." I drop a kiss on the tip of her nose. "And even better, I'm thinking about waking up next to you in the morning."

Liv laughs and shakes her head. "I wouldn't romanticize that, Linc. I can be pretty scary first thing."

I kiss her lips. "Never. You could never be scary to me. Even if you have the worst case of morning breath, it won't scare me away from you."

A pretty flush colors her cheeks as she steps away from me, and this time I let her. "We'll see. You haven't seen my hair before I get a chance to tame it."

She turns and leaves her bedroom, and I trail behind her down the stairs. I wait in the hall as she heads to her mother's bedside, checks her vitals and her breathing, and then returns to me.

"Still asleep?" I ask softly as I push my feet into my shoes.

She nods and curls her arms over her chest, glancing back toward her mother uncertainly. "She's doing that more and more lately. It feels... It feels like it means something." Tears shimmer on her lower lashes and I pull her into me, cupping the back of her head to hold it against my chest.

"It means she's tired, Liv. And that she's fighting. She's conserving her energy."

My woman nods against me, but she's still trembling, so I hold on to her a little longer, until her shaking stops and she takes deep even breaths. Only then do I pull back and look down at her sternly. "No baking tonight. Get some rest, okay, sunshine?"

She rolls her lips between her teeth and doesn't promise me anything. Which is enough for me to know she's going to ignore my order, so I lean closer to her. "If I ask Harvey tomorrow and he says there are new baked goods in this house, I will have to punish you, Olivia."

Her eyes go molten gold at the dark promise in my voice. "You know that's not really a deterrent, right?"

I lean in close until my lips press against the shell of her ear. "It will be if I get you worked up, on the edge of coming, and then stop. It will be if I finish myself off on your pretty tits and then leave you wanting. It will be if your punishment is that I do not touch you for three days after. Imagine it Liv, all that arousal with nowhere to go."

Her mouth drops open as she glares at me with denial in her eyes. "You wouldn't."

I chuckle, press a kiss to her ear, and rumble out. "Oh, baby, I definitely would." I pull back and snatch my coat off the hook by the front door. "Get some rest tonight, Liv, because you won't be getting any tomorrow."

Liv shows up to our work dinner looking like a wet fucking dream in a tight blue wiggle dress with a heart-shaped neckline, that hugs every single one of her curves, puts them all on display for the men we'll be dining with tonight.

A fierce, possessive pride fills me. *She's mine.* Fucking mine. And she looks so damn good when she pulls off that white coat I picked out for her, that countless eyes run over her. I step behind her, and help her pull the coat off her shoulders, fingers scraping along the column of her neck before grasping the fabric.

"If anyone but me touches you tonight, sunshine..." I don't finish the thought, but her head tips toward me and she nods so I know she understands. No one touches her but me, and if anyone does, she'll be punished for it.

She turns to me with a cheeky smile on her lips, running over my body in the same way I looked at her. My chest may puff out just the slightest bit at the desire that ignites. It's the same fucking suit I was wearing earlier, but with the way she's looking at me, you'd think it was a tuxedo or grey sweatpants.

"Ditto, Mr. George."

My smile turns wolfish. "Game on, Miss Hart."

Her eyes lower demurely and a flush spreads over her cheeks before her eyes flash up. I just barely move out of the way as the hostess, a pretty woman with deep red hair and the palest skin, tries to touch my shoulder to get my attention.

She looks at me with surprised blue eyes when my lip pulls back in a snarl at her. She pales even further. "I'm so sorry, Mr. George. I didn't-"

"Is our table ready?" I cut her off without preamble, earning a chastising scowl from my woman.

The hostess bobs her head. "Yes, follow me this way."

My hand finds Liv's lower back, stroking her through the silky fabric of the dress I picked out for her. I love that she wears the clothing I bought her. It has the possessive side of me rearing even more, and my hand drops to caress the curve of her ass, squeezing the plump flesh, as the hostess guides us into a private meeting room.

Olivia arches a brow at me, but doesn't smack my hand away, so I dip a little lower to the juncture of her legs, just as the hostess turns to us with an uncertain smile. "Will this be okay?"

The woman next to me seems to have lost the ability to speak, so I smile at the hostess and nod. "Yes, it should be fine, thank you." She leaves us and I round the table and then pull out a chair, ushering Liv into it. She sinks down and I take the spot next to her, not wasting any time to tug her chair closer to mine and sliding my hand onto her thigh.

She ignores my caress and pulls out her ever-present tablet, placing it neatly between our place settings with her stylus on top. By the time she's gathered all the things she'll need, the door opens, and we both stand facing the three men and three women who've joined us. With the table between us, it's easy to keep our distance, to not touch any of them as we greet them, just giving nods and smiles.

When we settle into our chairs again, Liv has Harry Green on her side, and I have the wife of Bert Friar on my side. Since we moved our chairs closer to each other, there's a bit of a buffer zone around us, but we still spend the entire dinner jerking away from everyone else in order to win the game.

Next to me, Liv shifts, and I catch sight of Mr. Green's hand hovering just over her arm, and she leans toward me, reaching with her left hand for her drink to keep him from touching her. "Good girl," I murmur low enough that I know no one else can hear me.

When Mrs. Friar slides her hand toward my knee, Liv watches its progress with an arched brow. To avoid the contact, I stand and smooth a hand down my tie while lifting my glass with my other hand. All eyes turn toward me. "A toast." I have no fucking clue what I'm saying, only that I don't want to lose the game because what I have planned for Olivia tonight is too delicious. "To new business ventures and old friendships. To building something we can all be proud of."

Yep. Absolute nonsense, but it does the trick as they lift their glasses and down the contents. Mrs. Friar turns to her husband with a pout. When I sit down, Liv leans over with the tablet in her hand and points at something on the screen.

My mouth curls into a smirk.

Good Bossypants is written in her swooping cursive.

The rest of the night goes on like this. By the time dessert has been served, neither of us has let anyone else touch us.

We stand as one, chattering and moving toward the coat check where we'll gather our things and then leave. Olivia purposefully pushes to her feet last, giving everyone else time to move through the restaurant ahead of us. Smart girl.

I'm right on her heels, so close I'm sure she can feel my body heat and my breath on her neck.

"Lincoln," says Mr. Green. "Good doing business with you." He holds out a hand for me to shake, but I ignore it in favor of helping Liv into her coat.

"I'm sure it will be beneficial to both of us," I say as Liv slides her arms into her jacket.

Mr. Green arches a brow at my refusal to shake his hand, and I'll probably regret it later. But also, my surliness is well known in the business community, so it's likely not that big of a surprise.

He turns his attention to Liv. "Miss Hart, as always, it's a pleasure to see you."

My lips curl into a smirk as her impeccable manners kick in and she slides her fingers into his, giving a firm shake, but not lingering in the slightest. It sets off a chain reaction, where everyone else shakes her hand to. I make note of each point of contact as victory sings through my veins.

I fucking won.

But really, we'll both get a prize.

19
Olivia

I try to look around Lincoln's house, to see what the personal space of this man I'm with looks like, but the only thing I really catch sight of is the chandelier hanging in the foyer and a fancy wooden staircase leading up to the second floor, before he's on me.

One hand hooks behind my neck, dragging me toward him, while his other grabs my hip. His mouth descends and the strap of my bag slides off my shoulder to land with a plop on the floor.

My eyes close as he kisses me, devouring my mouth, trying to get us as close as we possibly can be without him being inside me. "You are in so much trouble, sunshine," he murmurs, before hooking his hands under my thighs and lifting. I coil myself around him, arms over shoulders, legs around hips, and he goes back to kissing me while I try to figure out what I'm in trouble for… and what my punishment might be.

All thought leaves me when Lincoln pulls his mouth from mine and lets my legs drop, holding on to my ass as he carefully sets me on my feet.

I blink open my eyes to find us in a dimly lit room. There's a huge bed as the centerpiece with soft looking blankets and pillows. Dressers and bureaus line one entire wall. A knot forms between my brows as my gaze snags on metal hooks stuck into the ceilings and walls. "Is this your room?"

He smirks down at me, kisses the tip of my nose. "No, this isn't my bedroom. This is my playroom."

My brows arch. "Christian Grey's red room of pain."

He scowls at me. "No. Lincoln George's dark room of pleasure."

I laugh and press up to kiss him. "Sorry, didn't mean to offend you."

He deepens the kiss, hands gripping my hips and tugging me into him, grinding his erection against my belly. "Take off your clothes, Olivia," he murmurs. "And then kneel right where you are and wait while I prepare."

"Prepare what?" I ask, already tugging at the zipper of my dress. It's one of those stupid side zippers though and it doesn't go easily. Lincoln's fingers brush my hands out of the way, and the zipper gives for him, like a hot knife through butter, like it wouldn't dream of denying him something he wants.

He kisses my bare shoulder and then steps away from me. "You'll like it, I promise."

I believe him. I like everything he does to me. So, while he disappears into the dark corners of the room, I pull off my dress, and drape it over a nearby chair, step out of my heels, and tuck them under it.

"Everything?" I ask, glancing over my shoulder to where Lincoln is standing on the bed with a length of rope in his hands.

A shiver works its way over my body, pebbling my already hard nipples even more at the sight. I've never been tied up during sex before, but I think, based on that reaction, I like the idea.

"Everything," he confirms, without looking up from his work.

I shuck off my bra, panties, garter, and stockings, not trying to be sexy about it, because Lincoln is busy with his task. But he lets out a low groan as I add the items to the chair with my dress. "Goddamn, that is a fucking gorgeous sight."

A flush floods my chest and my cheeks as I turn toward him, and carefully drop to my knees, splaying them just the slightest bit. My palms come to rest on my thighs, and I lower my gaze to the floor.

I feel his eyes on me the entire time. "Have you done this before, sunshine?" There's a rough edge of possession in his voice, as though he doesn't like the idea of me doing this with anyone but him. "Because that pose is fucking perfect."

I don't lift my eyes. "I haven't. But I read a lot."

"Christian Grey's red room of pain," he murmurs, and then the room falls silent, the only sound the rope sliding against itself, as he ties knot after knot. Curiosity has me glancing up just as Lincoln wraps his hands around the rope and lifts his body off the bed, making sure the hooks will hold his weight. If they hold his weight, I shouldn't be a problem.

Satisfied, he turns toward me, one brow arched. He tsks when he sees me looking. "Couldn't resist having a peek, hmm?"

I quickly lower my gaze. "Sorry."

He chuckles. "I'll let it slide this time, baby. But in the future, when I ask you to kneel, keep your eyes on the floor."

I nod. "Okay."

"Good girl. Now come here." I do as he asks, just like I always do when we're together like this. He hums his approval as I crawl across the floor, then climb onto the bed with him. His hand slides to cup my jaw as he kisses me softly. "What's your safe word, sunshine?"

"Snickerdoodle," I breathe into his mouth. I doubt I'll use it. The only time I have is when I wanted to break off what we were doing entirely. It's more of a safe word for our relationship, rather than a safe word for the games we play in the bedroom.

"Good girl." I try not to preen under his praise, but it happens anyway. He sees it, a smirk pulling at his lips. Gentle hands urge me into position, kneeling much like I had been before he called me to the bed.

The first slide of the rope against my skin makes goosebumps ripple in its wake. I'd expected it to be rough, like most rope is, but it's soft as silk, pliable as he loops it around my body in a complicated pattern I don't even try to follow. Concentration creases his brows, his slate blue eyes focused. He kisses my wrists before he wraps the rope around them. "If at any point you feel uncomfortable, Liv, tell me. This is designed to gently restrict blood flow, not cut it off entirely. The last thing I want is to cause lasting damage."

I nod my understanding. "I will. I promise."

He grins. "Good." And then he stands and gets off the bed, where he finds one dangling rope and pulls. My arms stretch over my head. Another pull and the ropes tighten just slightly. One more pull and my body lifts off the bed, hovers only an inch or so.

Lincoln secures the rope and then looks at me. "Still good?"

I flex and wiggle, making sure I can still do so with every part of my body, and then nod. "Yes."

I expect him to start, to move after I've reassured him I'm good, but he just stands there, eyes running hungrily over me. "So fucking perfect," he murmurs almost to himself, shaking his head like he can't believe it.

I look down at my body as best as I can, at the soft black ropes looped around my breasts, over my hips, around my knees. He has me tied with my knees bent, splayed open. I can't straighten my legs no matter how I strain.

He rubs his fingers over his lips. "Baby, you look even better than I imagined. This is my favorite fucking sight ever." He drops his hand and saunters toward me, almost idly squeezing his cock through his suit pants. I frown at the realization that he's still fully clothed. Even his tie is still on.

"How about you return the favor? Give me my favorite sight ever."

He smirks. "Is that your way of asking me to undress, sunshine?"

"Yes." No reason to shy away from it.

A low chuckle rumbles from him as he slowly undoes his ties, sliding the silk off of his neck. He drops it on the floor. His shirt follows. I expect him to take off the pants next, but he leaves them on, before climbing onto the bed.

He kneels in front of me, one finger circling my pebbled nipple. "Are you ready for your punishment?"

I blink when he does the same to the other breast. "What am I being punished for?"

He tsks and shakes his head, bending to kiss the corner of my jaw. "Don't pretend like you don't know, sunshine. Playing innocent won't save you."

I shake my head. "But I don't know, Linc."

"Six times, sunshine," he murmurs against my neck. "You let six different people touch what's mine after I warned you not to."

I frown, trying to think of what he could possibly mean. But I can't. I'd gone to great lengths to avoid anyone touching me but him. I dodged hand pats, made myself look like a fool to avoid a hand to my lower back, leaned far too close to him to avoid having Mr. Green murmur something in my ear.

It takes me far too long for understanding to click in my brain. "The handshakes?"

He grunts in response, teeth nipping almost painfully against my flesh before he pulls back.

"Linc, you can't be serious! It was for all intents and purposes a business meeting! I had to shake their hand at the end of the night!"

"I didn't," is his reply.

If I'd thought my arguing with him would soften him up, the way his eyes narrow at me, the way his face turns into an emotionless mask has me second guessing it. Anxiety coils in my stomach as I tug at the ropes binding my wrist. But of course, they don't go anywhere. He's too damn good at what he does. My hips flex as I try to kick my feet, to straighten my legs, to stand, but I can't. I'm stuck here dangling from his ceiling, stretched taut, pussy on full display and dripping, because as much as I might argue with him against my need for punishment. I actually kind of love it.

His fingers grip my jaw and cheeks, pressing them in. "I gave you your rules at the beginning of the night, Olivia. You didn't follow them. You know that as well as I do. So now you're going to accept your punishment, aren't you?"

I swallow and nod, dipping my eyes down over his bare chest to rest on the button of his suit pants. "Yes, sir."

He bends his head and kisses me almost gently before he murmurs, "Good girl," causing a flood of arousal to seep onto my thighs. He leaves me there, dangling, and moves around in the shadows of the room where I can't see him.

He's gone so long that I know without a doubt that this is part of the punishment, the anticipation, the waiting, that makes my anxiety and my nerves ratchet up and up, until I'm literally squirming like a worm on a hook.

When I can't take it any longer, I lick my lips and whisper. "What's my punishment?"

The smack to my ass comes out of nowhere. I didn't even realize he was so close to me, close enough to touch. A moan leaves me as my head tips back, and he chuckles, climbing up behind me, pressing into my back, teeth on my neck again, in that spot he knows drives me crazy. "Fuck. You love that, don't you?"

His hand slides around my front, between my thighs, finding my clit as I gasp out, "yes."

Wait, that's not his finger. It's a vibrator. I look down and find him holding a small purple silicone toy. "What-" The question I was going to ask is cut off on a moan when he flicks it on. My hips buck up as best they can, trying to both get closer to the sensation and farther away as my already sensitive clit screams.

It's been too much today. I can already tell that. My body is wound up tight, on the verge of coming again with only a few seconds of pleasure. Lincoln slides his other hand up to grip my chin, tilts my head down until I have no voice but to watch as he swirls the little vibrator over my sensitive bundle of nerves. His breath gusts over me as my moans grow louder, the restricted movement of my hips more frantic. "Look at you, baby. Look at how responsive you are to me. Look at how wet."

I nod frantically, a long moan sounding from my chest as I fight against the ropes, straining toward release, and just as I'm about to come, just as I open my mouth and gasp out, "Fuck, Lincoln, yes. Yes," he pulls that little vibrator off my clit and leans away from me, removing all physical stimulation from my body, leaving me on the precipice that I want to fling myself over, but I can't. Not with the way I'm bound.

"What the hell?" The words rip from me in a whine, sounding far too needy. "Lincoln, please. I'm so close."

The faint brush of his lips over my shoulder through the fabric of my shirt. "I know." He sounds so damn smug about it, too. He doesn't explain further, just lingers behind me, while my body comes down from the almost orgasm.

"This is my punishment, isn't it?" I mutter, slumping against the ropes. "Orgasm denial."

He hums. "So fucking smart, baby." I preen under his praise even as I want to curse at him. This is not something I've ever wanted to experience. Why would I? The entire point of sex is to come, to reach that release, that moment of forgetting. "Six people touched you. So we're going to do that six more times, and on the seventh I'll let you come."

I let out a slow breath and nod. "Okay."

His hand grips my chin, tilting my head back so he can devour my lips, my mouth, my tongue. "If it gets to be too much," he whispers against me. "You can always use your safe word." It's a gentle reminder that this is a game. That he knows I don't have a lot of experience with this kind of thing and he's giving me an out if I want to take it.

"I'm good," I say. "I promise."

He kisses the tip of my nose before returning to my lips, right as he moves the vibrator back onto my clit, making me jolt at the sudden pleasure. He keeps his mouth on mine this time, keeps my head tilted back, swallowing every single one of my moans as he brings me to the edge of ruin again.

And once again he pulls away, making me sob into his mouth. He swallows that sound too, greedily, like my half pain, half pleasure is sustenance he needs to live, before he once again puts space between our bodies, letting me come down again.

Over and over, he does it, bringing me higher and higher. Sometimes with only the vibrator, sometimes he thrusts his fingers inside me, groaning over how I grip him, frantic to reach my orgasm, but he never stays.

By the time he murmurs, "that's six, sunshine. You're doing so fucking good for me, baby." I'm sobbing, tears flowing as freely down my cheeks as the arousal flows down my thighs. And that spot I love, the one where all thoughts cease and I'm just sensation? I've been there for *ages*. So much longer than that brief moment at the peak of the orgasm.

I'm pretty sure I've been babbling pure nonsense through the last two almost orgasms, demands, pleas, promises, anything my orgasm denied brain thinks might be enough to sway him, I've said.

Lincoln comes around to face me, smoothing my sweaty hair back from my face, wiping the tears from my cheeks. "You are so fucking beautiful like this, Liv." His lips brush against my cheek in a tender move that surprises the hell out of me, but in the next instant he's leaning back to look at me. "You ready to come, baby?"

"God, yes," I whimper, hips shifting toward him eagerly. "Please, Linc."

He moves away from me, and another sob pulls out of me. Why the hell is he leaving?

"Patience, sunshine." I watched dazed as he stands on the bed and kicks off his pants and boxer briefs. His cock springs free, bounces against his stomach, and my mouth waters when I see the glimmer of pre-cum smeared there.

I expect him to let me down, to undo the ropes, but he doesn't. Instead, he slides his hips between my splayed legs, still sitting up. His erection brushes against my over sensitive clit, and I whimper, jerking to get away. "Shh, I've got you, baby. I promise. I'm gonna make you scream so fucking good."

One hand goes between our bodies, positioning his cock at my entrance, and the other grips my chin. Our chests press together, mouths meeting but not really kissing. "Ready?"

I nod frantically, and he thrusts into me in one hard move. My body lifts farther off the bed, stars explode in my eyes, and I realize somewhat distantly that I'm coming after just one thrust from him. He groans but doesn't stop. His hips buck into me, fucking me through my first release. One of his hands grip my hip, holding me still to get a better angle.

The entire time he's speaking low, filthy words in my ear. "Fuck, yes, Liv. Just fucking like that. Squeeze my cock so good. Gonna fuck my sweet little pussy every fucking day. Gonna fill you up."

I nod along with him, helpless to do anything else but just hang there, letting him use me however he wants. Another orgasm builds, making me clench and pulse around him. He groans and reaches up to the knot just above my hands. "When I undo this, put your arms over my shoulders, okay, baby?" I nod, only halfway aware of what he's saying, and then the rope holding me suspended releases. My bound wrists drop right over his head and shoulders like he'd wanted. My fingers tingle as my whole weight falls on top of him, sending his cock deeper inside me.

He doesn't waste a moment rolling us until I'm on my back, still bound with my knees bent and thighs spread. I want to move, to help us both feel pleasure, but I can't. A whimper pulls from me, distressed and needy.

He shakes his head, all but grinning at me. "You just have to take it, baby. Take what I give you. "

I nod frantically. "I want it, please. Linc." Apparently already coming once already wasn't enough.

The pumping of his hips slows. He's no longer barreling us toward the edge. He's casually strolling along. "What do you want, sunshine?"

I growl and try again to move my hips, to change his pace with my body, but all that happens is the ropes bite into my skin and I move maybe a millimeter.

"Olivia. *Tell me*," he orders.

"Fine, bossy pants," I huff. "I want you. I want to come again. Please. I need it. Please. Linc, I need it. I need *you.*"

He groans. "Sweetest fucking words I've ever heard. I'm gonna give you what you need, baby. I promise. You trust me to take care of you, don't you?"

I nod, fingers scrabbling against his neck as much as they can while still bound. "Yes. I trust you."

Something flickers in his eyes, something that looks a lot like guilt before he sets his jaw in determination. "Good girl."

He pulls back as much as he can with my bound wrists around his neck. One of his hands loops around the front of my throat, the other around my hip. And then he really fucks me. My rope bound breasts bounce in time with his thrusts. His slate blue eyes move rapidly over me, like he can't decide where he wants to watch. My parted lips, my bound body, the spot where we're joined, his hand around my neck. "God, so fucking perfect. Why did you have to be so perfect, Liv?"

He sounds upset about that, accusatory, but I don't know why. We're trying, aren't we? We're together and trying. If he thinks I'm perfect, it can only be a good thing. Right?

"Come for me, baby." The hand on my hip slips until he finds my clit and circles it with a rough thumb. I scream, back arching as best as it can as the orgasm hits. My vision goes dark, my breathing stalls out as every muscle in my body tenses.

Above me I hear Lincoln grunt out my name, hips hitting an offbeat rhythm, like he can't focus enough to keep it even. His hand flexes around my throat as his movements stall out. I feel him pulse inside me, spilling his seed.

His forehead comes to a rest between my breasts, heavy beats gusting out of him, as I stroke my fingers through the hair at the back of his head as best I can. I jerk when his mouth closes over one of my nipples, sucking gently, before his teeth scrape over it.

"You did so good, sunshine," he murmurs against my skin, before pushing up. He's gentle as he pulls out of me, careful not to jostle me too much. And then he softly undoes the ropes, rubbing blood back into my limbs, kissing the indents he finds, rubbing muscles cramping from being in a bound position for so long.

I want to ask him about the resentment, the guilt I saw while he was inside me. I want to ask what's wrong, because even though we both came, I can't ignore those emotions, even if I want to. But he disappears before I can, moving to a closed door at the far side of the room. A flare of light makes me squint.

A moment later, he's back with a warm wet cloth that he uses to clean between my legs. "Linc," I start, and he looks up at me, brows raised.

"Yes, sunshine?"

He looks so deliciously rumpled, so gorgeously sated. And he's being so careful with me, showing me he cares with each soft brush of his hand, each gentle brush of his lips. The words die on my lips. I force a soft smile and curl my still lightly tingling fingers around his shoulder, tugging him up. "Kiss me."

He smirks as he crawls up my body, stretching the whole length of his against mine. I love the weight of it, love the feel of the light sprinkling of chest hair against my breasts. The kiss he gives me is as soft as his hands, long slow sipping kisses that make a fire start in my belly, a low simmering heat. Ridiculous considering how rung out I feel.

Linc slides off me, settles on his side, his wide palm on my stomach, right over a still fading indent from his ropes. "That wasn't too much?"

I tip my head to look up at him. "No, it was perfect." My teeth sink into my lower lip as I look at the rope still hanging from the ceiling. "I didn't know sex could be like this," I admit after a moment.

His finger traces along the path left on my skin from the ropes, circling first one breast the then other. "What was it like before?" I open my mouth to answer him, and he shakes his head before I can, cutting me off. "No, nevermind. I don't want to hear about you having sex with other men. It makes me feel unaccountably stabby."

I laugh, and he grins down at me. "Without getting into specifics, it was never this good. *Ever.* Sex has always just been a release. Usually quick, and I almost always would think about other things while it's happening."

He arches his brows as his hand stills on its path. "You think about other things during sex?"

My hand rubs up and down his forearm. "Not with you, Linc. It's the only time my brain fully shuts off."

"And that's a good thing."

I nod. "Yes. It's a very good thing. It's a gift. Thank you, Linc."

His nose wrinkles in a way that I've never seen before. "It's weird for you to thank me for sex."

I brush a kiss to his chin. "It's not just the sex, though. It's the... peace that comes after. The absolute lack of thought. When we're together, I'm not thinking about anything, and I need that. Especially now." Guilt pinches my stomach. "It probably makes me a shitty person."

His thumb smooths over my forehead. "You're not. Everyone needs a break now and then, sunshine. Even you. I'm glad I can be that for you."

"Me too."

He sighs and rolls onto his back, pulling me with him, until I'm draped over his chest. One of his hands strokes through my hair. "I don't normally sleep in here, but I'm too tired to move."

I ignore the pinch of jealousy about the other women he's likely had in here. We both have pasts. I don't need to think about it. "I'm fine sleeping here if you are."

He hums and pulls me closer, before somehow snagging a blanket and draping it over both of us. "If I get the energy, I'll move us later." Lips brush against my forehead. "Get some sleep, sunshine. I'll probably wake you up in a few hours to fuck you again."

My toes curl at the thought. "I'm fine with this."

I fall asleep with a smile on my face.

20
Lincoln

I tug Olivia closer to me, even though she's already as close as she can be without me being inside her. I'm on my back and she's splayed over my chest, head wedged under my chin, hands tucked under hers against my beating heart.

It's still dark out, night blanketing the city. But I'm finding it hard to sleep. Some part of me doesn't want to waste a single moment of my time with Olivia on something as insignificant as rest. I want to always be talking to her, touching her, fucking her.

I feel desperate.

Like there's a clock counting down our time together and once it runs out, that's it. That's all the time I'll have with her. Never to see or hear or touch each other again.

I try like hell to not let it affect my relationship with her, to not show her this worry weighing me down. But I am worried. Worried about where this is going, where it can go. It rears when I think about how much I need her, the number of times I've come inside this woman, how I can't keep my hands or mouth off her.

Her legs shift restlessly against mine and I know she's on the verge of waking up, especially when her body tenses into a stretch, pressing against me as her back arches just slightly. I tilt my head to watch her face as she comes to. It's one of my favorite moments of the whole fucking day. The sleep blurred look, her hair messy, the soft smile she gives me without fail before she presses soft kisses to my lips. We don't normally stay the full night together. Usually, she leaves before the morning so she can be there with her mom first thing.

And I haven't stayed the night with her because it would be impossible to be quiet with all the things I like to do to her. She seems to agree. The last thing either of us wants is to keep her mother awake by having noisy sex under the same roof as her.

Thank God, Olivia finally allowed me to pay for a night nurse. If I could, I would just move them both in here and have a full-time staff to take care of Caroline's needs. My house is big enough that Olivia and I could get up to what we want to and not have anyone else know.

But it's far too early in our relationship to try for that. Beyond that, the clock is ticking down. Soon she won't want anything to do with me.

Olivia breathes in deep, her feet pointing and flexing as she rubs her face on my shoulder, before peeking up at me. "Hi," she whispers softly, that sleepy smile on her lips that I love.

"Hi, sunshine." I press a kiss to her forehead, one of my hands coming up to stroke through her hair. She melts against me, peppering my skin with tiny nips and kisses.

"What time is it?" she asks eventually, sounding like she doesn't want to know.

"It's around three."

Her head shoots up to glare at me. "What are you doing still awake? Have you slept at all?"

I press her head back down to my skin before carding my fingers through her hair again. "I don't need sleep right now, Liv. I just need you."

She hums and kisses my nipple. "Who would have thought Lincoln George would say such sweet things?"

I smirk down at her. "Only for you, baby."

Her fingers stroke over my abs, drawing little shapes over my skin. "Why are you still awake, Linc?" She will not be dissuaded. "Tell me."

I sigh and tug her farther onto my chest, until she's laying on top of me, elbows on either side of my ribs, legs between mine. Her chin rests on the backs of her hands folded my sternum as she waits.

"I just…" I'm not sure where to start. "I'm in awe of you." A pretty pink flush moves over her cheeks. "I'm in awe that you want to be with me."

"Lincoln…" she starts, but I cut her off, pressing my finger to her lips to stall her words.

"Don't. Just let me get this out. Okay?" She nods and settles against me again, keeping those pretty honey eyes of hers on my face. "I'm the oldest of four siblings. There's me, Kyan, Zayne, and Francie. I'm… I have a different father from them. From when our mother was younger. She had a fling with an older man and was pregnant when she met the man that I think of as my father. He's *never* thought of me as his son, even though he adopted me."

A knot forms between her brows and I can tell she wants to ask about it, about why I think that, but she keeps her questions trapped behind her lips. "I didn't notice at first. I was a child. But when Kyan came along and got older, I started to notice the differences in how our father treated me vs how he treated Kyan. They would leave me at home, while he took Kyan out on playdates, just the two of them. He was never shy about reminding me I'm not his son, not really. He liked to do this specifically after I'd ask why I couldn't go with them."

Her frown deepens, and I use a finger to boop the end of her nose before sliding up the bridge to smooth the wrinkles between her brows. "My mother talked to him about it repeatedly. I remember the fights they'd get into, the screaming matches that would result in her crying, and Kyan crawling into bed with me. But things never changed. They only got worse when my mother died giving birth to the twins. His full evil side came out then. He tried to keep me away from my siblings, to poison them against me. But Kyan had seen enough at this point to know that he was an asshole. All those nights he spent screaming at our mother only solidified our bond together. The four of us, we're close. Well, as close as I can be with other people."

I can tell she wants to argue with me on that point, but she doesn't. Gratitude for her restraint floods me. I need to get this out. I need her to understand why I'm like this. Why I'm so resistant to letting people in, to feeling any sort of emotion. "He tried his damndest to separate us. Skipped right over me to groom Kyan to take over his company, but Kyan wasn't the least bit interested. Neither were Zayn and Francie. The only one of the four of us that had any interest in business at all…"

"Was you," she finishes for me, understanding filling her eyes.

"Was me," I confirm. "I wanted to prove to him I could be what he needed me to be. That I could follow in his footsteps even if I wasn't his biological son. I wanted to give my siblings a chance to follow their dreams and live without the pressure he exerted on them."

"He didn't give you that chance, did he?"

I shake my head. "He didn't. When I graduated high school, he told me I would never take over his family business, that I would never be his son, that I would never be good enough for him."

"Oh, Lincoln." Tears fill her eyes and spill over her cheeks, falling silently to drip onto my chest.

"Shh, baby," I smooth my thumbs over her cheeks, wiping away the moisture. "It's okay. It worked out for the best. I went to university, met Cabot, and was determined to build my own company. One that would rival his, that could buy and sell his company a thousand times over, and that is exactly what I did."

Of course, when my father found out about it, he said it was only because the Harkness name was attached. He diminished my accomplishments and then told me he was selling his company to someone else. So I would never get my hands on it. Even if he died, I wouldn't inherit.

The memory of that conversation still makes my stomach clench. The angry words and names he called me still ring in my ears.

Liv nibbles on her lower lip, tears still slipping from her eyes. "I'm sorry you had to go through that, Lincoln. I'm sorry that he made you feel like you... like you weren't enough. You are. You're more than enough. It's part of why I want to be with you."

A ragged breath blows out of me, and I hook my hands under her armpits to slide her up my body so I can kiss her lips, salty with her sorrow for me. She kisses me back, soft sweet kisses, and I swear I can feel her emotions flowing into me. Each press of her mouth to mine says, *it's okay. I'm here. I see you. All of you. I care for you, about you. I'm not going anywhere.*

I don't know if it's just wishful thinking or what she's actually trying to tell me, but either way, it helps. When she pulls back, she doesn't go far, pressing her forehead against mine. "My mother was my father's mistress."

I pull back as far as I can, pressing harder into the pillow to see her face as she drops that bit of knowledge on me. She doesn't look upset by the statement, her honey eyes warm and steady on my face.

"I didn't know that when I was a kid. I thought it was normal for a father to only come visit once a week. For him to spend a few hours with me, and then a few hours with my mom alone. It seemed normal to me right until I started school. Until I saw the other families, the other fathers pick their kids up from school, go on field trips and spend more than just a few hours a week with their children." Her eyes slide away from me, toward the window. "When I asked my mom about it, she didn't lie or try to hide it from me. She told me that Dad had another family that he had to spend time with, but that he still loved us with his whole heart. Which, you know, looking back at it now was definitely a lie. She told me if I ever saw him in public, with his family or without, I had to pretend like I didn't know him. That it was a game and the only way to win was to pretend that we were strangers."

"Jesus, Liv." My heart is breaking in my fucking chest for her. And right on the heels of that agony is the guilt. Because isn't that what I'm asking her to do? Pretend like we're less than we are to each other? Granted, it's mostly to keep her job safe, but I'm also keeping our relationship quiet for an entirely different, selfish reason.

She must see it on my face, because she gives me a soft smile, dropping a kiss on my lips. "Don't do that. What we're doing is different. We're being discreet because I work for you, but I know you're mine and that I'm yours."

Fuck. "Yeah, sunshine. You are mine." To prove it, I slide my hands down her body and cup her ass, pulling her tighter against me.

She giggles before she lifts a shoulder and shakes her head. "It worked for a while. The game. But… It was a small town. Everyone knew. I started to notice the looks they would give me and my mom when we were at the grocery store, at church, at the park. When I was at school, the other kids would bully me for not having a 'real' family, whatever that means. We endured the entire town's ire, while he was... celebrated. Everyone loved him." Her fingers toy with strands of my hair. "He was the mayor, had a ninety-seven percent approval rating, and could do no wrong in the eyes of the townsfolk. No, my mother bore the brunt of it. She was the evil seductress that wooed him away from his marital bed. Never mind that she was eighteen and working as an intern in his office. Nevermind that he told her he loved her long before they ever had sex. She was the evil in that situation, and by extension..."

"So were you."

She bites her lip and nods.

Fuck. I want to go back in time and find little Liv, wrap her in my arms and get her the hell away from anyone that ever hurt her before I raze that entire fucking town to the ground. But I can't do that, so I use my thumb to pull her lip from between her teeth, then lean up to capture it with mine, sucking it into my mouth to run my tongue over it. She whimpers and I swallow the sound before pulling back, sliding my hands into the hair on the side of her head.

"What happened?"

Her brows arch. "What makes you think anything happened?"

"Well, you live across the country from where you grew up, and you've never mentioned your father before. So something must have happened to inspire the move."

She sighs, presses her forehead into my chest like she doesn't want to look at me while she says it. "Middle school happened. Teenage boys happened. Mean girls happened. A school administration that did nothing to help me, because of how they perceived my mother happened."

I frown and use my grip on her hair to lift her eyes to mine. "Explain." It's only when she arches a brow at me that I realize how it came out as a demand. "I mean, if you want to tell me, I would love to know what happened."

She grins at me. "Better."

I smirk back at her. "See? I'm learning." Her gaze goes kind of distant, staring at the headboard of my bed, like she's remembering the events that led up to her mother moving her halfway across the country. "Sunshine?"

She doesn't look at me, but she starts talking. "I was in seventh grade, so like twelve or thirteen. And God, kids can be so mean. They started with writing things on my locker. Home wrecker. Whore. Slut. I reported it each time to a teacher, a counselor, and the front office. They never did anything. Only gave me the supplies to clean it off, like it was my fault there was a mess and I needed to learn my lesson by scrubbing the slurs off." My brows lower as anger bubbles in my stomach on her behalf. "When no one did anything about it, things escalated. I started getting body checked in the halls. The boys started groping me when they could get away with it. The girls called me names in hissed whispers when teachers weren't around. It got to where I dreaded going to school, and my mother noticed. When I told her what was happening, she called my father and told him to do something about it. He said it was out of his hands."

"What?" I whisper harshly, and her eyes finally turn back to me, surprise coloring her features, like she hadn't expected me to be so upset by this.

She shrugs again, fingers going back to my hair to stroke through it, like she's trying to sooth me. "He said he wouldn't step in, that he couldn't step in, because of optics. Because of how it would look to the town. He said it was just boys being boys and that I needed to learn how to stand up for myself. I might have done just that, if it hadn't been for a sophomore cornering me, and..." she shudders and closes her eyes. "Well, it doesn't matter what he tried to do, because I got away, ran to my mom and we left the next week."

Her pretty honey eyes open, and I see the pain in them. "I haven't seen my dad since. When mom got sick, I reached out to him to let him know. Left a voice message, but he never responded."

I stroke my hands up and down her back, smooth skin slipping under my palms. "What's his name?"

"My father? Mayor John Jenson." A furrow appears between her brows. "Or I guess maybe he's not the mayor of Hyatte anymore. I don't know. Never bothered to find out."

My hand slides up to cup the back of her neck. "And the asshole, the sophomore who tried-" I can't even bring myself to say it. If I do, I might fucking explode.

She narrows her gaze at me. "Why do you want to know?"

I meet her eyes and let her see my sincerity when I say, "because I'm going to fucking ruin him."

If I had any doubts about Liv being the woman for me, they would be laid to rest when a small smile pulls at her lips, and she nods. "Just wanted to be sure. I probably shouldn't tell you this, because I don't want you to go to jail—I'd miss you—but his name is Jason Barnes."

Jason Barnes. I lock that name away for later, along with her father's. If I could have her give me a list of every person who's ever hurt her, I would do it, and then work my way through it, but something tells me Liv isn't for retribution of that scale. So I'll settle for those two names.

I wrap my arms around her, cradle her on my chest, as she nuzzles into me. "What a pair we make," she murmurs eventually, back to drawing shapes on my skin with the tips of her fingers. "Who would have thought that two such damaged people would fit together so well?"

"You aren't damaged, sunshine. And even if you are, all your rough edges, all your jagged tears, they fit with mine."

She hums, lifting her head to look at me. "I like that. The idea that going through what we did makes us fit together."

I push her silky hair over her shoulder before pressing her head back to my chest. "Me too."

"Linc?" she whispers, eventually.

"Yeah, baby?"

"Thank you for sharing that with me. For telling me about your father." My arms tighten around her. "I know that wasn't easy for you."

"It wasn't," I say hoarsely. "But I want you to know those ugly parts too, Olivia. I need you to see them, so you know what you're getting into."

"There are no ugly parts of you, Lincoln," she murmurs, sounding half asleep even as she tries to make me feel better.

But her gentle reassurance only makes me feel worse. If only she knew what I'm keeping from her. If only she knew just how far I'm willing to go to prove my father wrong about me. If she ever found out—*no*, when *she finds out*—that'll be it for us. She'll want nothing else to do with me.

Liv's breathing evens out. The steady puffs of air on my chest let me know that she's asleep. I know I should try to sleep too, but my mind is whirling with new information about Liv, with plans for ruining her father and the asshole who tried to put his hands on her when she was still a child. I think about my father, and for the first time, I have an unfamiliar emotion regarding him. *Gratitude.*

I'm fucking grateful for the way he treated me back then. Because if he hadn't, if he'd accepted me as his son, took me under his wing, taught me what he knows, I never would have had to strike out on my own. I never would have created the relationship I have with Cabot, the company I built with him. I never would have met Liv, this incredible woman in my arms that makes me feel like a whole person.

I wasn't speaking out of my ass when I said that our broken bits fit together. They do. And I have him to thank for every jagged edge.

⋯⋯⋯⋯⋯♥⋯⋯⋯⋯⋯

I'm up before Liv the next morning. Not surprising since I hardly slept at all and it's a Saturday, so she has nowhere to be. I leave her asleep in bed and make my way to my home gym, where I run through a quick workout before showering. By the time she makes her way into the kitchen, wearing nothing but my shirt from the night before, I'm halfway through making her breakfast.

I turn as she enters, eyes sweeping from the top of her messy hair all the way to her bare toes. Damn, she looks good first thing, like I should take her back to bed and mess up that hair a bit more. "Morning, sunshine," I murmur before turning back to the pan of eggs.

Her arms slide around me from behind as she presses her whole body to mine, resting her cheek between my shoulder blades. "Morning." She sounds soft and sleepy. "I thought we'd wake up in bed together."

"Next time," I promise, moving the pan of eggs to a cool part of the stove and flipping off the burner. I turn in her arms and cup her cheeks in my hands before bending to steal a kiss from her lips. Her fingers dig into my sides, and a moan escapes from her as she presses closer, but I pull back, not letting her take it further.

She whines when I pull away, making me chuckle. "You need food, baby. I worked you over pretty hard last night. How are you feeling?"

Her eyebrow arches. "I'm fine, Linc. If it was too much for me, I would have said something last night. You know, when you had me strung up over your bed and were denying me orgasms? A little morning nookie is hardly going to send me running."

Another laugh pulls from me. I can't help it. She's just so damn adorable. "Breakfast first, then maybe if you're a good girl, we can have some morning *nookie*."

She rolls her eyes, but I can tell she's not going to push it. "If you promise we'll have sex again before I leave, I'll let you feed me."

I drop a kiss to the tip of her nose. "Deal. You want coffee?"

"Have you met me? Yes, *obviously* I want coffee, Lincoln."

"Don't be a brat. Or I'll have to punish you later." I point her toward the coffeepot and smack her ass to get her moving toward it.

She squeaks and then looks over her shoulder at me. "Will you punish me with sex? Cause that's not much of a punishment, if we're honest."

"Brat," I growl at her, and she giggles, before setting about making a cup of coffee for herself, singing that Limp Bizkit song about doing it all for the nookie under her breath.

We talk about our plans for the day as we eat—her spending time with her mother, weeding her flower beds and going grocery shopping, me figuring out the best way to hurt the assholes who hurt her. I don't tell her that, of course, instead I say I'm just going to get some work done.

She frowns at that. "Do you want to come with me instead? I know it's not thrilling to hang out with my mom and weed, but... I don't like how much you work." She rests her hand on mine. "You need a break every now and then."

I think about my plans for what I'm actually doing today, and about the stack of files I do actually need to go through. But do I? They'll still be there tomorrow or Monday. And spending the day with my girl, even if it is just doing chores around her house or running errands, sounds infinitely more satisfactory than being here alone plotting revenge.

Not that revenge won't still happen, it'll just happen later.

"If you come over, I'll make whatever baked goods you want. Brownies? Cookies? Croissants?" My grin grows with each of her suggestions, and I flip my hand over under hers, curling my fingers around hers.

"Crispy rice treats?"

Her brows arch. "And here I thought you didn't like sweets at all, but you like the most ooey gooey sweetest treat ever?"

I lift a shoulder. "It's not that I don't like sweets, Olivia. I just try to limit how many I eat. For instance, I don't need to eat a cookie every day to prove I like it."

She sniffs. "You don't have to, but why wouldn't you?"

I laugh. She laughs too, her brilliant grin splitting her face. She lifts my hand and folds it between both of hers, holding it close to her chest. "Yes, I will make you the best crispy rice treats you've ever had, Lincoln George. Will you come hang out with me today? Please?"

How the hell can I resist her? I use her grip on my hand to pull her closer. "Yes, Olivia Hart. I do believe I will."

21
Olivia

The recurring event on Linc's calendar has been bugging me. I haven't seen it until now, because Giovanna has had control of his personal calendar and I've only been allowed to see his work one in order to plan my schedule.

Every Thursday night, *'Dinner with A'* is repeated. I scroll back a year and then forward a year. It's still there. Who is A? Why doesn't he put in their full name? I try to think back on if I've ever spent time with him on a Thursday, if he's ever missed his dinner with them, in order to spend time with me.

Every Thursday. The day he wears a random tie. This morning he'd put on the one I picked out, even though he rolled his eyes at my choice—navy with pink and white flowers. He just kissed me and then wrapped it around his neck and smirked at me the whole time.

Now I'm remembering the conversation we'd had over his kitchen island, just before he'd pushed up my skirt and fucked me silly. He'd asked if I was going home tonight. I told him I was, that I needed to spend some time with my mom, and that he was more than welcome to come over too.

To which he'd politely declined, saying he didn't want to get in the way, and he wanted to give me and mom time alone together. He didn't mention a standing dinner with this illusive A character.

My teeth sink into my bottom lip as I glare at the event reminder and lean back in my chair and go over every possibility in my head. Lincoln has three siblings, Kyan, Francie, and Zayne. So it's not one of them. His only friend that I know is Cabot.

Maybe it's a typo that he just never bothered to fix?

"Gi?" I look up at the dark-haired beauty across from me as she holds up one finger and then goes back to typing. I wait while she finishes, already second guessing my need to figure this out, to ask her about it. It'll give too much away, I'm sure of it.

"Yes?" she asks, spinning her chair to face me.

"Mr. George has a recurring event every Thursday. A dinner. Justin Huntley from RHD reached out hoping to schedule a dinner next Thursday." *He did no such thing, Liv, you little liar.* "Do you know if that standing dinner is flexible?"

Gi shakes her head like she can see right through my lie. "Nope. It's not. He always goes. Though technically it's not going since, it's always at his house. It's been driving me crazy for years, trying to figure out who it is."

My jaw clenches. *It doesn't mean he's cheating,* I tell myself. *It doesn't mean he's keeping you as a side piece while he has a steady girlfriend.* It means nothing other than that he has a standing dinner. I mean, before he promised to try with me to open up, he was photographed all over the city with different women. No girlfriend in their right mind would be okay with that, right?

Now, if he's photographed at all, it's with me, but usually we're dressed like we're on a business outing and although there's speculation about our relationship, they mostly seem content to comment about how I'm not his normal type.

Which I guess I'm not. Too wholesome and sweet, where he is usually seen with sleek model types.

My point is, no woman in her right mind would put up with this for years. No woman would look the other way while Lincoln splashed his affairs all over the gossip columns. So even if this is a woman, it's not one he's dating.

I nod to myself, thankful that my logic won out over the panic that was climbing up my chest. I will put up with a lot of things, but being the other woman is definitely not one of them. I watched my mother do it, watched her struggle with the censure of those around her, watched her accept only pieces of my father before he went home to his wife. And I saw how it broke her.

Thank God, she reforged herself into something stronger and escaped. Though there are times I think that was more for my sake than hers. If I wasn't a part of the picture, I'm pretty sure she would still be in Hyatte, accepting pieces of my father. *Crumbs.*

Gi eyes me. "I wouldn't worry about it, Liv. It's been going on since long before I started here. Maybe it's... I don't know, therapy or something."

Therapy.

That could be it. He could be working on himself. But if he's been speaking to a therapist for years, shouldn't he be... more well-adjusted? I wouldn't have had to tell him he's worth getting to know that his father is an asshole, and he deserves love.

But then who am I to judge another person's damage, just because I want Lincoln to realize his worth, doesn't mean it's going to happen with a snap of my fingers.

My phone rings, my desk phone, not my cell, and I pick it up without thinking. "Cabot Harkness's office."

I know something's wrong as soon as I stop talking. The prickling sensation scrabbles over my scalp and down my neck when I'm greeted with just heavy breathing on the other side. I swallow and try to keep my voice professional as I say, "Hello?"

Please let them say something. Anything. A wrong number. Something. But it's not. In the next moment that same electronic, singsong voice from before sounds through the phone. "I'm gonna kill you. I'm gonna kill you."

My first instinct is to hang up. But I take a deep breath and reach for my cell phone instead, pulling up Lance's contact information and shooting him a text to let him know what's happening.

His response is immediate: Keep them talking.

"What do you want?" I whisper.

They cut off. "I want you dead, little girl." An icy chill rolls down my spine. "Dead and gone. Dead and gone."

I feel all the blood drain from my face. Giovanna's eyes are on me, concern pulling at her features. "What is it?" she mouths at me. I shake my head.

"Why are you doing this?" I say into the phone, not bothering to hide the fear in my voice. "What did I do to you?"

"You exist. That's enough. I won't be happy until you're dead and gone."

"Please stop," I whisper. "Please."

A hand curls over my shoulder, strong and solid and firm, and I look up into Lincoln's eyes as he slides his palm to cup the back of my neck and holds out the other one. "Give me the phone, sunshine," he demands. I shake my head, because Lance told me to keep them on the phone, and I have a feeling if Linc gets on the phone, they'll hang up.

He growls and tugs the headset from my fingers roughly, bending slightly to keep the cord from hitting my face. "What do you want, asshole?"

I shake my head at him. God, he shouldn't antagonize them. He needs to let Lance do his job and figure out who this is. He meets my gaze, thumb stroking over my pulse point soothingly. "Well, that's too bad. Because that is never going to fucking happen." I watch as all the blood drains from his face, and his fingers tighten just slightly, before he slams the receiver down in its cradle.

I jerk to my feet and his hand falls from my neck. "What did they say?"

Lincoln shakes his head and rubs his fingers over his lips. I don't miss that his hand is shaking. "Lincoln, what did they say?"

He looks at me, and I'm momentarily stunned by the emotion I see in his face, a combination of fear and anger and guilt. Why is there guilt there? This isn't his fault.

He opens his mouth, but no words come out. My phone rings on my desk, and he gets to it before I can. "What?" The word is barked.

I hear the inaudible murmur of a deep voice on the other side but can't make out the words. "Figure it the fuck out, Lance." I relax somewhat at hearing that it's not the creepy person on the phone. Lincoln glances up at me. "This can't keep happening to her."

I frown when he hangs up and turns to me. "My office. Now."

I don't bother to argue. His protective, possessive instincts are on high alert, and anything I say right now will fall on deaf ears. I look at Giovanna, who is watching us with wide eyes. "It's fine," I say to her. "Everything is fine." The reassurance ends on a squeak when Lincoln pulls me into his office and shuts the door with a click. A second later, his arms are around me, and my face is pressed into his chest. We're both shaking.

"You're okay?" he murmurs into the top of my head.

I swallow and nod, tipping my chin back to kiss the corner of his jaw. "Yeah, I'm fine. It's just a voice on the other end of the line. It can't really hurt me."

He pulls back, cups my face with his big hands. "But it can scare you, Liv. I hate the idea of you being scared."

I let out a breath as his forehead presses to mine. "I do too. But I'm okay. Lance will figure it out. This isn't going to go on forever."

His lips brush against mine. "Aren't I supposed to be comforting you?"

I shake my head, making the tips of our noses brush. "We're supposed to comfort each other. That's what being in a relationship is."

I want to ask again what they said to him, what scared him so badly. But he's just now starting to relax, to release some of the tension, like just holding me helps. I don't want to throw him back to that place, so I stay silent.

He guides me over to the couch, where he sits and arranges me on his lap sideways, with my head on his shoulder and my feet braced on the cushion. We're quiet. The only sound is our breathing and the occasional press of our lips together.

Eventually, there's a timid knock on the office door, and Gi calls out without opening it. "I'm so sorry, Mr. George, but you have that lunch with Mr. Kline." I tense at the man's name. He's possibly my least favorite person I've ever met. "If you don't leave now, you'll be late."

Lincoln sighs and kisses the top of my head. "I want you to stay here."

I straighten in his lap and look at him. "What? Why?"

"Because Jerome tends to undress you with his eyes, and he's persistent in his belief that eventually you'll cave to his advances. If he does that right now, I'll probably kill him. It'll be messy and I'll end up in jail, and you'll have to visit me for conjugal visits."

I don't know how I giggle after that call from earlier, but I do. Lincoln's mouth quirks into half a smile. "Besides, I know you hate him. You don't need to deal with him after what you just went through."

I face plant into his chest, and he wraps his arms around me. "Thank you," I murmur, before rearing up and kissing him. "Thank you."

He pushes my hair over my shoulder. "Don't thank me, sunshine. It's completely selfish. I don't want to go to jail."

Another laugh pulls from me, and he grins. "It might take a while, though. Will you stay until I get back?"

My fingers fidget with his tie, making sure it lays just right. "Will you take excellent notes for me to send to Cabot?"

"Of course."

"Then I'll stay."

He kisses me then. Long and slow and deep, before he groans and pulls back. "I have to go. I *hate* that I have to go."

I run my fingers over his jaw, before standing and slipping my feet back into my heels. "But you need to."

He follows me off the couch, adjusting his jacket. "You'll be okay?"

Placing my hand on his chest, I grin up at him. "I'll be fine." I glance pointedly at the clock on the wall. "You're going to be late. I know you hate that, too."

"I'm finding I hate it less and less when it means I get to spend more time with you." He bends and kisses me again before slapping my ass. "Be good." There's a cocky smirk on his lips as he steps out of the office.

I trail after him, heading to my desk when he hooks a left toward the elevators.

"What was that about?" I look up to find Giovanna watching me.

I should have told her about this a while ago, so I sigh and lean back in my chair. "I've been receiving disturbing phone calls for a while now. Security is aware of it, and they're working on figuring out who it is."

"What kind of disturbing phone calls? Are we talking *Black Christmas* from 1974 bad? *Scream* bad?"

I consider her question. "I don't think it's that bad, but I think it has the potential to get that bad. If they don't figure out who it is."

She nods, her lips tight. "And Mr. George was just checking on you?" The way she asks tells me she knows there's more to our relationship than either of us lets on.

"Yeah. Yes. He just wanted to make sure I was okay. Not too shaken up."

"Good. It's about time he became a decent human being."

A surprised laugh bursts out of me as I hear the elevator ding behind me. "Gi!"

She smirks. "What? It's true! That man has been an asshole the entire time I've known him. He's only gotten better since you started working with him."

Warmth glows in my chest. It feels like Giovanna just gave us her blessing, which is sort of weird because it's not as though we need it.

"Olivia Hart?"

I glance up at the delivery guy hovering near my desk. "Yes?"

"I've got a package for you." He holds out a clipboard. "If you could just sign here?"

I can feel Giovanna's eyes on me as I sign, and he slides a white box tied with a red ribbon onto my desk. I smile up at him. "Thank you."

"No problem." As soon as he's gone, Giovanna is out of her chair and next to me.

"You can't get personal deliveries here, Olivia. You should know better."

I roll my eyes at her. "Well, I didn't know I was getting a package. I didn't send this to myself, Gi."

She makes a disgruntled sound, but I ignore her, pulling the ribbon on the box to untie it. Maybe I shouldn't open this here? If it's from Linc, like I suspect, maybe I should wait until I get home. He might not want this to get around the office. But then why would he have sent it to me at work?

It's probably nothing. Or at least not something he'd mind other people seeing, otherwise he would have sent it to my house.

Decision made, I pull the lid off and Giovanna screams.

"Miss Hart?" The officer across the table from me calls my name to get my attention back on her. She's an older woman, gray at the temples of her slicked back brown hair. There are small wrinkles at the corner of her hazel eyes, and around her mouth, that I have the feeling are from frowning more than smiling. Right now, she has an apologetic wince on her face. "I'm sorry, I know this is a difficult time for you, but if you could just go over the events for me one more time. Please."

I swallow and nod, fisting my still shaking hands in my lap. "Of course, Detective Hayes. Whatever I can do to help." I don't tell her this is the fourth time we've gone over my version of events. She knows this. She's been with me the entire time. "The package was delivered at around-"

The door slams open and I feel him before I see him. It takes everything in me to stay where I am, to keep my hands clenched in fists, rather than reach for him.

"Sir, you can't be in here," Detective Hayes says.

Linc's hand comes to a rest on my shoulder, squeezing gently, before he takes the seat next to me. "I can be in here, actually. You are in my building questioning my employee. I have the right to know what exactly is going on."

"Actually, Mr. George. You don't have that right when it concerns a criminal investigation."

I'd been fine until now. Well, not fine, but keeping my emotions under control. But now, with him next to me, I'm on the verge of losing it entirely. I don't look away from Detective Hayes. "Actually, I don't mind if he stays." I tell her. "Unless it's... illegal for him to be here? I'd like him to stay."

She eyes both of us; her gaze lingering on Linc longer. I chance a glance at him, and see him staring her down, daring her to say he can't stay. She doesn't. Instead, she clears her throat and looks back down at the pad in her hand.

"Do you mind me asking what the nature of your relationship is?"

I stiffen at this question, but Linc just leans back in his chair relaxing into it, now that he knows she's going to let him stay. "I'm not sure if that is any of your business," he says, splaying his legs until his knee bumps against mine.

Detective Hayes probably thinks he's manspreading, trying to take up as much space as he can, but I know it's his way of offering support to me when he doesn't think more intimate touching is appropriate.

Detective Hayes's eyes flick up to us again and then back to her notepad. "Well, we had been thinking that this incident had to do with Miss Hart specifically, but if," here she hesitates before continuing. "If you have a more *intimate* relationship, then this might be an attack on you as well, Mr. George. Maybe a past lover trying to warn Miss Hart away from you. Someone you wronged in the past trying to scare you and her."

I glance over at him, wanting to see what he thinks of this, willing to follow his lead. I'd be lying if I didn't say that my heart was pounding in my chest, eager to see what his reaction is, what he's going to say. Will he claim our relationship? Reach over and lace his fingers with mine? Will he look Detective Hayes in the eye and say I'm his?

I realize with a start that I want that. Probably more than I've wanted anything. I want him to say on the record, 'she's mine.'

His gaze flicks in my direction, and then back at her. "Miss Hart is my employee. She works directly under me on behalf of my business partner, Mr. Cabot Harkness. Nothing more."

Well, shit. In this scenario, I'm not even his PA. I'm still working for Cabot Harkness. He's separated himself from me as much as he possibly can, while my desk is outside his office.

Detective Hayes looks at me, gauging my reaction to this statement, and *God,* I hope that the pain that's lancing through my chest isn't showing on my face. I'm pretty good at masking my emotions, at pushing them away. My hands are shaking again, and I know I'm blinking heavily, fighting back tears. Hopefully, she'll chalk that up to exhaustion after a scary situation.

"Is that true, Miss Hart?"

My tongue darts out to wet my lips as I nod. "Yes. That's true." I can feel his gaze on the side of my face, but I don't look at him. He's set the tone for the way this is going to go. Now the only thing I can do is power through. I shift until our knees are no longer pressed together, tuck my hands under my thighs to hide their shaking. "Mr. George is just my employer. Nothing more."

Damn. I'm a good liar. I almost believe me.

Though I guess if I look at it from this moment going forward, that is the truth.

"Liv? Livie! Where the fuck is she?" The knot in my chest, the one that I hadn't even realized I was holding onto so tightly loosens at the sound of Claire's voice in the hallway. I can't make out the indistinct murmur of the response. But I sure hear her shriek at whoever is keeping her from getting to me.

"I swear to God if you do not let me in to see her right now, I will take that taser and shove it so far up your ass-"

Oh, God, she's going to get herself arrested. I'm out of my chair and yanking the door open before either Detective Hayes or Lincoln can stop me. "Claire! Stop threatening the nice police officer. He's just doing his job."

She rushes toward me, her arms open wide. I let out a little choked sob as her arms close around me, my head buries itself in her shoulder. "I've got you, babe," she murmurs against my head. "I got you. You're fine. You're going to be fine."

I sob into her jacket, the events of the day suddenly overwhelming me with the arrival of my best friend and safe space. I don't lift my head from where it's resting as she glares over my shoulder.

"I'm taking her home. You've been talking to her for nearly three hours. That's long enough. Especially when she's the *victim* here."

There comes the murmur of voices, words I can't make out over my sniffles and then Detective Hayes says louder, "that's enough for today. If you think of anything else, Miss Hart, please call me."

I sniff and raise my head to give her a watery smile. "Sorry about the waterworks. You did an excellent job of keeping me on track. You're a phenomenal police officer, Detective Hayes. I hope you know that."

She stares at me for a moment, and then a faint flush spreads over her cheeks. "Yes, well, thank you for saying that, Miss Hart." She gives me a kind smile. "Take care of yourself."

I nod, flick my gaze at Linc, only to look away just as quickly as Claire guides me down the hall and back to my desk to gather my things. We've almost made it when his voice stops us. Well, it stops me, but not Claire, who takes a few more steps until she realizes I'm not following. "Miss Hart, may I speak to you in my office for a moment?"

I don't turn to look at him. Claire does, a glower on her face. "No. You may not. She's taking the rest of the afternoon off. Anything you have to say to her can wait until tomorrow… Or Thursday. Whichever day, she decides to come back."

"Claire," I mumble. "Don't."

"Don't what, Livie? This asshole has treated you like shit since the moment you started working for him. He can't give you one day to deal with an-"

"Claire's right," he cuts her off. My best friend's mouth hangs open at the concession, even though it's not true. He hasn't treated me like shit recently. He's been caring and thoughtful, even if it is behind closed doors. "Of course, Miss Hart can have the rest of the afternoon off. I merely wanted... I wanted a moment alone to check on her."

I turn around slowly, looking at him full on for the first time since he left the office this morning. I'm not sure what I was expecting after his words, maybe a little concern showing on his face, maybe something to show that he cares. But it's not there. His face is just *blank*. His hands tucked into his pockets, the picture of nonchalance.

He'd looked at me with more concern this morning after that phone call.

"May I have a moment of your time, Miss Hart?" My heart crumbles at his polite tone of voice, his careful wording. What I wouldn't give to hear him call me sunshine or hell, even Olivia, but he's back to Miss Hart.

I feel Claire looking between the two of us, reading both of our body language. I'm sure she knows exactly what I'm thinking. She's been my best friend since high school and she knows me as well as my mother. But I have no clue what she's reading off of him. I can't read a damn thing and I've had his cock in my mouth.

"I think I just want to go home." I say softly, looking away from him, only to be pulled right back in. His jaw tightens, and then he nods once.

"Very well. I'll call a car to take you home."

"No. Thank you, Mr. George, but we'll just take an Uber." His jaw tightens even more as I offer him a small, tense smile. "Wouldn't want anyone to think you're playing favorites with your employees, now, would we?"

I turn on my heel and move the short distance to my desk, scoop my purse and jacket and the stride out of the office, Claire trailing me.

But I am definitely done for the day.

22
Lincoln

I am pissed.

At the cops currently tramping through my fucking office, like the answer to the mystery of whoever threatened my girl is going to be in the accounting department.

I'm pissed at the fucker who sent her such a grisly gift.

I'm pissed at the girl herself for not giving me the chance to make sure she's okay, to talk to her, to take care of her. No, she just had to stomp out of here with tears on her cheeks and pain in her eyes without giving me the chance to explain, to make her see. She wouldn't even let me make sure she made it home safe, refusing my offer of a driver.

I'm pissed at myself for the major fuck up I created in that room when faced with the opportunity to claim Olivia, the only fucking thing I've wanted to do since I laid eyes on her, and I ruined it. As soon as Detective Hayes said this might be happening to my girl because of me; I knew it was true.

Right now, as far as this asshole knows, I'm just fucking her. What would he do if he found out what's really happening? That I crave her, want her, need her. She's the best part of my fucking day and not only when I'm fucking her mouth or her pussy. No, every fucking moment I spend with her is a goddamn gift. She makes everything better. Makes my life worth living. I hadn't even realized how much I needed someone like her. No, not like her. How much I needed her, specifically. Only her.

It's time to admit to myself that I'm falling in love with Olivia Hart.

Whoever this is, they can't know that. Not if I'm the reason this is happening to her.

Just about the only person I'm not pissed at is Claire. Even when she was tearing me a new one, I knew she was doing it because she cares about Olivia as much as I do, maybe more. And thank God, she raised a fuss and got her out of there. Four hours is too long, especially when Olivia is the *victim*.

The elevator stops and the doors slide open. I stride down the hall and open the door to our security center without knocking. I called down earlier to warn them I would be coming and what I needed to see.

The lanky blond guy behind the counter stands up from his chair and salutes me, like I'm a goddamn general, before his cheeks go pink and he drops his hands. "Sorry, sir."

I grunt in response. "You have what I need?"

"What? Oh, yes, sir. I do. If you want to-" He motions for me to come around the desk until I can see his screen. I do and he waits until I'm situated before hitting the spacebar to make the video play. It's not very long. The way the camera is situated, it looks right over Olivia's shoulder. I try not to think about how at certain angles the security guards might get an eyeful of her tits, but make a note to have the camera position changed.

I watch as a man approaches her desk carrying a white box with a red ribbon tied around it. It looks like one of those boxes from a fancy flower shop. Her lips curl into a pleased smile as she signs for the delivery. *Fuck.* She probably thought I'd sent her something.

Olivia hesitates before pulling the ribbon, like she isn't sure she wants to open it with Giovanna hovering over her. And when she lifts off the lid, my stomach lurches. Nestled in a bed of white glittering plastic grass, the kind put in children's Easter baskets, is a heart, bleeding into the white, staining it pink and red. At the top of a box is a piece of paper that says in bold black writing, *A heart for Miss Hart.*

I can't tell if it's a threat, or a really fucked up love note to my girl, but it doesn't matter either way. Because she's mine, and I'm going to fuck up whoever the hell this is.

My cell phone rings, and I yank it from my inner suit jacket, jabbing the answer button when I see who it is. "You better have some good fucking news for me."

Lance sighs on the other end of the line, sounding as frustrated as I feel. "I don't. I tracked down the bike messenger who brought it. His boss contacted him, picked up the package on the front stoop of a condemned building. I spoke to the boss, and the person paid cash, no credit card."

I swear and run a hand down my face. "Did you get a description?"

"I did. It was a man, wearing one of those face masks from the pandemic, and a ball cap for the Guardians. Not too tall, shorter than me, and on the small side. Like he works out, but not to bulk up. Brown or dark blue eyes."

I card my hand through my hair. "None of that means anything. There must be thousands of guys that fit that description. We didn't get a name or anything?"

"Nope."

"Fuck."

"Yeah."

"How the hell did it even make it to her desk, Lance? All deliveries and mail go to your office first to avoid this very fucking thing." I feel feral, like a wounded wild animal snapping at everyone and anyone who has the misfortune of getting anywhere near me.

My head of security sounds pissed as hell as he says, "I have no clue, but I'll find out. And whoever let this slip by will be dealt with."

By that he means fired, but if he beats the shit out of them first, I have no complaints about it. "Good."

He says something to someone else on the other end of the line. "My guy just let me know Olivia made it home okay. Claire took her to a coffee shop, presumably to help her calm down, before taking her home to her mother. Caroline doesn't need the added stress."

Something itchy crawls over my skin, like there is no reason for Lance to know so much about Oliva and her mother, like he shouldn't know her well enough to presume anything about her actions. I have to talk myself down from snapping at him all over again.

It's his job to know these kinds of things. It's what I pay him for.

"Thank you," I say, running a hand down my face. Only vaguely aware of the security guard watching me with wide eyes. I nod at him and head out of the security office.

"No problem, boss. I'll have my guys stay on her, keep an eye out, just in case. You should get some rest. It's late."

Is it late? I look around with some surprise to find that night has indeed fallen. "Yeah, maybe I'll do that."

The office is still full of people. Cops are still interviewing my employees. What they're hoping to uncover I have no idea, but it seems like everyone knows Liv and has a kind word or a story about her. The few conversions I overhear tell me that no one has any ideas about who would do this to her.

I should probably wait until they all go home, but I can't stay put. Everything is urging me toward a small robin's egg blue house on the outskirts of town. I want to see Liv, to hold her, to let her know I fucked up earlier. I should have told Detective Hayes what she means to me.

The last thing I want to do is hurt her.

All I can see is the pain on her face as she told me she didn't want me to play favorites with my employees. Yeah. I fucked up.

Despite that I want to go to her, I don't. She's at home with her mother and it's late. The last thing she needs is me showing up at this hour, making her mother wonder why I'm there. I've already done that once. I don't need to do it again.

I'll text her when I get home and make the trip across town tomorrow first thing.

My determination to give Olivia space lasts for as long as I take to go home, shower, and change into a pair of sweats and a hoodie. Almost as soon as I'm dressed, I'm out of the house again, climbing into the car I rarely drive, and heading to Olivia's.

I'll just park down the street from her house and keep an eye on it to make sure nothing else happens. I ignore how much of a creeper that makes me. Frankly, I just don't give a shit. I don't care that Lance has someone watching her house already. *I* need to make sure she's okay.

I park two houses down from Liv's in front of a two-story cottage that looks like it's seen better days. At around ten, Claire leaves, and I settle in to watch Olivia's house for the rest of the night. I expect the lights to turn off after Claire leaves. But they stay on. *Every* light in the house stays on, even the ones upstairs in her bedroom. I see the shadow of Liv's silhouette pass by the windows, one pale hand checking the latch to make sure they're locked.

She does this repeatedly—at least five times—while I watch. My heart aches. But at least I can tell she's not physically hurt. I tip my head back against the headrest and keep my eyes on the lit up windows, wishing like hell I was inside.

I shouldn't have left her alone today. As soon as I heard that voice on the other line, I should have bundled her into my office and never let her fucking go. Especially when the voice threatened to tell her the thing I've been keeping from her. Hearing that scared me more than the creepy electronic voice.

How they even know about that is a mystery. Though it gives us a direction to look. Because there are only a handful of people privy to the information they threatened me with. Though anyone with access to our H&G files would have been able to find out if they just did some digging.

Fuck. How have I not thought of that? Olivia would just need to flip through a few pages of the Moreau file to find out that I've been lying to her.

I can't let that happen.

Pulling my gaze from Liv's house, I grab my phone and type out a text to Giovanna, telling her to grab the Moreau file and put it on my desk. When I get to the office tomorrow, I'll put it in the locked drawer that only I have a key to and leave it there until it's needed.

Which, with any luck, won't be for a very, very long time.

By the time midnight rolls around, all the lights in her house are still on, and I can't stay put. I slide my phone into my coat pocket and push open my car door.

23
Olivia

Claire stays with me until I kick her out at around ten. My mom is asleep. Harvey is long gone, and I am exhausted. But I can't sleep. I've walked around my house, checking to make sure all of my windows and doors are locked at least five times, but it's not enough to make me feel safe. I'm not sure I'll ever feel safe again.

My mom is asleep in her bed, chest rising and falling gently as I curl up in the corner of the couch. She doesn't know about the delivery I received today. I'd made it clear to Claire that I don't want to worry her any more than necessary, and this isn't necessary, not yet.

Claire argued the entire way home, but eventually relented. I know I won't be able to keep it from my mom forever. I'll tell her when we have more information, when we know who it is, and I can give her good news along with the bad.

I sit bolt upright at the sound of a quiet knock on my door, heart thundering in my chest as sudden panic overtakes me. I must have dozed off, because for one moment I'm not totally sure what's going on, but then the memory of the box containing a bloody heart being delivered to my desk hits me and I scramble up to my feet. My fingers close around the baseball bat I keep for occasions such as this, and I edge toward the door, glancing over my shoulder to make sure my mom is still asleep.

The knock comes again, and a glance at the clock on the stove tells me it's nearing midnight. My heart hammers harder in my chest as I slowly creep toward the door, lifting on my toes to check the peephole. My breath whooshes out of me and I open the door, but don't relent my grip on my bat.

"What are you doing here?"

Lincoln looks up at me, dark circles under his eyes. "I wanted to make sure you're okay."

My gaze narrows. "I'm fine."

Linc's slate blue eyes drift down to the bat in my hand and then back up to meet mine. "You don't look fine." I don't know what to say to that, because he's probably right, and I don't feel fine either. "Can I come in?"

I step back from the door, granting him entrance. As soon as the slab of wood clicks shut, he pulls me into his arms, head pressing into my shoulder, face against my neck. The bat clatters to the ground as my arms wind around him, clutching at his coat.

We stand there in the foyer, just holding each other, soaking in the comfort of the hug. He pulls back, hands sliding up to frame my face, gaze running over me like he's making sure I'm not hurt.

"Are you okay?"

A humorless laugh pulls from my chest before I face plant between his pecs. "It's all relative, isn't it?"

Lincoln cards his fingers through my hair, pressing me into him, as my arms wind around his waist. "I suppose it is," he murmurs against the top of my head. "Liv, I'm sorry I-"

I shake my head and pull away from him so quickly he doesn't have a chance to stop me. "Don't. You don't have to explain. I understand."

I fold my arms over my stomach as I pad into the kitchen, flicking on the electric kettle more for something to do than because I want tea. Lincoln trails behind me, leans a shoulder against the frame of the wide door. "You do?"

I lift a shoulder. "Sure, I'm technically still your employee. It wouldn't look good for me to be dating my boss. People would question if I actually deserve my position." I'm halfway lying to myself *for* him, making it seem like he did this for me, and not for him. But I don't have the energy to be upset about it. I'm wound tighter than a spring, ready to jump at the slightest provocation, and I can already tell I won't sleep tonight. I need to preserve what energy I have.

"Liv." I glance up at him before turning to pull two mugs down from the cabinet. He's behind me in a flash, pressing me into the counter, lips on my neck, hands braced on either side of my hips. "Will you let me explain?"

I shake my head. "No."

"No?"

"No. I already said you don't need to. I'm not mad. We agreed to try, that you'd give me more than you were before. And you are, Linc. I see that." I turn in his arms and fist his shirt in my hands to emphasize my point. "It's okay that we can't proclaim to the world that we're together. I understand your reservations about that. You're still here, with me every night, hanging out with my mom, flirting with her to make her feel young again. You talk to me. It's not just about fucking like it was before. Maybe in the future, when I'm back to working under Cabot, or hell maybe I'll move to a new job entirely, then you'll feel ready to give me even more. I'll be ready when you are."

His mouth opens like he's going to respond, but then he snaps it shut and his jaw tics, keeping whatever he was going to say behind his teeth. "It's okay," I whisper to him. "I understand."

He gives a jerky nod and then reaches behind me to flick off the kettle. I glance over my shoulder at it, and then up to him, one brow arched in question. "You don't need tea, sunshine. You need sleep. Come on, let me put you to bed."

The command is far gentler than any he's given to me before, but it doesn't make it any less effective. I let him guide me up the stairs and into my rarely used bedroom, where he pulls out a pair of sleep shorts and an oversized t-shirt for me to change into. That done, he drops a kiss on my forehead and leaves me to change, while he goes back downstairs to check on my mom and turn off the lights.

I brush my teeth and then just stand in the middle of my room, waiting for him, exhausted and dazed, staring out the window at the dark street. Lincoln's hands on my shoulders pull me over to the bed, where he tucks me in before stripping and joining me. He sighs as he pulls me into his chest, one arm around my waist, the other around my shoulders with his hand buried in my hair, holding me against him. One of his thick legs wedges between mine, holding me in place. "Okay?" he asks, his voice soft and sleepy.

I hum my assent and wiggle closer to him, eyes falling shut as my breathing evens out. It feels so right being in his arms, so safe. "See?" I murmur. "You're already giving me more."

His arms tighten around me, almost reflexively. "This is nice," I sigh as I slip into oblivion, but not before I hear him whisper into the top of my head.

"It is."

I wake up cradled against a hard body for the first time in... years. At least four, probably longer. Sure, I dated while I was in college, but it was more along the lines of late night hookups that never stayed over. I didn't have time for anything else. Certainly not a full-time boyfriend and lazy mornings and sleeping in.

I still don't have a lot of time for things like that. It's part of why I haven't minded so much that Lincoln kept his distance, didn't push for more than he could give. My entire focus has to be on my mother for the next few months, at least.

Lincoln and I have slept together, but he's always out of the bed when I wake up, already halfway ready before I've even stretched and blinked my eyes open. I've never begrudged him that. He's busy too, and since we're trying to keep things relatively hush hush, it makes sense that he'd slip out with the dawn.

The closest we've gotten to waking up together is when I stayed at his house, but even then he'd obviously been up for hours before I made my way to his kitchen.

I thought I didn't need it. But this is... nice.

Really fucking nice.

Lincoln is curled around me, head pressed against my shoulder, one heavy leg draped over mine, both arms wrapped securely around me, like I'd tried to escape in the middle of the night, and he'd pinned me down to keep me from fleeing.

I blink against the light streaming through my window, momentarily confused. I never wake up when it's light out. Haven't for years. I'm wound too tight to have a late morning. And I usually need to check on my mother a few times during the night. I don't even have to set an alarm to do it. My body just wakes me up every two hours like clockwork, but not last night.

No, I slept straight through the night.

And God, it feels amazing.

So freaking amazing.

I stretch a little, arching against Lincoln, and he tightens his grip on me, nuzzling into my hair and taking a deep inhale before he settles again. I wish I could let him sleep, but I need to get up and in order to do that, he needs to let me go.

"Linc," I whisper, fingers trailing over the forearms banded just below my breasts under my t-shirt. "Linc, I need to get up."

He shakes his head. "No. You're staying right here." His voice is all husky and sexy with an early morning roughness. It makes my thighs shift against each other, but I ignore it. I have responsibilities.

"My mom-"

"Is fine, sunshine," He sighs, rolling me over so I'm on my back. I continue the motion until I'm facing him. "I got up about two hours ago and checked on her. Harvey is already here. They're having coffee and scones."

My heart clenches in my chest. "You did that?"

Half his mouth quirks into a smile as he brushes a strand of honey blond hair out of my face. "Of course I did. You needed sleep. I know you don't get nearly enough."

I tip my chin up and ignore that we both have morning breath to give him a soft, sweet kiss. "Thank you." His hand tightens in my hair as he pulls me in for a second kiss. I wait for him to deepen it, turn it from lazy, soft sipping to something more carnal. I'm prepared to tell him we can't have sex under the same roof as my dying mother. But after one slow, languid kiss, he pulls back, presses his forehead to mine and seems content to just lay here with me. Despite the stiff length I can feel poking my thigh.

"How are you feeling this morning?" he murmurs.

I don't meet his gaze, instead watching my fingers brush over the light dusting of hair on his chest. "Okay, I guess. I just wish we knew who was doing this."

He hums and pulls me closer. "The cops will figure it out, sunshine." He doesn't sound convinced. "And if they can't, I have my security team working on it, too."

I frown. "What would they be able to do that the police wouldn't?"

"There are less legal ways of tracking down stalkers. Lance and his team are looking into it."

I nod and slip my hand around his waist, burrowing into his chest as he curls his arms tight around me. "You think it has something to do with you, don't you?"

"Yes," he admits, fingers stroking through my hair, carefully working through any snags he finds. "You worked for Cabot for a month before you started receiving any sort of threatening messages or items."

I tip my head up to meet his gaze. "I worked for you for two weeks before anything happened. Maybe it's not related to you at all. Maybe it's someone I met-"

He cuts me off with a kiss, one that has me moaning into his mouth, but when he pulls back, I continue. "What if it's Jerome? That guy gives me the creeps."

He makes a noise between a chuckle and a growl, like he can decide if he wants to be angry about how Jerome so blatantly ogled me the first time we met and has continued to do so at every meeting we have, or if he needs to laugh it off. "You and me both, sunshine. But I don't think he'd do this."

My brows draw low, and I let out a breath. "I didn't... Um, I didn't say anything because-"

Lincoln draws back when I trail off, slate blue eyes running over my face. "What happened?"

My nose scrunches as I look up at the ceiling to avoid his gaze as the words spill from me. "He may have called a few times to ask me... well, not on a date, because he's married. But I guess just to fuck him. He was pretty persistent there for a while."

"Why didn't you tell me?" Lincoln grinds out, hands flexing where they're holding me.

I lift a shoulder. "I handled it. Told him a firm no every time he asked. Didn't leave room for doubt. It seemed like he got the hint eventually and stopped asking." A little shudder rolls through me. "Maybe he just changed tactics, though."

I don't know what he would think would happen if he scared me away from my job, from Lincoln. It's not like I would just fall into bed with him, but it's a possibility. I'll call Detective Hayes later and tell her. Maybe it'll help.

But then Linc is rolling, reaching for his phone on the bedside table, and I watch as he pulls up a text chain with Lance. He only sends two words: Jerome Kline. Lance sends back: On it.

Lincoln sets his phone back on the bedside table, and rolls back toward me, only to find me watching with an arched brow. He shrugs. "He'll look into it. If there's anything there, he'll find it. If not... We'll handle him in a different way."

He sounds so menacing when he says that, that I can't help the giggle that burst out of me. "You really have that whole evil genius thing down. Did you know that?"

He grins at me. "You think I'm a genius?"

"I think *you* think you're pretty smart," I quip back. He throws his head back and laughs, before lunging forward, hands slipping under my t-shirt to tickle my sides while I thrash under him, wildly. He's relentless though, continuing tickling until I get my legs around his waist and both his wrists in my hands, holding them wide of my body.

"Stop," I gasp out through giggles. "No more. I can't take it."

I know he could break my hold if he wanted to, but he doesn't. Instead, he flattens his palms on the bed next to my head and rolls his hips, grinding against me. "I think you can take anything I give you, sunshine."

A soft whimper pulls from my chest, and he grins wickedly down at me. God, he's so handsome like this... he looks... happy. It's with a jolt that I realize I don't think I've actually seen him happy before.

Maybe he needed this as much as I did. Maybe he needs a moment, a break to just *be*.

I release my grip on his wrist to trace the outline of his smile, almost reverently. It only lasts for a moment since it breaks when he puckers his lips against my fingertips, trailing soft kisses over them. "Are you happy?" I blurt out. My cheeks immediately flush with embarrassment, and my hand drops to my chest. "Nevermind."

Lincoln drops down until his chest presses against mine. He weaves his fingers through my hair, holding my head steady as he drops gentle kisses all over my face, murmuring words between them. "I am happy, sunshine. You make me happy. A lot happier than I have the right to be." A knot forms between my brows at that seeming offhand comment. "I'm just soaking it in while it lasts."

The little bubble of peace I'd been in ruptures, and I feel my body go stiff, even though I will it not to. The backs of my eyes sting as he pulls back, looking down at me with a furrow that matches mine. "I didn't mean it like that, Liv," he tries to reassure me.

Swallowing, I push on his shoulders, trying to get him to move off me, but he stays put. "Sure you didn't, Linc."

"Olivia. What I'm saying is I'm an asshole. I'm lucky to have someone as sweet and kind and caring as you in my life. But I know at some point I'm going to fuck this up. I'm going to do something that is going to piss you off, and you are going to leave me. Rightfully."

I stare up at him, torn between wanting to tell him that will never happen, to reassure him with words of love, because I *do* love him. I've tried my hardest not to let it get to this point, not yet. But I can't help it. I love him even if it makes my heart throb in my chest. Even though I can tell he's not fully in this with me.

But I also want to point out that he's already putting distance between us. "This will never work," I mutter, and watch as his face crumples. It makes my heart hurt, seeing the pain I just caused him.

"Liv, sunshine-"

"Let me finish, okay? Let me say what I need to say, please." His jaw tightens, but he gives a jerky nod. "This is never going to work if you keep one foot out the door, Lincoln. If you keep waiting for the other shoe to drop, keep waiting for me to come to my senses and leave you." I curl my fingers over his shoulders and give a little shake. "I'm in this. Fully and completely in this with you. You need to give me the same."

He sighs, forehead dropping to rest between my breasts as my arms slide around his shoulders, holding him to me. "I'm trying, Liv. So fucking hard. The last thing I want to do is hurt you."

I blow out a breath, lacing my fingers in the hair at the base of his skull. "Me too."

He lifts his head and meets my gaze. I'm entranced by what I see there, a reflection of what I feel in my heart, all warm gooey feelings. His lips part like he might give voice to those feelings and my heart flutters, but then his phone chimes with an incoming text message and the moment breaks.

He sighs, kisses me one more time and rolls off me, reaching for the device. Whatever he finds there has a furrow forming between his brows. "I have to go," he says, distracted, but then he lifts his gaze to mine and a smirk on his lips. "Duty calls."

Fuck. *Work.* It's Thursday and late in the morning, so I'm sure everyone is already there. I move to get up, throwing the blanket off me. "I'll get ready so we can go together." But Lincoln is already pushing me back against the pillows, tucking the blanket around me.

"No, you're staying home today. Rest. Relax. Hang out with your mom. I'll call you later." He drops a kiss to my forehead and then turns to gather up his clothing, yanking on his sweatpants first and then his t-shirt. "If you're up for it, would you want to come to my house tonight? I'll cook."

I blink up at him. "You cook?"

He chuckles, low and sweet, as he bends at his waist to kiss me again. "I cook," he murmurs against my lips. "I'll call the night nurse so you can stay."

I shake my head. "No, I don't want to impose."

"It's not imposing, sunshine. I'm offering because I'm a selfish bastard who wants to spend all night fucking you in a proper bed. Not on a couch or on my desk. A bed. *My bed.* Since we can't do it here."

I huff out a laugh and nod. "Fine. Yes. I will come to your house."

He beams down at me before burying his face in my neck and kissing me repeatedly while I shriek under him. When he pulls back, he reaches for his wallet, pulling out a single key and pressing it into my hand. "Just in case I run late tonight," he murmurs against my lips as he kisses me again. "The code to the alarm is 0228. You have thirty seconds to punch it in, okay?"

I nod my understanding as I finger the key. "Do I get to keep this? Is it mine now?"

He bites his lip like he's trying to smother a grin. "Yeah, baby, you can keep it."

I blow out a breath, feeling light in my chest. "That's kind of a big deal, isn't it?" I whisper.

"It is," he whispers back, but it ends on an oof as I lunge up, throw my arms around his neck, and pull him back to the bed with me, peppering kisses over every part of him I can reach while he laughs.

"You should stay," I urge between kisses. "Stay."

He groans. "You're too tempting, sunshine. But I have stuff I need to do today. Maybe if you're very lucky, we can both take tomorrow off."

I regard him with wide eyes. "Like play hooky together?"

He bobs his head. "Yeah."

"You're a bad influence, Lincoln George. What will my boss say?" I tease.

Another laugh bursts out of him. "I think he'll be just fine." He smacks a kiss on my lips, then another on my neck. "I have to go. I'll see you tonight." He taps the tip of my nose as my lower lip pushes out. "No pouting, baby. I'll work today so we can play tomorrow. Deal?"

I roll my eyes and sigh. "Fiiiine."

He chuckles as he scoops his zip up hoodie off the chair. As soon as he opens the door, I'm on my feet, trailing behind him to the front door and out on the porch.

He turns to face me with an arched brow. "I thought I told you to stay in bed."

I shrug. "Just kissing my man goodbye before work."

He growls and lunges toward me, kissing me senseless with my arms around his shoulders and his arm looped around my back. I gasp when he smacks my ass as he pulls away. "Go inside, Liv. I'm the only one who gets to see you like this."

I pirouette back toward my door. "Well, you and Harvey." I can't help but tease him about how he thought me and Harvey were a couple when we first met.

"Brat," he chuckles, walking backward down my walkway.

I wiggle my fingers at him as I push open the door, feeling his eyes on me until I close the door between us.

I'm so glad he came over last night, so glad he didn't just leave our relationship the way it was after he didn't tell Detective Hayes that we're together. I draw a deep breath through my nose as I head to the kitchen to pour a cup of coffee, even though I don't feel like I need the caffeine.

For the first time in a long time, I feel refreshed, like I actually got enough sleep. And despite what happened yesterday, I feel lighter than air.

I suppose the love of a good man can do that.

24
Lincoln

"You're sure you want to do this?" My gaze trails from the window up to meet Lance's eyes in the rearview mirror.

"I don't have much of a choice, do I?"

He looks back at the road and shakes his head. "Look, it's really not any of my business, but Olivia-Miss Hart," he corrects himself when I all but growl at him for using her name. "She doesn't deserve this, Linc. You know she doesn't deserve this."

I nod. "I know."

"You need to tell her."

I do. I do need to tell her. But I can't. Not yet. Not until I know I'm not going to lose her because of this. I need her more than I need air in my lungs and food in my belly. She's the only light in my life, my sunshine. I can't lose her.

"Not yet," is all I say as I look out the window.

"When?"

I don't have a good answer for that. I'll never

have a good answer for that, because breaking Liv's heart isn't high on my list of things to do. Things are so fucking good with us right now, despite the asshole stalking her. I want to savor what we have, give it time to grow into something with solid roots before I have to try to knock it down with my bullshit.

No, I don't have any answer for him, so I revert to my asshole mode. "I don't pay you to question me, Lance. I pay you to protect me. Do your fucking job and shut the hell up."

I hear the steering wheel creak as he tightens his grip on it. "You added protecting Olivia to my list of duties, Lincoln. This is me doing my job."

Well, shit. "You know your job description doesn't extend to her emotional well-being."

His jaw tics. "I say it does."

I want to fire him right on the spot. I hate that he's pushing this. That he's calling me out on my bullshit. He's not wrong about any of it. Everything he's said to me is the truth. Everything he's pointed out, I've thought to myself. I just don't want to hear it from him, either.

When I'm with Olivia, I can push the guilt away. I can convince myself that it's worth it if I get to be with her. I bask in her light and in her presence and fool myself into believing that what we have is strong enough. But when I'm alone, that's when the voice of my father comes out, snarling at me that I'm not good enough, that I will never be good enough. That I'm a failure.

I've worked my whole life to prove him wrong. It's part of why I'm in this goddamn fucked up mess. I hate I might prove him right.

The car slows to a stop outside Niche, and I eye the facade of the building like it will tell me what's waiting for me inside. It doesn't.

"Liv is coming to my house tonight. I want you to go pick her up, make sure she arrives okay," I say, still staring out the window at the happy couples moving in and out of the restaurant.

"Whatever you say, boss." Lance doesn't sound happy about this in the least.

"It goes without saying, or at least it should, but don't say anything to her about this." I know there's a hint of pleading in my voice, and I know Lance can hear it. He meets my gaze in the rearview mirror and nods, even though I can tell he hates it.

I do too.

I push open the door and step out of the car, smoothing my suit jacket as I go.

Alicia's already at the table in the middle of the restaurant, a romantic candlelit table. She's wearing a cream-colored dress that shows off her cleavage. Her hair is styled in soft curls around her face, her lips painted a dark red. She smiles as I approach the table, seemingly happy to see me. Her head tilts, offering me her cheek to kiss, but I ignore it. Even that relatively innocent sign of affection makes me feel uncomfortable now.

Her eyes narrow as I squeeze her shoulder and take my seat across from her, looking around at the other diners before meeting her dark brown eyes. "Why are we here?"

She arches a brow and takes a sip of her white wine. "It's nice to see you too, Linc."

I sigh, finger the glass of bourbon already at my place setting. Alicia knows what I like to drink. "Hello, Al. It's nice to see you. What are we doing here?"

She chuckles and shakes her head. "I thought a change of pace from our normal Chinese take-out eaten at your kitchen island would be nice. We used to go out all the time."

I lift a shoulder and look away from her, taking a drink of alcohol that burns so good down my throat and into my belly. I'll only have one drink. I want to be sober when I go home to Olivia. I have plans for her.

"We decided that the media attention was too much, Alicia. Why are we here *now*?"

Her lips thin out as she meets my gaze, then she reaches into her bag, hanging off the back of her chair and pulls out a small black box. My stomach lurches as she slides it across the table to me. "You know why we're here, Lincoln. I think it's time you asked me, don't you?"

I swallow thickly, eyes latched onto the box, before I scan the restaurant again. There in the corner a camera, a photographer setup to capture the moment. I have no doubt that the image will be all over the media sites tomorrow. *Breaker's Point Bachelor Finally Settles Down.*

I don't reach for the box. "I already asked you. You already said yes." Giving her the ring weeks ago had been the equivalent, right? Sure, I hadn't made a big deal about it, because this isn't supposed to be a big deal. It's just… business.

She leans forward, bracing her forearms on the table. "We need to make a public announcement, Lincoln. We need the world to know that this is happening."

She means Liv. Liv needs to know this is happening. This is her fucked up way of forcing me to tell Olivia. Either I do it tonight, or Liv will find out tomorrow along with the rest of the city.

Alicia is one of my oldest friends, but I hate her at this moment. *Oh, how I hate her.*

She scowls. "Don't look at me like that. It hurts my feelings."

I down the rest of my drink. "I don't know how you expect me to look at you. You're forcing my hand here."

She scoffs. "I'm doing no such thing. This is what we agreed to, Lincoln. If you're feeling guilty or upset, that's on you. You chose to have your little fling, knowing how this would end."

My hand tightens on the glass and it's a wonder it doesn't shatter. *Little fling.* To hear what I feel for Olivia reduced to those two words is enraging. It's so much fucking more than that.

But Alicia is right. I did this to myself.

I feel sick. I'm going to throw up at any fucking moment, all over this fancy restaurant. What a headline that would be.

"It's only going to get worse if you drag it out, keep her hanging on. Don't you think?" Alicia says, reaching across the table and covering my hand with hers as if she's sympathetic to my plight.

I flinch away from her, tucking my hand into my lap where she can't reach it. "I don't see why we need to rush anything."

Alicia gives me a look like I'm smarter than this. "Lincoln, we agreed to this. *You* agreed to this. It's not fair to her. You're lying to her, promising her a future she can't have."

I shake my head. "No. I never promised her... anything." My stomach lurches and I have to look away from the beautiful woman across from me. I should have known something was up. I should have known when she suggested dinner at Niche that she was planning something.

Sure, we meet for dinner every Thursday, but it's usually at her house or mine. We don't need the gossip rags catching on to our relationship, turning it into something it's not. It's worked in both of our favors, especially since we haven't had a sexual relationship since sophomore year in college. This way we can sleep with whoever we want and keep our business arrangement.

Alicia tsks, and leans back in her chair, lifting her wineglass to her lips before setting it down. "You might not have promised her anything, Lincoln, but believe me, she is thinking about it. Thinking about a future with you, what that's going to look like once you go public about your relationship. Hell, she's probably imagining the wedding, the house, the kids. She seems like the kind of girl that would do that."

The slight curl of Alicia's lip tells me just what she thinks about those types of women. The ones who dream of a family, or security, of a happy home and a happy life. Alicia is only driven by professional success, by taking what her father built and growing it, making it better, putting her own stamp on it. I used to be the same. Though my focus was proving my father wrong, on building something of my own. It's part of why we became what we are. We shared similar goals.

Shared being the operative word here. Now, I care less about proving my father wrong, and more about giving Liv everything she needs to be happy.

The waiter arrives with the starter salads and Alicia smiles her thanks at him before she levels me with a look. "You can't get out of this, Lincoln. It's a binding contract. You know that. You're really only hurting her here by not telling her."

I can't help but notice that Alicia only refers to Olivia as *her* or *she*, like saying her name would humanize her.

"And if she really cares about you like you say she does, then maybe it doesn't have to end in disaster. You know I don't give a fuck what you do after. If she loves you, she can accept this. It'll be unorthodox, but in these modern times."

I blink at her, wanting to laugh and cry all at the same time. She has no fucking clue what she's talking about. I know Olivia loves me. I can see it shining out of her pretty honey eyes when she looks at me, all soft and sweet. She hasn't said it yet though, hasn't voiced those three words out loud, but I know she feels it. The same way I feel them for her.

The knowledge is like a gunshot to the chest, so powerful I nearly double up on myself, curl over my plate of lightly dressed greens and gasp for breath.

I love Olivia Hart.

I've probably loved her since the first I laid eyes on her, ill-fitting clothes and all.

I can't lose her. I can't.

Alicia just watches me. When I meet her blue eyes, she lifts a shoulder. "We can talk to her together. I'll explain everything, what we need and what it means for your relationship. If she's as level-headed as you make her out, she'll listen, she'll understand."

I let Alicia's words soothe me, let them spark a hint of hope in my chest. Liv is level-headed when she needs to be. She'll at least hear us out, hear *me* out. She'll be upset, understandably, but she'll see that this can work.

She'll have all the parts of me that matter. The ones that make up a relationship. She'll have my body, my heart, and my soul. She'll have every bit of me I can give her.

And Alicia will have the rest.

I think about Olivia telling me about her father, about how he treated her mother, showing up once a week. I think about how Olivia said her mother loved him enough to take those bits of him he was willing to give, but Caroline Hart loved Olivia more. When the assholes of the town started treating Liv like trash, Caroline had enough, and moved her daughter across the country, leaving the man she loved behind. Liv hasn't seen her father since.

But this… we wouldn't be like that. I could live with Olivia, be with her every second of the day. Fall asleep next to her, wake up with her cradled in my arms. We could be a family, a real family in everything but name.

It could work. She'll see that we can make this work. She'll understand that I made this deal before her. Before I realized what it felt like to truly love someone.

She loves you.

She'll understand.

Doesn't make it any easier, knowing the blow I'm going to deal her, knowing a piece of her heart will fracture. I just hope she'll let me put it back together when this is over, that once she sees it's the only way, she'll forgive me and let me build a life for her we can both thrive in.

You're lying to yourself. That voice sounds suspiciously like Caroline Hart. No idea why Olivia's mom is speaking in my head right now. But I suspect that she's right.

Alicia gives me a blinding smile as the server comes to whisk away our salad plates. "So we're in agreement, then? We'll go forward with the plan? Tell her sooner rather than later?" I give a jerky nod and she beams at me before nudging the velvet box in my direction. "Good. Now ask me."

I pick up the ring and flick it open, hating every second of this. My lips part, but she cuts me off. "Down on one knee, Lincoln. Make it look good."

My body makes robotic movements as I push up from my chair and round the table. Alicia has a look on her face like she has no clue what I'm doing, and I'm sure I look equally as dazed. My knee hits the floor.

It'll be okay, I think to myself as I hold the box between us. *It'll be fine,* I reassure my racing heart as I say, "marry me?" to the sound of a camera going off rapid fire. *She'll forgive you,* I lie as Alicia throws her arms around my shoulders and accepts, before kissing me on my lips in front of so many witnesses.

When I slip the ring on her finger, my nose burns, and my vision blurs as panic claws at my chest. Alicia keeps hold of my hand, tugging me into her body for a hug. "It'll be okay, you'll see. Everything will work out like it's supposed to."

"I can't lose her, Alicia. I fucking can't." My voice is hoarse with emotion as I pull away from her.

She squeezes my hand, giving me a sympathetic smile. I look down at where she's still holding me, at the ring on her finger. The ring that Olivia helped me pick out.

I am such a fucking asshole.

I can't lose Olivia.

But I think I'm going to.

25
Olivia

The sound of the door opening wakes me. I hadn't meant to fall asleep on the couch. No, I meant to get naked and kneel in the bedroom for Linc to find when he got home, but these late nights and worry over my mother has made me even more tired than usual.

I'm so groggy it takes me a moment to realize that there are two sets of footsteps entering the house, two voices echoing in the foyer. One I recognize, as dear to me as my mothers, the other is vaguely familiar and female.

Don't jump to conclusions, Liv. You know he meets with other women. It doesn't mean anything is going on. He invited you here, remember? He gave you a key to his house and the alarm code. That's a big deal. I glance at the clock over the mantle. *No, there's a perfectly logical explanation about him bringing a woman to his house at 11:30 pm.*

They move toward the living room, and I jump to

my feet, heart pounding unnecessarily, like they caught me doing something wrong when I'm not. He invited me here. He gave me a key and told me to let myself in.

I run my hands down my jeans, over my thighs to smooth them out and hope like hell, my hair isn't sticking up all over the place. But it probably is, and I probably have creases on my face from sleeping on a throw pillow.

They come to a stop when they see me, freezing just inside the entrance to the living room. The woman—who looks like a goddess by the way all tall, statuesque beauty with long, shiny wavy dark hair, perfectly arched eyebrows, deep red painted lips and cheekbones for days—gasps when she sees me, one hand going to clutch at her chest like I scared the shit out of her, while the other hand latches onto Lincoln as she moves closer to him, pressing her full breasts into his side in a move that feels far too familiar.

"Miss Hart." Linc's voice sounds hoarse, like he's swallowed glass and is trying to speak around it. There's emotion there, but I can't focus on it, because I'm stuck on the way he called me 'Miss Hart.' Not Olivia, or Liv, or Livie, or sunshine. *Miss Hart*, like I'm just his secretary, his employee. "What are you doing here?"

I stare at him, willing him to remember that he told me to be here, demanded that I come and wait for him here. He stares back, face impassive, as he waits for my answer. Embarrassment floods me, as I realize that maybe this is why he brought me here. So I would catch him with another woman. So I would see just how little I actually mean to him. That he isn't willing to try or give me more than crumbs.

That everything I thought we were building together has been a lie. Every touch, every kiss for the last few weeks. It meant nothing to him. Even that soft look in his eyes this morning, the way he'd looked at me like I meant something, like I was important.

That's couldn't have been real, not if he's standing here with another woman pressed against his body in the middle of the night.

I was a fool to ever think this could work.

I don't know how the hell I didn't see this coming. He's too good a liar.

I blink against the stinging in my eyes and lick my lips, before smoothing a mask of indifference over my face, polite professionalism. The same one I use when we're with clients or potential investors. "I brought the files you wanted to go over, Mr. George. I fell asleep while waiting for you. You must have *forgotten* that you asked me to come."

The woman's eyes rake over me, no doubt taking in my jeans and ragged band t-shirt and wondering why, if this is a professional meeting, I'm not dressed, you know, more professionally. "You're Olivia."

I turn my attention to her, reaching up to tuck my hair behind my ears and push my glasses up my nose. She's too pretty, and I'm too messy. "I am. I'm sorry to interrupt. Just give me a minute and..." I look down at the ground, searching for where I kicked off my black ankle booties. "I'll get out of your hair."

My voice cracks on the last word, and I internally curse myself for breaking before I can escape. For letting him see how much he's hurt me. My chin wobbles as I duck my head even further, yanking on first one boot and then the other.

My purse and my jacket are hanging in the closet by the front door, where they've hung countless times before, where I'd gotten used to them being. But now they'll probably never be there again. *And fuck.* My overnight bag is upstairs in his bedroom. The one with my change of clothes for tomorrow because I'd thought-

I cut off the thought and force my legs to move, to push by them, feeling their gazes on me, hers heavy with pity, his with some emotion I don't want to look at too closely. God, I wish they wouldn't just stand there watching me. I wish they'd fucking go and do something else while I make a hasty retreat. It makes me feel itchy and pathetic.

You are *pathetic, Liv. Look at you. Look at you being so gullible as to think that he might actually care for you.* Pathetic *doesn't begin to describe what you are. You weren't good enough for your father, and you sure as fuck aren't good enough for Lincoln George.*

Tears are threatening, making my movements harried. My fingers feel strangely numb and shaky as I yank my coat off the hanger, followed by my purse. I don't bother putting either on my body, just hug them to my chest as I turn to offer them a watery smile. "Have a good night."

"Olivia, wait." I wish like hell that it was Lincoln saying my name, but it's not. It's the woman. I turn halfway, not wanting to fully look at either of them when my chest feels like it's shattered, and my heart is on the floor. "I just wanted to introduce myself, since we'll be seeing more of each other."

She approaches me with her hand out, like she wants me to shake it, and Lincoln stands behind her, hands shoved into his pants pockets, just *watching*. Watching while this perfectly coiffed woman reaches into my chest and tears out my heart with her next words. "I'm Alicia Moreau, Lincoln's fiancée."

My mouth goes dry and I can't get a breath. Not a single goddamn breath into my lungs. Once when I was a kid, I was hanging upside down on the monkey bars, trying to do some kind of flip that you only attempt when you're a kid because you think you're invincible. I fell, landed hard and had the wind knocked out of me. It hurt and was terrifying not to be able to breathe. I'd laid there gasping for air, and sure I was dying, but this is worse.

So much fucking worse.

"Fiancée?" I finally gasp. I'm sure my expression is one of horror, of agony and defeat. I'm not polished enough to hide what I'm feeling at this moment, not broken enough. Tears spring to my eyes and Alicia just keeps standing there, smiling. Either not at all aware of the blow she just dealt me or enjoying it far too much.

My watery, shimmery gaze finds Lincoln. "How long?"

His jaw tightens, and he looks away, refusing to meet my eyes. "Just tonight," Alicia answers for him. "He told me you helped pick out the ring. You have excellent taste."

"I- What?" I pull my eyes off the man standing stoically behind her, letting his fiancée trample all over my fucking heart, just standing there saying fucking *nothing* at all. My gaze latches on the ring on her hand and I realize that yes, in fact, I did pick it out, though he'd told me it was for his sister. *His fucking sister.*

Back before he told me he'd try. Back before we started our actual relationships. He's know this was coming the entire time we were together. He's been planning this, keeping me on the side while he wined and dined another woman, while he planned a future with her and strung me along.

"Well, you aren't Francie," I mutter, blinking to remove the moisture from my eyes, refusing to cry.

Alicia's smile falters just the slightest bit. "Pardon?"

I ignore her. I am so fucking done with this. So fucking done with everything. "You are such a fucking asshole, you know that?" I say to Lincoln before turning a pain filled smile to Alicia. "Congratulations on your upcoming nuptials."

And then I yank open the front door and throw myself through it.

I hear him say my name, *finally,* but I ignore it. The door slams shut behind me. And I all but sprint it down the stairs and onto the sidewalk, glancing left but heading right. If he comes after me, he'll assume I'm heading for the subway to catch the last train home. But I don't want to risk seeing him at all, so I head farther away from my house, from my mother, from where I should go when my heart feels like it's breaking.

He doesn't come after me. Of course he doesn't. He got what he wanted. He had his fun, played his games with me, and now he has the polished woman he can present to the world, the woman he can be proud of.

I will never be that woman. A college dropout. A failure. An assistant at his company. His freaking employee.

Of course, he's not going to choose me.

After about ten minutes, when I know he's not coming after me, I find a bar called Poison and duck inside. I'll call a rideshare and head home where I can huddle in the shower and silently cry my eyes out, so I don't disturb my mother.

I weave through the crowd to the bar and hop onto a stool, hoping like hell I don't look as raw as I feel. While I wait for the bartender, I pull out my phone, halfway hoping it'll be filled with messages from Lincoln and halfway hoping he hasn't reached out.

The screen is blank. No messages.

My heart twists and squeezes in my chest as I stare at the empty screen. This is it then. This is really the end of us. I gave him a second chance, was idiot enough to take him back, to trust that he'd be willing to give me more, to give me the whole cake and not just the crumbs.

But I was wrong.

So fucking wrong.

A strangled sob pulls from my chest as tears fill my eyes.

"What can I get you, hon?" My head shoots up, and embarrassment floods my face that this stranger has caught me sobbing at a blank screen. But the woman who looks my age, but has a gray streak in her black hair, right up front, and tattoos twisting up her arms only reaches out and pats my forearm. "Oh, sugar. I got just the thing for that."

Without saying another word, she grabs a glass, pours two fingers of whiskey into it, and slides it over to me. "Drink up and then tell me all about it."

I half laugh, half sob as I pick up the glass. "I don't think you want to hear my literal sob story."

She lifts a shoulder before crossing her arms and leaning onto the bar. "I'm a great listener, and I get the impression that's something you need right now." She flicks the glass in my hand. "Come on."

Sighing, I relent, gulping half the glass, and gasping at the burn as it blazes a path down my throat. "What's your name?" I ask when I have my breath back.

"Nadia," she answers while pouring a drink for the guy next to me.

I swallow the second half of my drink. "Well, Nadia, have I got a story for you."

"That motherfucker," Nadia says, sloshing another shot into my glass. I'm pretty sure this trip to the bar is going to cost me half a month's mortgage, but I'm so heartbroken, I can't really bring myself to care. That's a problem for Future Liv. Right Now Liv needs to drown her sorrows in cheap whiskey and bad techno.

I've lost track of how many times Nadia's poured for me. Lost track of the time, lost track of fucking everything. I am sloppy drunk right now, elbow braced on the bar, chin propped on my palm, pushing my cheek up toward my eye. I'm pretty sure if I tried to stand right now, I'd fall over.

But the outrage on my new friend's face on my behalf is worth it. "He's been with her the whole time?" She practically shouts, shoving the drink at me.

I nod, face nearly hitting the wooden bar as my chin slips off my hand. "Yeah. Yeah, he must have been right? I mean. It's only been a few months that we've been," I can't bring myself to say 'together.' That *we* were together, because it makes it sound like a relationship and if tonight has proven anything to me, it's that it was not a relationship, no matter what I thought while we were in it. "Fucking," is the word I settle on since that's all it was to him. "You don't just get engaged to someone after a few months, right? He was dating her in public and fucking me behind closed doors. He had me help pick out the engagement ring! How fucked up is that? I just read too much into everything."

"Liv, no. Fuck that!" The man next to me is named Josh and has been listening to my entire story. He's big and burly and looks like a trucker who could kick some serious ass if he wanted to, but he's been sympathetic while

I cried my eyes out to him and Nadia, so I'm not intimidated by him at all. A calloused hand brushes the tears off my cheeks. "He's the asshole. He led you on. He made you think there was more here than there was for him."

I nod along with his words because they're true.

Linc never took credit, but I know for a fact it was him that changed my health insurance so I could afford to pay for a night nurse, or he covered the additional costs himself. There's no way that Natalie in HR suddenly realized that eighty percent of the cost of a second caregiver would be covered by my insurance, after months of me fighting with them about it.

At the time, I thought it meant he cared about me, about my mom, about easing the load on my shoulders. But now I have to wonder if it was just a way to free up more of my time so I would be available to play with him when he wanted, a way to manipulate me into letting him control me.

"Yeah," I breathe. "Yeah, Josh. You're right." He gives me a sweet, sad smile. "Maybe I should date you."

He chuckles and drops his hand from my face. "I'm flattered. But I think my wife would have a few things to say about it."

My cheeks flush. "Oh, shit. Sorry."

He waves off my concern as Nadia slides a glass of water in front of me and whisks away the glass of alcohol. I let out a sound of protest, but she shakes her head at me. "You just propositioned a man who looks like a grizzly bear. Trust me, you'll thank me in the morning."

I run a tired hand down my face. "You're probably right." My forehead hits the sticky bar as I groan. "What am I supposed to do? I fucked my boss and now he's engaged."

Josh's big hand comes to a rest between my shoulder blades and rubs a soothing circle while Nadia tsks in front of me. "You want to know what you do, Livie? You don't let that asshole see he broke you. Don't give him the fucking satisfaction. You march into that office tomorrow." I groan at the thought, and she chuckles. "Or the day after, and you prove to him that he isn't worth the shit on your shoe. He doesn't deserve you, hon. You show him that."

Her words light a spark in my chest, and I nod against the bar, ignoring how my skin sticks to it. "Yeah. Yeah. I'm not going to let him ruin my job for me. I'm not going to run with my tail between my-"

"Olivia."

My rant cuts off on a choked gasp aimed at my tits, because I'm still face planted on the slab of wood. No. No, he can't be here. He can't see me like this. I'm supposed to prove he didn't hurt me the first time I see him.

Josh's hand stills its motion, and he leans into my side, a warm solid presence. "You just said that out loud, Liv."

I wince, and my head shoots up to look at him with wide eyes. "What part?"

"The bit about proving I didn't hurt you," Lincoln says from behind me. I don't turn to look. I can't. If I do,

I'll break all over again, and I'll never be able to pick up the pieces.

On the other side of the bar, Nadia all but snarls. "This is him?" She doesn't wait for me to answer. Just points an imperious finger at him. "Get your ass out of here, douchebag. We don't like your kind around here."

I don't have to look to know that Lincoln is giving her an unimpressed look, likely with his brow arched condescendingly. "My kind?"

"Yeah," Josh says, stool scraping back from the bar as he stands to his full height. "You know, assholes who take advantage of their position and coerce an impressionable young girl into having sex with them, treating her like a dirty secret."

I frown. I'm not that young or impressionable, but everything else is spot on.

"Is that what I did?"

Nadia scoffs, reaching under the bar and producing a baseball bat. "I've known Liv for all of two hours and I can already tell she's way too fucking good for you. That girl has a heart of fucking gold, and you broke it, so get the fuck out." She lifts the bat like she might actually take a swing.

I stumble to my feet, swearing when the alcohol hits me harder and I sway, but I still manage to slip between Lincoln and my staunch defenders. He might be an asshole, but that doesn't mean I want to see him with his head caved in or anything. Also, I don't want Nadia to go to jail. She's a little spitfire and I think we could actually be friends.

But that could also just be the booze talking.

I hold up a hand to both of them. "Everyone, just calm down." I sway again and Josh, the closest to me, reaches out to catch me, propping me up with an enormous hand under my elbow.

"Get your hands off her," Lincoln growls in a tone so full of possession that I can't help but turn my blurry gaze to him. He's dressed in a pair of army green joggers and a t-shirt with a charcoal cardigan thrown over top. My heart clenches all over again, because Lincoln George is damn handsome in a suit, but he's devastating like this, dressed down and casual, looking relaxed. I used to imagine waking up to him looking like this, to being privy to a side of him that no one else is.

His slate blue gaze remains focused on where Josh is still holding me steady, a knot between his dark brows. "Let. Her. Go." He demands, again.

Josh doesn't and thank God for that because I'm pretty sure I'd fall if he wasn't supporting most of my weight in his one hand. "I don't think I will."

Linc takes one threatening step forward, and that's enough for me to intervene again. "Nadia, put down the bat. I like you and I don't want to see you in jail." Nadia arches a brow at me before she nods once and hides the bat back under the bar. "Josh, thank you for keeping me from face planting, but I think I'm okay now." The big man releases me at my request but doesn't move away. I take a deep breath and lift my gaze to Lincoln. "You should go home. I have nothing to say to you."

He doesn't move, just stares at me and then he says, "You might have nothing to say to me, but I have plenty to say to you." He holds out a hand. "Let me take you home and explain. Please, sunshine."

I shake my head at him while wagging a finger in the air between us. "No. Snickerdoodle. Snickerdoodle. Snickerdoodle. I'm *done*."

His finger hooks around mine and he uses it to tug me just the slightest bit closer. "Olivia, please. This isn't a game. I'm not... I'm not trying to dominate you into following my orders. I'm not planning a scene. I just want to talk to you."

"You didn't have anything to say earlier while your finance introduced herself to me."

He winces and tightens his finger around mine. "I panicked. I didn't know how to say how to make it right. How to explain it to you. I'm sorry I hurt you, baby. So fucking sorry. You have no idea. But I think if you'll just listen, I can make this right."

I see now that the amount of alcohol in my veins is a mistake because I'm softening toward him. I feel myself waver in my anger, in my pain, and a little voice at the back of my head says, *give him a chance. You owe him that much. Look at him. He looks as torn up about this as you feel.*

"Fine!" I say to my inner voice, exasperated with myself. "Fine," I say to Lincoln, narrowing my gaze at him. "We can talk."

"Thank you." He lets out a breath and slides his hand up mine until he's gripping my wrist, like he's worried I might run from him again. Smart move because I actually might. "Where're your things?"

I hook my freehand over my shoulder and point with my thumb at the seat I'd been on. But Josh is already moving, grabbing up my jacket and bag and carrying them over to me. "You sure you want to go with him?" He asks as he holds my things hostage. "I don't have a problem kicking his ass if you need me to."

I grin up at him and pat his arm. "I'm sure. Thank you, though." I lean toward him, and he bends down until I can whisper to him. "Honestly, I'm so drunk right now I'll hardly register anything he says. He'll get it off his chest, and I'll probably forget about it by morning."

Josh chuckles. "I think you said that louder than you meant to, Livie." Then he reaches into my purse and pulls out my phone. "Unlock that for me." I do without question and then watch as he adds himself and Nadia as contacts, and then snaps a picture of Lincoln and sends it to both of them. "Text us when you get home. Let us know you're safe."

Tears prick my eyes at the concern this virtual stranger has for me. Two strangers. Both Nadia and Josh. Two hours in their presence and I already feel like we're going to be the best of friends.

Without thinking, I wrap my arms around the big man and squeeze. "Thank you."

His big hand swamps the back of my head as he presses me into his chest. "You're welcome." I feel him shift his attention to Lincoln. "We've got a picture of you.

We know your name. If anything happens to her, we're siccing the cops on you."

My chest glows warm with the warning, even as I chuckle and pull away from him. "Linc won't hurt me. At least not physically," I reassure him. I believe that. He might be upset or angry—though if he's mad at me right now, he can go fuck himself—but he would never hurt me.

Josh keeps his eyes on my face, like he's making sure I actually believe that. I meet his gaze with determination to reassure him. He nods slowly and releases me, fingers uncoiling one at a time, ready to catch me again if I need it.

Lincoln moves closer, puts his hand on my shoulder and pulls me away from the big man. I shrug him off, scowling, before turning to wave at Nadia. "Thank you."

"Anytime, hon. Remember to let us know you made it home, okay?"

I nod and spin on my heel, leading the way out of the bar. My steps are steady and sure, not the least bit wobbly. I'm congratulating myself on that when I bump into a table, and it nearly goes down, taking me with it. Lincoln swears, catches me and the table and then keeps his hands on me as he guides me out of the bar.

I suck in a deep breath of the chill night air as we step outside. "How much have you had to drink, sunshine?"

I scowl at his use of my nickname. "Don't call me that," I snap. "And the amount of alcohol I've had is none of your business."

He runs a weary hand over his face. "Jesus, you're slurring your words. Let's go back to my-"

"No!" I shake my head, making the world wobble precariously. "No. Fuck no. I'm not going back to the scene of the crime." I lurch away from him, toward the subway entrance that will take me home. He catches me before I make it too far, guiding me to a car idling on the side of the road. I bend down to look in the front seat and find Lance behind the wheel. He gives me a sad smile, and my heart lurches.

He knew. Lance knew. How many other people knew I was a goddamn idiot?

I viciously flip him off with both fingers.

Linc pulls me away and maneuvers me into the back seat of the car, pushing me until he can slide in next to me. I scoot over until I'm pressed against the far door to avoid touching him, but he just follows me, reaching over my shoulder to tug the seatbelt across my chest.

The gesture makes tears well in my eyes, and I slap my hands over them to keep the offending moisture at bay. I will not cry. *I will not cry.*

"Why?" I gasp out. Really more of a sob that a gasp. "Why would you do this to me?"

Lincoln slips an arm over my shoulders and tugs me into him. I let myself enjoy it for about a second before I get both my hands between us and push with all my might.

"Don't touch me!" I shout, pushing him again because it felt good to physically show him how angry I am right now. "Don't ever fucking touch me again!"

Lincoln holds his hands up between us, like he's trying to tell me he won't, but then his hands dart out and catch my cheeks, swiping away the tears that are still falling from my eyes. He's so tender, so gentle. "Please, don't cry, sunshine. Please. It guts me when you cry."

I jerk my face away from him, turn my entire body toward the door, stare out the window as tears keep falling. He doesn't say anything else, doesn't try to touch me, and I tell myself that is a good ling, that I don't want him to comfort me right now.

The car pulls to a stop and Lincoln opens the door, waits with one foot on the cement. I swipe at my eyes and look around.

We're in Lincoln's neighborhood. In front of his house. Without looking at the man next to me, I push the button to lower the partition. "Lance, can you take me home, please?"

He twists around to look at me, while Lincoln growls out. "No, he can't take you home. You're staying here tonight."

I ignore him, keeping my eyes on his head of security. "Please, Lance."

His gaze darts to Lincoln, and then back to me, before he nods. "I'm not in the habit of kidnapping women, so, yeah, Liv, I'll take you home. And Lincoln is going to let me."

I can feel the tension radiating off Lincoln, can practically see him shouting he's going to fire Lance in his head. But after a moment he sighs and slides back in, closing the door and putting up the partition again.

He doesn't say anything as the car pulls away from the curb. I can feel him watching me, feel his gaze on the side of my head. I keep expecting him to break the silence to explain. That's why he's here, isn't it? To explain away what happened tonight. But he remains silent, just like he had the entire time that woman—*Alicia*—tore out my fucking heart and stomped on it with her Louboutin's.

I'm tossing out every pair Lincoln bought me first thing in the morning. I'll put them on the curb with a free sign. In fact, I'll have a garage sale where everything he ever gave me is up for grabs. First come, first served as much as your arms can carry, you can take.

We're almost halfway to my house when he finally speaks. "I didn't want this to happen."

I don't look at him. "Well, it did." I frown. My voice is still slurred and thick with tears. "You made your choice, Lincoln. Just like my dad. You picked someone else."

"Baby," he breathes, shifting toward me, pausing when I press further into the door to keep him from touching me. "I didn't pick her. I pick you. I choose you."

I turn my head toward him, hope flaring in my chest. His pretty slate blue eyes look at me with such tenderness, running over my blotchy face and swollen eyes like I'm the most beautiful thing he's ever seen. "You… choose me?"

He nods, reaching to cup my cheek. "I'll always pick you, Liv. Always."

I swallow down the emotion that wants to crawl up my throat at those words. "So you aren't marrying her?"

His lips thin, pursing together, and that's enough for me to know the answer. I slap his hand away from my face. "I told you not to touch me."

"Just let me explain, sunshine, plea-"

He cuts off when my palm connects with his cheek, frustration and hurt and anger bubbling until they need an outlet, and apparently that outlet is me slapping him.

He blinks at me, mouth hanging open in surprise. I'm surprised too. I'm not a violent person, I don't strike out at people. The only person I've ever struck was Jason when he tried to force himself on me. It's definitely not my first instinct in a conflict.

But I just want Lincoln to *hurt*. To feel some small amount of the pain that he's caused me. I obviously can't hurt him emotionally. He doesn't care enough about me to have that be the case, but apparently, I can hurt him physically.

Even if that hurt doesn't compare, and my palm throbs and tingles from the impact. "Don't. Call. Me. That," I grit out. "Don't call me anything."

He swallows and leans away from me, against the door. "You're angry and hurt. I understand that," he says in an even tone. I scoff. "Being drunk probably doesn't help."

I shake my head. "I beg to differ. Being drunk helps. It numbs some of the pain. Pain *you* caused me, Lincoln. I'd be broken right now if I wasn't drunk."

I see him flinch out of the corner of my eye. "We'll talk tomorrow," he says. "When you've had a chance to- to calm down and sober up. We'll talk tomorrow." He repeats. I'm not sure if he's trying to convince me or himself.

"Nothing you say will change what you did, Lincoln," I murmur, my voice surprisingly even. I must be slipping farther into the numbness. Self-preservation kicking in. I have to be numb, or the all-consuming agony will swallow me whole. And I can't afford that. I have too much shit to do. I have to take care of my mom and focus on work.

Oh, fuck. *Work*.

How the hell am I supposed to work with him?

I push that worry away. That's a problem for Future Olivia. Future Olivia will reach out to Cabot and see when he thinks he'll be back. Future Olivia will come up with the best ways to avoid Lincoln. Future Olivia will start looking for a new job.

Right now, I just have to focus on getting out of this car and away from this man.

Thankfully, right as I have that thought, Lance pulls to a stop outside of my house. I have the door open and my seatbelt off before Lincoln can so much as blink. I stumble up the pathway, fumbling through my purse to find my keys, and am not surprised when Lincoln trots up next to me. "Liv," he starts. "Please."

"Please what, Lincoln? Forgive you for breaking my heart? For making me think that you actually cared? For making me lo-" I cut that off. He doesn't get those words. He doesn't get them from me, not anymore. Never again.

He stares at me, his slate blue eyes intense. "Please, promise me we'll talk tomorrow."

I find my keys, hooking them on my finger and then continue toward my front door. My booties thunk up the front steps. "I'm not promising you anything. I might be willing to talk tomorrow, I might not be. Unlike you, I don't make promises I don't intend to keep."

I shove the key into the lock and twist. He stops me before I can open the door with a gentle hand on my wrist.

"Olivia, *please*." The pleading in his voice almost breaks me. It's almost enough for me to crumble and tell him, '*yes, fine. We can talk tomorrow.*'

But I harden myself against it. He doesn't care that he hurt me. Why should I care if he's hurting? Some vengeful part of me wants him to hurt. To feel bad.

It's that vengeful part of me that shoves open the door and steps inside.

It's that vengeful part of me that looks into his eyes, his pretty slate blue eyes, so he can see my sincerity.

It's that vengeful part of me that whispers, "I could have loved you, you know," just before I close the door in his devastated face.

26
Lincoln

This must be what Hell feels like.

27
Olivia

The knock on my door comes far too early, considering the hangover pounding through me. I wish I could say that as soon as I closed the door on Lincoln last night, I also closed the door on our non-relationship. But instead I sucked it up, found the night nurse Lincoln hired, told her to go home, locked the door behind her and sank to the floor in the foyer where sobbed silent tears into my knees, before falling asleep there.

So when there's a knock on the door, I am in a unique position to hear it. But it also means I can't just roll over and ignore it. I'm literally right there.

I groan as I push to a sitting position, muscles and head screaming at me. I'm sure I look like shit, but I don't have it in me to care. The knocking comes again, followed by a gruff, "Olivia, I know you're in there."

Shit.

Fucking goddamn bloated, hungover, head

pounding, shit.

I blink at how blurry my vision is, and then swipe my hands along the floor to find my glasses, before shoving them on my nose and glaring at the front door. "Come on, sunshine, open the door."

A growl of frustration erupts from me, because how dare he still call me that? How dare he sound like he means it when he obviously doesn't? I stand abruptly, ignore the way it makes my head pound and my eyes water, and yank the door open.

There he is, the bane of my existence on the other side of the door, hand raised like he was about to knock again. "What?" I whisper-shout at him and then regret it because my voice is all croaky and weird.

His eyes rake over me, from the top of what I am sure is a rat's nest of hair over the outfit I was wearing last night, and down to my toes. His expression cracks, softens. "Baby," he breathes, reaching toward me like he's going to hug me, pull me into his chest and wrap his arms around me. I stumble back, shaking my head.

"No." I hold up a finger at him. "No. Don't. Don't do that."

He ignores me, hooking his finger around mine and using it to pull me closer. "Olivia, please. I fucked up, I know. But please don't shut me out. Let me explain."

He catches my wrist and pulls me in, and like an idiot, I let him. I'm so damn tired and weak. This man *makes* me weak. He pulls me in until my nose presses against his soft t-shirt, until I'm breathing in the now familiar scent of him. His arms wrap around me, holding me even though I refuse to hold him back. Tears spring to my eyes, soaking into the fabric under my cheek. His chin presses into the top of my hair as I take long shuddering breaths and try to get myself under control.

After I don't know how long, he sighs. "Can we talk?"

Fresh tears leak out of my eyes, but I nod against his chest before pulling back. "But I need to check on my mom first." And freshen up because I know I can't possibly smell good at the moment, with morning breath and alcohol seeping out of my pores.

He slides his hands up my back and over my shoulders until he's cupping my face. "Whatever you need." His lips brush against my forehead in a move that is so freaking tender it makes my heart ache. I pull away from him quickly, not wanting to let this apologetic, gentle version of Lincoln soften me toward him.

He made his choice, and he broke my heart.

He follows me inside and lingers by the kitchen with his hands tucked into the pockets of his jeans. "I'll make coffee. You go do what you need to do."

I bob my head and hurry down the hall to the living room to peek in on my still sleeping mother. I watch the steady rise and fall of her breath before turning and retreating the way I came, darting up the stairs to freshen up.

By the time I come back down, over twenty minutes have passed. I've rinsed off in the shower, brushed my teeth and my hair and changed into clean clothes. I also swallowed some painkillers and about a gallon of water from the bathroom faucet. So, I'm feeling moderately more human as I step into the kitchen and find that Lincoln has tidied up while also making coffee and laying out a few of the leftover pastries I cooked earlier this week.

I take in the spread and then look up at him. He's watching me with something close to uncertainty in his eyes, hands stuffed in the pockets of his jeans, zippered hoodie hanging open. I get that same pang I got last night at seeing him dressed down.

"I didn't even know you owned a pair of jeans."

He blinks at me, before a small smile curls his lips. "I own several, actually."

Moving to pour myself a cup of coffee from the pot, I hum like I don't believe him, even though he's wearing the evidence right now. He's quiet while I add cream and sugar to the bitter brew and use a spoon to combine it into a pale brown. I take a sip before using the mug to motion to the dining room on the other side of the house. "Should we sit?"

He gives a jerky nod and then picks up the plate of pastries and carries it over.

I wait until he's settled and take a seat facing him, keeping the table between us on purpose. He's too in tune with my body, and I'm too inclined to forget all the shit he's pulled if he touches me at all. So this is better.

He doesn't start talking immediately, sliding the plate back and forth with nervous fingers, before abandoning it to spear his fingers through his hair, mussing it up in a way that I've only seen after we've had sex.

"Are you going to start?" I ask before taking a sip. "Or should I?"

His slate blue eyes lock onto me, assessing. And then he sighs. "I'll start. I think you made yourself fairly clear last night when you drunkenly told me you'd never let me touch you again, and that you could have *loved* me." His voice cracks just slightly on the word loved, almost like it was hard for him to get out.

I try like hell to not let that tiny tell of his emotions break me. Instead, I arch a brow and wait, sipping my coffee like I have all the time in the world.

"Alicia and I met in my senior year of college. She was a Junior. We dated for a while, but ultimately decided that we worked better as friends. We've been meeting at least once a week for years. Our families know each other. We run in the same circles. We've spent holidays together, vacations. Her father owns Moreau Industries. She's his only child, set to inherit the entire company."

I carefully set my cup down to keep myself from spilling the contents as my hands shake.

I get the subtext here. I get what he's saying. It's the same thing I thought last night. She makes sense in his world. The perfect socially acceptable wife. The woman born to money. Someone on his level, at least on paper. Whereas I—I glance around my shabby little house that I've tried so hard to upgrade, to turn into something it's not—I'll only ever be a struggling college drop out.

"I told you about my father, about him selling his company to ensure that I would never get my hands on it. Moreau Industries bought it."

Revenge? This entire thing is about revenge on his father?

"I approached them about selling it to me, offered them a hell of a lot more that it was worth. They countered with a total merger, with combining our companies. It seemed like a good idea, bringing together two powerful corporations. I would finally have control of the company that my father built, and I could choose to do whatever I wanted with it. The... the marriage was something they wanted added to the contract."

"Something they wanted, but not you?" Why the hell is my voice so hoarse?

"For years, Liv, I didn't think I would find anyone that I wanted to spend my life with. I thought Alicia was the best I could hope for. A marriage based on years of friendship and mutual respect, with the intention of merging our two companies when the time came."

I swallow hard and force myself to ask. "Do you still feel that way?"

He shakes his head. "I don't know. I don't think so. It kind of depends on you, I guess."

"Me?"

He nods slowly, bracing his forearms on the table in a move that I recognize from meetings with clients. "Yeah, I think we could be something more. You said last night that you could have loved me. Is that still true?"

I nudge my coffee cup nervously, shifting it left and right like he'd been doing with the pastry plate. "I don't know, Linc. You got engaged last night. *To another woman.*"

He licks his lips. "That doesn't have to change anything with us."

My gaze narrows on his face. "How?"

He laces his fingers together and straightens his back, his face smoothing out. "Alicia and I don't have a romantic or a sexual relationship. What we have is a partnership, based on respect and a contractual obligation-"

"I'm sorry there are already contracts involved?"

His brows narrow as he looks at me. "We signed contracts for the merger of our companies before you and I-"

"So you are *contractually obligated* to marry her?" My voice comes out in a whisper, but shrill. I can't believe what I'm hearing. I can't believe this is real. Who the hell does this kind of thing?

He meets my gaze and nods. "Yes. Her father only agreed to the eventual merger with the understanding that she and I would be married. But she and I have talked about what that means for us. We don't love each other, we never will. We agreed to be married for the sake of the merger but to be open to finding someone outside the marriage to be intimate with, to spend time with. Essentially, she'll live her life and I'll live mine."

The pieces fall into place, like little knives stabbing into me. Death by a thousand cuts. "So," I say slowly, like I'm not shriveling up and dying on the inside. "You and I can be together because she won't care if we're fucking."

He winces. "Don't call it that."

My brows arch and anger hits hard and fast. "What? *Fucking?* But that's what it would be, right, Linc? You'd be married to her. To the whole fucking world, you and her would be husband and wife. You'd continue to spend holidays together, vacation in the Maldives, go to charity events and family dinners together. And then you'd come to me every Friday night in whatever hole you stashed me away in. Just like my father. I'd be your dirty little secret. We'd fuck and then you'll go back to your wife. I could keep working for you though, right? So we'd have that too. We can fuck in your office, on your desk, in the copy room. We can let the whole fucking company know that I'm a home wrecker, the woman who knows you're married and just doesn't give a fuck."

"Olivia, baby."

I shake my head at him. "We wouldn't have a relationship, Lincoln. We would never actually *be* together. You'd be giving me crumbs. And I already told you I don't want that. I deserve more."

His jaw tightens and I can practically see him shoring up his walls, building them back up because he knows I'm right. He knows he wouldn't be able to take me out to dinner or on a date. He's well-known enough that the gossip rags would see and latch on to it. It would be a fucking scandal.

"I don't know what else you want me to do, Liv. This is the best I can do. This is what I can offer you. I can't break the contract."

Right, because the future of his multibillion-dollar company, which really doesn't need another acquisition to survive, is more important than me, than *us*. He reaches across the table, stretching one hand toward me.

"Please, Liv, let's at least try it." The pleading in his voice hits me in my chest.

Oh God, I'm tempted, and I hate that I am. I hate that I'm sitting here considering letting him diminish me, hide me away. I saw what that can do to a woman, watched it happen to my mother even though I was too young to fully understand. But looking back, I know what being in a relationship with my father cost her, to be the *other* woman, to have the entire town know who she was and look down on her for it.

I lived this scenario already.

"What if I get pregnant, Linc? What then? You gonna treat our children the way my father treated me? You gonna see them a few hours out of the month? Will you explain to them what our relationship is really like? Why it's like that? Will you tell them that their mommy doesn't mean enough to you to fight for her? To be with her one hundred percent?"

With each word I say, I can see him withdrawing farther from me, can see the reality of the situation sinking in. The reality of what he's asking me to do sinking in.

"Why didn't you tell me? Why didn't you give me some kind of warning that this was coming? Why did you make me pick out her fucking engagement ring?" My chest aches at the memory, at how I'd briefly entertained the thought of him asking me to marry him, even when I knew we were over.

He rubs a hand over his face, slides the tips of his fingers over his lips, like he's trying to stall for time to come up with an acceptable answer. One that won't make him vulnerable but will still satisfy me.

"Let me guess," I say before he formulates a reply. "You never thought that we could be anything more than fucking, right? You figured we'd play games until Cabot came back to the company, and then you'd tell me it was over, and you'd never have to interact with me again. Even when I told you I wanted more, when you said you'd try, you never actually thought this would work, right? You were never actually in this."

"Right." The word is harsh, and it makes me flinch. Hearing him confirm it tears at my heart, makes it hard to get a breath.

"So then, what are you even doing here, Lincoln? You were right. You got what you wanted. You don't have to force this or try to manage me. I was fine before you. I'll be fine long after. So why are you even fucking here?"

"Because I fell in love with you, Olivia!" He bursts out, sounding fucking angry as hell about it. "I fell in love with you, and I can't see myself living a life without you in it. I need you."

Oh, God. *Oh, God.*

A declaration of love is supposed to feel good. It's supposed to make your heart race and your stomach flutter with butterflies. I'm supposed to want to say the words back to him, shy and bashful and *happy*. I'm supposed to feel happy.

But I don't. I just feel angry and hurt.

"*Liar,*" I spit out. "You are such a fucking liar, and you don't even realize it."

Lincoln's jaw tightens, his hands fist on the table. "I'm not fucking lying. I love you."

I scoff, shaking my head. "Oh, you love me, do you? You love me so much you'd keep me a secret from your family? You love me so much you'd ask me to share you with another woman? To get only a quarter of your time? Is that how much you fucking love me?"

"Liv, I love you. I just can't give you more than that. I have responsibilities. I have-"

"Contracts." I lean back in my chair, shaking my head. "What in the very limited time we've spent together gave you the impression that I would be okay sleeping with another woman's husband? That I would be your mistress."

His eyes go hard, his jaw sets. "Well, you do like it when I call you a *whore* while I fuck you. I didn't think *mistress* would be that far off."

My body goes cold. I think I might sway, but I'm not sure. I feel detached from my body numb, except for the shame that is buffeting me. There's something wrong with me, I knew it. I knew it wasn't normal. Even if Lincoln never made me feel bad about it, embraced it even. But here he is, throwing it in my face, using it to hurt me.

My face heats in shame, and tears of hurt fill my eyes.

His face falls as he realizes what he just said. He reaches toward me. "Shit, Liv-"

"Get out," I whisper, tucking my chin and standing from the table.

His jaw tics. "Olivia."

My hands fist at my sides. "Get out, Mr. George," I say with more force. "I don't want to see you anymore."

"*Olivia.*"

"In fact, you can take this moment as my resignation."

"I refuse your resignation. I don't accept it."

My chin tips up, but I don't meet his gaze. "I don't think you can do that, but regardless, I will not be coming in for work any longer. Eventually Giovanna will report me to HR, and I will be fired. The result is the same. I will not see you again. Now, get the fuck out of my house."

I can see that he's not going to let this go. I can tell that he's going to push this, and I brace myself for his assault.

"Olivia-"

A voice, sharp as a whip, cuts him off. "I believe you heard my daughter, Mr. George."

"Mama!" I cry, the sight of her shaking me out of my numb state. I push by him out into the hall to find her leaning heavily against the wall. "You shouldn't be out of bed."

My mother hardly pays me any mind as I wedge myself under her armpit and loop an arm around her too thin waist, taking her weight onto me as best as I can. It's not much to begin with, so I manage just fine. She continues to glare at Linc like he's the antichrist. "Please leave."

Linc runs a frustrated hand through his hair, slate blue eyes burning over me as I carefully shift my mother around, guiding her back down the hall. "Let me help at least," he says, and I hear him take one step forward, like he's going to put his hands on my mother, take her weight from me, place her gently in her bed. Like he cares enough to do that. I pin him with a glare over my shoulder, keeping him in place with the force of it.

"How many times do I have to tell you to go away, Lincoln? We are done. For good. Forever. Never a-fucking-gain. I don't need or want your help. Now leave."

I whip my head back around and practically carry my mother back to her bed as she pants out. "You heard her. Get!"

I've just lowered her onto the side of the bed when I hear the front door click closed with a finality that makes my heart break all over again. My mother is silent as I guide her back to the pillows, lift her legs up to the mattress and cover her once again with her blanket.

"Olivia-"

"Are you hungry?" I ask, fluffing her pillows that in no way need to be fluffed. "I think there's some bone broth left, or if you want something a little more filling-"

"Olivia Jane, look at me."

I shake my head as my chin wobbles. "Nope. No ma'am, not gonna happen." If I look at her, there is no chance of keeping the tears at bay and she doesn't need me sobbing all over her.

Soft, cool, bony hands cup my face and make me meet her sad eyes. "Tell me what that was about."

I sniff hard, swallowing down tears along with a fair amount of snot, and force a smile to my lips. "It's nothing. Work stuff."

She snorts, not letting me go. "Sweet pea, if that was about work, then you might as well call me Mother Teresa because I'm a saint."

I wrinkle my nose because that didn't make any sense. "You are a saint, mama."

She tsks and pats my cheek. "Tell me, shug."

I sigh and drag the chair closer before settling down. "How much did you hear?"

She settles back on the pillows now that she's sure I'm going to spill the beans. "I heard you come home last night crying. I heard you fall asleep on the floor in the foyer. I heard that boy call you a whore and suggest you be his mistress."

I blink at her. Jesus, I underestimate this woman. She knows a hell of a lot more than I thought.

Also, my mother now knows some of my sexual preferences and that I'm not normal. My mother pats my hand before leaning back against her pillows. "I'm not one to judge, sugar. You know that. I was your father's side piece for years, and it was enough for me. To have pieces of him. I loved him so much that I couldn't imagine life without him in it. But I saw what it was doing to you. How sad you'd get when someone snubbed you, called you a name, made fun of you for not having a real dad." Her eyes flash with anger. "And then that little shit, Jason, did what he did, and I knew I couldn't stay anymore, knew we couldn't stay anymore."

She reaches over and laces her fingers with mine. "I loved your father, Olivia. But you are the love of my life. You are my reason for being. I couldn't make you stay in a situation that was unsafe."

I blink against the stinging in my eyes, lower lip quivering as I take a ragged breath. "If not for you, I would probably still be there," she admits, with a small, fond smile on her lips. "But that type of life would never be enough for you."

I swallow around the lump in my throat. "I know. That's why I told him to get lost."

My mother's honey-colored eyes latch onto my face. "But you love him?"

I swallow again and give a jerky nod. "He just doesn't love me. Not enough."

She picks up my hand and squeezes. "What's enough, Liv?"

"Enough to be his number one priority. To be on his arm and introduced to his family. Enough for him to want to marry me, spend his entire life with me, not just parts of it. Enough to give up a vendetta against his father."

She nods along with every word I say, and when I'm done, she gives me a smile. "I think he *does* love you like that, sugar. How could he not? He just doesn't realize it yet. Give him time, give him grace, he'll come around."

I snort and shake my head. "I don't want him to. Not after he suggested I be his mistress while he marries someone else."

She hums, brushing her knuckles against my cheek. "Keep lying to yourself if that's what you need to do, sweet girl. But do me a favor and when he does come to his senses, give him a chance. Don't hold yourself back from happiness because of fear."

I frown at her. "I wouldn't do that."

My mother just arches a brow at me and settles back against her pillows. "Sure you wouldn't. I know I didn't give you a good example of what a healthy relationship looks like, Olivia. I know I failed you as a mother when it comes to that-"

"No, mama, that's not-"

She shoots me a wry look. "Sugar, I was with a man who didn't put me first for fifteen years, and I never dated when we moved here. I failed you in that. I can't blame you for being scared. But you're strong. Stronger than me. You know what you deserve, Olivia. You know what you can handle."

I frown, not understanding what she means, but I don't want to argue with her, either. "What I deserve is to be put first."

She nods and pats my hand. "Yes. And if he offers that to you, I hope you can overlook this mistake and allow him to make you happy. A forgiving heart is a happy heart," she breathes the last few words, as her eyelids flutter, worn out from the excitement of the morning, from getting out of bed by herself for the first time in months.

I lean forward and brush a kiss over her forehead. "Get some rest, mama."

She nods as her eyes drift closed all the way, but when I move to get up, they fly back open, piercing me with an intensity I haven't seen from her in ages. "You deserve love, sugar. You deserve the whole fucking world. And I think Lincoln George is just the man to give it to you."

I sit with her until she falls asleep, holding her hand and considering her words.

A forgiving heart is a happy heart.

If I'm honest, I want to forgive Lincoln. I want to be with him and to really try. I want to tell everyone that he's mine. We both deserve a second chance at this.

She's right that I'm strong, that I know what I deserve, what I'm worth. I just have to hope that eventually, Lincoln will see it too. Hopefully, before he marries someone else.

28
Lincoln

I've fucked everything up.

I should have never suggested Olivia be my mistress, should never have equated her kinks in the bedroom to her being anything less than wife material. I should never have agreed to this stupid contract with Alicia. Why the hell had I done that? We could have made a contract that was simply business and merged our companies together as friends.

At the time, I hadn't envisioned meeting someone who would make me feel... well, *anything*. Anything at all.

And Olivia Hart makes me feel all the things. Love and lust. Frustration and joy. Strength and tenderness. Happiness before. Misery now. A desire that flares so hot, I'm halfway surprised we didn't burn each other while satisfying it. She makes me feel cared for, possessive, gentle, and kind. Goddamn, how she wove herself into my very make up, I have no idea. Just that now she's there, I can't get her out.

I don't want to.

I want to drown in all

the things Olivia makes me feel.

"Mr. George?" It takes everything in me not to snarl at Giovanna as she sticks her head into my office, tentatively. I don't blame her for being cautious. The last few days have been rough, and I've definitely reverted back to my assholish ways. I glare up at her as she pushes the door open farther and moves into my office. To her credit, she doesn't shrink away from me, and she doesn't let her eyes wander over my shoulders and chest like she used to. "I was wondering if you might want to put money in the pot?"

My brows lower. "What pot?"

"For Olivia." The sound of that name is almost enough to send me into a hurt filled rage. Almost. But I make myself focus on what she's asking. Money for a pot for Olivia. *Why?*

"What the fuck for?"

Giovanna stumbles back a step at my tone of voice, her fingers twisting in front of her. "I thought you knew. Liv's mother passed away two days ago. We're taking up a collection to send her flowers and anything left over we're going to just give her. It's not much, but we wanted to do something for her."

She keeps talking, but I've tuned her out. Ms. Hart passed away? How had I not known? Fuck. Liv must be hurting so bad right now. An ache forms in my chest, thinking of her all alone in her house. I rub at it, but of course that does nothing.

Silence stretches and I realize Giovanna is looking at me expectantly, waiting for my answer. "No. I don't want to put money into the pot to buy Olivia flowers." I want to do so much more. I'm *going* to do so much more.

Giovanna's mouth falls open, and a red angry flush spreads over her tan cheeks before she snaps her lips closed and shakes her head. "Olivia cared about you, about all of us. She deserves better than this. I cannot believe that you would be this unfeeling."

I lean back in my chair and cock a brow at her. *Unfeeling?* I'm feeling more than I've ever felt before. Unfeeling is the last fucking thing I am.

I let out a weary sound, spinning in my chair to look out the window. "Get the fuck out, Gi."

It takes a moment, but eventually I hear the door click shut. As soon as it does, I'm moving, swiping up my phone and dialing numbers. Olivia might not want me anymore, might not trust me to take care of her, to give her what she needs, but that will not stop me from doing what I can for her, to help ease her suffering in whatever way I can.

She'll just never know it's me.

I blink against the glare as I step out of my car, before nodding to my driver and smoothing a hand down my black suit jacket. Across the expanse of green grass and headstones, I find the small gathering of mourners. Surprise hits me when I realize a fair number of them are employees of mine, likely here to support Liv rather than mourn her mother. I watch as Giovanna approaches a small, slumped figure in all black, sitting front and center of the freshly dug grave.

My heart tugs in my chest as I watch her crouch in front of Olivia, hands resting lightly on knees covered in black tights. God, I am both dying to look at her face, to see her with my eyes, and also dreading it. The last thing I want to see is Olivia weighed down with the agony she must be feeling at the moment. I've often thought she should always smile, that she should always be happy, because she shines when she does. When Liv is happy, she makes everyone else around her happy, too.

"Were you planning on watching like a creep from over here?" A feminine voice asks. Two bodies accompany the question, joining me in looking over the cemetery.

I twist my head just enough to glare over Cabot at the tiny woman with her fingers wrapped around his arm. "Verity."

"Lincoln," she says back, eyes focused on Olivia. "I wish I could say it's good to see you, but that's almost always a lie. Especially so right now."

"Rose," Cabot says, softly, drawing her closer to his side. "Now is not the time to discuss this. You can give Linc the dressing down he deserves later."

She hums and presses up onto her toes to brush a kiss against Cabot's cheek before she moves toward the mourners, toward Liv.

I keep my eyes on her. "What did I do this time?"

Cabot sighs, shifting to face me just slightly. "I think you know. I received Olivia's letter of resignation, Lincoln. Verity is pissed about it, angry at me for leaving her with you. She really cares about that woman. And you fucked it up."

My throat goes tight, like my heart has lodged itself there, and my nose stings. "Yeah," I agree softly, shoving my hands into my pockets. "Yeah, I did."

I don't wait to see what his reply is, taking off with sure steps toward Olivia. I'm aware of the looks I get, of the glares from Claire and Harvey sitting on either side of my woman. They no doubt know all the sordid details of what I did. I ignore them in favor of the woman between them, looking pale, and devastated and so fucking beautiful even in her heartbreak that it literally steals the air from my lungs on a gasp.

She's talking with Verity, nodding along to whatever my friend's wife is saying. Tears form along her lower lashes, spill over to wet her cheeks. Verity uses her thumbs to wipe them away gently, and then squeezes Olivia's hands and steps away from her.

Red-rimmed honey eyes find mine. "Linc-Mr. George." Her voice is hoarse, tight with tears, and I watch in horror as her chin wobbles more, like she's on the edge of sobbing, because I came to her mother's funeral.

Fuck. I didn't want to upset her further, I just wanted to make sure she was okay, make sure she knew I was thinking about her, supporting her, *loving* her, even if it's from a distance. Even if she doesn't want me anymore.

But Verity was right. I should have watched from the cars like a fucking creep.

"Olivia," I say, and my voice also sounds tight with emotions, hoarse with unshed tears. How the fuck did this even happen? I haven't cried in years, not since my asshole father threw me out and told me I'd never make anything of myself. And here I am, ready to kneel at her feet in the dirt and sob into her lap.

She holds out one trembling hand and I take it gratefully, even as my heart thumps painfully in my chest. This is Liv in a nutshell, so kind, so effortlessly graceful, so damn forgiving. The knot behind my ribs releases just slightly as I slide my fingers into hers, as I feel her skin on mine for the first time in days.

Her teeth sink into her lower lip to stop its wobbling as she looks up at me, gold eyes asking me something I don't have an answer for. "Thank you for coming," she whispers.

"I'm sorry for your loss, Liv. Your mother was… She was amazing." That tightness is back in my chest, squeezing my ribs, needing an outlet.

"She was, thank you."

Fuck. I don't want this to be how it is between us. Stilted. Full of polite social niceties, none of the passion or care we'd become used to showing each other before I fucked it up. Before I lashed out in anger, before I ruined the feelings blooming between us.

I need to fix what I can. I need to show her I still care, that I will continue to care for her even if we're not together. The need to comfort her, to hold her broken pieces together when she can't, overwhelms me.

I use my grip on her hand to slowly carefully pull her up out of the chair, giving her plenty of time to resist. If she does, if she pulls away even the slightest bit, I'll let her go, release her hand, and walk away.

But she doesn't.

Olivia lets me pull her from the chair and right into my arms where she belongs, where she should always fucking be. A little sob puffs out of her as I hold her against my chest, one hand in her carefully curled and styled blond hair. The other hooked around her back, fingers brushing her rib cage, where I can feel the beat of her heart.

Liv's hands slip inside my suit jacket and around me, fisting the back of my shirt as another little sob shakes her body. "She's gone, Linc," she whispers against my shirt, voice muffled and aching. "She's gone."

My cheek presses into the top of her head, as my hand moves to stroke up and down her spine, right over the zipper of her black dress. "I know, sunshine," I murmur, hating the pain in her voice. Nothing I say will make it better, But I have to try. "I know. I'm so fucking sorry, sunshine."

I mean those words in more than one way. But she doesn't need to think about the bullshit I put her through right now. She needs to focus on her grief, on working through it, on figuring out life with her mother's presence no longer in it. I just hope like hell she'll let me be a part of it in some way. In *any* way.

Because if I've learned anything over the last few days, it's that I need Liv. I need her in my life, and I'll take her in any way that I can.

I'm not sure how long we stand there, wrapped up in each other, Liv leaning heavily against my body, gripping my shirt like I'm her lifeline. But eventually she pulls back, swipes at her cheeks with one hand, while the other stays at my waist. She doesn't look up at me, instead she frowns at my shirt. "I got makeup all over you," she murmurs, hand sliding over the white fabric that is indeed smeared in black and brown and pale tan. "And people are watching."

"I don't care, Liv." My hand slides to capture another tear with my thumb as it falls. Our position is intimate. We exist in this little bubble that is just her and me. I know there are people outside the bubble. People that might judge us, how close we are. My employees. Cabot. Hell, even Verity might have a problem with this. But I just can't bring myself to care about anything, about anyone, but Olivia Hart.

A small smile curls her lips, there and gone in a flash as a knot forms between her brows. A wave of sadness washes over her face, making her expression crumple. Almost like she feels like she shouldn't have smiled, shouldn't have had a moment of peace today of all days. But she should. God, she should. She deserves every moment of peace, especially on a day like today, when her broken heart is on display for everyone to see.

But I watch as she builds up her walls again, one brick at a time, hardening herself against me again, back to where she was in her hallway when she told me we're done forever. She takes a deep, shuddering breath and drops her hands from me. I do the same, even though everything in me is demanding that I scoop her up and cradle her on my lap through this whole ceremony, through watching them put her mother in the ground.

"Thank you for coming," she says, moving back a step until her legs bump into the chair she'd been sitting in. She sinks down, still so graceful, even in her grief. Then she looks away from me, dismisses me, just like that.

I nod, run a hand through my hair. "Of course, Olivia. Whatever you need."

Next to her, Claire snorts and narrows her eyes at me, but Olivia's best friend doesn't say anything. I honestly wouldn't blame her if she did, but she keeps her mouth closed around the words she wants to say to me for Olivia's sake, I'm sure.

If I want to have any sort of relationship with Liv, I'm going to have to make it up to more than just her, prove myself to the people that care about her too.

I tuck my hands in my pockets and move away from her, skirting the crowd and the curious looks to stand at the back, but still in a place where I can watch Olivia, keep my eyes on her. It's not long before Cabot and Verity join me. Verity tucked against his much larger frame with her back to his chest, his arms draped over her shoulders.

"Do you want to talk about what the hell that was?" Cabot asks, giving me some serious side eye.

I swallow and shake my head, gaze still latched on Olivia's blond hair. "Nope."

Verity reaches out and links her fingers with mine, giving them a supportive squeeze. "I'm sorry I called you an asshole."

I arch a brow and look away from Liv long enough to give her a questioning look. "You didn't call me an asshole."

She sighs and shakes her head, looking regretful as hell. "Well, not out loud, but I definitely did in my head. I also called you a bastard, a waffle stomper, and a douche canoe. And I'm sorry about that, too. There's obviously more to the story than Olivia just got tired of your bullshit and quit."

I nod and look back at the girl in question, at her bowed head, at the curve of her shoulders, the way her body shakes as she cries quietly. "No, she did get tired of my bullshit," I mutter. "And I can't blame her for it."

I can feel both of their eyes on me. "So what are you going to do about it?" Cabot asks, eventually.

I open my mouth to respond, to say there's nothing to do about it. I have a contract to marry Alicia, to expand our company to make it more successful, to prove to my father that I can be something, that I'm not a fucking disappointment. I can't offer Olivia more than crumbs, and she doesn't want crumbs. She wants the entire cake. She *deserves* the entire cake. She deserves to be with someone that shouts from the fucking rooftops that she's theirs. To not be a dirty little secret.

Fuck, she deserves that and so much fucking more.

But if that is the goal, I can't see a way forward for us. Not when I have the contract I signed two years ago hanging over me. Not when I have my father's voice ringing in my ears.

Still, I can't bring myself to say goodbye to her, to close the book of Olivia Hart and Lincoln George. She may have told me we're done forever, but I can't bring myself to believe it.

And if the way she was holding onto me is any sign, then she doesn't believe it either.

29
Olivia

My house is too quiet. I have the TV turned on just for the background noise, but it still feels quiet. My mom didn't make a lot of noise to begin with. She spent a lot of her time sleeping, watching Tv, reading when she had the energy. So it's not the amount of noise that's missing, it's just her.

It's been a week since my mom passed away quietly in her sleep. A week since I held her hand and whispered goodbye to her. A week since she cupped my cheek and told me she'd be keeping an eye on me from above or below. Wherever she ended up, she'd be watching me, heart full of love and so proud of everything I accomplish.

I'm not sure she'd be proud of the way I've holed up in my house, of how I haven't cooked or cleaned, of how I haven't showered in three days, not since the morning of the funeral. I knew it was coming—we did—I had time to prepare, to say goodbye, to create new loving memories with her. But it doesn't make the ache of her loss any easier to bear, doesn't make it easier to remember she's gone.

It's worse when I forget. When I wake up suddenly in the middle of the night and blearily make my way to the hospital bed still in the living room to check on her, only to stare at it with tears on my cheeks as I remember all over again, that she's gone.

The one constant for my entire life is no longer in this world with me. I'm not sure what I'm supposed to do with that. All the preparation in the world can't ready you for the truth of it, for the loneliness. The grief.

God, I feel so fucking alone right now.

Next to me, my phone vibrates. I'm not even sure why I've kept it charged. It's not like I look at it, or answer any of the messages sent to me. I may feel lonely, but the idea of interacting with anyone makes me feel exhausted, worn down and wrung out. I can't be bothered to try to be okay for other people. To try to convince them I'm fine.

The only time I've been tempted is when *Bossy Pants* flashed across the screen. The pull to Lincoln is strong, the urge to just fall into his arms, to have him take control of my body, to use his commands to pull me out of my mind and away from my grief, to let me just have one moment of peace from the ache of loss that's constantly buffeting me.

But then the need to see him is swallowed up by guilt. Because I shouldn't be seeking a way to escape my grief or the memory of my mother. I need to feel this pain, every ounce of it, because I love her, and she deserves to be mourned. She deserved so much more than to get cancer and die in her mid-forties. She should have lived a full fucking life. She should have moved on from my father and found love again. And she should still fucking be here with me.

So yeah, anytime I forget that she's gone, anytime I have a moment of peace or happiness, it's immediately followed by guilt. Guilt I know she wouldn't want me to feel. But I can't help it. Just like I couldn't help the guilt I felt for smiling at Lincoln at her funeral, brief as it was.

Lincoln at the funeral...

I hadn't expected him to come, had prepared myself for the disappointment of it. I wasn't particularly nice to him the last time we'd spoken, and I wouldn't have been at all surprised if he'd kept his distance.

But I can't deny the relief I felt when I saw him looking somber and handsome in his black suit. It had taken every ounce of my self-control, and Claire and Harvey's hands on me, to keep me from throwing myself at him, and begging him to please, please just take me away and make me forget, even if it was just for a moment.

I'd kept myself in check and managed to remain polite until he pulled me out of my seat and gave me the best hug of my damn life. It wasn't even really a hug; it was... a tether, a safe space for me to fall apart.

For so long, Claire was that for me. She was there whenever I needed her. Her arms around me let me know it was safe to feel whatever I was feeling. That she would help me pick up the pieces when I was done. That's the kind of friend she is.

But now... Now I think somehow, Lincoln George has become that for me. *How?* How in the world is that the case? Especially now, when he's marrying someone else to maintain a merger? How does he still feel like the only person I want to talk to? The only person who can make me feel anything but this all-consuming grief?

I pick up my phone and navigate to the text chain that has *Bossy Pants* at the top with a picture of him. I should have deleted his number and blocked him ages ago, as soon as I broke things off and gave my verbal resignation, but I can't bring myself to do it.

Some small part of me is hoping that he might... change his mind. That someday there will be a call or a text from him that will say he made a mistake, that he wants me. *Only me.*

My finger hovers over the text bubble for so long the screen goes dark.

I sigh and set the device down again before swiping it up and typing out,

I miss you.

I stare at the words. They feel too raw for me, too exposing. And what do I hope to accomplish by sending it? To make him feel guilty? To piss off Alicia?

Tears fill my eyes and spill unchecked over my cheeks. I lost the two people that mean the most to me in such a short amount of time, within a week of each other. It's not fair. I can't tell my mom that I miss her. I can't let her know I'm thinking about her every day. God, I wish I could, but she's not here for me to do that with.

Lincoln... Lincoln is here. He's just not mine anymore.

The constant ache in my chest throbs, painfully.

I delete the last word of the message and type a new one.

I miss her.

I don't know why I feel okay sending that to him. I don't know why I feel in my bones that I need to tell him something, open the door to something. But I do.

The message is marked as read immediately. The three dots appear.

**BossyPants:
I know, sunshine. I know.
I'm sorry.**

A strangled sound leaves me as I curl over myself, hands pressing the phone to my chest, as if that will help with the pain.

It doesn't.

"How are you holding up, hon?" Nadia asks, bumping her hip against mine as she pauses next to where I'm cutting limes and tossing them in a small plastic bin.

"I'm... good," I say slowly, before nodding and saying with more conviction. "Yeah, I'm good. Better."

Her head tips to rest on my shoulder for a second. "I can tell. Sometimes you just need a break from the normal."

My lips twist into a small smile. She's not wrong. Working at Poison is *not* my normal. Living without my mother is my new normal, but I'm still not used to it. Living without Lincoln... Well, that's still an open wound. One that I poke at every so often, by searching his name in Google or walking by his house on my way to or from work.

It's getting easier, but it still hurts.

"Oh, I almost forgot," Nadia says, reaching into the front pocket of her apron. "This came for you."

I frown down at the red envelope she offers me. It looks like there must be a card inside. One of those really fancy ones that have like a 3d effect to them, because it's thick.

There isn't an address, just my name written in a vaguely familiar scrawl. It's not Lincoln. I know that much. Not from Claire or Harvey, or hell, even Gi.

"You gonna open it?"

Licking my lips, I drop the knife and dry my hands on a towel before reaching for the envelope. Then I just stare at it. "How did it get here?"

Nadia shakes her head. "I don't know. I found it wedged in the mail slot that no one uses anymore."

Well, that's not creepy or anything.

I let out a breath as I flip it over and slide my thumb along the closure, cracking the seal. A customer farther down the bar calls out and Nadia gives me one curious glance before she hurries away to take their drink order.

I watch her retreat and then slide the card out, frowning at the romantic tone of the front. There's a bouquet of roses with swooping glittering white font that says, *for my love.* My frown grows as I flip the card open, and my breath stalls in my chest. Nestled between the cardstock is picture after picture.

Me and Linc hugging at my mother's funeral.
Me leaving my house looking haggard as hell.
A shot of me through my living room window.
Behind the bar at the Roost.

Me on the sidewalk outside of Lincoln's house, because… well, I'm weak and sometimes just want to be a little stalkerish.

One of me bent over in Lincoln's office with my ass red ad cum dripping down my thighs.

I recognize this one. It's from Lincoln's phone. He snapped it one day after absolutely wrecking me.

The photos drop to the bar and my eyes move to the words scrawled inside the card.

How will I kill thee?

Let me count the ways.

My vision blurs and I can't make out the rest of the words written in what looks like dried blood. But it can't be blood, right? Because that's crazy. It's just fucking insane.

My heart thunders in my chest and there's a ringing in my ears and I just stand there staring at the card at the pictures on the bar. My phone buzzes in my back pocket and I woodenly pull it out, answering the call and holding it to my ear without looking to see who it is, but I can't make my mouth work.

"Liv?" Nadia says from next to me, one hand curling around my upper arm, trying to get my attention, but I'm just staring down. She sucks in a sharp breath when she follows my line of sight.

Then in my ear, through the phone, I hear Lincoln say urgently. "Olivia? What's wrong?"

My composure cracks and my lip wobbles. *"Linc."*

"Baby, where are you?" He sounds frantic. Apparently, the way I said his name is enough to cause him to panic. "Tell me. I'm coming."

My head shakes and I can't make my mouth form words. I don't know if Nadia can tell how much I'm struggling, but she plucks the phone from my limp fingers and I'm mildly aware of the people around me are giving me curious looks, of Nadia gripping my arm, and pulling me into the backroom, all the while talking to me, murmuring words I only half make out. She puts on a pair of latex gloves and carefully removes the card and its contents from my hands. I want to ask her what she's doing, but after a moment my brain clicks that she's trying to keep from putting her fingerprints on the items, because they are evidence. Lincoln must have coached her on what to do. I watch as she slides the card into a plastic zip bag and then discards the glove in the trash.

"I need to call Detective Hayes," I say tonelessly.

Nadia plops onto the couch next to me and laces her fingers through mine. "It's already done. Lincoln called them. He's on his way too."

I nod, and she presses her cheek into my shoulder, keeping me close. I blink down at the top of her black hair. "You don't have to stay with me, Nadia. It was just getting busy out there."

"Shut up, Olivia. I'm not leaving you here alone when you are obviously in the middle of having a breakdown or a panic attack."

Am I having a panic attack? It doesn't feel like it. I don't feel panicky or frantic. Not like Lincoln had sounded. No, I just feel numb. Wrung out. How much is one person expected to endure, you know?

The door slams open and then Lincoln is there striding toward me, hair standing up like he'd run his fingers through it on the way here. He drops to his knees in front of me, big hands engulfing my bare knees, thumbs swiping back and forth.

I blink at him, wanting to reach for him, to have him wrap me up in his arms and hold me against his chest. I want him to tell me everything is going to be okay. Even if it's not.

His slate blue eyes stay focused on me, while his thumbs move back and forth in a soothing motion. He looks like he hasn't slept. Dark circles rim his blue eyes. He looks paler, his normally golden skin bordering on gray.

There's a thick scruff clinging to his jaw, like he hasn't shaved since the last time I saw him at my mother's funeral weeks ago. His hair is a mess, and although he's in a suit, it's not tidy. White shirt wrinkled, top button undone, tie loose around his neck.

I frown at that. At the tie. Before I know what I'm doing, the tip of my finger is brushing against the knot. "It's light blue."

His mouth quirks into a half smile before it's gone. "What is, sunshine?"

My finger strokes over the silk again. "Your tie. It's light blue, and it's a Friday. You always wear black on Friday."

He shakes his head a little. "The color of my tie is the least of our worries, baby."

My jaw clenches at the endearment, and my hand drops, landing with a soft thud on my thigh.

"I thought it was over," I whisper. I really did. They've been quiet, lost interest. There's been nothing since I stopped working for Lincoln, since before that, actually. I suppose it's possible they're still sending threats to the office, but I haven't seen them.

He frowns, slides his hands up the outside of my legs, over my cutoff jean shorts, until his hands frame my waist. "I know. I did too."

"Um, boss?" Kevin's voice comes from just outside the office. "The cops are here. I told 'em we didn't have any fights or anything."

Nadia pushes up from the couch, squeezes my shoulder as she does. "I'll go direct them back here and give my statement. Hang tight, shug."

I swallow and nod. "Thanks, Nadia."

She waves off my thanks and then leaves me and Lincoln alone, far too close for my fragile state. We sit there, staring at each other, his fingers rhythmically tightening and releasing my waist, his chest pressed against my knees, a solid comforting weight.

I can feel his eyes on me, running hungrily over every inch of me, from my loose wavy hair to my t-shirt and jean shorts. "Besides this, how are you doing, sunshine? You look…" He swallows and glances away from me, eyes sliding shut for a moment before he's right back to drinking me in. "You look like you're doing better."

My hands fist on my thighs to keep from reaching for him, pulling him onto the couch with me to have him stretch out on top of me. Not for anything sexual, but so his weight can help ground me, comfort me, make me feel safe and whole.

"It's all relative, isn't it?" My voice is hoarse. "How's Alicia?"

I want to call back those two words as soon as they're out of my mouth. It's far too telling, gives him too much insight into how I'm still hurting, how jealous I am. He opens his mouth, presumably to answer, but I slap my hand over his lips. "Nevermind. I don't want to know. I really don't want to hear about her or your wedding planning or… anything."

I feel him smile against my palm, feel his cheeks plump and see his eyes crinkle at the corners. His shoulders slump, just the slightest bit, not in dejection, but in relief. Like he's pleased that I sound jealous as hell.

One of his hands leaves my waist to curl around my wrist and slides my hand down, pressing it to his chest over his heart. "Liv," he starts, but then the door opens and Lincoln pushes to his feet, spinning hands raised like he's going to attack whoever is interrupting us.

Detective Hayes enters, her eyes on the notepad in her hand as she jots down a few more thoughts, but she pulls up short when she sees Lincoln towering over me, looking like he's ready to go to battle. Her eyes flick to me, and then back to him, as her brow arches. "Mr. George. I didn't expect to find you here."

He relaxes marginally. "I'm the one that called you."

She nods, looking down at the little pad in her hand. "Right, but seeing as the last time we spoke, you maintained that you and Miss Hart only had a working relationship, and she no longer works for you, I'm surprised. How did you know Miss Hart received a new threat?"

I shift on the couch, leaning forward to intervene, because it sounds an awful lot like Detective Hayes thinks Lincoln had something to do with this. And although we aren't on the best terms at the moment—we aren't on any terms at all—I know in my bones he didn't.

But Lincoln doesn't seem offended, he just widens his stance and crosses his arms over his chest, settling in for the barrage of questions. "I called Olivia just as she received the letter. Her manager let me know what was happening. I called you and came as quickly as I could to make sure she's okay."

Detective Hayes nods. "And how did you know she would receive a threatening message?"

I make a noise in my throat as I push to my feet, frustration bubbling in my stomach. "He didn't do this," I protest, moving forward to get my point across.

Lincoln catches me around my waist before I can move between him and the officer, turning me to face him. His hands coming up to cup my face, make me meet his eyes. "She's just doing her job, sunshine. I'd rather she be thorough than have something slip through the cracks. Your safety is more important than any discomfort I might feel at answering a few questions."

I frown, but nod slowly, before shooting a glare at the Detective. "For the record, I know he didn't do this."

Her sharp gaze moves between the two of us before she notes something on her pad of paper. "Noted."

Lincoln tucks me into his chest and wraps me up in his arms. "I was calling Miss Hart to beg her to meet me for dinner. There have been a lot of changes in my personal life recently and I wanted to discuss them with her."

A knot forms between my brows at that, and I want to ask what he means, but bite my tongue to keep the words inside. I don't care. I don't care about changes in his life. I don't care about anything with him. Not anymore. He made his choice, and I made mine.

Those choices will not allow us to be together.

I wouldn't be able to live with myself if I become his mistress. He has a dumb idea that his company needs this merger, so he needs to fulfill his contractual obligations. He's choosing business over me.

No matter how heartbroken I am, how much I feel like half a person. I can't give in to him. Even if his arms feel like heaven. Even if he holds me like I'm the most important thing in the world to him.

"Is that normal? To discuss your personal life with your ex-employee?"

I swallow and tip my chin back to look at Lincoln, wanting to see his face as he answers this question. His slate blue eyes flick to meet mine, giving me a soft smile, and then he looks back at Detective Hayes. "Olivia is so much more than just an ex-employee. She's my best friend. My confidant. My light in the dark. She is *everything* to me. The most important part of my life. So is it normal for me to discuss my personal life with an ex-employee? No. But it is normal for me to do so with Olivia."

I blink against the tears that want to spill, hold back the snort of disbelief that wants to leave me. Detective Hayes makes a noise in her throat. Half hum, half scoff. "So I take it when you told me that Miss Hart is only your employee and nothing more, after someone sent her a bloody heart in a box you were lying?" She levels me with an unimpressed look. "You *both* were lying."

My heart rate picks up. Shit. That's a crime, isn't it? Obstructing justice or something? We should have told her right from the freaking start, we should have told her.

Lincoln must feel the tension in my body because he squeezes me tighter. "Miss Hart took her cues from me. I should have told you we were together, that we'd been sleeping with each other, but I… panicked. I got worried if anyone found out how I actually feel about her, the asshole stalking her would up their game. I thought… they would take her from me. So I lied and said she was nothing." His lips brush against my temple. "But that couldn't be further from the truth. She's *everything*," he murmurs against my skin. Then he straightens again and levels Detective Hayes with a look. "However, I do believe that my original assessment is true. This is happening to Liv because of me."

She arches a brow and shifts her weight. "Oh, really? And why is that?"

His arms tighten. "I recently got engaged to another woman." Detective Hayes's arms drop by her sides in shock. "Since then, the threats on Miss Hart have stopped. There have been no deliveries to the office for her, none to her house. No text messages or letters."

"Except for this one." Detective Hayes moves over to the desk, where Nadia left the card carefully covered in a plastic bag, before pinning him with a hard look. "What changed?"

Lincoln sighs, kisses my shoulder, and then says. "I broke off my engagement yesterday."

30
Lincoln

I feel the tension riding Olivia. Every muscle in her body is taut, her heart is beating hard in her chest, vibrating through her ribs and into mine. She stiffens further when I say the words I wanted to tell her in private, when I could look her in her gorgeous honey eyes and tell her I love her. I choose her. I want to spend every second of the rest of my life with her, making up this monumental fuck up to her.

I want to tell her that the month away from her has been torture, that almost as soon as she left, I started working on a way out. Out of the strangle hold Alicia and her father had on my company, out of the contract. I only kept my distance because I didn't want to go to her until I knew I could offer her everything she deserves. The entire fucking world. The whole cake, not just crumbs.

She deserves that, and so much more.

Slowly, so fucking slowly, my girl twists her head to look at me.

"What?" I smirk at her, at

her wide eyes, filling with tears. "Lincoln, what did you just say?"

I shift her around, turning her in my arms so we're looking at each other, so she can see that I'm telling the truth. "I broke off the engagement to Alicia and the contract that required it."

Liv swallows, shakes her head. "No, but... You said you needed the merger... you said..."

My thumb presses into her mouth, quiets her protests. "I know what I said. They were the biggest lies I've ever uttered. I don't need the merger, I don't need H&G. I need you. You're the only thing I need, Liv." I press my forehead to hers. "I want to talk about this to tell you everything, but maybe we can wait until it isn't a part of a police investigation?"

A small, strangled laugh pulls from her chest, and she tips her chin up to brush her lips against mine in the smallest briefest of kisses. So quick I'm halfway convinced I imagined it, but then she's pulling away from me, turning to face Detective Hayes.

I lift my eyes to the detective while curling my body over my woman, keeping her close. "I think the person behind this is Alicia Moreau, her father Jacques, or someone hired by them."

I know without seeing it that Liv's gaze narrows. "Why would Alicia want to freak me out?"

Detective Hayes flicks her gaze from her to me. "That's what I would like to know."

I straighten, just slightly, meeting the officer's gaze. "Our engagement and subsequent marriage was part of an overall contract to merge Moreau Industries and H&G. Moreau Industries acquired my father's company some years back, and I wanted to take possession of it. But on top of that, the merger made sense. Both companies were seemingly successful and have aligned priorities and goals. The notes and letters Olivia received were aimed at scaring her away from me, keeping us from getting close. Every time we took a break or a step back, they would pause, but as soon as we were together again, they would pick up. My first thought was that it was a woman I'd slept with. Maybe one I didn't break it off with as kindly as I should have."

Detective Hayes is jotting things down in her notebook before she looks up at me. "And the reason you suspect the Moreaus is because she's one of those women?"

I shake my head. "No, it's because their company is practically bankrupt. They kept it quiet, falsified documents to show they're in the black, when really they're so far in the hole that the only way for them to get out of it is a massive influx of capital."

"Like they would receive from becoming a part of H&G." Olivia says, understanding washing over her. "They were trying to scare me off, so that what happened wouldn't." She shifts just slightly, tipping her head back to look at me. "Why would the marriage need to be a part of that? They could have just suggested a merger."

I lift a shoulder. "I couldn't even pretend to know. But maybe it has something to do with hoping it would give Alicia greater power over both companies? I don't know. I don't care." Unable to resist the pink bow of her mouth, I dip my head and brush her lips with mine.

Detective Hayes snaps her notebook shut. "Well, I'll reach out to the Moreaus and see what they have to say about it." She picks up the plastic bag containing the card. "If I have any other questions, I'll reach out."

I nod. "The head of my security team, Lance Bigelow, will be in contact. He has the results of our private investigation, including the true state of the company. It might help with questioning."

Detective Hayes's mouth tightens, and she blows out a breath. "I should arrest you for obstructing justice. If you had told me your suspicions from the start, then maybe you both could have saved yourselves some heartache."

Olivia jerks, like she's going to protest, but the detective is already waving her hand. "But I'm a romantic at heart, and the last thing I want to do is separate you when you've just found each other again." She gives us both meaningful looks. "But I expect only the truth from here on out. We can only help you if we have all the facts."

Olivia nods emphatically. "Yes, of course, Detective Hayes. I'm so sorry."

When I don't immediately apologize, Liv jams her elbow into my side, making me wince, but I do as she so clearly wants. "Yes, I apologize as well."

The detective rolls her eyes and strides out the door, leaving me and Liv alone for the first time in a month.

Almost as soon as the door shuts, Liv starts crying. I hurry to wrap her in my arms, tugging her against my chest again. "Shh, baby, don't cry. Please, I hate it when you cry."

She balls up her fists and slams them against my chest, not hard enough to actually hurt, but enough that I know she's mad at me. "You asshole!" she wails into my shirt. "I can't believe you did this to me."

I pull back enough to look at her tear-streaked face. "Broke off my engagement for you?"

"Got engaged in the first place!" She wails, face scrunched up with pain. "How could you do that? We're supposed to be together, Lincoln. That's like a fact of the universe and you almost ruined it!"

A chuckle rumbles from me, and Liv's tears dry up in favor of a scowl. "Don't laugh at me!"

I cup her face and smooth my thumbs over her cheeks, wiping away her tears. "I can't help it. You're so fucking adorable when you're upset."

Her scowl deepens, but then she leans into me, pressing her face into my chest, as my hands slide around her, one into her hair, the other clasping her opposite shoulder. "I missed you," she murmurs. "So much."

I bow my head over hers. "I missed you too, sunshine." We stay like that, just holding on to each other until there's a knock on the door and then it's pushed open slowly. Nadia pokes her head in.

"Sorry to interrupt. I just wanted to tell you to take the rest of the night off." Olivia shakes her head, but Nadia points a finger at her in warning. "Yes. Take the fucking night, Livie. You just had a traumatic experience and the two of you have a lot to talk about. We will manage here just fine."

Liv bites her lower lip. "You're sure? It's a Friday."

Nadia nods and flaps her hands at us. "Yes, girl. I am sure. Get the hell out of my bar."

"Come on, baby," I murmur into her ear. "Let me take you home. Let me take care of you."

Liv melts against me while Nadia cocks an eyebrow in my direction. "I'll grab my things."

Liv presses up to kiss me on my lips, a brief press of our mouths together before she slips past her boss. Who crosses her arms over her chest and leans against the door frame with her shoulder. "You fuck this up again and I will kill you."

Her tone is perfectly pleasant, but I see the warning there. I nod and run a hand through my hair. "If I fuck this up again, I'll hand you the knife."

She tilts her head, running her eyes over me from top to bottom, and then nods once. "Deal." She straightens. "But I think you dying would actually truly break Livie, so just don't fuck it up."

"I don't intend to."

"Good."

Nadia turns toward the hall with a smile on her face and a second later, Liv appears with her bag and her jacket. She flashes me a shy smile as she tucks her bag into her side. "Shall we?"

I can't help the grin that spreads on my face. She's here, coming home with me. We're going to talk and she's going to forgive me. I know it. I move toward her, lace my fingers through hers. "We shall."

When we enter my house, Liv looks around like she can't quite believe that she's here. There's a flicker of agony on her face as her eyes latch on where Alicia and I were standing the last time she was here, but it fades almost as soon as it appears. She folds her arms over her chest and moves farther into the house, heading straight for the living room and the bar along one wall.

She points at a bottle of bourbon. "Do you mind?"

I shake my head. "Not at all."

I don't know what to do with my hands, or my body or *anything*, as I watch her drop her bag to the floor and then grab the bottle and two glasses. She carries them over to the couch and plops down before pouring two generous glasses and nudging one toward me.

"Sit down, bossy pants."

My heart swells as soon as she uses the nickname, and my hands leave my pockets. "Quite demanding of you, Liv. Now who's the bossy pants?"

She rolls her eyes and swipes up her glass before leaning back on the couch and taking a sip. I watch as she relaxes in increments, sinking further into the cushions, before I move to sit next to her. I leave about a foot of space between us, even though what I really want to do is cradle her on my lap. I need to remember to keep my hands to myself and let her control how quickly we move.

I'm the one that hurt her.

I'm the one asking for forgiveness.

She's the one in control.

She finishes her drink and then slides the crystal glass onto the table before eying me. "So you broke things off with Alicia."

Nerves assault me as I nod and run a hand through my hair. "I did. I never should have let it get to this point, Liv. It kills me that I did. As soon as I started…" I take a deep breath and barrel through. "As soon as I realized I loved you, I should have broken things off with Alicia, should have forgotten about the merger, about my father's company. I should have…" I trail off and slide my hand over the couch toward her, hoping like hell she'll reach back.

"It doesn't matter what I should have done because I didn't do any of it. What matters is that I hurt you. I wasn't there when you needed me. And I'm so fucking sorry about that, Liv. I know it's not enough. It's not nearly fucking enough, because they're just words. But I hope you'll give me the chance to show you, to prove to you that I mean it when I say I want to be with you. Only you, for the rest of my life."

Liv eyes my hand resting on the cushion between us. *Please. Please reach back.* She doesn't. "You broke my heart, Linc."

I swallow hard and am not the least bit surprised when my voice comes out hoarse. "I know. And I know I don't deserve it, but I'm really hoping you'll forgive me and give me another chance."

Liv looks at me, arms crossed over her chest, then leans forward and snatches up the bottle to pour herself another drink. "What about your father's company?"

I arch a brow, surprise rocketing through me. "What about it?"

She takes a sip of the alcohol and spears me with a look. "You've been working so hard to get to a point where you could take it, own it. I'm guessing that Alicia and her father aren't going to go forward with the merger if you don't marry her."

I shift a little closer, not missing how she sounds the tiniest bit jealous when she says my ex-fiancée's name. "She won't, but I think I can get him to come around. But even if they tell me fuck no to my face and shove me out the door, it won't matter. I'll happily give up the company of the man who never loved me like he should have, if it means I get to spend forever with you." My hand slides closer, brushes against her thigh, right where her cut-off shorts end.

She flicks her gaze down to where my fingers touch her and then back up. "And I suppose if they're behind the threats against me, then it doesn't really matter if they play ball or not."

My gaze narrows. "If they're behind the threats against you, sunshine, I will use every penny in my bank account to put them behind bars for the rest of their fucking lives."

Half her lips curl into a smile. "I believe that."

Relief flows through me. *Progress.* "Good. You should. I would do anything for you, Liv. I'm sorry I didn't see it before."

She stares down at the amber liquid in her glass. "I'm scared."

The words spoken so bluntly, so easily make me reach for her, gather her onto my lap, and I'm relieved when she doesn't push away, just cuddles closer into my chest with a weary sigh. "Why are you scared, sunshine?" I already know, but I think she needs to say it.

"I told you about my father, about the way he treated me and my mother. We were never his first choice, always the runner-up. I told you how it felt to be the second option." I want to tell her she'll always be my first option, even when I was going to marry Alicia. My life would have been with her, but I know that's not how she would feel. "And then you asked me to do that, to be okay with sharing you with someone else. And that's... That's really not okay. I'm scared—fucking terrified—that if we give this a shot, you'll keep me as a second option. Not your first choice."

"No, baby-" I protest, but she puts her fingers to my lips, stalling out the words.

"I lost you and then I lost my mother within a week of each other. I'm not going to lie. Losing her overshadowed losing you." That makes sense, so I nod. "And after, when I started coming back to myself... I realized I missed her like crazy, that I still wanted to talk to her, to see her. But I can't. I'll never be able to see her again." A tear escapes her eye and flows over the curve of her cheek. "But you... You're here, alive, breathing. And I miss you almost as much as I miss her. I-I ache for you, Linc."

My heart throbs painfully in my chest, and my lips pucker against her fingers involuntarily, needing to soothe her, to kiss her.

She smiles softly at me, rubs her fingers back and forth before dropping them. "I can't do anything about missing my mother but breathe through the pain of it. But I can... I can do something about missing you."

Hope lodges in my chest, makes my stomach flip as I straighten slightly, eager to hear her next words. "What does that mean, Olivia?"

She cups my jaw, tears shimmering in her pretty honey eyes. "It means even though I'm so fucking terrified, I'm willing to give you another chance. I want to be with you."

I let out a whoop of triumph before I slide my hands into her hair to hold her in place as I lunge up and claim her mouth with mine. She's just as sweet as I remember, even with the salty taste of her tears mixing in. One of her hands curls in my tie and pulls me closer, while I try to fucking inhale every bit of her I can.

She pulls back long before I'm ready to, long before I've had my fill of her lips. "This means we're together, Linc," she says like a warning. "You're going to have to take me on proper dates and introduce me as your girlfriend to people."

I grin up at her. "I can't fucking wait, sunshine."

She smiles back and tips forward, hands diving into my hair as she presses her mouth to mine. "Good. So I'm your girlfriend and you're my boyfriend."

"Yep." Nothing has ever sounded better to me in my entire goddamn life.

"Hmm…" She trails her lips over my jaw as my head tips back. "I think my boyfriend should take me to bed."

Fuck yes. I've never moved so fast in my life. Looping my hands under her ass and shifting her so her legs can wrap around my hips, I lunge up from the couch and carry her up the stairs. I bypass the playroom and head to my bedroom.

We don't need any games tonight. We just need us.

I stop in the middle of the room and let her legs fall to the floor, her converse sinking into the throw rug as she slides down my body. Her fingers go to work on my tie, sliding the silk out from under the collar of my shirt.

As soon as she's done, my hands dive under the hem of her t-shirt with the Poison logo on the front, yank it up and over her head. When I see the lacy bra underneath, offering the perfect swell of her breasts to me like a feast, I groan. My arm loops around her back, making her arch toward me as I bend my head to run my tongue over the tops of them, before lapping at first one nipple through the lace and then the other.

She gasps and moans at my attention and then she pushes me back, trembling fingers going to the buttons of my shirt. "You have too many clothes on, bossy pants. Need to feel you."

Well, fuck who am I to deny her? I push her hands away, grab both sides of my shirt and rip it off me, sending buttons flying. Olivia looks up at me with wide eyes. "Linc! That shirt had to cost more than a small car!"

I chuckle. "I can buy a new one, Liv. Now get the fuck over here."

She doesn't do what I say immediately, arching a brow and reaching behind her to undo the clasp of her bra. When it falls to the ground, she steps over it and right back into my arms. We both groan at the slide of our skin against each other.

She feels fucking perfect. Better than I imagined, better than I remembered. "Like a fucking dream come true."

She giggles and her fingers latch into a belt loop on my pants, dragging me over to the bed. "Can't wait," she says as she stops next to the mattress and shimmies out of her shorts, kicking off her shoes. "I need to feel you inside me, Linc."

I shed my pants as she climbs onto the bed, shimmying backward until she's on the pillows.

I crawl up after her cock hanging heavy between my legs. "I can't wait either. Later, I'll lick your pussy until you scream, and I fuck you with my fingers. Later, I'll kiss every inch of this fucking perfect body. But," I swallow hard and settle between her legs. "Right now, I need to be inside you."

Olivia gives me a soft smile before reaching between us and grasping my dick in her hand, squeezing and stroking a few times. "Fuck," I hiss, as she guides me to her entrance, notching me in just slightly. Then she grasps my shoulders as I sink down on top of her, holding my weight on my forearms, so as much of our skin is touching as can be.

I look into her pretty honey eyes. "Ready, baby?"

"Yes," she breathes.

I push slowly into her, making us both groan at the tight fit. Her hips roll slightly to ease the way, but she's already so fucking wet for me, so it's easy to push until I'm fully seated. We stay like that, getting used to the feel of each other again, while holding eye contact. I feel her gaze all the way down to my soul and know that this woman is it. There will never be anyone else for me. Only Olivia Hart.

If I fail this chance she's giving me, if I fuck up somehow, and lose her forever, I'll never look at anyone else. Liv is all I fucking want in this world.

My woman's eyes go soft, a gentle smile curling her lips as she lifts to kiss me, tongue sweeping into my mouth. "Everything's going to be fine," she breathes. God, I want to believe it. "Now fucking move."

I chuckle but give her what she wants. Pulling my hips back before slamming in again, making her mouth open on a pant as her knees curl closer to her chest. "Oh, fuck yes," she moans. I live for that sound. I'm going to make her moan every single day of our life.

I push up enough to curl one hand around her knee, pulling it up higher, opening her to me more. "Like this, baby?"

She nods frantically, hands gripping, pulling, urging me to go faster, deeper, harder. "Please, Linc. Remind me what it's like to be yours."

I growl and all bets are fucking off at her words. "Yes, Liv. You are mine." I punctuate each word with a thrust of my hips, watching as her breasts bounce. "You're fucking mine, baby. And I'm never letting you go again."

She rears up and captures my lips with hers. This isn't a soft kiss. It's a battle, a promise, and a challenge. "Good," she gasps out, teeth scraping my shoulder. "I'm not letting you go, either. You're mine, Lincoln George."

We don't talk anymore, our entire focus on our bodies, our pleasure, on reaching that peak together. It's almost like we're trying to see who can make the other come first, a race to the finish line. But Liv will always, always come before me. There isn't a force on earth that could make it otherwise, even her perfect pink pussy gripping me so fucking tight.

I slide my hand down her stomach to that bud between her legs. She screams when I circle it, her hips moving frantically as my name falls from her lips in a constant perfect litany. "Linc, Linc, Linc. Yes. Oh, fuck yes. Linc!"

"Look at me, baby," I growl at her, fucking into her harder. "Look at me when you come. I want to see it."

She peels her eyes open and meets my gaze, keeping them focused on my face as I pinch her clit and she detonates. Her whole body tenses, head tipping back as a loud moan comes from her chest. She clamps down on me like she can't stand the thought of letting me leave her body, even just an inch. The feel of it, of her eyes on my face while she clenches rhythmically around me, sets off my own orgasm. I call out her name as I fill her, and I swear that as soon as my cum touches her, she comes again, helping to milk me even more.

I collapse on top of her, open mouth resting against her pulse point. Her arms loop around me, stroke up and down my spine, until eventually she pats my shoulder and I take it as a sign she needs some air. I roll to the side, but don't go far, staying right next to her, with my arm looped over her stomach as she stares up at the ceiling, dazed.

I drink in her profile, her gorgeous features, her honey hair spread on my pillow where it should have been all along. God, I want this. I want her here every fucking night. I want to wake up to her every morning, sleep rumbled and sweet.

I bury my face in the curve of her neck. "Move in with me," I murmur against her skin. "Please, Liv."

Her fingers tangle in my hair and tug gently, lifting my eyes to hers. "Isn't that… fast? Shouldn't we take time to-"

"Fuck time," I growl out. "I've spent enough fucking time away from you. I want you to move in with me. I want you here when I get home from work. I want your clothes mixed in with mine in the laundry. I want your products in my bathroom and your baked goods in my kitchen."

She arches a brow and laughs. "Is that a euphemism?"

I chuckle. "No, baby, it's the truth. I want my life with you to start right now. Please, move in with me. Or I can move in with you if you'd rather stay in your house."

Her teeth sink into her lower lip. "Yeah, about my house..." I tense, knowing what's coming. "You paid the mortgage."

I shrug and trail my fingers over her collarbone. "I didn't want you to worry about it while dealing with the arrangements for your mother."

She blinks at me. "You paid the entire thing, Lincoln. Not just a month or two."

My tongue swirls around her pink areola. "I did. I have the money. You needed the help."

She hums and strokes her fingers over my hair, while her back arches, lifting her breasts further to my mouth. "And the hospital bills?"

"Insurance covered them," I'm quick to say because I do not want her to feel like I did too much. I know my girl and she doesn't want to be taken care of all the time. She wants to be an equal partner. The problem is, I make a hell of a lot more money than she does, and I like spoiling her.

"Really, even the past due ones?"

I nod before moving to the other nipple. "Yep."

"Lincoln." I lift my eyes to hers and sigh.

"Look, your insurance should have covered those from the beginning. Your mother was your dependent. It's not your fault that the health insurance provided by your employer at the time didn't cover it. I simply corrected an oversight in my company, Liv. It's fine."

She hums, tightens her grip on my hair and tugs until I'm close enough for her to kiss. "I'll pay you back."

I laugh and kiss her. "No, you won't. At least not financially. If you want to pay me back, you can move in with me. It'll be more than enough."

My girl sighs, shakes her head, looks down and then back up, a small smile on her lips. "I'll... *stay* with you for a bit. Until we get the issue with the... with my stalker resolved. I'll feel safer being here with you. And it will give us a chance to see if this will work long term."

I frown, not liking that she feels like we need a trial run, but then I guess I can't really blame her. I fucked things up between us, nearly ruined what we have. Of course, she's going to be cautious. I've been working toward us being together for a month. She's only just now coming up to speed.

"Okay, it's a deal," I say. "But I have free rein to convince you that you belong here with me, okay?"

She laughs. "Okay."

I lunge up and kiss her, stealing the sweet sounds that fall from her lips. "First up," I say, gripping her knee and opening her to me. My cock settles against her slick heat and we both groan. "Orgasms. I'll give you so many fucking orgasms, sunshine." My hips shift, and she moans as I slide into her. "*All* the orgasms."

Her fingers clutch at my shoulders as she arches to meet my thrusts. "Hmm. That does sound nice."

I nod, my hair failing to brush her forehead as I grind against her. "If we live together, I can bend you over whenever I want. I can strip you bare and lick your sweet pussy until you come all over my face. I can wake you up in the middle of the night and fuck my good little whore like she likes to be fucked."

Olivia moans, head tipping back as her hips roll to meet mine. I nibble and lick along the length of her throat, drawing out more and more cries, until she's pleading with me to let her come.

"Baby, you don't need my permission for that. Not right now. If you need to come, come."

"Linc," she whines. "Please. I need you to fuck me harder. Please."

I bite my lower lip to keep from grinning at her. "No, baby. I'm not fucking you right now. I'm making love to you, soft and slow and sweet."

Her pretty honey eyes widen as they meet mine. "Love?" she asks, and apparently the idea of that is enough to ratchet her pleasure up even more because she clenches around me, the little flutters telling me she's so goddamn close.

"Yeah, sunshine. *Love.* I told you I loved you and I meant it. You're it for me, Liv. You're all I want in this life or the next. Forever. I fucking love you forever."

"I love you too," she moans. "Fuck, Linc!" Her body shudders around me, clamping down as her orgasm hits, sweeps her under sweet bliss. I'm right there behind her, calling out her name to the ceiling as I spill my seed inside her.

I collapse on top of her, boneless and sated. Olivia doesn't seem to mind, just strokes her hands up and down my spine idly, kissing my shoulder, my neck, my jaw.

Eventually she murmurs, "So orgasms, huh? That's a pretty compelling argument in the for column."

I chuckle against her neck before lifting my head to sip from her lips. "I know. Who would have thought it, hmm?" I smooth the hair back from her face and hope she can see my sincerity as I continue. "I'm going to spend the rest of my life making you so happy, Olivia. I'm going to make sure you don't regret giving me another chance."

Her honey eyes go soft and sweet, and she leans up to kiss me again before whispering, "I believe you."

31
Olivia

I wiggle my fingers at Lance as I push through the door, feeling his eyes on me until it shuts. I'm pretty sure he stays on the other side of the door until he hears me activate the alarm, too.

As soon as I do, my shoulders slump, relief flowing through me. I hadn't realized how tense I'd been all day, just waiting for something to happen, for the next sick delivery to arrive, for a shadowy figure in the corner of my eye.

It's only been two days since the card was delivered. Nadia told me to take the weekend to recover, told me to take the entire week if I needed, but my shift today, was the opening shift, starting at eleven and finishing at six, so I figured it was okay to go since I would be home before the sun set.

Lincoln begged me not to. He wants me to come back to work for him and Cabot and H&G, but it just doesn't feel right. Not now when he's actually my boyfriend and we're trying to live together. If we're not going to try to hide it, then I shouldn't work for him.

Besides, I actually like working at the bar. It's fast-paced and fun. I love Nadia. The customers are an easy going bunch. Josh shows up nearly every evening, sometimes with his wife in tow.

But today has been difficult, and I think that maybe Nadia and Lincoln were right. I hate the idea of letting Alicia and her father dictate any portion of my life, but maybe I should take a break from working at Poison just until we know that the danger has passed.

Lincoln will be so pleased.

I tuck my jacket and my purse into the closet after fishing out my phone and sliding it into the back pocket of my jeans before wandering toward the kitchen, where I Lincoln should be. He promised to cook tonight.

The house is quiet, too fucking quiet, making my hair stand on end as I pass by the darkened den. Why are all the lights off?

"Lincoln? Baby? I'm home." I call out, feeling silly and cliche, even as a shiver of dread moves over my body.

Movement out of the corner of my eye has me whipping my head toward the living room. It's shadowy and dark and I can't make out much of anything, just the black forms of the furniture.

"Lincoln?"

Faint light from the kitchen filters through the room. I take slow steps, inching toward it, turning the corner into the large open space, but staying right by the door. The light over the stove is on, but nothing else. Taking a deep breath, I reach out to the light switch.

A scream pulls from me as my eyes adjust to the light. Between the dining room table and the couch is a wooden chair with arms, one of the ornate ones I made fun of Lincoln for having at the head of his table. Sitting slumped over with blood dripping down his face is Lincoln.

"Linc!" I start toward him, my feet moving over the hardwood floor rapidly.

A loud bang as me ducking, hands over my head as I freeze, heart thundering in my chest. *Was that a fucking gunshot?*

"Leave him," a feminine voice says. I look at Lincoln for a moment longer, torn between closing the distance between us so I can make sure he's okay, and staying right where I am. I keep my eyes on his chest and see the gentle rise and fall with each breath. He's alive. Though obviously not well. The blood darkening the collar of his shirt is proof of that.

"Hands up," the voice says, and I turn toward her, holding my hands in front of my chest, like that will stop a bullet if she decides to shoot me.

Alicia stands against the wall, tucked away so I couldn't see her with the lights off. Smart. She looks as put together as the one time I've seen her, long dark hair curled to perfection, wearing a pair of tight dark wash jeans and a silky white blouse with tiny pearl buttons.

"What are you doing?" I ask, my voice strained around what feels like my heart lodged in my throat. "Why are you here?"

Alicia taps the gun in her hand against her thigh. "Why do you think I'm here, Olivia? You tried to take what *belongs* to me."

My eyes dart in Lincoln's direction, hoping like hell I'll see his slate blue eyes, but his chin is still slumped to his chest. "So," Alicia says, lifting the gun, drawing my attention back to her. "Now I'm going to take your life."

I watch horrified as she shifts her finger to the trigger, and I don't have the chance to move before the gun fires, the bullet exploding from the barrel with a deafening sound.

The shot goes wide, but I swear I still feel it whizzing right by my head, feel the force of it lift my hair. Alicia curses and tightens her grip on the gun, bringing up her left hand to steady it as she points it at me again.

My hands shoot up. "Okay, just... calm down. Okay?" I wince because I know it's the wrong fucking thing to say. No woman in a rage likes to be told to calm down. It will almost always make the situation worse.

"Calm down," she spits. "You expect me to calm down when some hayseed hick college dropout has ruined all of my plans? Do you have any idea what it took to plan this, to get Lincoln to agree? I got rid of girl after girl in college. Years of planting seeds of how unlovable he is to everyone but me. I bought his father's fucking company for this. I had to work on him for over a year to get him to agree to marry me."

I frown, brows drawing low, trying to make sense of what she's saying. "Wait... This isn't about saving your father's company? I thought-"

"You thought I did all this for a company? No, I did it because I love him. For six fucking years, it's been him and me. I could overlook the one-night stands and constant parade of women, because every Thursday night he was with me. Every. Single. One. I was the only woman in his life for so fucking long. I thought it was only a matter of time before he realized he loved me, too."

Lincoln groans from where he's tied up, head lifting just slightly as he comes to. Alicia swings the gun wildly in his direction, and a little sound of fear squeaks out of me. I thought it was bad when she pointed that gun at me, but this is worse so much fucking worse. Especially since he can't move.

"Don't. Please," I whisper. I didn't mean to, but it slips out. Alicia doesn't look at me, keeping the gun trained on the man I love with my whole heart. *"Please."*

Lincoln's gaze snaps up. He doesn't focus on Alicia, though. His slate blue eyes slide right over her and find me. A pained expression crosses his face when he finds me. "Sunshine," he groans out. "I'm sorry."

Tears sting my eyes, and I shake my head. "It's okay. We're going to be okay." My phone is burning a hole in my back pocket. I just need to reach it, call someone. *Anyone.* I give Lincoln a reassuring nod, sliding my hand behind me slowly, trying like hell to not draw Alicia's attention.

"Don't look at her," Alicia snaps. "I'm the one who's been with you for years. I'm the one who loves you."

I keep my eyes on Lincoln as I slowly drag the phone out of my pocket, flashing it to him, and his eyes spark with recognition. While he turns his attention to Alicia, giving her what she wants, I press and hold the side button and a volume button down.

"Why are you doing this, Alicia?" Linc grinds out, and I can tell by the way he's moving that he's trying to undo the ropes binding him. If I can tell, I'm sure Alicia can too. He needs to stop.

"I told you why. I love you, Lincoln. For years, I've loved you, since the first moment I saw you. You just never saw me that way, never wanted me that way." On my screen, the SOS option appears. My heart thunders in my chest as I carefully slide my thumb over, staring until it connects. "I was fine with it because you never seemed to want anyone like that. But I knew, as soon as you started fucking *her*, it was different. I could tell she was going to be a problem."

I move so slowly as I bend to set my phone on the side table. I should have probably just slid it into my pocket again, but I want them to hear what she's saying, to have a record of it.

"You sent the pictures, the first ones of us in the elevator?" Lincoln asks, gaze flitting to me briefly before landing on her again. "How did you get access to our security feeds?"

Alicia waves her free hand and the one holding the gun trembles as she does. "It was easy. All I had to do was tell people I needed access for the merger. You really need to tighten up your security, Lincoln." She glances over at me, and I freeze, the phone on the table in front of me, screen down. "I don't like you over there, where I can't keep my eye on you."

I hold up my hands and inch toward Lincoln, which is where I want to be, anyway. I want to be next to him, feel him close to me, even if he can't wrap his arms around me. "Okay, okay, just... maybe you can put the gun down?"

"Mm, I don't think I will. That's far enough." I stop three feet from Lincoln and its torture. Fuck. I need to be right next to him. My hands ache with the need to hold him, and I know that if we could touch, even for the briefest of moments, it would soothe us both. I take one more step toward him. The gun swings in my direction, and Alicia lets out a sharp, "*stop.*" And Lincoln makes a pained noise in his throat.

He probably feels the same as I do. It's worse having the gun pointed at the person you love. I stop with my hands still raised and my heart thundering in my chest.

"Alicia, please," Lincoln tries. "We're friends. We've been friends for years. Don't do this."

The crazed woman lets out a humorless laugh, shaking her head. "*Friends.*" She spits the world like it's something distasteful. I suppose, to her, it is. Especially when it comes to this man. She brings the gun up and smacks it against the side of her head a few times. "I never wanted to be your *friend,* Linc. Never. But it was all I could have from you. So I took it because it had to be enough. But not now. Not anymore." The gun lowers and points directly at his head. At this range, it's not likely she'll miss.

My heart crawls up my throat. "If I can't have you," she says, her voice deadly serious. "No one can."

32
Lincoln

I want to look at Olivia. If these are my last moments on this earth, I want to spend them gazing at the girl I love, reassuring her. Showing her with my expression that I fucking love her. I want her sweet honey eyes to be the last thing I see, but instead I'm staring down the black barrel of a gun with an insane woman taking up most of my field of vision.

I can't look away. No matter how hard I want to.

"Wait," Olivia's voice comes from next to me. My eyes slide shut at the tremor in her voice and the need to hold her slams into me so fucking hard, it steals what little breath I have left. "Alicia, just wait. Okay? You can- You can have him." She offers. I know she's lying through her teeth, know she's stalling for time. She called the police, someone will be here soon, I just hope Alicia doesn't completely lose it and kill both of us.

"Please don't shoot him. Please."

Alicia turns her attention to Olivia, and it is so

much fucking worse. The feral animal in me rears up, needing to get rid of the threat to my woman, my love, my fucking life. But there isn't a damn thing I can do about it at the moment.

Focus, Lincoln. Focus on what you can do.

The rope. I need to get the knots undone. Once I've done that, I can assess the situation and figure out the next steps. While Alicia looks at Liv, I twist my hands, trying to get my fingers on the knot, trying to loosen it enough to let my hands slip free.

Alicia used my rope. The same rope I tied Liv up with, suspending her over the bed in the playroom. It's silky and soft, designed to flex and bend so it doesn't hurt too badly. Alicia probably thought she was being clever, but really, it's going to work in my favor. I can get out of them. I know I can.

"You wouldn't just give him up. Not now," the madwoman snarls.

Olivia nods vigorously, shifting a half inch closer to me. "I would. I swear I would. If it'll save his life, I'll give him up. I'll leave town. I love him enough to do that. Please, Alicia."

The woman who has been my friend since college hesitates, then she shakes her head. "No. No. I don't think you would give him up, and I'm positive he won't be content to just let you go." She sighs like the whole situation is a hassle she just has to suck it up and deal with. "I guess I could shoot you, hmm? With you gone, he'd be more likely to embrace me."

I try not to bark out a laugh, try not to draw attention back to myself. The ropes are loosening, and I need just a little longer to get them off totally. But the idea of me overlooking that Alicia killed Olivia and somehow falling into bed with her is laughable.

So fucking laughable.

Beside me, Olivia tenses, body going eerily still.

Alicia's expression turns furious. "You think this is fucking funny, Lincoln? I have a *gun*."

I swallow and nod, before tipping my chin up to look her right in the eyes. "If you kill Olivia, you're going to have to kill me too, because there is no force on this earth that will keep me from tearing you the fuck apart. Do you hear me, Alicia? I will fucking *end* you and smile while I do."

The gun comes up, taps against her lips like she's considering. "I suppose you're right."

And then she moves too quickly for me to track, dropping the gun and firing. I brace for impact, brace for the pain of a bullet tearing through my flesh. But it never comes and when my eyes open, I find Alicia still standing in front of me, but the gun… the fucking gun isn't pointed at me.

No.

No. No. No.

I jerk against my bonds as my frantic gaze finds Olivia, still standing where she was, with her mouth open in a surprised 'o' as she looks dazedly back at me. Her hand presses against her stomach. She's pale and shaking.

I scan her body again, still struggling against the ropes. There's no blood that I can see.

Did Alicia miss?

But then Liv stumbles back a step, knees bending slightly before she straightens them, and I see it, blooming against her the white t-shirt with Poison's logo on it. A roar pulls from my chest, and Alicia, who had been standing there, just as dazed as Olivia, jumps, swinging the gun toward me.

I don't look at her; I don't pull my eyes from Olivia, who looks right back at me, mouth opening and closing, before she just... crumples.

Another gunshot rings out. But again, there's no pain. And I become vaguely aware of more bodies flooding the room. Of Lance kneeling in front of me, checking me for injury.

"I'm fine," I grind out, still staring at her unmoving form. "Liv. Help Liv, please."

He nods, but still pulls out a knife and cuts the rope holding my hands before pressing the hilt into my tingling fingers. Once that's done, he's gone, crouching next to Olivia, who's stretched out on the floor now. I can't see her face, but I can see her feet shaking and moving restlessly.

I don't waste time before cutting the rope on my ankles, stumbling from the chair, only to have my legs give out, unable to support my weight. I don't fucking care, though. Nothing is keeping me from getting to my girl. I drag my ass across the floor, crawling, until I'm on the other side of her, staring down at her beautiful face. Her honey eyes find me, and a relieved smile curls her lips before it's swept away. "Linc, you're okay," she whispers.

"Yeah, sunshine," I choke out. "I'm here. I'm right fucking here. And you're staying right fucking here too. You hear me?"

She gives a jerky nod, even as her body tightens up in pain. "I hear you, bossy pants."

I bend my head and press a kiss to her forehead. "Good girl." I look over at Lance, who has his hands locked over the weeping wound on her stomach. He meets my eyes with tight lips, eyes serious.

"We need to get her to the hospital," he murmurs.

I nod frantically. Yes. Of course. Of course, we need to get her to the hospital. They'll fix her. Fix this.

"Paramedics are on their way," someone says from behind Lance, and I look up to find a uniformed police officer. I nod, but can't seem to focus enough to say anything, not to them. Everything in me is focused on my girl, on willing her to live, to stay with me.

My forehead drops to hers, while my fingers clutch hers. "Stay with me, baby. Promise me you'll stay with me." A weak breath puff over my face, there's a wheeze in her lungs that shouldn't be there. "Olivia. Please."

"I-I'll try. I'm trying."

I shake my head. "No trying. Do it. Stay with me."

Out of the corner of my eye, I see Lance move back, and a second later, I'm pushed out of the way. Olivia's eyes widen in panic, her hand reaching for me, and I snarl, lunging forward to get to her again, only to be held back.

"Let them do their work, Linc," Lance orders me. "There's nothing you can do for her right now. Let them save her."

I want to argue with him, especially when Liv is still reaching toward me, but then my sight of her is cut off as they swarm around her body, pulling various lifesaving instruments from bags.

"Linc?" she calls, and I lunge forward again. Lance wrestles me to the ground.

"I'm here, sunshine," I call hoarsely, hoping like hell she can hear me over the noise around her. "I'm right here. I'm not going anywhere."

I ride with Olivia to the hospital in the back of the ambulance, where one of the EMTs patches up the cut on my forehead with a bandage. He says I might need stitches, but they'll have to wait until we reach the hospital. Olivia is still on the stretcher, passed out or knocked out from the pain meds they gave her. But there's a steady *beep, beep beep,* from one of the monitors that lets me know her heart is still beating.

I focus on that sound, letting it soothe me as I hold her hand the entire way. Every so often she blinks up at me with bleary honey eyes, like she's checking I'm still there, like I promised.

When we get to the hospital, they make me leave her, pulling my hand from hers as she's whisked into an operating room, behind a door that says 'no entry' in big red letters. It takes two orderlies or nurses or whatever you want to call them to hold me back.

I can't hear the sound of her heartbeat anymore. That *beep, beep, beep* was the only thing keeping me sane. I'm muscled into a chair in an exam room, where a nurse stitches up my forehead and then I'm led to a waiting room and told to wait.

It's a nightmare.

The only thing I can think about is the feel of her blood on my hands. The fragile breath against my face, the wheeze in her lungs. I curl in on myself, my now clean hands pressing into my face, my eyes, like that will erase the sight of the woman I love, my entire fucking life, bleeding out on my hardwood floor.

A body takes the chair next to me, a big broad hand rests between my shoulder blades. I don't have to look to know who it is. "Lance called you?" My voice is hoarse.

Harvey's hand moves in a circle. "Yeah. Claire too. She's on her way, but she was out of town for a conference. So it'll be a while."

I nod. "Liv will want to see her when she wakes up."

Harvey shifts his arm, sliding over my shoulder to tug me sideways into his chest. "She's going to be okay, Lincoln. She's a fighter. And she has so much to fight for."

I take a deep, shuddering breath and try to let his words soothe me. It doesn't help. "Does she?"

Harvey's quiet and I think maybe he won't answer, but then he says, "yes, she does. She has Claire and me. She has friends who love her. She has you. She has a lot of love in her life, Linc. And that is worth fighting for."

"I'm not worth fighting for," I mutter into my hands. "I'm the asshole who broke her heart, who ruined her."

Harvey's hand pauses in its gentle soothing, his body going stiff beside me. I tip my head up to look at him, but he's staring straight ahead, toward the doors that says, 'No Entry.' "You better pray she feels differently, Lincoln," he says grimly. "Because we need her to fight right now. We need her to fight to come back to us."

Minutes bleed into hours. Every second feels like an eternity. And there is nothing for us to do but wait. The seats around me fill up. Nadia and Josh. Lance. Giovanna. And finally Claire. Everyone that loves Olivia is here. I'm sure that even Caroline is in this hospital, watching over her daughter.

The world outside has turned from dark to light by the time the doctor finally comes out. "Hart family?"

I lurch to my feet, sweeping my eyes over the doctor to find not a single speck of blood on him. The people around me stand as well. "Who's next of kin?"

"She doesn't-" I start, but find the words get tangled on my tongue. Harvey steps up next to me.

"Olivia doesn't have any blood relatives nearby. But we're all her family." The doctor nods in understanding, but he doesn't look like he's going to tell us anything.

"I'm her fiancé," I say. "I'm going to marry her." It's the truth even if I haven't asked her yet. Every ounce of me knows that eventually she'll be mine. I'll be hers. We'll have the whole white dress and tuxedo ceremony.

The doctor looks down at his chart. "You're Lincoln George?"

I nod. "Yes. Please, is she- Is she okay?"

The doctor smiles. "Yes. She's going to be just fine." My knees go weak at the statement, and I nearly crumple to the floor, but Harvey is right there next to me, propping me up, as the surgeon keeps talking. "She came through surgery without a hitch. We've just been waiting for her to wake up from the sedatives so we could verify with her who she wanted us to talk to. As soon as she did, she started demanding to see you."

I blink against the tears in my eyes, taking shaking breath after shaking breath. "I can see her?"

He nods. "Yes. Follow me."

I glance at everyone else in the room, hesitating. They all love her too. Shouldn't they also get to see her? Harvey claps a hand on my shoulder. "Go tell her we love her. We'll be here waiting."

I nod, squeeze his forearm before jogging after the doctor. He brings me behind the no entry door, guiding me through countless halls until we come to a private room with a closed door. "I'll give you a moment alone with her," the doctor says before disappearing.

I don't go in right away. Instead, I take a moment to get my emotions under control. I don't want to overwhelm her as soon as I step into that room. I need to be calm, to be her rock, so she can focus on just healing, getting better.

When I feel like I have a solid mask on, I step into the room.

All the hard work I just did evaporates in a heartbeat. My nose and eyes sting as I take her in. She looks tiny, frail, like the life has been sucked out of her. Her skin is still pale, lips dry and chapped. There are countless monitors around her, attached to cords and tubing. Her eyes are closed.

But that steady *beep, beep beep* is back, and I find that, more than anything, soothes me.

Her eyes flutter open. The same warm honey brown meets mine. "Linc?" God, her voice is barely more than a whisper, but it's enough to propel me across the room until I'm by her side. I want to touch her, but I don't know where to do it without hurting her. So my hands just hover over her, until she lifts one limp hand and tugs on my wrist, urging me onto the bed with her.

"You're crying," she says, softly with concern.

I nod as I shuffle up the bed, curling my body over hers while still keeping one foot on the floor. "I am."

She brushes the moisture away. "Don't cry, baby. I'm okay."

Hearing the words from the doctor had been a relief. Hearing the words from Olivia herself is like a balm to my tattered soul, mending all those rips and tears that had happened the moment the bullet pierced her flesh.

With a sob, my forehead falls to hers, pressing in close. "Fuck, Liv. I thought I lost you. What would I do without my sunshine?"

Her hand curls loosely in the fabric of my blood-stained shirt. "You didn't lose me. I'm here." She swallows thickly and tears shimmer along the bottom of her eyes. "I thought she was going to shoot you, to kill you right in front of me."

I nod, making our noses bump. "I know. And she shot you in front of me instead. Worst moment of my fucking life. I hope you're prepared for me to wrap you up in bubble wrap and to never be out of my sight again."

She lets out a pained giggle that ends in a groan. "Don't make me laugh. It hurts."

"I wasn't trying to make you laugh, baby. I meant it. You are never leaving my sight again. Or if you do, you'll have three fucking guards with you at all times. I'm not risking you again."

She hums, fingers the buttons on my shirt. "Does that mean I get to do the same to you? Can I pick out a security team for you?"

Half my mouth quirks up. "So long as you don't put Lance on it, because he's the head of yours."

She flattens her palm over my left pec, feeling the beat of my heart as her eyes drift closed. I think she might doze off, but then her eyes fly open. "Alicia?"

"She was shot when the cops showed up. I didn't ask about her condition. I don't give a fuck if she lived or died. Either way, she's never coming near you again."

Her body relaxes, and her eyes close again. "Good. That's good," she sighs, sounding already half asleep.

"Get some rest, baby." My lips press into her forehead, and I resist the urge to climb fully onto the bed with her. I don't want to knock into any of the monitors or disconnect the cords. Also, the bed isn't big enough for the both of us.

I make a mental note to look into bringing in a bigger bed for her while she's here, one we can share while she heals. I move to get off the bed, to pull the chair in the corner closer, but Liv's hand shoots out, holding on to me.

"Not yet," she murmurs. "Stay just a little longer."

I settle back into position, with my forehead pressing to hers, fingers laced together.

"Linc?" she says, sounding half asleep.

"Yeah, sunshine?"

Her eyes flutter open and she pulls back as much as she can, pressing farther into the pillow behind her to meet my gaze. "I love you. I wanted to be sure I said it. I want to be sure that you know I love you."

My eyes fill and spill over again. Her gaze narrows as she reaches to wipe the tears away with one trembling hand. "I didn't mean to make you cry."

I catch her hand and press my lips into her palm. "These are happy tears, baby. So fucking happy."

A small smile curls her lips. "Good. I'm going to sleep now. Please be here when I wake up."

I kiss her palm again, speaking against her skin. "Nothing could drag me away."

Epilogue
Lincoln

I'm not typically a nervous guy. I'm pretty sure no one has ever looked at me and thought, *man, he is anxious today*. Today, if someone looked at me and thought that, they'd be one hundred and fifty-eight percent correct. Because today, I am a fucking mess of nerves.

A hand claps on my shoulder, squeezing gently before Cabot rounds my body to stand in front of me. "You're going to do fine. You got this," He reassures me.

I nearly roll my eyes at this. "I suppose you were completely calm, cool and collected when you did this?"

Cabot laughs and shakes his head. "Hell no. I was a mess. But it all worked out, and it will work out for you too."

I shake my head. "I think doing it like this is a mistake."

He chuckles again. "No, it's not. She's going to love it."

I'm doubting everything today because it needs to be perfect. Everything needs to go just right.

Another hand falls on my other shoulder and I glance over to find my brother, Kyan, standing there. We've got the same blue eyes and dark hair, inherited from our mother, but he's bulkier, rougher. His hair is longer, almost enough to pull into a knot at the top of his head. The tattoos on the backs of his hands and the leather jacket on his shoulders only enhance that look. "Relax, Linc. Olivia's going to love it because she loves you."

My heart swells at his words. He's not wrong. She does love me. She tells me every day, multiple times, just how much. I do the same to her. How could I not after nearly losing her? If I were to die today, or God forbid If I were to lose her, I want her to know beyond a shadow of a doubt just what she means to me, what she will always mean to me.

"Will you stop?" Francie's voice cuts through the air, and for a moment I think she's shouting at me, but a moment later she continues. "Not every girl wants to hop on your dick, Zayne. She's working. Leave her the hell alone."

I turn to the door as she storms through, dragging her twin after her. "Stop flirting with anything in a skirt."

Zayne shrugs his shoulders. "She wasn't in a skirt, Fran."

The one and only George sister whips her narrowed gaze around and glares at her twin. He jerks back almost instinctively. I don't blame him. I've been on the receiving end of Francie's glares on more than one occasion, and I know the power they have. "What was that?"

Zayne shrugs, flicks his gaze to me and Kyan, see's he won't be getting help from us, and then says slowly, "I'm just saying she wasn't in a skirt, Fran. She was wearing pants."

Our little sister jerks her pointer finger to jab in his chest. "You listen to me Alexander James George. Today is not about you. Today is not the Zayne show." She wiggles her fingers int he air. "Today is about our big brother and the love of his fucking life. If you set a single toe out of line, I have absolutely no problem releasing those pictures of you from summer camp to the press."

Zayne's eyes widen and he clutches at the space over his heart. "You wouldn't."

"I *would*," she confirms before spinning on her heel and grinning at me and Kyan, hands clapping together excitedly. "Yay! I love a party!"

Nerves grip me all over again. Today is Olivia's birthday, her first without her mother, and I need everything to go perfectly. So far, there have been no hiccups. I woke her with my head between her thighs, gave her two orgasms, and then made her stay in bed while I got up and made pancakes for her. They weren't as fluffy as the ones she makes, but she ate every last bite, happily humming the whole time. Then I fucked her in the shower and, when she was dressed, sent her on her way with Claire, Nadia, and Giovanna, of all people. The girls were under strict instructions to keep her occupied all day. Almost as soon as the door shut behind her, the preparation started.

Furniture was moved. Decorations put up. A small stage built. Caterers took over the kitchen. Now it's nearly time for the party to start. I know Liv and the girls arrived at least an hour ago, but they were rushed upstairs.

I haven't seen my girl since this morning, and I miss her.

"He looks like he's going to throw up," Zayne says, eyeing me.

Francie elbows him hard in his ribs. "Shut up, ass. He's going to be fine." She moves closer to me, gripping my arms and peering into my face. "Take a deep breath, big brother. This is just a party, like any other party. Everything is going to go perfectly because I'm going to make sure that is the case. "

I shake my head. "I want you to enjoy the party, Fran."

She grins up at me. "Please, organizing and making things run smoothly is nearly orgasmic for me."

All three of us brothers grumble while Cabot barks out a laugh.

"Never, ever talk about orgasms with us, Francie. Please, I'm begging you," Kyan says, with real pleading in his voice.

She chuckles and shakes her head. "You know I've had sex before, right?"

"No! No stop. Stop it!" Zayne growls. "We don't want to fucking hear about it."

Amusement sparks in my little sister's eyes, and she grins up at me. "But you might learn something. I've had some fantastic sex-"

My palm smacks over her lips. "No more, Fran," I growl out. But I know she's just needling us to help me get over my nerves. I give her a small smile and a nod of acknowledgement.

She beams back at me from behind my palm. She squeezes my forearms and steps back. "Okay, T-Minus five minutes. I'm going to go check on our girl, make sure they got her into the right dress."

The right dress. Fuck, with that one comment, Francie undoes all the calming her teasing did. But my little sister saunters out of the room, unaware of the havoc she's wreaked.

"This is a mistake," I mutter again, and the three of them close ranks around me.

"It's not," Cabot reassures me.

"I can't imagine being with the same woman for the rest of my life," Zayne says, running a hand over his lips like he's wiping away the notion. "But with the two of you, it makes sense."

Kyan grips my shoulder and gives me a little shake. "She's going to say yes, brother. She loves you."

She's going to say yes. I let those words sink into me, soothe me.

Because today isn't just my sunshine's birthday, today is the day I'm going to ask Olivia to marry me.

Olivia

Today has been the best. Well, as good as it could be with my mother absent from the festivities. She would have loved every second of the party Lincoln threw for me, all the custom cocktails and the food. The people gathered around to wish me a happy birthday.

He's been perfect all day, starting this morning when he woke me up with a stack of pancakes with a candle in the middle, just like my mom used to do every year without fail before she got sick. He'd then told me my first gift was to spend the day getting pampered at a spa with Claire, Nadia, and Giovanna, while he did all the last minute set up for the party.

We'd arrived back at the townhouse with our skin glowy and muscles relaxed, only to be swept up by a team of stylists who finished primping us with blow outs, professional makeup, and designer gowns. I felt like a princess, even if it was a little over the top.

Now the party is in full swing. Zayne's band, Brigades of Menace, have just finished their set, and there's music being piped through the sound system. Everybody looks happy and content and it makes me happy too, the buzz electric.

The one downside to all these happy people is I've hardly seen the man responsible. I've been pulled from one conversation to another all night. I miss him, have missed him since this morning.

Thankfully, I've just sotted him alone, at the edge of the crowd.

"I told you I didn't need anything big today," I murmur to him, slipping my arms around his waist and leaning against his back.

He hums, wrapping his big hands around my wrists and turning to face me. "You deserve it, though."

My mouth quirks up. "Do I?"

He nods solemnly. "Yes, you deserve big parties, and to be treated like a queen all the fucking time. But especially today."

I laugh, winding my arms around his neck while he frames my waist with his fingers. "You did my mama proud today, Mr. George."

The grin he gives me is bright and so fucking happy it's almost out of place on his face. I'm getting more and more used to seeing it, though. It's been making a recurring appearance in the last few months, especially once I fully healed from being shot and the surgery that followed. Now it's on his face more often than not.

"Well, I'm not quite done yet." My toes curl in my shoes at the dark promise in his voice. "As soon as these losers clear out, I have one more surprise for you."

"Hey!" Claire says from nearby. "I heard that asshole!"

Lincoln grins at her. "I wanted you to, Claire bear."

My best friend lifts her middle finger at him, but she's grinning. I'm not the least bit surprised at how well they get along now. They are almost scarily similar. Both fiercely loyal, willing to do anything for those they love. And they both love me, so I'm a damn lucky girl.

Still, I pinch Lincoln's side, making him wince and glare at Claire. "Both of you play nice."

Claire laughs and slips away from us, weaving through the party. I see her pause every so often to chat to people, and eyes flick to us, and then away. I frown. "What's she doing?"

Lincoln wraps his arms around me from behind. His chin rests on the top of my head. "Probably kicking people out for us."

He doesn't sound upset about my best friend breaking up our party. I sigh and lean against him. "She's a good friend, being the asshole for us so we can…"

I trail off as Linc nuzzles into the hollow behind my ear, before his tongue darts out, flicking over my pulse. "What can we do, sunshine?"

I swallow the whimper that tries to escape as he licks and bites at the spot. "Whatever-Whatever you have planned." Between my legs clenches at the idea. Over the last few months, as soon as the doctor gave the all clear, Lincoln has been… expanding my knowledge of the games he likes to play in the bedroom. It's not all the time, not like it was at the beginning. He's just as likely to wake me up to make love to me soft and slow as he is to bind me with ropes and use a paddle on my ass.

It all depends on his mood and what we've been doing. Or, sometimes I ask for it. Ask for him to take control, clear my thoughts for a bit. He's always happy to comply.

I have no doubts at all that he has something planned for tonight once everyone has left, and I honestly can't wait to give myself over to him and let him bring me pleasure.

"Who says I have anything planned?" He murmurs right against my ear, making my scalp tingle.

"Please. You always have something planned."

He chuckles and kisses my temple before pulling away. "You're right." And then he raises his voice to be heard over the music. "Okay, party's over. Everyone out."

My hand slaps over his lips, to stop the flow of words, but I'm laughing so it doesn't have the right effect. And the damage has been done already. People are gathering their things, coming over to say goodbye before heading out the door.

I hug everyone, thank them all for coming. My friends and his siblings are the last to leave, along with Verity and Cabot. We embrace. Every one of us. Kisses are pressed onto cheeks, promises are made to call each other the next day, and more than one person beams at me like they know something I don't.

I just beam right back because my heart feels light.

I miss my mother every day, and I knew today would be especially hard, since for so long it was just the two of us. But with Lincoln and these people, my chosen family, around me, I'm not sure I could be happier.

Claire is the last one to leave, winking over her shoulder at me. "Love you, babe! I'll see you soon."

I give her a finger wave and then turn with a chuckle to Lincoln, only to see him standing watching me with a pleased smile on his face. But there's a flicker of something else there too. *Trepidation,* maybe? It's gone a moment later, so I push it to the side.

"Well, Mr. George. What next?"

Without answering, he holds out a hand to me, and I slip my fingers into it without hesitation. I would follow this man anywhere in the world.

Lincoln guides me over to the dining room table and I tilt my head when I see it's already cleaned of all the food and drinks. But then, I guess that might be part of the catering service he hired. I turn to Lincoln with questioning eyes and stop when I see how nervous he is. Why is Lincoln so nervous?

He shoves his hands into his pants and nods at the table. "Climb up."

Oh, okay, so this is going to be like I'm the meal sort of thing. My fingers go to the zipper on the side of my dress, readying to pull it off, but he stops me. "Leave it on, baby."

I arch a brow at him, but do as he says, kicking off my heels before putting a foot on a chair and boosting myself onto the table. Lincoln holds out a hand to help me as I gather my skirts around my legs before settling onto the tabletop.

"Just sit there," he says, pointing at me, like that will help get his point across more.

I have to bite my lip to keep from smiling at how obviously nervous he is. "I'll stay right here."

He eyes me, nods once and then strides out of the room, running a hand through his hair. It's that nervous move that makes me think something is really up. Worry gnaws at me. Is it Alicia? They sentenced her to life in prison, but I know her father has money and connections, so maybe she got a reduced sentence somehow?

I'm not worried about her coming after us, not anymore. But I hate the idea of her being free, of being on the same streets as I am.

Okay, yeah, maybe I am worried about her coming after us again.

I hear him return, and twist to look at him, needing him to just rip the band aid off and tell me. "Linc-"

The words die on my lips as I take him in. He's changed into a green sweater vest striped with red and gray, over a dark green button up and jeans. In his hands is a pale pink cake with candles sticking out of the top.

He smirks as he saunters toward me. "Happy birthday, beautiful."

I look down at my dress, pale lavender chiffon, bunched up around my knees,, the sweetheart neckline, the slightly vintage feel. Things click into place when he slides the cake in front of me and then climbs up to sit with his legs crossed, facing me.

Sixteen Candles. He's giving me the ending of *Sixteen Candles* like I always wanted. I'm dressed in an updated version of Molly Ringwald's dress, and he's dressed like Jake Ryan.

Tears fill my eyes as I look up at him. "Lincoln George, you perfect, perfect man."

His smirk grows into a full-blown grin. "I'm hardly perfect, sunshine." He reaches across the table and catches a tear as it slides down my cheek. "Happy tears, right?"

I giggle and swipe at my other cheek with my hand. "Yeah, happy tears. How could they not be?"

He leans forward slightly, and I lean in too, thinking he's going to kiss me over the cake like the end of the movie, but he pauses with two inches between our mouths. "I think I might be able to give you even more happy tears if you look at the cake."

I frown, not following what he's saying, and my eyes drop to the cake that I'd barely even looked at. It's pale pink with white roses. There are sixteen candles stuck in the top and scrawled across the top in bright pink frosting are the words, *Marry me, sunshine?* My mouth drops open, tears flood my eyes as my hands come up to press into my face.

Lincoln uses a knuckle under my chin to lift my eyes to his. He has a ring in his hand, but I don't look at it. My entire focus is on him, on his pretty slate blue eyes, on the smile on his face, the tears lining his lashes.

"Olivia Hart, my love, my world, my sunshine. I have loved you since the moment you called me bossy pants in that sweet southern voice of yours. I tried so damn hard to resist you, to resist this, because I knew I wasn't a good enough man for you. But you make me want to be a better man, Liv. No, you just make me a better man, by giving me your love and support, by believing in me, in us. I never thought I would find someone that completes me, makes me whole and happy. But I did and couldn't be more fucking grateful. I can't imagine my life without you in it. I don't want to. I need you so fucking much." He holds the ring out to me. "Marry me."

It's not a question, but a demand, and I can't help but laugh a little at that. He seems to notice because he adds somewhat sheepishly, "*please.*"

I'm nodding before he's tacked on the word, dropping my hands from my mouth to curl around his. "Yes, bossy pants. Yes, I will marry you."

He grins, takes my hand in his, and slides the ring on my finger. I recognize it. It's one that I tried on for him ages ago, back when he told me we were shopping for Francie, but really he was buying an engagement ring for Alicia to fulfill their contract. I loved this one. I suggested he buy it but thank God he didn't because now it's mine.

Lincoln uses his grip to pull me closer to him while moving the cake over to the side so it's not between us. Our mouths crash together, tongues meeting and sliding. I curl my hands in his sweater vest and pull him closer, pressing onto my knees to crawl into his lap. His hands grip my hips and my arms drape over his shoulders. Our mouths never leave each other. Well, they don't until he pulls back, breathing heavy. His forehead presses to mine. "I love you so fucking much, Olivia. I can't wait to spend the rest of my life with you."

Fresh tears prick my eyes and I nod against him, making our noses bump together. "I love you too, Linc. You make me so happy."

His grin grows, and he tips his head back to shout at the ceiling. "She said yes! She fucking said yes!"

At first I think he's just celebrating, just happy. But then the faint sound of cheering reaches my ears, along with countless feet pounding toward us. Realization strikes. "They're still here?"

He pushes my hair back over my shoulder and nods, the tip of his nose rubbing against mine. "Yes," he confirms just moments before the entrance to the dining room is filled with all the people that love us. Every one of them is smiling, cheering. I tip my head back and laugh. I should probably climb off Lincoln, should accept their congratulations, but I don't want to let him go yet.

So I don't. I slide my arms around his shoulders and squeeze him tighter, burying my face in his shoulder with a laugh.

"God, I'm so fucking happy," he murmurs into my hair, hands stroking up and down my back.

I sit up and beam at him. "Me fucking too."

Tana Rose Books

The Pantheon Series
Completed
Kiss
Marry
Kill

Personal Demons Series
Completed
The Haunting of Sophie Covey
The Revelation of Sophie Covey
The Demise of Sophie Covey
The Rapture of Sophie Covey
The Sedition of Sophie Covey

Septem Stellae University
Hand and Tome
Blade and Tether
Cross and Spider
Dagger and Crest
Shadow and Veil (2023)

Dark Everafter
Once Upon a Dark Turn
Untitled #2 (2023)

Standalones
No Rest for the Wicked
He Sees You When You're Sleeping
Bossy Pants

Printed in Poland
by Amazon Fulfillment
Poland Sp. z o.o., Wrocław

36124610R00266